CONJURE

VOODOO VIXENS

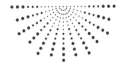

J. MOON

TO BE NOTIFIED OF NEW RELEASES, CONTESTS, GIVEAWAYS, AND
BOOK SIGNINGS VISIT FACEBOOK.COM/JMOONWRITES

For information contact :

jmoonwrites@gmail.com

Book design by: Jeremy R. Dixon

Cover design by Oddball design

Edited by : Noir literary

ISBN: 9781732081338

GUIDING LIGHT

"Is solace anywhere more comforting than that in the arms of a sister?"

Alice Walker

PRELUDE TO A STORM

I cannot die like this.

The thought echoes in her head, as Amina lays helpless, sprawled on the dusty wooden floor, crimson streams seeping from her side. Her face is frozen in fear as she stares up at the ceiling, her arms stiff as a porcelain doll. To her left she hears the sounds of the Brooklyn streets. If only she could call for help. The thought crossed her mind, but she knew no one would hear her, and no one would wander into this abandoned house where she had been shot and left for dead.

Magnum had planned this with precision.

Amina groaned as the pain shot through her, bringing tears to her eyes. She shifted into a sitting position and peered at her right shoulder. Blood trickled from the wound down her back and onto her thighs. She pulled herself up, took a step towards the door, and collapsed. She cursed as a blurring pain reverberated around her shoulder. This is nothing, she thought. It's barely even bleeding, she tried to convince herself. But even with positive thoughts, still she lay crumpled on the floor.

Over the years she had committed so many sins, some she regretted and others she did not. Her family would probably say it was just so predictable that she would turn up dead in an abandoned house. She was always the bad sister, the up to no good troublemaker, the rotten apple in the bunch. It had been six years since they stripped her powers.

She ran away that night.

And swore vengeance against her sisters.

Amina refused to give them the satisfaction of being fully rid of her. She would stay alive if only to spite them all. With her eyes closed she began to chant. Amina knew there was only one way out of this. She must call on a spirit that only the damned or desperate would invoke.

At this moment she was a bit of both.

Even though she no longer had her gifts, she hoped against all else that she could still tap into her magic. With everything she had, she prayed for the dark spirit to come to her. The only way she could defy death was to summon a demon, and not just any demon. One of immense power...one that was a part of the Petro Loa.

A keeper of the dead.

She chanted for what seemed like an eternity, with each word almost feeling like her last. The rhythm of her voice hummed low like a silent prayer. Just as she was about to give up hope, she heard movement in the corner of the room and an icy wave of terror shot up her spine. Suddenly an ominous red fog worked its way into the room and panic rose in her chest. Amina looked incredulously at the figure that stood before her, surprised that her spell had worked and terrified at the sight of the demon.

Shrouded in shadows and darkness, he came to her, appearing almost as a vision of the slaves. He wore a crisp black tuxedo, with a white shirt unbuttoned to expose the many tattoos written across his gaunt chest. His skin black as tar, and his face covered with a pasty white ash. Papa Samedi sat in the corner just a few steps from her, lighting up a cigar. Amina stared into his emerald colored eyes as he blew smoke. She struggled to breathe as fear sought to rob her last breath. His lips curled into a frightening grin, revealing decaying yellow teeth. Amina blinks and in the lick of a flame, Papa Samedi is on his feet and reaching for her. He yanks Amina by her right foot, and pulled her across the floor.

"My… my… Ms. Lawson. How long have I waited to collect your soul cher?" he bellowed in a Cajun accent. Papa Samedi's voice was a raspy and southern heavy baritone. It's the kind of voice that could only exist in nightmares.

"I've always liked devouring the souls of witches. But I always loved me the taste of an evil witch," he slurred with a malicious smile.

Papa Samedi cocked his head to the side and sighed. "Come now gal, I'll be takin' you to hell," he said as he dragged her along the floor. Violent winds whipped the fog as a part of the floor crumbled and tortured voices called from below. Demonic sulfur wafted up into the air and tiny daggers of fear stabbed Amina's spine.

"Wait!" she cried as she writhed on the floor like a worm. "I can help you."

With a jolly whistle, Papa Samedi continued to drag her, giving her his back. As he lugged her along, the blood from her wound created a smudged red trail on the wooden floor. "Help me how? You have no real power."

"It was taken from me. If you help me, I can get you real power."

He paused and glanced over his shoulder. "I'm listening."

"Save me and restore my powers. Then I can help you get the greatest power there is." Amina drew a deep aching breath, as she thought of home, and everything she had been running from. "I can get you the power of all the Lawson sisters, power of the Bennu... the Phoenix."

A sinister grin swept across the demon's face as he dropped Amina's legs. He whirled around with his dusty coattail billowing in the darkness. He whisked his hands and Amina levitated up from the floor by dark emerald streams.

"I think you got yourself a deal," he hissed before pulling her into a kiss.

1

MOTHER

"Makayla are you up?" Patrice shouted as she ran down the stairs like a mad man. She thundered down half dressed, half ready to go, and her thoughts muddled by the foggy haze of sleep. The storm was over, but peace was nowhere to be found. And it had been that way for a long time.

Ever since they left New Orleans.

Ever since Katrina.

Since then a strong dread settled into Patrice's stomach and latched onto her like a leech. It kept her awake every night, chanting and praying. It kept Patrice waiting for the winds to stir, the earth to move, and the storm to come again. And this restlessness couldn't have come at a worse time. She needed to be at her best for the new client meeting this morning.

Patrice ran her hands through razor straight Brazilian hair that cascaded down her back. "Makayla!" she called up the stairs. She shuffled around everything she carried in her left arm to check her phone.

"Oh god," she moans.

It is already eight o'clock. She'd definitely be late. "Makayla!" Patrice shouts again, this time with a hint of anger in her voice. The last thing she needed was to drag her sister out of bed.

Makayla sat downstairs, curling her long honey-blonde streaked hair. "I'm in the kitchen!" she called back.

Patrice put on her earrings and eased a foot into one of her black pumps. "Are you already dressed?" she asked as she took another step down.

"Yeah!" Makayla responded with an attitude. She turned to Yolanda, who ate fruit and Greek yogurt in big spoonfuls. "You better get your sister. She must think I'm still a child," she sassed out of the side of her mouth.

Patrice caught wind of that last part, and had a good mind to go upside Makayla's head like Gran would've. "Excuse me?"

Makayla looked upward. "Oh nothing."

Patrice strolled in the kitchen and brewed herself some coffee to go. "Thank God you are ready, because I am already late."

Makayla rolled her eyes. "Peaches, you need to get some sleep."

Patrice clicked her heels to the other side of the kitchen. "Trust me, I know."

It wasn't until Patrice had almost finished packing her lunch that she noticed her bright eyed and olive-skinned middle sister Yolanda. "Yolanda what you doing here? Ran out of food at your dorm?"

"Yup. As usual," Yolanda called back. She finished her yogurt, pulled out tarot cards, and proceeded to divide them into three stacks.

"What are you doing?" Patrice asked.

Yolanda patted at her hair, which was braided into a halo of beautiful natural brown loveliness. She flipped over the cards. "I have been working with the tarot cards to develop and control my visions. I've also been using rocks and crystals as well. The cards, the rocks, and crystals have all been saying the same thing for the last week. Something big is coming."

Patrice poked her head from around the refrigerator. "Yes. They are called bills. Some bills are coming. So you need to focus on graduating so you can help me with some of these expenses."

Yolanda cackled, "Don't worry, big sissy. I'm doing just fine in that department. I am supreme in bio-chemical studies. Now I want to be supreme within the spirit realm and master how to discern the signs the spirits show me. And the signs are all pointing to something or someone big headed our way."

A doorbell cut their conversation short. Patrice dashed to the kitchen table, as she tried to stuff everything into bags. She turned to Makayla, "Can you go get the door?"

Makayla sucked her teeth, "Do I look like the help?"

Patrice shot her a nasty look. "If you're staying in my house and not paying any bills, then yes. You are the help." She shook her head. "I'm not in the mood to play with you this morning."

With a sigh, Makayla dropped the curler and sluggishly trekked to the door. "Yes sir master. Issa going." Of the four sisters, Makayla was the shortest but her attitude made her seem a foot taller easily. She was a radiant young beauty that was full of confidence and quick wit. The latter often got her into trouble or annoyed whoever was on the receiving end of her jokes.

Patrice cut her eyes towards Makayla. "Girl, hush and grab the door."

*M*akayla answered the door, and bustling through came Aunt Dot, the only relative the Lawson sisters had left in this world. Aunt Dot became essential to Patrice for undergrad to attend Spelman. For that, Patrice was always grateful. But together, all of the sisters dreaded her visits, because they are accompanied with requests to do root magic for either Aunt Dot's friends or someone she was indebted to. Based on the way Aunt Dot pooched into the kitchen with her Newport cigarette in her hand, they could have assumed she had another job for them.

Aunt Dot was an outspoken woman. One could tell this from looking at her sunset-orange hair styled into a short buzz cut and the loud yellow scarf she wore, that matched her maroon colored sweater.

"Hello my beloved. I got some work I need you girls to do," she rasped with an airy tone before taking a puff on her cigarette.

Patrice sighed heavily as she slipped her bag on her shoulder. "For the millionth time, Aunt Dot. We don't have time for that anymore."

Aunt Dot held out her hands in protest, "Now Peaches, my dear…. I hear you. But my neighbor Ms. Tina—her son Jayshon got caught selling drugs again! And they will lock him up for good this time unless you help." She took a long puff on her cigarette. "I already told her it would cost her around $500. That's $300 for you and $200 for me. I gotta' have my Bingo money," She said as she erupted into a dry cackle.

Patrice side-eyed her aunt before laughing. Like all of their family members, Aunt Dot had gifts of her own. It was the gift of Empathy, the ability to sense and discern the emotions of others. It was a gift many Voodoo priest, priestess and prophets manifested.

Back in New Orleans, Aunt Dot was someone who would seek out clients for Gran. The same grandmother who had raised the girls at an early age, was the most powerful witch of all. She was known as Mother Phoenix. It was a title that was only given to the highest Voodoo priestess. Marie Laveau had been the first, and tragically Gran had been the last. The magic in their family could be traced all the way back to Egypt. The ancient Egyptians worshipped the entity known as the Bennu. A creature of fire and magic known in the western world as a phoenix. The Phoenix was the spark of life. The creator reborn out of fire. The all-birthing mother from which all blessings flow.

People would come from all over the world for help in their situations from the powerful Mother Phoenix. But you couldn't talk to the Mother without talking to Aunt Dot first. Aunt Dot also runs a small candle and hoodoo shop downtown, where she sleeps in the back.

Patrice glanced over to her baby sister "Makayla, grab your bag and let's go." Then she turned to her Aunt Dot. "I'm sorry Aunt Dot, I can't help you. I don't do that anymore. You're going to have to tell her you made a mistake."

"I ain't made no mistake," Aunt Dot protested. "Your grandmother trained you to be the next Mother Phoenix. You're the heir to the throne, honey. Why are you ducking your destiny?"

Her words only invoked a painful past in Patrice. One she'd do her best to protect her sisters from.

Free of danger.

And free of magic.

Patrice stopped in her tracks, and shot a chilling glance towards her aunt. Aunt Dot didn't comprehend so Patrice wanted make her stance crystal. "Destiny doesn't pay bills, Aunt Dot. We don't practice magic in this house. That's just the way it is. And if you want to continue to come over here, then you need to be clear on that." Patrice's tone was tough and firm. It was always in her nature as the eldest to speak in authority. This carried over to her work and non-existent love life. She demanded control and to hell with anyone who questioned her say-so.

Yolanda and Makayla paused to look over at her. When she talked like this, she meant business. Aunt Dot's face softened, and Patrice could tell her words had cut too close.

She took a quick breath to summon calm. "Now we'll talk to you later because we are late," she said as she walked past Aunt Dot.

Yolanda could sense the situation going from zero to one hundred quickly, so she stood up and moved to usher Aunt Dot toward the door. "Come on, Aunt Dot. She has to go to work."

Aunt Dot snatched her arm back and outed her cigarette against the wall. "Well, I know she has to work but she could still hear me out. Back in my day I would've worked a hex to snatch that heifer bald. She doesn't have to talk to me like that." Aunt Dot was still shouting as Yolanda pushed her out the door.

"Just meet me at my dorm tomorrow. Like we usually do," Yolanda whispered so her sisters couldn't hear.

All anger erased from Aunt Dot's face as her lips curled into a smile. "Okay beloved, I'll see you later."

Patrice had stopped doing magic years ago and prohibited the others from doing so also. Yolanda was the only sister who had learned from their grandmother but it was so long ago and she was so young that she didn't truly benefit from Gran's teaching.

"Makayla let's go!" Patrice shouted as she dashed towards the door.

Behind her, Makayla strolled along with her long and elaborately styled honey blonde hair swaying into the wind. "I'm coming."

~

*M*inutes later Patrice was pulling up along the curb of North Central High. Patrice turned to her sister. "Now Makayla, promise me you will think about what you say before you say it. Don't go in there today showing off," Patrice preached in a low stern voice.

Makayla frowned. "But you don't understand. Some of these girls be trying me. If you throw shade my way, then I'm going to throw fists your way."

Patrice shook her head. "I know, sis, but violence is never the answer. You just got off suspension for fighting. All your life you're going to have to deal with girls like that Erica. You have to rise above it."

"But you don't understand," Makayla interrupted. "Miss thang called me a THOT," she shouted with a look that suggested she was highly appalled.

Patrice side eyed her sister, "A THOT? What is a THOT, Makayla?"

"That Ho Over There," Makayla answered while pointing out the window.

"What... who is that?" Patrice asked, confused.

"No, it stands for 'That Ho Over There.'"

Patrice sighed. "Really Makayla, you know how many names people have called me. It's not what people call you— it's what you answer to. Listen, I work hard so I can provide a life that is comfortable for all of us. You know where we came from. You know what we went through. We are the only Lawson girls left and I want to leave a legacy that has nothing to do with magic." She reached over and pulled Makayla's hand off of her phone. "Promise me you will focus on your school work. If they come for you... pay it no mind."

Makayla remained silent as she shook her head while staring into her phone.

"Makayla...promise me," Patrice repeated.

"I'll try," Makayla said before leaning over to Patrice and hugging her.

"That's all I ask, baby girl," Patrice said before patting her on the back. "I love you and I always got your back, but Makayla you have to stop being so sensitive," she murmured as Makayla got out of the car.

Makayla walked into her school as Patrice drove off. Even though Patrice's bossy nature sometimes annoyed her, she stilled respected Patrice because she was the only mother she'd ever known. She waved Patrice goodbye as she pulled away from the curb, and sped down the highway.

2

THE NEW CLIENT

*E*arly morning Atlanta sun stung Patrice's eyes as she lowered the blinds. She could see the whole city from her office, and it was one of the delights she enjoyed. The Coca Cola sign stood profoundly in the far left, as twin peak towers glistened in the distance. She looked out to the distance and could practically feel the pulse of the city. Just when Patrice thought the day couldn't get any more chaotic, she came to work and everyone was buzzing around to prepare for the big client visit.

As always it was up to Patrice to lead the ship. Word around the office was that she would get lead on this project. And it was a no brainer after the success of the fifteen million dollar contract her team secured with the government. It was only Patrice's second year at ITN and she could feel a management offer within her grasp.

A high pitched shriek from behind stirred her out of her flowing thoughts.

"Hey girl? You ready for this one sis?" Nicole said as she

stood idle by Patrice's K-cup machine. Nicole is a very petite girl, with a bone-straight asymmetrical bob that rounded her narrow face. Patrice had told her she could use it once, but she's been coming into her office ever since to use it.... and often unannounced at that. It annoyed Patrice.

Patrice folded her arms. "How much is this contract again?"

The machine finished with a loud hiss, Nicole grabbed her mug. "Are you kidding me? This is twenty-two million dollars. Twenty–two sisters honey." She took a sip of her cup and frowned before grabbing the sugar and pouring.

Nicole discarded the used k-cup. "Come on girl you should know this. Mr. James will be here any minute. He is the new hot-shot millionaire who created ExFit, the app that allows you to search for a personal trainer and book them. He just moved here from New York. And he is trying to expand ExFit."

A throbbing pain stabbed the right side of Patrice's head. "You're right...I'm just a little off. This morning has been crazy," she replied as she massaged her temples.

Nicole stirred her cup. "You know Patrice, you really got to get you some sleep. You've been off your game lately."

"Trust me, I know." Patrice said as she sat on the side of her desk.

Nicole pulled out her phone, "But get into this tea honey. Not only is he rich, successful, and single but girl, the man is fine. Yes, God!" she said raising her free hand.

"How do you know?" Patrice asked.

"What do you mean how do I know? I follow him on Instagram, Twitter, and Facebook. I know his net worth, his likes, his hobbies and what he likes to listen to when working out. If you give me one more day, I can find his nudes and social security number."

Patrice laughed, because she knew her friend was proud to be the office gossip and took her job reporting the news seriously. Initially many at ITN didn't think Nicole would last long when she first started working there but then Patrice took Nicole under her wing. She figured as the only two black women in the company, they needed to stick together.

Patrice leaned in as Nicole scrolled through pictures of their client. On his page she saw various angles of his well-sculpted body as he worked out at various gyms across the world. Patrice was even more impressed when they scrolled through shots of him visiting Bali, touring the streets of London, eating dinner on a yacht in Cape Town, and partying in L.A.

They scrolled past more shots of his body, in particular, one of his bulging chest.

Her nipples hardened.

Out of instinct, Patrice clasped her pearls. "Well somebody looks like a snack."

"A snack?" Nicole repeated. "That man is a whole damn meal," she said causing them to laugh.

A serious thought crept over Patrice. She couldn't remember the last time she had a date, it was probably around the time her sister Yolanda graduated high school. Yolanda was about to graduate from Clark Atlanta in a year, so it had been a long time. Patrice knew men found her attractive, that wasn't the problem. She had flawless brown skin, dark black hair that fell down to her back and a walk that made men fall to their knees. She graduated with a Bachelor's from Spelman and an MBA from Emory. Success and excellence were two words that had driven her life. Between working, going to school part-time, and taking care of her sisters, Patrice had little time for dating.

Patrice noticed the door opening out of the corner of her eye where in walked Oscar Petrov with a crowd following him. Very quickly, Patrice put on her best smile to welcome the suits as they spilled into the office. Oscar Petrov was a balding middle aged Russian man, with pale skin and sparkling brown eyes. Brown eyes that sparkled with money and greed.

"And here she is, Mr. James...our senior consultant Ms. Patrice Lawson."

He walked into the room and her body cried out yes.

Patrice looked up and came face to face with the man whose photo she'd been staring at on the phone. She looked into his hazel brown eyes and lingered, "Hello, Mr. James," she greeted in a very demure tone.

He took her hand, "Please, Ms. Lawson, call me Lorenzo."

His voice was deep and rugged. It pleased Patrice.

She smiled, "You can call me Patrice, that's fine," she said almost blushing under the heat of his gaze.

Lorenzo James looked even better in person. He stood around six foot four with broad shoulders and burly muscles etched by his well-tailored navy suit. He had a chestnut skin tone that complemented Patrice's light toffee brown, very well. Patrice continued to drink in his features as he smiled at her. His hair was trimmed into a dark black wavy Caesar, and his beard was groomed to perfection.

On Instagram she had noticed he had several tattoos, but standing in her office he had them all covered up.

A professional man who had the soul of a hustler.

He had her attention. She studied him with intent.

Lorenzo's face was sculpted, not like a model but more like

an actor, one of the action stars Patrice had always adored. There was a ruggedness to his swagger that did something for her. She was still clasping his hand as she stared at him. The smile on his face now growing wider told her he was admiring her as well.

"Nice to meet you, Lorenzo," she gushed after noticing she was still holding onto his hand. She pretended she had to scratch her neck to snatch it back.

Mr. Petrov cleared his throat. "I was telling Mr. James that you will lead the team consulting on his account. I also told him you were the best."

"Right of course," she said snapping back to reality.

Beads of sweat bubbled at the top of her head. A sudden wildfire swept over her body. Patrice fanned herself before looking over. Why did she do that? The sunlight hit Lorenzo's eyes at just the right angle, and her knees buckled making her stumble back, but before she could fall Nicole caught her from behind.

Lorenzo unbuttoned his blazer. "Your reputation precedes you, Patrice. I look forward to working with you."

Her lips parted but nothing came out. For a moment she felt as though a moan was about to escape her lips.

"Yeah...me too," She said falling over her words. *Get it together girl. This is embarrassing*, Patrice thought to herself.

Oscar cast a sidelong gaze at Patrice before ushering Mr. James away. "Come on Mr. James let's leave these two ladies to their work."

Lorenzo nodded, "It was nice meeting you ladies and I look forward to working with you."

Nicole waved him away. "Yes sir Mr. James we are extremely excited."

Nicole watched them leave as she continued to look down. She cackled and said, "Yes Mr. James we can't wait to work right under you, especially Patrice."

Patrice smacked her shoulder. "Hush."

"And see you talking about a snack. That man was a three piece, a biscuit, and two sides girl. Enough for dinner and lunch the next day."

Patrice shook her head. "You are terrible."

"No that's you." She corrected.

"You're right, but I'm gone get it together."

Nicole snapped. "You better, because we need this coin."

Patrice took a breath and sat down at her desk. "Okay let's get it."

3

SHIFTS IN THE SPIRIT

For Yolanda, being a conduit for the spirit realm wasn't easy. She had been dealing with the dead ever since she was a little girl. Of all her sisters, she was the most sensitive to the shift of good and evil energy. The others naturally had a little bit of this, but not as much as she did. That's why it didn't set well with her that she could feel something coming.

But what it was, she had no clue.

The strange feeling reminded her of when she first met her best friend Abigail. Abigail was a runaway slave who died in the 1800s. She had drowned in the swamp not far from their old house. Yolanda was looking for her doll one day in the backyard, when Abigail picked it up and introduced herself. At first Abigail's pale drenched skin, and tattered clothing frightened her but Abigail's innocent smile melted away all of Yolanda's concern. Outside of her sisters, Yolanda had no one else to play with so they became friends.

Yolanda and Abigail had so much fun together, they would

chase each other in the woods, braid each other's hair, and play hand games. Yolanda tried to introduce Abigail to the other kids in the neighborhood, the ones who were mean to her but she was the only one who could see Abigail, and that did nothing but make the kids think she was even weirder.

Eventually she grew out of Abigail in high school. Abigail was still a nine-year-old girl when Yolanda turned sixteen. On the day of Yolanda's sixteen she felt a dread like never before around Abigail. She could sense a shift in the dead girl's spirit. Soon after she tried to tell Abigail they could no longer be friends and she saw another side of Abigail.

The angry side of her spirit.

Yolanda had no choice but to call Gran on Abigail. And Gran laid Abigail's restless spirit right and proper, yes indeedy.

Gran had said, "Yolanda, you are an sensitive old soul. The spirits touched you when you were born my dear. Just like they did me. And yous' got a responsibility to serve them. To help them, because no one else will."

Yolanda still carried Gran's words with her to this day. Most people walk this world aimlessly without a purpose but Yolanda had one. She was a guide for the spirits, and darn proud of it too.

This spooky feeling still weighed heavily on her mind. It even prevented her from enjoying this rare occasion where her sisters had dinner with Aunt Dot. As someone who didn't grow up with a mother or father, she usually appreciated anything resembling normal family time. Yolanda was with all her lovelies and she couldn't be happier. She smiled wide just from looking across the table at her lovely family. Yolanda fanned herself to keep from gushing, then she rubbed between her glasses and nose.

Calm down Yolanda, she thought to herself.

On most nights it was just Makayla and Patrice. For the last three years they have lived in a four bedroom, three and a half bathroom, stone-sided Craftsman located in awesome Alpharetta, a suburb outside of Atlanta. Patrice cooked her famous lasagna and she even made a vegetarian version for Yolanda. Makayla was on her phone texting. Patrice was sipping red wine after having finished the work she'd brought home. Aunt Dot was just sitting down at the table and the sight of her family brought joy to Yolanda's heart. On the inside she knew there was a missing piece to this pretty picture. Just as her mind ran across the missing piece of the puzzle, the doorbell rang.

Yolanda was the first to spring up. *Who could it be?* She wondered. She wiped her hands on her jeans, and opened the door to a sight so shocking that it made her want to fall out.

"Amina!" she shouted, barely recognizing her sister.

Designer shades concealed Amina's eyes and a sleeve-length rose tattoo adorned her right arm. She wore her hair in long, dark Senegalese twists, and had a septum piercing that reminded her of the black hipsters at Clark Atlanta. A sudden chill swept over Yolanda and made her hand tremble over the doorknob. She looked at her sister and saw blackness in her aura, it was an armor invisible to most but not Yolanda.

Six years is a long time.

Yolanda had a feeling not much had changed.

Amina lowered her shades, "Well, aren't you going to let me in?"

Yolanda leapt out of her river of thoughts. "Of course, come in sissy," She chirped, returning to her usual bubbly demeanor.

As soon as Amina stepped in, Yolanda pulled her into a

long, warm embrace and rocked her sister side to side. She buried her nose in her shoulder. Amina smelled of exotic spices and brown liquor. The scent of alcohol was so heavy on her breath that it made Yolanda's nose twitch.

"It's good to see you," Amina said in a low voice.

"You too," Yolanda returned with a smile.

Amina looked around the house with a look of repulsion. "So where is everybody?"

"In the dining room. Follow me! "Yolanda said as she pulled her sister after her.

"Who is it?" Patrice called from around the corner at the table.

"You will never guess!" Yolanda shouted back. She turned the corner to walk into the dining room and reveal Amina. "Remember when I told y'all I felt something coming? Well, here she is?"

Everyone stared at Amina as if they'd seen a ghost. At first they didn't know what to say, so they just stared in awe as silence strangled the room. Makayla was the first out of her seat. "Boy stop! You mean my big boss ass sister Amina came through? I can't believe it." She rushed from around the table to pull her sister into a hug.

"Wow little bird, you are so big now," Amina said as she hugged her sister back.

"I know. I missed you so much," Makayla said in her sister's ear.

"Me too," Amina said halfheartedly.

Little bird was a nickname Amina gave her little sister for the chirping sound Makayla used to make when she cried as a baby. Then just as love filled the room, it went cold the moment Amina's eyes met Patrice's.

Patrice sipped from her glass of red wine and greeted her coldly, "Hello, Amina."

Amina's eyes narrowed. "Peaches."

Silence fell back over the room. Everyone stood frozen. The shade between the two sisters was so thick, that Aunt Dot looked back and forth at them uncertain who was going to be the first to throw daggers.

Aunt Dot coughed, "Well let me go ahead and fix my plate. This is going to get good." She said with a raspy dry laugh.

4

HERE COMES THE HURRICANE

*G*ran realized that her granddaughters Amina and Patrice were two polar opposite personalities at very young ages. Patrice had always been the apple of Gran's eye. She had a Type A personality from the moment she started kindergarten. Patrice always strived for perfection, she took charge, was considerate of others, she was well-mannered and possessed all the attributes of a fearless leader. Patrice had been on the A honor roll since her first day of school, she was also the class president from elementary to high school. Then she was valedictorian in college and business school. She excelled in sports as a member of the track and volleyball teams. Plus, she often volunteered and mentored other young black girls in her spare time. Overall, she was known as a proper role model, not only to her sisters but the community.

Amina on the other hand was a rebel without a cause. She had always been the black sheep of the family—getting into fights, being expelled from school, hanging with a crowd of thugs, she also cursed like a sailor and drank like a fish. Amina had spent most of her life in the cold darkness of Patrice's shadow. Her resentment ran deep. It ran deep until it became sorrow. And that sorrow brewed rage.

A rage that became the source of her power.

Through magic, and even through natural maternal instinct, Gran did her best to give Amina the love she needed, but she was stubborn and insisted on finding her own way.

Yolanda was the first to cut the tension in the room. "Amina, why don't you have a seat? We are having lasagna and salad," she said as she pulled out a chair.

Amina sat with her eyes still keen on Patrice, moving slowly, cautiously. "No thanks, I don't eat meat." She adjusted her chair in a prissy and pompous manner.

"You too? Don't worry we have a vegetarian option," Yolanda said gleefully.

Amina smiled. "Thanks, that sounds good."

"No problem. It's nice to not be the only vegetarian in the family." Yolanda said, smiling before turning the corner to fix Amina's plate.

In her head Patrice decided for once she was going to be nice to her younger sister. "So where are you coming from and where are your bags?" she asked low, with her voice almost dropping to a feminine tenor, as it often did.

"New York," Amina said placing her hands uncomfortably in her lap. "And I didn't bring any. I ain't staying here. I got a room downtown at the W Hotel."

"Hmmm. Okay," Patrice said nodding.

Makayla sat next to Amina, beaming. "So what's up superstar? Ms. Video Vixen. What rapper are you dating now? What brings you to town? And what did you bring me?" She fired one question after another rapidly. "Let me guess, you are in town to shoot a music video?" she said grabbing Amina's shoulder in excitement.

Amina cackled as she raked her twists to the side. "No video. Not this time. I came because I missed you guys." She forced a smile.

Patrice rolled her eyes. She was almost slammed back against the chair. "Really? You missed us? Six years and no phone call, text, tweet or letter—but you missed us?" Patrice leaned in closer, "You are not fooling me, Amina. After six years you show up out of the blue. Why are you here?"

"Well, I don't know about you, but we talk all the time," Makayla spoke up.

Patrice turned to Makayla, "Really?"

Makayla nodded her head. "Yes, we FaceTime every other day. I told her about the new house."

"Well that's good, but back to you," Patrice said shifting herself back to Amina. "Why are you here?

Yolanda returned from the kitchen and placed a full plate in front of Amina. "Not going to lie it's good to see you...but I'm just a bit curious myself." Yolanda smiled before settling back down in a chair across the table.

Aunt Dot peered up from her plate as she munched on her salad, a huge piece of lettuce wiped her bottom lip. Makayla batted her long, feathery eyelashes. All eyes were on Amina waiting anxiously for an answer.

She cracked a smile as she reached for a fork, "No, really I miss you guys. I have been traveling all over the world with my boyfriend Magnum, and I got tired of being on the road. He's on tour and I was alone in our spot in New York so I thought this would be a good time to visit my sisters." Amina picked at the food on her plate.

"That's so cool," Makayla commented.

Everyone resumed eating and then Patrice cut through the sounds of forks hitting plates with, "Bullshit. I don't believe you." She rested her chin firmly on her fist. It was an action that meant yes I said it, now what are you going to do about it.

Everyone looked up from their plates uncomfortably. Again the tension in the room became unbearable.

Amina continued looking down at her plate, "Really Patrice, I haven't been here five minutes yet and already you are starting with me." She looked over to Patrice and in usual Amina fashion, her anger was written all over her face. Amina was never one to hide or fake her emotions. As soon as you pissed her off you would know it from an arched brow, a wrinkling of the nose, or the cutting of her eyes. Of all the sisters she was the darkest in skin tone. The insecurity of feeling less beautiful than her sisters, coupled with the feelings of being an outsider amongst the group had shaped the tough armor that she carried daily. If anything her skin tone did not take away from her beauty, it strengthened it. She was the most beautiful shade of twilight and this made her carry herself like she was amongst the stars. Amina cocked her head, "Are you going to start with me already?"

"I'm not starting with you, little sister. I just don't believe you." Patrice gripped the edges of the table. "You may fool them but you don't fool me. I know you."

Amina cut her eyes at her sister, "Really? You know me?"

Patrice leaned in closer, "Yes, I know you." She sat back in her chair and folded her arms. "You are always up to something. And I feel this time is no different. You…showing up out of the blue. Do you owe someone money? Are you in a trouble? What's your game, Amina?"

"Hey!" Yolanda shouted as she raised a hand. "Be nice."

Dull anger came to Amina, making her right foot tap. She tossed her fork on the plate and it landed with a loud clink. "Here we go again. Ms. Perfect thinks she can judge me. You think you know me but you don't. I know you though."

"You know me?" Patrice asked.

"Yes," Amina shot back. "You are a controlling workaholic who can't keep a man to save her life," she spat with as much venom as she could.

Makayla gasped, "Shade heifer!" she shouted before covering her mouth. Yolanda and Aunt Dot glanced over at Patrice speechless.

Yolanda pointed her finger towards Amina. "Be nice."

There was that acid tongue of hers. When Amina felt offended, it often lashed out of control. And when it was out of control, she was liable to say anything to cut whoever opposed her. Amina wasn't one to go for soft blows, she always went for the jugular. And for that not only was she known as the troubled sister, she was known as the shady sister.

"Well of course, I can't keep one with skanks like you around," Patrice returned, meeting her level of lowness.

"Peaches!" Yolanda interjected, upset that her sister was about to make things go from bad to worst.

Amina pushed away from the table. "I know you are not talking about Robert," she asked with her face curled into the ugliest of frowns.

Patrice stood up at the table. "Yes, I'm talking about Robert. He was my boyfriend and you are my sister. I don't understand how you'd believe that what you did was right."

Amina waved her hands. "How many times do I have to apologize to you? For the millionth time, I'm sorry." With a hand on her hip, she leaned in. "But when you think about it...I was doing you a favor. Robert was community dick anyway. You thought he was the love of your life but so did every other girl."

Patrice leaned across the table. "Look Amina, I don't know why you're here but I'm going to let you know that I'll be damned if I let you do anything that will harm this family. You need to be clear on that."

Sensing the anger in her sister's voice, Yolanda stepped in "Peaches come on let's just sit down and enjoy dinner."

"What the hell are you talking about?" Amina shouted. "You know what your problem is?" Amina asked pointing her finger at Patrice. She waited for a beat to choose her words carefully and talk through the rising tides of her anger. "You think you are our mother. Well, I got some news for you, Peaches...you are *not* our mother. You are not Mom and you are not Gran neither."

Patrice's eyes watered. And her face stiffened.

There it is. That was the blow Amina was looking for. A sliver of a wicked smile spread across her lips. It made her feel so good.

"I may not be Mom or Gran, but I've been here. Where the HELL have you been? Besides selling yourself for a bag and getting shots in your bottom. How dare you speak to me like that? After all that I have sacrificed for this family." Patrice's voice shook, it was full of emotion.

"And we appreciate you," Yolanda murmured in a small voice as she rubbed Patrice's shoulder.

Patrice picked up her glass and took a big gulp. She paused then looked back at her sister. "You know...you are just like her. You are just like Mom. Selfish and reckless."

That was the button that didn't need to be pressed; it sent Amina into a fury. "How dare you, Peaches! Mom might not have been the perfect mother, but she was still our mom."

Patrice shook her head. "Get out of my house!"

Amina leaned forward. "You want me out then make me leave."

Patrice leaned forward on the table until they were breaths apart. "Trust me. This is not what you want."

A fire ignited in Amina's hands and she could feel the storm brew within. She aimed her steely gaze towards Patrice, "I command the mighty winds to stir, come forth in the place and protect me from my enemy. Come now, I conjure thee."

Suddenly, a fierce gust of wind blew through the doors and lifted open the windows. Amina's eyes glazed into a milky white color as currents of electricity ran up her tattooed arms and sparked from her hands. Amina's long dark twists blew all about as the powerful gusts swirled around her body. There was a rush of wind, a force so powerful that it swept the plates off the table and blew them into the air. It was both obvious and shocking to the sisters that it was Amina who was channeling the powerful winds around her.

Amina swirled her hands. "No, this is not what you want?" she mocked, challenging her sister.

"Okay, that's enough, girls," Aunt Dot shouted above the rattle of the blinds as they knocked back and forth on the window.

Wind stirred all around them and wisps of electricity danced through the air. Total silence fell across the room as the winds lifted Amina into the air. As powerful winds bent to her will, she became wraith personified.

Beauty and terror at all once.

A living hurricane.

Makayla looked at Amina in fear. "Yo sis-chill out."

Patrice stood frozen in shock. "How in the world did you get your gifts back? We bound them." She said, recalling the hex they'd done to strip Amina of her powers, in fear that she was turning to the dark side.

Amina smiled devilishly, "Let's just say I'm more powerful and more connected to the spirits than you think."

Patrice huffed at her. "Well I don't know how you got them back but I want you OUT!" she bellowed, her voice rolling like thunder. The power of her words sent Amina flying all the way from the dining room table and around the corner to the front door. Amina hit the door with a loud bam before she crumpled to the floor.

"Peaches!" Yolanda shouted in disappointment. "I can't believe you did that." She hurried from the dining room to check on her sister. The swirling winds immediately subsided.

Aunt Dot let out a hearty dry laugh. "I know that's right, Peaches. You will not come talk to me any type of way…in my house…that I pay bills in…not on my watch." She hit the table and continued laughing.

Amina picked herself from off the floor. "Some things never change," she said as she grabbed for the door.

Yolanda tried to race after her, but she was too late. Amina was already out the door.

5

MIDNIGHT

*A*round midnight that night, Amina strolled through a nearby graveyard seeking an audience with her savior. Papa Samedi had kept his promise. He had healed her body and returned her gifts. Now it was time to fulfill her part of the deal. How Amina was going to do that without harming her sisters, she had no idea.

Like always, her plan was to con her way out. As she walked, the Georgia air became humid and thick as a rolling fog swept across the graves around her. Surrounding her were the noises of the creatures of the night—the hum of insects, the call of night birds, and the rustling of small animals. For most people, this would be unsettling but Amina felt right at home. A part of her always felt like a creature of the night.

Amina hugged herself. She shivered in her t-shirt with her belly exposed. Above her rose moss-draped trees, stretching up to misty clouds that covered the moonless sky. Mosquitos buzzed all around Amina's face as she walked across the overgrown grass of the graveyard.

Despite the mosquitos Amina still thought it was beautiful out in the cemetery. Weathered ivory statues covered in moss littered the graveyard and Amina had felt herself back in New Orleans for a moment. Somehow throughout the mess she could picture the graveyard in its splendor before. Yes indeed it was beautiful, but she figured it would've been better if she weren't here alone.

If she had a lover.

A thug.

Magnum.

Just like that, a vision of Magnum sauntered to her mind. That man was so damn fine to her still. He was 6'3, dark skin, big lips, chinky eyes, thick eyebrows, and tattoos everywhere. Just thinking about his prison muscles made Amina's body moist and quiver. Magnum was her type down to the T. She loved men with that fresh out of jail look.

It was sexy.

Magnum was the rare type that appeared hard upon first glance, but boyish in the next, whenever he smiled. She missed the magnetism of his embrace, the way he pulled her hips, grabbed her ass, held her body against his.

And she knew he'd probably take her face down out here with no questions asked. He would make her come at least three times. A dick game that was untouched. It was the only thing that made her feel the electricity of her lost magic. After years of scamming and stripping, Amina lucked up with a baller who could make her come. Then she fucked it up by crossing him. Normally she was the type to never catch feelings. Securing the bag was the main mission. Always. This time she slipped up, and it cost her.

I still can't believe he shot me, she thought to herself.

He cheated on her with random groupies.

She stole his money and leaked his music. Amina thought it was a pretty even trade.

Hot tears of anger bubbled in her dark eyes. Magnum would pay as soon as she shook the demon.

Midnight was the time when the ancient Voodoo priestess believed magic was at its highest. Amina could feel this untamed energy in the air. It was a tingling sensation, the power surging through her. As she walked farther into the graveyard, goosebumps formed on her forearms, right along her tattoo sleeve. She shuddered as she sensed a dark presence.

Amina spun around. Papa Samedi materialized behind her, whirling through shadows. "How did it go, cher?" he asked in a menacing voice as he gripped his cane.

Amina circled him, "I'm in there but like I said it's not going to be as easy as it seems."

"Well, let's make it easier," the demon said as he retrieved a diamond-studded blade from his side. "This is the dagger of shadows. Stab it through the hearts of your sisters and it shall remove their powers."

Amina looked down at the blade and frowned. "I know what that is. And I'm not using that on my sisters."

"Pardon me?"

With a flick of his wrist, the angry Loa made Amina fall to the ground in uncontrollable convulsions. Amina flopped and rolled through mud and grass. "Don't tell me you're going soft on me now. We made a deal and I want what's mine... witch."

In uncontrollable pain she pleaded, "I know and I plan to keep our deal. I have another way. I can get them to relinquish their gifts without killing them."

Satisfied, Papa Samedi released his hold on Amina. "You had better. I'm not playing with you witch. I want that power. With all the powers from the Lawson sisters combined, I should have access to the powers of the Phoenix."

Amina cautiously eased herself off the ground. "I promise you. I won't fail you."

"You better not," the demon hissed.

As Papa Samedi watched Amina walk out of the graveyard, a yellow boa constrictor slithered its way toward him. The snake stretched almost six feet long. He turned to the snake, "So what do you think?"

Morphing out of the yellow boa constrictor came a six-foot tall demoness covered in pale yellow scales and eyes red as fire. Protruding from her forehead were curving horns, thick as an elephant's tusk that twisted upward, and her hair was pulled tightly into many knots. She was known as Mama Brigitte, and she was another member of the dark Loa. She was also Papa Samedi's wife.

"I think she can't be trusted," she said as she slinked closer to his side.

"Exactly," Papa Samedi agreed before holding his hand out. "Follow me."

Mama Brigitte followed him until he came across a grave that was covered with weeds. "Here lies Thomas Gaines. A rapist and mass murderer. One of the best souls I ever collected. The demon sliced into his hands with his long talon and bled out blood as dark as night on the grave.

Rising through sand and mud came a casket. Thomas burst out of the casket with a thunderous fist and leapt to his feet. Papa Samedi had the ability to bring back the dead. It was through him many Voodoo practitioners prayed to for help in necromancy rituals. Whatever was left of Thomas was gone; he was now a puppet to Papa Samedi.

A zombie.

Papa Samedi handed Thomas the shadow blade. "I have a job for you. Run this blade into the heart of the youngest Lawson sister and bring me her power. Do that and I'll let you roam this earth in your old body. Fully alive and healed."

Thomas nodded in agreement.

Mama Brigitte looked to her husband. "What is the meaning of this? Why don't you just have him kill Amina…take her soul and be done with it."

"I can't!" he spat back. "The soul is power. And for eons now we have maintained our existence by the feasting on damned souls and worship from fools. This is a meaningless existence. I want more."

"More?" she questioned.

"With the deal, I have with Amina, I have felt power I have never felt. A taste if you will. I restored her powers and now her soul is bound to mine. She grows stronger and so do I."

Mama Brigitte looked worried, "What are you saying, love?"

"With the gifts of all four sisters. I'll have enough power to rival the Phoenix. I can become The Creator."

"That's blasphemous!" Mama Brigitte declared.

"No. To continue existing in a world of darkness is. As The Creator, I can create a new existence or conquer this one." Papa Samedi railed before he laughed with an evil scoff.

Mama Brigitte shuddered as she stared into the eyes of her lover.

Papa Samedi took her hand and kissed it. "As always I can't do anything without you, my love."

She lowered her head. "I will be by your side, as always."

6

GET READY

*P*atrice let out a tired sigh as she rocked back and forth on her porch. It was a little past midnight and, as usual, she couldn't fall asleep to save her life. All was quiet in her neighborhood. Fall winds blew and she shivered underneath the handmade quilt she'd wrapped around herself. Amina had brought trouble back to their front door. Patrice could feel it. This time it wasn't her being paranoid or over-protective. *God knows what that girl is up to,* she thought. She reached over to her right and sipped at her peppermint tea. Aromatic notes of mint danced in her nose as the warmth of the tea soothed her soul. It was nippy outside for early fall in Georgia, but she loved it out here. There was something about the crisp air and quiet of the community that brought her peace. Not enough to sleep but just enough to stop worrying.

On nights like this she did the only thing that could ease her mind. A ritual for protection. While everyone slept the night away, Patrice laid lines of rock salt in the corners of her house and burned frankincense and myrrh outside. Her grandmother had performed the same ritual every night when Patrice and her sisters were little girls and had taught it to her.

Even though she no longer practiced magic, she couldn't help but continue Gran's ritual for protection. She had her sisters to protect. They were the most important thing in her life. Twin plumes of smoke swirled into the air, as the incense lay burning in a small pan of aluminum foil beside her ivory rocking chair. When the fire from the incense dimmed, Patrice grabbed it and strolled back into the house.

As Patrice entered she was swept away by the warmth that enveloped the home. She paused to listen. All was quiet except for the ticking of an antique grandfather clock that rested by the kitchen door. Striding into the kitchen she placed her mug in the sink and tossed the foil of burnt incense into the trash can. She was folding her quilt and preparing to go upstairs when a small, still voice called out to her. At first she thought it was nothing since the voice started as a whisper. But the voice called louder.

Peaches... Peaches...

As she listened closely, she noticed that the voice didn't call her by her government name but by the nickname given to her by Gran. Leery, she followed the call of the faint voice. She followed the voice out of the kitchen, down the hall, and to the basement door. Patrice opened the basement door, still leery but hopeful.... hopeful somehow that her grandmother had found a way back to her even through the afterlife. Patrice turned on the basement light and trekked down the stairs.

The light bulb flickered as she trotted down. *I told Makayla to change that bulb a week ago,* she thought. Patrice rolled her eyes.

When she arrived downstairs, the voice fell silent. Patrice

circled the basement until she came to a bunch of old stacked containers. A grey container rumbled underneath the stack, causing the others to buckle against the wall. Suddenly the container sprung to life and slid across the room to her feet. Patrice leapt back as her heart pounded. Without hesitation, she sprinted back up the stairs.

"Peaches…. Peaches," Gran called again.

Patrice turned around. She descended the stairs again, took in a deep breath, and fell to her knees as she opened the container.

Buried underneath old clothes, candles, and photographs from their home in New Orleans, she found a book she hadn't seen in a long time. It was called the Legacy, a magical tome that chronicles the rituals and history of her ancestors. Five hundred seventy-two wonderfully crafted and illustrated folios, bound in brown leather and covered in gold. Created by Marie Laveau in the 17th century, it is one of the most coveted magical books in existence and almost four hundred years old. Depicted on the cover was a tree—its roots, symbolizing the continual growth of the family line based on the wisdom of their ancestors.

It had been years since Patrice had last seen the Legacy. She remembered it being more illustrious then but after being in storage for years, it had lost its beautiful golden color. The Legacy was the most important heirloom in her family. Marie was the beginning of their bloodline. Her power flowed through Patrice's veins and her sisters. Most voodoo practitioners and witches spent decades trying to achieve the power the Lawson's had, which they called gifts. Patrice could move things with her mind and conjure fire. Born after Patrice was Amina, who could conjure storms. Yolanda, the third sister, was clairvoyant and touched by the spirits. And her youngest sister Makayla had yet to manifest an active gift. Patrice expected Makayla would come into her gifts any day now, especially since she'd just turned sixteen, the age gifts manifest. That was another problem Patrice would have to deal with.

"Get ready," Gran murmured and the sound of her voice was so clear that Patrice could've sworn the old woman was over her shoulder.

Patrice pulled the Legacy out of the container. It was heavy and the dull gold plating felt cold as marble in her hands. She set it on her lap and it had the weight of a newborn baby. As it laid in her lap, the pages of the Legacy flipped and fell open to one particular ritual.

To Conjure the Spirit

To call the spirit of the most high, Phoenix, one must gather the ingredients, dress the candle, burn in a bowl and recite the spell. You will need:

o   Rattle Snake Blood
o   rosemary
o   thyme
o   Dragon blood oil
o   High john the conquer root

Patrice shook her head, "Gran, what are you doing?" she asked out loud.

It had been years since she had practiced real root magic, the rituals Gran had taught her and the spells she worked for others, to pay for her college education. Even now she kept some items for rituals in the house. But why did Gran want her to conjure the Phoenix? As she wondered what Gran was trying to tell her, the light bulb flickered again. On and then off. It burned bright and eerily dimmed. Then suddenly the lights went out in the basement, and darkness loomed all around.

Patrice shuddered. Her bones stiffened. She blinked and when she opened her eyes, the basement was red. Patrice stood up gingerly. Red shrouded around her, thick and murky red, like a fog. The hair on the back of her neck stood upright like soldiers as survival instincts slammed into her head. A dark spirit was in the room. She could sense it. Goosebumps pricked her arm as the room became frighteningly cold.

Without warning, the Legacy sprang up off the floor. Patrice grabbed the book with cat-like reflexes. An unseen force yanked back, almost snatching the book out of her grasp, so she pulled back harder. Patrice and the unseen entity played tug of war with her family's most precious heirloom. Nothing, and no one, was going to take the Legacy. She wouldn't allow it. Patrice snatched the tome back, and across the room she slid on her behind.

A raw scream erupted from her throat as her back slammed against the wall. She stood up, her legs throbbing in pain. Patrice raked her gaze around the basement and she almost jumped out of her skin when she saw the silhouette of a man cast against the wall. He was the dark spirit. She knew that in her bones. But how did he get inside the house? How did he get pass the barriers of protection? In her head she remembered the words of her grandmother. *Never show fear in the face of evil. Talk to it like a man if you have to. Show your strength.*

Patrice swallowed her fear and summoned strength. "I will only say this once. Get the hell out of my house!"

The shadow laughed at her. His dark voice rolled around the walls of the basement, like a tumbleweed blowing in the wind. Patrice peered closely at the shadow. She saw something through the red. Through the darkness. Lips that curled into a malicious sneer. Although she couldn't make out a face, she could tell he was grinning at her, mocking her, and taking delight in her fear. The shadow moved and suddenly a towering presence loomed behind Patrice. Her blood ran ice cold. Warm breath blew on her neck. Rough hands ran down her shoulders. Her lips quivered at the inkling of his touch. It was a touch so cold, it felt like death itself. The man in the shadow was behind her. Don't turn around, she thought. Don't look.

Lips lowered to her ears. "I come for your powers," a heavy Cajun voice whispered.

Patrice swung her fist. "Get out!"

Nothing was behind her. The shadow was gone. As she looked around the basement, something tugged her arm to the other side.

"Get ready!" Gran uttered with her eyes glaring, both hands on Patrice's shoulder almost shaking her. The look on Gran's face told Patrice her grandmother had to fight from the other side just to say these two words to her. Her eyes watered. Fear and hope struck her at the same time. Gran vanished before she could get a good look at her. She was there only for a second, only long enough for Patrice to get a glimpse at her face, only for her to see the urgency in her eyes.

"Peaches!" a voice called.

The light bulb flickered and the lights came on. And the red faded away along with the man in the shadow.

"Peaches, are you down there?"

Patrice glared up to the basement door. Makayla stood in the doorway with a baseball bat in hand. She still had the fog of sleep in her eyes as she stood there in her pajamas and hair wrapped with a pink scarf.

"Peaches is that you? What are you doing down there?" Makayla asked, her voice still filled with sleep.

"Just looking through some old stuff," Patrice said as she placed the Legacy back in the old grey container. She grabbed the railing of the stairs, but before she walked up, she glanced back and made the container slide back across the room with her mind.

"What are you doing up?" she asked in her motherly voice.

Makayla rested the bat on her shoulder. "Girl, I thought somebody was robbing us. If you hadn't answered me, you would have gotten all of this bat action, okay."

Patrice shrugged. "Robbed in this neighborhood? C'mon let's go back to bed."

"All right," Makayla said as she trekked back upstairs.

The storm was over or so she thought. After six years of a magic-free existence, evil had found its way past the doorstep and into the house. There would be no sleeping for Patrice that night. She settled in her mind that she would burn and chant all night long if necessary. As Patrice closed the door to the basement, she looked behind as she thought back to the sound of her grandmother's voice. The lost hope. Maybe one day she would hear from her Gran again.

7

A DOLL'S DILEMMA

hy her?

It was the question Makayla always asked herself whenever she saw them. Makayla felt hopeless, standing at her locker watching and wondering what Devante could ever see in Erica King. Yes, it's true Erica has a big ole butt. But to Makayla what else was there? If you asked her she would tell you that Erica King is a dusty looking girl with a loud mouth, and a nasty gap between her teeth. In her mind there was no comparison between the two of them.

But yet, there he was with her.

Makayla had been in love with Devante ever since he moved into town from Florida two summers ago. Devante Wilson is a vision of tall muscles wrapped in caramel skin, with perfect curly hair styled into a faux hawk. He plays on the varsity basketball team and he is the "It boy" of North Central. That's why she was so baffled as to why he's been dating Erica King. In her mind she figured he needed someone as equally popular and beautiful at his side. Someone who would hold him down. Makayla wasn't necessary the "it" girl of North Central yet... but she wanted to be. Makayla stood watching their every move.

Erica pulled Devante into a kiss, and Makayla could only dig her nails into her book bag strap to keep from punching the girl. As he kissed Erica, she cut her eyes towards Makayla. Makayla's rage intensified. She thought about stomping over there and snatching Erica to the ground before dragging her across the hall. She entertained the idea for a moment, but realized Patrice would kill her after another suspension.

"Look at her... she thinks she cute." Wallace said as he leaned into Makayla's ear. Wallace is a tall pimply boy, with curly brown highlighted hair. His bad acne and feminine ways often got him picked on but his quick wit was often enough to back away any of his haters. Most important of all he was well dressed, extremely intelligent and was the only person in the school who had a love for fashion that could rival Makayla's.

Makayla curled her lips, "I don't know why with that late outfit, looking like she went to Citi Trends to get her fashion for less. Mmkay?"

"Yass," Wallace shouted.

They laughed together in sync. Both throwing their heads back and chuckling as if they were the rich & famous. Overhead, the bell rang making the crowd of students in the hall stir.

Devante and Erica walked towards them. His arm wrapped around Erica's shoulder while her arm rests comfortably around his waist. Devante glanced over to Makayla, and time slowed down to match the hard thump of her heart.

Makayla turned towards the hall, brushed her hair down and across before waiting in anticipation.

"What's up Makayla?" Devante said in his smooth southern drawl.

Makayla's heartbeat went into overdrive. A heat wave flashed over her buttery brown skin but as this all happened, she remained cool as a cucumber. Batting her eyes, she replied. "Hey Devante."

Erica smacked him on the chest, "Don't be speaking to her." She grumbled. Erica's lips curled into the ugliest of frowns, as she sized Makayla up with her eyes.

Makayla folded her arms. "Girl, fix that face."

Erica sucked her teeth. "Fix that horrible weave," she shot back. Her little minions Brittany and Amy laugh at her joke, and join her from behind.

"Y'all better keep walking!" Wallace shouted.

After a few more eye rolls they continue down the hall to disappear into the mass of students. Devante pulled her closer to him, and a sharp pain stabs Makayla's thumping heart.

Makayla turned to Wallace, "It doesn't matter if we think she's cute or not…. he does." The words came out in a whimpering moan.

"But I mean why be with a five when you can get with a ten," Wallace said as he looked his best friend over. "My bestie is fab."

Makayla smiled, "Thanks bestie." She looped her arm into his and they strolled down the hallway together.

"Makayla what happened to our plan?" he asked. "By now we should be dating all the boys on the basketball team and running this school. Instead we are just some struggling sophomores."

Makayla placed a finger over his lips, " Let me stop you right there, before you continue on with these lies. Honey, the doll doesn't struggle. She is fierce!" She said as they continued to stroll down the hallway. "We just have to make sure everyone knows it." She said with the suggestion lingering in the air like a question.

As they strolled by a bulletin board in the hallway, a light-bulb went off in Makayla's head. She ripped off a flyer from the bulletin board. "I got it. Let's join the North Central cheer-leading team."

"Okay, I'm here for it. That sounds like fun." Wallace squealed before coming back down to earth by a sudden conclusion. "But wait... isn't Erica the cheerleading captain."

Makayla nodded her head, "She is for now. But after me and you turn it for this audition... she won't be for long."

Together they laughed on cue.

Wallace looked at the flyer closer. "But wait the audition is this afternoon."

Makayla sighed, "That means we have no time to waste. Come on, this is a good excuse for us to go to Starbucks for lunch and watch YouTube clips from Bring It On, so we can pump out a quick routine." Makayla counted the tasks on her fingers. "We meet up to brain storm for lunch, put something together at Starbucks, then come back and turn it out. It's really simple."

"Bet, count me in love." Wallace said before double kissing Makayla's cheek. "You have a nice day and be sure to text me before lunch."

"Oh I will darling."

They hugged it out and parted ways. Everything Erica Kane had, Makayla wanted and she determined that she would bring her enemy down one way or another.

8
LOVELY

*Y*olanda thought about doing something cute with her hair before her next client was to come over. She had a little over an hour to waste and figured in no time she could do some cute twists and maybe get some studying done. When she passed by the mirror she became transfixed with her own beauty.

Becoming a vegan was one of the greatest things I've ever done, she thought to herself. She was free from all the nasty, harmful chemicals on her hair and in her body. Plus every time she looks into the mirror, she was reminded of how much weight she lost.

Yolanda adjusted her large red glasses and delighted in the image before her. She ran her fingers through her hair, a wild bountiful bush that shimmers in the light. Her pale yellow skin glowed just as bright her aura. She lifted her CAU sweatshirt to look down at her stomach.

Flat like never before.

Blowing out hard she pushed out her belly button as far as it could go, then smacked it. "Ow!" Yolanda said before chuckling.

Yolanda was a rose that finally blossomed. It took her a long time to get here, in her mind. She could confidently say *I am beautiful,* but it also helped that she wasn't standing next to any of her sisters. After all she used to think she was cursed growing up. In her mind she was the sister that got screwed out of the good beauty genes and stuck dealing with the dead.

Yolanda thought about it carefully. Patrice came out of the womb looking like America's Next Top Model. Then Amina had the amazingly big knockers, and this was before the surgery. Now she was a certified video vixen with an hourglass frame. Even Makayla came into her beauty much quicker than she did, damn.

"The glow up from high school was so real." She whispered out loud. She came a long way from being the chubby light skin girl, always red in the face, with frizzy hair, and dressed in a thick sweater. High school was the worst. Yolanda grabbed a pillow and fell back onto the bed with a moan. Once the kids found out her middle name was Myrtle they used to make fun of her. They called her Myrtle the snapping turtle. Mostly because of the shape of her mouth. This was before the braces.

Oh no.

Just the thought of the name made her turn red and cry. She snatched off her glasses and dabbed at her big round eyes. High school was hell for Yolanda, and the first year of college wasn't all that great either. But now things had changed.

She had changed.

And that change didn't just come from becoming vegan. It

had come from love. She had met Malcolm, her little love Mochi, the day she made the big chop, about a year ago. The first thing Yolanda did was head to Eternal Sunshine, the best vegan soul food café in the city.

There she met a six-foot even, chocolate Jamaican king with a perfect mane of locks and white straight teeth. Strangely she always had a thing for nice straight teeth on a man. Yolanda believed teeth to be a good indicator of health, and that's important. Ever since that day, the two of them were inseparable.

She was convinced Malcolm had been sent to her by the Gods. He was smart, down to earth and spiritual. In many ways he was different than Yolanda but yet he still understood her. He didn't look at her like she was crazy, which most people do. Malcolm was the one who introduced her to the powers locked into different crystals. Their natural uses had been something he'd been studying for years. And not to mention he has had experiences with the other side before. Once he told her about the time the ghost of a previous owner haunted his childhood home, she knew she could trust him. More importantly she could be herself around him.

Whether that's Harry Potter and K-pop obsessed Yolanda, all natural soul sister Yolanda, or fight the power Black Lives Matter Yolanda.

Just as Yolanda buried her head into her pillow, thinking about her love bug, she heard a knock at the door. She tossed the pillow to the side and walked over to answer it. When she opened the door, before she could say hello, he was kissing her. He held her close, blessed her lips for a long time, kissed her as if he'd return from ten years at war.

"Queen," He said after finally releasing Yolanda from his hold. He walked in as she closed the door behind him. "What are you doing here so early?" Yolanda asked following behind. "I didn't expect you for another hour or so."

Malcolm flashed that infectious smile of his, accented by pearly white teeth. "I needed to spend some alone time with the Queen. Is something wrong with that?"

"Aww baby thanks, but I was going to study." Yolanda moaned, dragging her feet over to the desk, before leaning against it, and propping her foot up on a chair.

Malcolm loomed over her. "You don't need to study. All you need to do is relax and let me comfort you." Then he grabbed at Yolanda's sides and tickled her until laughter tore through her body.

He did that every time they were together and by now you would think she would expect it. "Stop," Yolanda said in a dry heave. She was laughing so hard, that tears streamed from her eyes. "Stop it! I'm being serious this is for a major class."

Finally, he stopped and said, "Yolanda, baby you worry too much. You will do well on your exam."

"I will do well? How do you know?"

"Because you are the queen," he said as he positioned himself between her legs.

Yolanda beamed all over. So much so, that she had to take her glasses off to wipe the sweat from her eyes. "You know Malcolm I love you so much. Do you know that? I don't think I can ask for a better man than you. You are always at my side encouraging me, cheering me on, and motivating me to use my gifts to help people. Hell you believe in me more than I believe in myself. Baby you're awesome."

He took Yolanda's right leg in his hand. "Uh huh."

She raised an eyebrow at him. "Uh huh," she repeated. "Is that all you have to say?"

Malcolm shrugged. "That's all that needs to be said. Yolanda you know how I feel about you. You are the most powerful and gentle soul I've ever met. I can't help but to love you."

Yolanda buried her face in her hands to hold back the happy tears.

Malcolm slid back the right leg of her sweat pant so he could place a kiss on her thigh. "Now let me taste that cat."

Laughter tore through them.

Once the chuckling subsided, he cleaned up his statement. "But real talk... how can I make you feel good?"

"Take off these socks and suck these damn toes." Yolanda commanded. Usually she never liked to talk dirty but with Malcolm she was comfortable to do whatever.

He started suckling on her big toe and it felt so good that she touched herself.

"Is that what you want?" Malcolm asked with his voice dropping an octave.

"Yes," she answered in a hiss.

He traced his long wet tongue across the ridges of Yolanda's toes. Tingles traveled up her spine as his tongue crossed each one. Her nipples ached fiercely.

With her eyes closed she whispered, "That's nice."

"That's nice huh?"

"Yes."

He slipped all five toes in his warm mouth and a wave of pleasure made her gasp. Yolanda's chest heaved almost as if someone punched her in the back. "Baby," She squealed.

Malcolm chuckled. "That's right girl tell daddy how good it

feels." He took off the other sock and Yolanda presented her left foot for him. Malcolm held her foot as if he was about to put a glass slipper on it, instead he ran his tongue between her toes and suckled each one.

The man never ceased to amaze her. She grabbed the edge of the desk and fixed her eyes towards the gods. "Baby that's enough," she said. "Make love to me."

In one swift motion, Yolanda was lifted off her feet, and carried to the bed. They undressed each other as they kissed. He pulled Yolanda's sweatshirt over her head and ran his hands down her spine. She pulled his basketball shorts to his knees and wrapped her legs around his waist. Then he laid her on the bed and pulled off her sweats.

So much passion, heat, and sexual energy sparked beautiful colors around them. Yolanda's aura had always been the faintest shade of lavender while Malcolm's was silver. But as they kissed, held, touched each other, she saw bursts of magenta with exploding golden sparkles.

"Stay right there for mi baby." Malcolm said as he got on his knees.

Yolanda laid back and watched as he pulled down her panties. Malcolm parted her legs and kissed her in the most intimate places. "Moan for mi baby." He whispered.

"Ooh baby."

Malcolm put his tongue on Yolanda's pussy and her soul left her body.

Suddenly all of the walls of the room folded, and she was sent spiraling somewhere amongst stars. Pitch blackness surrounded her as she ascended higher and higher, to another plane. She looked back and saw herself on the bed, Malcolm between her knees. *I am still there yet I am here*, she thought.

Malcolm's tongue slid further as he parted her legs. Although she was as two, she could still feel his pleasure. His love. It overwhelmed her.

"Are you with mi baby?"

"Yes."

Malcolm shifted, spread her wide, put both his hands to legs as he lapped at her wetness. His tongue went deep, exploring further as he started a rhythm that sounded like churning butter. Then he added a finger.

Touched her here and there.

By now he knew the spot and how to get to it. He was torturing her. Yolanda never knew that a woman could have to struggle to keep her hands off a man, and she never figured she'd be that type of girl. But he was so rude.

And it turned her on.

"We got any more condoms?" He asked.

Yolanda pointed to the desk. "In the drawer," she said. Tears of an angel ran between her legs as she stared at his blessing, stiff and swinging between his legs. She giggled devilishly as she stared at him.

Malcolm looked over his shoulder and Yolanda's desire magnified. "What's so funny baby?" He asked, dreads perfectly flowing down his glistening back which ran down to a perfect ass. An ass that Yolanda thought could win a worldwide competition. Her baby had run track since high school, and that muscle milk butt of his was her favorite feature behind his smile, until he rolled down the condom and rightfully it became her third favorite.

Just looking at that thing made her think how nervous she was their first time. Especially since she was so inexperienced. When she saw it and how it grew, she said *no way jose*. Yolanda measured it herself. It was eleven and a half inches exactly. She didn't think that men in the real world were blessed like this. She had only seen two penises before. One with her first, Treyvion, who popped her cherry in his grandma's basement. The other from a dirty magazine Amina showed her once. Yolanda concluded Malcolm was the best she'd ever seen.

"Ready for mi baby?" Malcolm asked.

The Yolanda on Earth rubbed her nipples. While the Yolanda in the higher plane ran her fingers through her hair. "Yes," they both said.

Malcolm climbed on top of her. He kissed her passionately, grabbed a fistful of her aching breast, and took her right leg in the crook of his elbow. Malcolm entered her on a wailing groan, making her ascend higher amongst the stars. He was powerful in the way he took her. His first stroke was enough to shatter mountains. Malcolm filled her deeply, he kept his smoky eyes on hers, he wanted to see each gasp, witness each hiss of breath from the strength of his hips. His erection grew even inside of her, opening her up, spreading her womb wider. Deep inside her he held her close and sang her praise.

"Oh baby you're so deep. Take it easy."

Malcolm slowed his pace. He was a patient lover and he had to be. "Deep breaths. Baby breathe."

"Sweet gods," She murmured.

He kissed her and she nodded for him to continue. His pace quickened and her body loosened, welcomed him. Yolanda moaned as he fucked her to a peaceful weightlessness.

Fire swept through his lungs, she felt it the moment it swept through hers. It was something magnificent and powerful, waves of pleasure and orgasm crashing one after the other. It was something so powerful that it forced him to cry out as he pounded her, juices splashing from her womb. Her soul plummeted back to her body. All the stars fell. His blessing spasmed and spewed like a hose. His body jerked on top of her, he moaned, and then fell on top of her in a lump.

Our love is poetic, she thought.

It is magnetic.

It is made of the things that shatter stars.

Yolanda basked in the feeling that came from satisfaction of the flesh. She felt at ease, it was the spiritual release that came with orgasm. Malcolm's love always takes her to another place, to different worlds, where stars reign.

They laid that way for a moment, her fingers stroking his locs, his arms wrapped around hers, his strong muscled legs against her soft legs. As Yolanda laid in the comfort of Malcolm's arms she knew two things to be true. She had been put on this Earth to battle it's evil and she was made to love him.

Right then, a vision flashed before her eyes like lightning.

*Y*olanda was looking down and the sun glistened behind her. Malcolm's hands were covering hers. And she was gazing down at a child.

A girl.

Yolanda was not the same. She was much older. This is the future, she thought. Malcolm turned her cheek. She was smiling.

"Let's call her Lovely," he said.

Yolanda caressed the girl's soft round cheeks. Her eyes were sparkling diamonds. "Lovely?" She repeated. Then Yolanda opened her eyes.

"What did you say baby?" Malcolm asked.

Yolanda shook her head. She peered up to him. "I love you."

"I love you too," He says.

Their legs vibrated due to Malcolm's phone. "She's here," Malcolm said as he read the text.

9

THE SKULL

*I*t took Yolanda no longer than about five minutes to get ready for the client. She wrapped her hair in a gorgeous purple hair wrap. She pulled out her little green storage bin and tossed a black table cloth over it. Then she arranged pillows around the bin. The setup was nothing fancy but it got the job done.

She went to her desk and retrieved a lighter to burn smudge incense. Just as soon as she twirled the smudge around the room, she heard a knock at the door.

Malcolm entered slowly with a tall red haired girl that was about as yellow as Yolanda. "Rachel meet the ear to the gods, Yolanda The Supreme."

Rachel smiled as she stuck out her hand. "It's nice to finally put a face to the voice. Your reading over the phone was spot on. I had to meet you."

Yolanda moved her hand out of the way and hugged the girl. "Come beloved and have a seat." She pointed to the pillows around the bin.

Yolanda sat on a pillow with Malcolm behind her, and Rachel sat on the other side. Her red hair glistened in the faint light, it was the first thing Yolanda noticed upon meeting her. Yolanda placed her tarot cards on top of the bin. The cards she used were vibrant blue at the center, edged in gold and illustrated in vivid detail.

"Don't be nervous Rachel. I promise you Yolanda is the best." Malcolm said as he sat on the edge of the bed leaning in.

Yolanda chanted over the stack of cards then placed them on the makeshift table. "Okay Rachel, I need you to cut the deck into four."

Rachel did as told and split the huge deck of cards into four. She glanced back up at Yolanda for further instruction. With her eyes closed, Yolanda started with the first deck from the left. "The blinded fool," she said as she flipped the card over. "Well, this is obvious. You wanted to know if Ray is cheating on you and that's yes. I mean he is a football player so come on."

"I knew I couldn't trust him," Rachel grumbled underneath her breath.

Yolanda went to the next card, "Eight of Pentacles that's good news because in spite of Raymond you are excelling in your classes. And I see a new scholarship might be heading your way. Are you a graduating senior?"

"Yes," Rachel answered nervously. "I'm trying to get into Morehouse Medical."

Yolanda smiled, "Well I see you getting in with a banging scholarship at that."

Rachel clapped, "Okay that's good news. That's what I want to hear."

Yolanda's smile widened. Using her gifts to help people was

something she was genuinely passionate about. She glanced over at Malcolm and he kissed her on the forehead. When she first told Malcolm about her gifts, he took it as a joke. He didn't believe her until she warned him about taking a trip to South Africa with other students for alternative spring break. The plane malfunctioned and crashed, everyone on the flight died. Since then he encouraged Yolanda to help people in spite of Patrice's warnings. Patrice saw their gifts as an invitation to evil but Yolanda saw her gifts as a way to help the innocent.

Yolanda didn't know how she was going to break it to Patrice. She knew Patrice probably wanted her to graduate and get a job or go to grad school. But Yolanda knew that wasn't going to happen. She was going to marry Malcolm after graduating and travel the country solving supernatural mysteries together. She had spent most of her life believing herself to be crazy, it only made sense she married the man that could see her for who she was.

Queen. Ear to the spirits.

Yolanda flipped the card on top of the third stack. "Butterfly!" She exclaimed. "This is very good. A butterfly symbolizes transition and transformation. It means you are becoming a better person and you are about to enter a new season."

"Keep going," Rachel cheered.

Yolanda flipped the card out of the final stack and gasped as she revealed a skull.

Rachel jerked her gaze to Yolanda whose face went ghostly pale at the sight of the card. When she saw the skull, she became just as frightened as Yolanda did. Rachel stood up, "Huh? What does this mean? Am I going to die?"

"Not necessarily, it could mean the death of bad habits or old relationships." Yolanda tried to reason but she was still startled. There was a bad feeling whirling in her gut that made her nervous.

Yolanda picked the card up to examine it closer and as she did a ghastly vision came to her. It slammed into her head so hard that it made her hair extend out and loosen from the scarf. In it she saw Makayla frightened and scared out of her mind. She was being cornered by a massive man who was wielding a weird knife. Makayla was in a locker room with nowhere to go. Her attacker had his hands wrapped around Makayla's neck as he pinned her against the wall. Just as it came, the vision left her abruptly the same.

In fright, Yolanda hopped up and screamed. Rachel did the same. "It means death. I can't believe it. I don't want to die. Fuck that Malcolm I'm outta here." She shouted as she exited the room, leaving the door open behind her.

Malcolm grabbed a hold of Yolanda who was still screaming in fear. "What is it? Baby what did you see?" He asked.

"Makayla... Makayla," Yolanda hiccupped. repeatedly. She ran to the corner of the room and grabbed her phone. She had to call her big sister, Patrice. "Peaches Where is Makayla?" She asked but Patrice ignored and asked her about coming over to dinner. "No listen to me," Yolanda insisted. "We got to go get Makayla. I had a vision and baby girl is in danger."

"Stay calm. I'll drive by to get you in five minutes." Patrice said in a confident voice over the phone.

Yolanda shook her head, "Okay."

"What is it? What did you see," Malcolm asked again.

"No time. My sister is in trouble." Yolanda said before grabbing her purse and dashing out the door.

~

*A*cross the city at North Central High, Makayla sat beside Wallace on the bleachers of the gym as they watched the other students try out. Sitting at a long wooden table decorated in school colors, the black and yellow of the North Central stallions, was Erica, Brittney, Amy and a few other cheerleaders.

Wallace turned to Makayla, "I know we got this."

Makayla leaned in his ear, "Of course. Because where is my best friend?"

Wallace pointed to himself. "He is right here."

"Where?" Makayla asked again.

"Right here," Wallace repeated before the two busted out into laughter.

"Can you be quiet up in the peanut gallery," Coach Watkins shouted as she glanced back at Wallace and Makayla.

Coach Watkins was a large ruddy looking woman, with dripping wet Jeri curls, and moles polka dotted across her face. Embarrassed, Wallace placed a hand over his lips while Makayla zipped hers. Coach Watkins was not amused.

"Next!" Erica roared.

Saddened, a bubbly Puerto Rican girl walked off the gym floor with a frown. All evening long it was looking like slim pickings for North Central High School's next cheerleading superstar. The fifteen girls and guys who tried out were getting chopped by the panel left and right.

"Makayla Lawson," Coach Watkins Called out.

Makayla walked out onto the floor and locked eyes with a glaring Erica. Still, she felt confident. In the bleachers she could see Wallace, he was snapping at her. I got this, she thought.

"Just press play," Makayla said as she handed over her phone to be connected to the speaker.

Brittany an olive skinned girl with curly hair sighed as she played the track.

As the music came on, a hip-hop beat, Makayla went into an intricate call and shout routine. She stomped like an elephant, strong and elegant. Her hand movements were long and concise, and she cheered with the aggression of all the girls she watched from the YouTube clips. She ended her routine with a round of backflips that she landed into a split. She received a few claps at the table and a thunderous applause from her best friend Wallace on the bleachers.

"Good stuff Lawson. I know you had to have some spunk to match that loud mouth." Coach Watkins said with the coldness of her tone making the compliment sound almost like an insult. Just as Coach Watkins opened her mouth to call in the next person, all the lights inside the gym went out. Everyone in the gym gasped.

"All right, stay calm folks. It's probably a broken fuse. Stay where you are." Coach Watkins ordered.

Wallace climbed down from the bleachers and went to Makayla, "What is going on? " He looked around in all the darkness. "I'm scared."

Makayla sucked her teeth, "Scared of what? Boy stop!"

Coach Watkins turned to the panel of cheerleaders. "There are flashlights in the girl's locker room. I'm going to grab one and then go check on that fuse. Make sure everyone stays here and does nothing crazy." She said with a huff.

"No problem you know I got this," Erica said.

Twenty minutes had gone by and there was no sign of Coach Watkins. Makayla was tapping her foot as her bladder called her, along with the urge to charge her dead phone.

She turned to Wallace, "I'm going to the locker room to charge my phone and use the bathroom."

"But Coach Watkins said stay here," Wallace protested.

Makayla brushed him off with a wave, "Boy I'm just going to get my charger. I'll be right back." She said as she grabbed her phone off the table and then pranced towards the girl's locker room.

Erica turned to Brittany, "Uh where does she think she is going?"

"She's just going to get her charger," Wallace responded.

Erica stood up from the table and leaned over to call down the court. "Excuse me little girl but Coach Watkins said to stay here."

Makayla glanced over her shoulder and curled her lip before facing forward and continuing her walk toward the locker room. Erica called after her again but Makayla paid her no mind.

Once she entered the locker room, Makayla felt strange. There was a certain unease she couldn't explain. A drip drop of the showers and hiss of the steam room surrounded her. She went straight to her locker and plugged her phone into the charging bank. She toggled off her do not disturb icon and received a flood of notifications. Eight missed calls from her sisters Yolanda and Patrice. *What do they want*, Makayla wondered. She was dialing Patrice back when she heard shuffling near the entrance and her spine went cold.

"Wallace is that you?" She called out.

Makayla was met with no answer. Her battery was low and

her fear was palpable. Sweat coated her palms and her hands trembled as she called Patrice again. Suddenly she heard shifting behind her. Makayla whirled around, "Who is that? Erica? Don't play no games with me girl." She said as she walked further into the locker room.

I must be tripping, she thought to herself. She declared there was no one in that locker room but herself and her nerves. All this stress to make the squad and the drama back at home with Amina's return has got her tripping. Shrugging, Makayla peered down at her phone as she waited for Patrice to answer. Something caught her attention in the far corner to the right. She looked over.

Makayla felt her body go stiff with terror as she found Coach Watkins faced down in the showers with several stab wounds in her back. She covered her mouth and let out a loud resounding scream.

*S*he stopped screaming when she heard heavy footsteps behind, then her heart plummeted to her gut when she felt a looming presence so close she could feel breathing on her neck. To her left, she saw a long shadow cast against the locker. Covered in fear, Makayla turned around and shrieked in terror as she stared at the rotting corpse.

Sourness filled the back of her throat, as she looked closer. Makayla noticed that his jaw was dislodged and half of his face had already deteriorated. His left eye dangled just below the socket with no skin covering it. The rancid smell coming off of the corpse almost made her stomach do cartwheels. The dead had risen back to life. Makayla was standing face to face with a zombie.

Makayla's mind raced. Where had this man or monster come from?

"Awe hell no!" she shouted in terror.

Slowly Makayla backed away. She was terrified. His presence made the blood freeze in her veins. Brute and aggressive, the creature lifted a bench and tossed it to the side. Makayla screamed and continued shuffling back. His eyes were rotting and the stench of his body made Makayla want to puke. He tossed another bench to the side and again Makayla screamed.

Panic rose in Makayla's chest. She reached blindly behind her but Makayla was backed up against the wall. With nowhere to go. The zombie gripped her by the throat and slammed her against the wall. Makayla's feet strained for the floor, her toes dangled inches above the tile. Tears strolled down Makayla's pretty brown eyes as she whimpered and pleaded for mercy. He wrapped cold hands around her throat and yanked her up to his eye level against the wall.

He was pressing against Makayla's windpipe, now choking off her air supply. His rough hands descended around her neck with terrible power. Makayla saw the knife reflecting as he raised it high in the air. Makayla's heart was pounding. She shrieked as he raised the knife and it whooshed through the air as it came down.

10

GIRL, WE'RE IN DANGER

*M*akayla winced as she fell hard on her bottom. She opened her eyes. She was in the middle of the hallway, sitting down. *But how?* She wondered. As she searched her mind for answers, she realized somehow she must have discovered her gift. Makayla stood up and when she did, the zombie crept around the corner. He moved toward Makayla with a stiff, walk that made her blood run cold.

"Oh my god!" Makayla shrieked. She turned to her left, "Somebody help me!" she cried out to an empty echoing hall.

Pounded footsteps sounded in the hall towards her.

"Somebody help me please!" She cried again.

Zombies can't run, she thought. So Makayla ran as fast as she could. But to her surprise, this monster ran with the stride of a lion. Despite being half decomposed, the zombie's body moved like a predator chasing its prey. He came lunging after her with swipes from his knife. He missed, but just by inches. Makayla dodged him again and as he slashed at her, she fell through the wall, a set of lockers and into a classroom. She couldn't wrap her mind around this gift, somehow it was as if she could become intangible like a ghost.

To her left the door shattered into splinters, as the zombie burst through with knife in hand. She looked around and realized she was trapped. On her right was a set of three windows with a view of the student parking lot. She recognized the room as her Advanced Spanish class, located on the third floor. Makayla raked her gaze back to the zombie who was quickly shoving desks out of the way as he charged forward. With nowhere to run, Makayla weighed her options, and it was either through the window or death. She let out another sharp scream as she ran full speed ahead towards the window.

And to her surprise, she went straight through the wall. What happened next came so sudden that it was hard to fully process. First, she gasped as she plummeted down to the pavement, kicking and screaming. Next came the sound of shattered glass as the zombie followed. When she hit the ground, her body phased through the pavement, and she bounced back up, standing on both feet. She stumbled back as she tried to regain her balance, the whole experience had felt like jumping on a trampoline.

The zombie fell close beside her in a crumpled lump. Makayla whirled over her shoulder to witness the monster get back up with no inkling of pain. She turned to run when she was forcefully yanked back by her hair.

"No! " She screamed as the Zombie wrestled her down to the ground. "Please, please stop," Makayla begged.

Patrice and Yolanda pulled into the parking lot, just in time to see the giant corpse cowering over Makayla with a knife in hand. Patrice jumped out of the car and with her hands burning red and outstretched, she tossed him with her power.

Makayla popped her head up and looked back, "Peaches help!"

Patrice and Yolanda ran over. "Makayla are you alright?" Yolanda asked, her voice awash with worry.

Makayla breathing heavily, "Watch out!" she warned.

Yolanda was snatched by her hair and tossed back a few feet with ease. With an intense blow he knocked Patrice off her feet.

Patrice sprang back into action. The thought of her sisters in danger erased all fear and Patrice came charging at the zombie with her voice at a full yell. She shoved a knee in his gut to grant herself some room to work her magic.

"Fire, I command you to destroy my enemy," She bellowed with her deep alto echoing across the lot. Crimson embers exploded in her hand and she threw a ball of fire towards the reanimated corpse. Flames engulfed the zombie and he stumbled around with his arms flailing.

Finally, he fell again and this time for good. Patrice waved away the dark cloud of smoke that billowed before her, then she looked down and found a peculiar looking knife. She picked it up, deciding in her head it could be helpful in identifying his master.

She went back to Makayla's side, "Are you okay?"

Makayla shook her head, "Not hurt just scared. I'm so happy you guys came. I don't know what would've happened," Makayla said before burying her tears in her big sister's shoulders.

"That's all thanks to Yolanda," Patrice said as she scooped them up. "Come on let's go home."

*T*he three sisters soon found themselves back home downstairs in the dimly lit basement, light bulb still flickering as they tried to make sense of this horrible attack. Patrice held the Legacy in her hand while her sisters stood at the base of the stairs. To say the mood was tense would be an understatement, everyone was on edge.

"What the hell was that thing," Yolanda asked Patrice who was flipping back and forth in the book.

Patrice was digging through the pages of the Legacy looking for a clue. "I have no freaking idea," Patrice responded as she examined the diamond-encrusted dagger he left behind. "It looked like some sort of reanimated corpse. Like a zombie. Somebody has been working some black magic. But who or what in Atlanta could have that type of power?"

Makayla was sitting on the bottom step with her head burrowed between her knees. "I don't know who or what that thing is but all I know was that it was trying to kill me. Specifically, it tried to stab me in the heart." She stood up and stomped her feet. "It just got real out here. We are in danger!"

"We're not in danger," Patrice declared nonchalantly.

"Yes we are," Makayla argued. She pointed her finger towards Patrice as if to say you don't know what you're talking about. "That wasn't no regular zombie. I watch the Walking Dead. I know a zombie when I see it. That thing was on a mission. He was going to kill me and nothing was going to stop him. He was like Freddy, Jason, Michael Meyers and all of em' combined."

Patrice continued flipping through the pages of the Legacy, "Makayla calm down."

Yolanda grabbed Makayla's hand. "Just breathe sissy.

Breathe with me. Deep breath in and big exhale out. Let go all of the fear and negative emotions."

Makayla lifted her head. "And what are you doing? Shouldn't we be googling the number to the ghost busters or something? What is that?" She pointed.

Patrice kept her gaze towards the book. "It's the Legacy and it has a wealth of magical knowledge. Hence I am looking through it."

Makayla placed her hands on her hips. "Patrice Lawson, we have a whole damn book of magic in our house and you just weren't going to tell me that?"

Yolanda tugged her hand. "We were going to wait until you got your powers. Tell you about our family's history that way. I was planning to burn candles and do a nice ceremony."

Patrice shook her head. "You were planning to dance naked in a graveyard. I didn't tell you because I didn't want you to do anything stupid like a love spell or casting a curse, without knowing the laws of magic."

"Ms. Patrice Lawson you must still think I'm a child!" Makayla shouted. "It is dangerous in these streets and you would have me out here looking like boo boo the fool without magic."

A part of Patrice was just as scared as Makayla. Yet another more resilient part of her, told her to be strong for her sisters. Focusing on that strength she found an illustration of the dagger in the book, "The Legacy says this dagger is used to steal powers from witches." Patrice fell silent, pondering, and then turned back to them. "So this zombie was just a tool."

Yolanda sat forward, "What do you mean just a tool?"

"I mean a puppet. Someone obviously brought it back to

life. But whether they sent it after Makayla or just unleashed it remains to be determined."

Makayla stood up, " I told you! We're in danger, this is not cool."

"What are we going to do now?" Yolanda asked, very scared.

Patrice buried the book back in the grey container, "Don't worry about it. I will find out and take care of it."

Makayla folded her arms and side-eyed her older sister. Yolanda opened her mouth to speak but Patrice cut her off.

"I said I will handle it," She said louder so they could hear it all the way in the back. Patrice thought for a moment and she didn't want to sound so harsh. "Look guys I bust my butt everyday so we can have a happy normal life. I didn't want my life to be all about Voodoo, demons, and evil spirits. I want to enjoy life." She walked closer to her sisters and stuck a reassuring smile on her face. "We are going to do what we have always done. We are going to stick together and everything else will be alright. That's just the way it is and will be. We'll be fine." She started reaching for explanations, literally, with her hands reaching out to the sky. "Maybe some school girls were playing with dark magic and conjured something they had no business messing with. And Makayla you were the only thing next to it and it attacked you."

"I mean ….. I guess," Makayla answered. She said with a frown."One good thing I can say came out of this is I received my gift tonight," she said with pride. "Well I think I did," she corrected.

Yolanda glanced at her with a smile, "Really… what is it?"

Makayla shrugged. "To be honest I don't know. One minute the zombie had me pinned against the wall and the next I fell through the wall to the floor. Then when it was chasing me I walked through another wall out to the parking lot. So maybe I'm like Casper the fabulous ghost or something. I don't know."

"You think you can turn into a ghost?" Yolanda asked with a sarcastic uncertainty.

"Well whatever it is, " Patrice cut in. "We will help you with it. We will stick together. We will be alright." She preached in her authoritative tone.

"Speaking of sticking together, " Yolanda interrupted. "You really need to talk to Amina. You guys did the most, last night. And regardless of how she acts sometimes…. she is still our sister. The only family we have. Think about what Gran would do."

Patrice fell silent. As much as she didn't want to admit it, she knew Yolanda was right.

"I will go to her hotel and talk to her sometime this weekend," Patrice reasoned.

"Good." Yolanda settled. It truly bothered Yolanda's spirit whenever there was a fight amongst sisters. And even though she agreed with the decision to bind Amina's powers, she had regrets that Amina stayed away for so long. Now that Amina was back she saw this as an opportunity to get all of her sisters back together and Yolanda was determined to make them work it out some way somehow.

"We are sisters and we have to stick together. If something or someone is after us then we have to close ranks," Patrice asserted before marching up the stairs. Yolanda shot a look of uncertainty to Makayla. Reluctantly they followed Patrice back up the stairs.

11

RUNNING

*I*t seemed to Patrice that trouble was slowly heading her way. No matter what she did to protect her sisters, evil somehow managed to find its way to their door. She woke up early Saturday morning to a dusk orange sky. Fresh dew was still on the grass tops, birds were chirping and the air smelled crisp from last night's shower of rain. Patrice liked her early Saturday morning runs around Piedmont Park; those three miles were essential to her sanity, and almost necessary for her soul. While her sisters slept in, she got to lose everything weighing her down along the trail.

Patrice walked to the trail with her pink shaker bottle in one hand, and iPhone in the other. She was dressed in an Under Armour sports bra, colorful yoga pants, and dark red running shoes. With her Drake workout playlist ready to go, she pressed play and allowed the energy of the music to fuel her. Glancing around, she noticed the park was pretty empty except for an older white couple who sat on a park bench. She started stretching, pulling her knees to her chest, and then slowly touching her toes. By this time now the sun was still on the rise, and it beamed on her brightly as she scanned the trail. After loosening all her joints and muscles, she took off running.

As the early morning air hit her face, blowing her ponytail, she thought of the zombie they faced a few days back. This wasn't some regular Voodoo gone wrong, that monster was sent with a mission. *But why Makayla* she wondered. It nearly burned a pit in her stomach to lie to her sisters, but she concluded to herself that it was a necessary evil. Patrice had been a guardian for her younger sisters nearly thirteen years to the day; it was a weight and burden she was used to by now. As she considered it for a moment, the burden of taking care of her sisters was a lot lighter than the burden to be the next Mother Phoenix. Sure, she loved Gran dearly but the old woman was tough on Patrice, especially when it came to her magical training.

A part of her couldn't help but feel Gran was that much tougher on them all, after seeing how reckless their mom became. Patrice dropped her head down as she took in a deep breath, exhaled, and increased her speed. She didn't even want to think about her trifling ass mother, no-not even for a second.

The question that befuddled her the most, was who or what in Atlanta could wield that amount of magic. Resurrections were tricky and only an immensely powerful sorcerer could accomplish such a feat, then suddenly a chill came over her. Not of fear but of realization. She thought of that night in the basement when she was attacked by a shadow and warned by Gran. Certainly all of these things combined weren't a coincidence, something malevolent and powerful was after them.

Her heart was beating faster as her mind was bombarded with horrible images. Again she pictured the blank and soulless eyes of the zombie along with the sight of his half rotting face. It was one of the ugliest creatures she had ever seen. Truly despicable and evil. Then her mind drifted back to when she first came face to face with evil.

*S*he was nine years old and Gran was performing an exorcism ritual on one of her neighbors. Patrice could never forget Miss Lillie Mae Green. Miss Lillie owned a hair salon that Gran always used take them to on Saturday mornings after breakfast, and before they all went out shopping. She was a lively petite woman with radiant cocoa brown skin, and long flowing tresses that she kept pinned back off of her face in elaborate hair styles. Miss Lillie was always so nice to them, always complimenting them all on how pretty they were and giving them each mint candies after doing their hair. Patrice remembered that sometime before summer, the salon fell on hard times, Miss Lillie had lost half of her clients to a newer salon around the corner, and some days she couldn't afford to keep it open because she couldn't pay to keep the power on.

Eventually Gran found out the woman sold her soul in the graveyard for some money to keep the shop afloat, Patrice didn't know what the Petro Loa were at the time, but she quickly figured it out after what happened to Miss Lillie. The Petro Loa were tricksters. You sell your soul to them and you get what you want, but it's often at a great price. That was one of the first lessons in Voodoo Gran taught them. Nothing in Voodoo was free, either you will pay in the front end or back, but often there is a cost. This is most significantly true when it came to black magic, and sometimes grey magic, which was called gris-gris. Miss Lillie Mae got the money she wanted, but it was through the tragic death of her husband, and to make matters worst, the demon came back early for his prize.

Patrice could still hear the screams the fragile old lady made. She was strapped to a bed, screaming and clawing as she hollered in pain. The demon was wearing her out. There were at least twenty people surrounding her bed, chanting and praying to weaken the demon who had taken a hold of her. Miss Lillie had always been a pretty woman but after the demon had taken ahold of her she looked entirely different. Her hair fell out in large bleeding clumps, once vibrant skin became pale and sweaty with green veins protruding out. Just recalling the smell in the room was enough to make Patrice cough up a sour liquid.

That day one of the women told Gran that Miss Lillie could not be helped, and to just let her die. But Gran, the Mother Phoenix at the time was unyielding. Patrice was on the side of the bed when Miss Lillie lurched up and stared Patrice in the eyes. It was there for the first time Patrice saw evil. All the sweetness of Miss Lillie Mae's personality had been absent and instead she saw dark, cold, empty eyes, void of human emotion. Even though Miss Lillie was silent, that stare was enough to hunt Patrice for the rest of her life.

As Patrice cowered back, her grandmother splashed Lillie Mae with a lash of herbed water.

"Get out demon!" she shouted.

Miss Lillie Mae yelled out a blood-curdling scream that made a young Patrice tremble in fear.

Patrice was crossing the bridge, the lake glistening underneath her with the early morning sun reflecting in her eyes. She watched the sunlight ease across the water, sparkling as it touched waves created by the morning breeze. *Such a beautiful way to begin the day,* Patrice thought as she picked up her pace.

With Atlanta shining to her right, Patrice thought about her first time fighting evil.

She was sixteen and scared out of her mind. Her uncles had her surrounded and trapped with a man possessed with a reptilian spirit. Drums pounded as her heart raced and adrenaline surged. Gran's demon fighting days were long over and as Mother Phoenix in training, it was Patrice's duty to pick up the slack. Patrice was eating a face full of dust after the demon sent her spiraling with a sharp kick to the chin.

"Focus Peaches!" Gran called as she stood up from her throne. She was dressed in a rich purple and gold traditional garment, her hair pulled back in an elaborate hair wrap. "Get up cher. Use your gift just like I show you. You can do this."

Patrice was huffing as she flipped up and raised her fist in a fighter's stance. She kept her eyes on the demon before her in the pit. She kicked the dust of her jeans as she lunged her fist towards her opponent. He dodged her punch and countered with a kick to the side of her head. It connected with a loud thud that made Patrice see stars. She stared at the demon who looked like a disfigured man. Hard brown scales replaced flesh on his face and his eyes were an eerie brown. Again she lunged at him with a series of punches, and he countered, missing every blow by seconds. With a fierce paw to his chest, Patrice used her powers to send the demon flying outside the circle.

"Now!" Gran shouted.

Patrice looked to her left, and a Spanish sword etched in gold flew into her hand. In a swift fluid motion, she leapt up into the air to take off the demon's head with a swift slice of the blade. The drums silenced and were replaced with applause. Gran took Patrice in her arms. "I know you will make a fine Mother Phoenix one day Peaches," She murmured.

Suddenly the song playing in Patrice's ear faded. She peered down at her smart watch. Already she had run a mile and a half. Indeed it seemed evil was heading their way but like always Patrice knew she would be ready... ready to fight.... ready to protect and do whatever was necessary to keep her family safe.

A presence loomed behind her, massive and towering. Survival instincts flared up in her head and sensing danger, Patrice spun into a roundhouse kick.

"Whoa hold up!" Lorenzo shouted as he caught Patrice's leg.

He had her ankle on his shoulder and he pulled her thigh closer to his chest. Patrice was mortified. "Oh my god! I'm so sorry."

"I bet. That's one hell of a roundhouse you got." Lorenzo said laughing.

Patrice blushed as her embarrassment multiplied tenfold. She raked her eyes across his body. His chest was massive, brown, bare and covered in sweat. He had a firm grip on her thigh. She braced herself on his chest to keep from failing. *Damn he is fine*, Patrice thought. And she also noticed he was very warm. His chest felt like it was on fire, touching him was like standing too close to an oven.

And as they stood there in the park, smiling with her ankle caught in his hand. There was a timeless and seamless desire between them. Lorenzo admired her shape. She leaned in and before she allowed herself to fall for his charms, "Can I have my leg back?"

Lorenzo chuckled. "You might need that right?" he asked, his tone dripping in a cockiness.

Patrice shook her head, "Yes I do." She sat her leg down,

lingering glances between them both. "What are you doing here?"

"I heard Piedmont Park was a nice place to run. I love working out in the park. Fresh air and freedom," he said as he turned out to the openness. He looked back at her, with lust in his eyes. "Do you mind if I join you?"

Patrice was hesitant, "Sure." She gave him her back as she started running.

Lorenzo trailed behind her softly. "Ms. Lawson I couldn't help but admire your body. You seem to be pretty fit."

"It's Patrice, remember? And Mr. James are you flirting with me?" She asked looking back.

A devilish smirk appeared on his face. "How can you tell?"

"Because yesterday you were talking to my chest."

Lorenzo laughed. "And today I'm talking to your ass."

Patrice turned around to catch Lorenzo's line of sight, zooming in on her rear end. Patrice's body was curvaceous yet toned, it was a work of art that brought her pride as an athlete. She had a body that most women would pay for. So did her sisters. All the Lawson girls inherited almond eyes, excellent cheekbones, radiant skin, bomb hair, and voluptuous figures. He was enthralled by her Beyoncé type booty that was no silicone, no surgery, but all natural New Orleans homegrown.

Annoyed, she shoved him in the stomach. She did it so quickly that she forgot Lorenzo was a client. Patrice stopped dead in her tracks. "Look Lorenzo I'm a professional. I don't usually behave this way with clients. I don't think this is appropriate."

"Well I am too. And I don't usually behave this way with women. But there is something about you that has a brother tripping."

Patrice folded her arms, she found that hard to believe. "Oh really."

Lorenzo nodded. "You seem like a badass. You take no shit. I think you are very strong and beautiful. Scratch that, gorgeous. And I would love to take you out tonight for dinner."

Patrice closed her sweet brown eyes and allowed the offer to settle. "I'd have to think about it. Like I said I don't like to entertain relationships with clients."

"Look it's not like I'm asking you to come over for Netflix and chill. Just say yes," he said giving her the full Lorenzo James thousand-watt smile, with his swagger on one million.

Patrice thought hard. She wanted to get to know him and yet she was frightened of where that might lead. Lorenzo looked at her intently, waiting for an answer. The seriousness displayed on his face made her chuckle

Lorenzo took her hand, and chills traveled up her arm. "Talk to me Patrice. It's just dinner. So what's up?"

His persistence was like a heaviness in her chest. Was she truly ready to jump back into dating? It was a question she had to ask herself. Patrice couldn't help wishing she were truly ready, but she wasn't too sure. Why am I fighting him? Patrice questioned silently. Lorenzo was fine as hell, ambitious, and had a swagger that made her melt.

"Okay," She finally answered

"Okay?" He repeated.

She smiled and nodded, "Okay."

Lorenzo pumped his fist. "Alright bet. I'll hit you up later!" he shouted before running off.

$\approx$

houghts of home collided with Amina's next slow sip of champagne, clean and sweet. She was admiring the radiant morning sun from the balcony of her room at the W overlooking the city. It didn't matter what city she was in, every morning she woke up and thought of New Orleans. She could almost feel the heat of the sun and hear the horns from the infectious Cajun music that filled the streets, played on the radio, and became the soundtrack of her childhood. There was a void in her heart. She missed her house in the ninth ward. She missed her sisters. She even missed Gran who always used to proclaim that she was wasting her life away and would end up either dead or in jail. Amina shivered as her mind went back to the night Magnum shot her, the hopelessness, fear, and anxiety all attacked her at once. *Gran was right*, she thought.

She smiled at the thought of Gran, the woman who gave her many whippings, but still loved her dearly. Amina was a handful growing up, and she can accept that now as she looked back over her life. Gran often referred to her as a fast girl with a loud mouth. Even though they may have had rocky times, Gran was the only person who loved Amina despite her slick tongue and fiery nature. Amina could recall that one time when she broke into a gorgeous all black Mercedes by hitting it with a jolt of lightning. Gran was so powerful back then that she could sense when her girls were acting up. Amina didn't know where Gran was at the time, she could've been sitting at home under the dryer for all she knew but somehow miles away, before Amina could even hop into the car, she was yanked back by some invisible force. Gran's voice slammed into her head.

"Bring your narrow ass home!"

Amina laughed out loud at the memory as she pulled herself away from the balcony. Even though she knew her grandma would be shaking her head in disapproval at her right now, she still wished she could see her, hold her, and be wrapped in her protective arms.

Once thoughts of home faded away, her mind began to reflect on the events that had led her to being inches away from death. After running away from home for the millionth time, Amina had finally gotten a taste of the life she always dreamed of in New York. But before she knew it the same problems that followed her in L.A and Chicago, began to plague her in New York. Her usual hustle of money making schemes, credit card scams, and stripping led to her collecting enemies in the city.

She was ready to move on until one night she caught the eye of a notorious drug dealing rapper. His name was Magnum and he made Amina feel like the baddest chick on the planet. While dating Magnum she was adorned with lavish gifts, taken on trips around the world, and after just a few months she moved into his condo in Manhattan. She appeared in several of his videos and soon after, gained a following of her own through social media. Then things went sour. Magnum shot her after finding out she was leaking his songs and stealing his money.

Once she figured out how to shake Papa Samedi and had her gifts fully restored, she decided Magnum would be first on her hit list.

Amina was sipping the rest of her champagne and checking TheShadeRoom when she heard a soft tap on her door. She opened the door to find Patrice on the other side. Amina sighed, "Can I help you?"

"Can I come in?" Patrice asked.

Amina moved aside with her hand motioning Patrice to come in. "So I'm surprised to see you here." Amina spat as she closed the door.

"Trust me I am too," Patrice said as she stood by the bed. "Look Amina I know we have never been able to see eye to eye. And I might've been a little bitchy the other day."

"You think? Really or nah?" Amina sassed, raising her eyebrows and folding her arms.

Patrice could sense Amina's defenses flipping up. "I don't know how to say this but," A nervous laugh came out of here lips. "I'll just say it. I'm sorry. Amina when you came it took me by surprise and I didn't know how it was going to be with us, especially with how you left last time. But what I realized," Patrice started before placing a compassionate hand on top of Amina's. "We are sisters. Family. Like it or not, all we have is each other. I'm not going to lie; I've missed you. So instead of spending our time fussing and fighting why don't we for once try to be nice to each other?"

Amina's face softened and she peered down before she spoke. "I'd like that," she said with a hesitant and awkward smile.

Patrice smiled as well. "Also the girls and I would like it if you stay with us. All the Lawson girls under one roof."

Amina chuckled, "All the Lawson sisters in one roof. Wow Peaches. I'd love it."

As laughter filled the hotel room, the sisters came together for a loving embrace. To Amina's surprise, she began to shed tears. It was a strange relief. "Maybe it can be how it was when we were little."

"Like when we were kids?" Patrice asked. The mere thought took her back to memories of the Lawson girls growing up at Gran's house in the ninth ward. Amina clung onto her sister tighter. Amidst the tears came a malicious smile. She was in. Now it was time to put her plan into motion.

ETERNAL SUNSHINE

"*H*urry up! We don't have all night," Makayla yelled from the bed.

Patrice poked her head around the corner. "I'm coming, just give me a minute." Patrice must've tried on a dozen outfits, trying to figure out what she was going to wear on her date with Lorenzo. She was looking into the mirror unsatisfied with the frumpy sheer blouse that she paired with black leggings and stilettos. Patrice turned to Yolanda and Makayla, who shook their heads in disapproval. Cursing under her breath Patrice ran back into her closet.

"Forget it! I'm calling him to cancel. I have nothing to wear." Patrice said as she dove back into the pile of failed outfits.

"Not so you can be single for the rest of your life. Peaches you better go get this man. That clock is ticking honey," Makayla said as she stood up and toyed with her hair in the mirror.

Yolanda shoved Makayla, "Stop it!"

"What?" Makayla asked nonchalantly. "I'm just trying to keep it real with her. Lord knows she has been single since forever."

Patrice poked her head from around. "Hey! I heard that."

Yolanda paid Makayla's nonsense no mind, as she started to play with all of the bangles, bracelets and other accessories Patrice had displayed on the nightstand. "So where are you guys going again?"

"Some Reggae lounge in midtown called Patty Patty Boom Boom."

Makayla picked up a dress that was laying on the floor, "Sounds like fun to me. You know the doll loves to get her whine on," she said as she danced to silent music.

"Whine up!" Yolanda said joining the dance.

As the two sisters continued to dance around, Patrice was reaching up top for another pair of heels, when a photo fell down. She bent down to pick it up and smiled as she turned it over; it was taken over thirteen years ago. Patrice had just graduated college that May and was beaming with her diploma in hand. Gran was kissing her on the cheek. She was so surprised to see Gran, after all moving to Atlanta for under-grad had been the one time she defied her grandmother.

Patrice thought about how much easier life was then. She was so determined to forge a life far away from New Orleans and Voodoo, but she never figured in leaving home, she would lose her home. Soon after, in late August, Hurricane Katrina hit. When the levees broke she lost her home and most of her family. She was supposed to spend that summer celebrating the last of her innocence before joining the working world. At twenty-two, she had three younger sisters to take care of. Quickly she had to assume the role of mother.

To the outside world, the catastrophe of Hurricane Katrina was a natural disaster. But Patrice knew the truth. Katrina wasn't natural at all. It was caused by magic, a ritual that went terribly wrong, that resulted in men being slaughtered, people losing their lives along with their homes. All of this destruction caused by her wicked mother and her incessant greed for power. Patrice switched her thoughts. She could never go back, and she didn't want to. It was hard to think about the events of that terrible day, so she thought of the future, onward and upward, as Gran would say. Never dwell on the past.

Patrice shoved the picture back up top and whirled around the corner. Immediately both sisters gasped at how fine their big sister was. Patrice had picked out a short black spaghetti strap dress that had Bob Marley on the front with yellow pumps, accessorized with bangles on her wrist.

"Well that looks like a winner to me," Makayla said with a snap.

"And to that sissy, I would agree," Yolanda chirped with a nod of approval.

Makayla walked around Patrice examining her from head to toe. "Cute fit, check. Body on fleek, check. Accessories on point, check. Heels, check. Face beat, check. And hair laid like the river of Jordan. Peaches I think you are ready to go."

Patrice placed a modest hand across her heart. "Well thank you," she said as she bowed.

Makayla nodded with a smirk on her face. "You're welcome. Do you like your makeup?"

Patrice looked in the mirror and smiled. "It's fabulous."

"See!" Makayla shouted. "You can learn a lot on YouTube."

Yolanda sat up off the bed. "Turn around," she commanded with her hands.

Patrice did as told and Yolanda pulled her into a big hug. "This man better watch out because my big sister ain't playing no games!"

Patrice grabbed her purse and sashayed out of her room with her younger sisters following close behind. She was staring down the stairs when it hit her. This was really happening, she was going on a date. Patrice's heel was mid-step when she turned around, "Yolanda, you are going to stay over tonight, right?"

"Nope," she said proudly with a smile on her face. "I'm meeting Malcolm to check out this indie film on campus."

"Okay," Patrice murmured as she continued downstairs. She glanced over her left shoulder." And Makayla don't invite Wallace over. I don't want you two getting into any trouble while I'm out."

"Excuse me. This is not the first time I've been home alone." Makayla replied as she chased after her sister.

Patrice grabbed her coat as she reached the bottom of the stairs. "I know I just want to be sure". Patrice was in such a hurry that she almost bumped into Amina who was coming around the corner from the kitchen.

Amina caught her sister before impact. "Well, you look cute. Good luck on the date."

Patrice smiled, "Thanks. I'm mad I'm going to miss this. You girls are going to have so much fun."

"I'm just happy I get to spend some time with my sisters," Amina grinned.

"I know," Patrice said before heading towards the door. "Okay girls I'm gone. Wish me luck."

"Bye," the sisters sang in harmony, as Patrice went through the door.

Patrice popped back inside. "Again remember if anything happens call me."

Yolanda nodded, "We will. Bye."

Patrice left, then she opened the door again. "And don't forget to activate the alarm before going to bed."

"Will do Peaches don't worry," Amina answered this time.

Patrice slammed the door on her way out. Then she swung it wide open as she popped back in again. "I feel so bad for going out and leaving my sisters hanging. Should I stay so we can do something together?"

"Girl, will you leave already? We got everything under control," Makayla said.

Patrice huffed and threw up her hands. "Okay Bye."

Patrice left and the three younger sisters were left alone to their own devices. Makayla turned to Yolanda, "So what are we doing? What's the move?"

Yolanda reached into the adjacent closet and grabbed her backpack. "The move is I'm going to check out an indie film on campus with my bae." Yolanda headed towards the door and looked back at her sisters. "Deuces Chicas!" she said as she slammed the door.

Makayla threw up her hands, "How she just gone leave like that."

Amina pulled Makayla to her hip. "That's okay. Just me and my little bird. That sounds like fun to me."

"Well I guess," Makayla returned as they headed upstairs.

~

*I*f you asked Atlanta locals about Eternal Sunshine Cafe, many would call it one of the city's best hidden gems. College students from Georgia State, Clark Atlanta, and the collective Spell House would say the food changed their lives. It was in fact one of the first vegan soul food restaurants in the area. Most newbies who wanted to dip into the waters of veganism were advised to go there to try the fried chicken meal, which wasn't chicken at all, the jerk tofu, or the vegetable lasagna.

It was a nice sized shop nestled on a small corner on Peachtree st. As soon as you walk inside, the smell of fresh baking coco bread and jerk chicken wafted into your nose. To be a relatively indie shop it was spacious on the inside. There was a small bookstore inside on the right side of the entrance with a few shelves of African-American and Caribbean authors and the dining area was on the far left corner, right beside the door.

Eternal sunshine was a haven for healthy foods, indie authors, college students and at night, the Voodoo culture of Atlanta. Specifically, it was the main base for the Night Scar Clan. There was a door, on the side of the office that lead to a backroom. Around nine pm the backroom had been turned to a place of worship, where the sounds of chanting and drums overtook the night. Five men lined the back wall, beating on drums, as four women in white danced in a tight circle, holding candles and dashing the altar with oil, every few seconds the beat changed. An altar stood in the center adorned with fruits, a roasted pig, oils, herbs, spices, and candles. On this night, the Night Scar Clan had planned to focus on calling healing spirits for one of their own who was battling cancer. It was the clan's leader Josiah, who brought the rum, the cigarettes, the hot peppers, and the blood to conjure the Petro Loa.

Josiah took the rum in his hand and took a big swig, "Dark spirits we call you lord." The rum dulled his senses, and made him stagger, as he swayed to the hypnotic beat.

Someone placed three cigarettes in his mouth, he puffed from all of them, and blew smoke from his nose, "Dark spirit we call you lord!" He beckoned making the energy in the room stir, with the dancers adding in their calls, and the drummers adding to his chant.

A hot pepper was taken off the fire, and presented to Josiah. He took it with his mouth, and smoke wafted from his lips as the pepper hit his tongue. There were shouts in the crowd as this happened, he was showing his willingness to endure pain, he had wanted to hear from the Petro Loa, and indeed they came. Shrouded in shadows, Papa Samedi made his way to the backroom. Lights flickered all around, yet still the drummers kept drumming, and the chanters didn't stop chanting.

Papa Samedi visited them, and he saw that there was one amongst the clan who could be of use to him. He decided to make his presence known by mounting Josiah. Papa Samedi's spirit entered Josiah as if he walked through a door, Josiah immediately fell to the ground and trembled, as the dark spirit took control of his limbs. Several hands reached to usher him up. "Get off of me!" Papa Samedi shouted through Josiah. The true diabolic splendor of his voice made all drumming and chanting stop. All eyes focused on Josiah and he looked at them with his eyes wild and bulging. "Rum! Where is some rum?"

A heavy set woman with buttery brown skin and curly hair,

offered a bottle to him. He looked at her, snatched the bottle in his hand, and turned it up. They all watched in awe as he drank the whole bottle in mere seconds. Once the last drop touched the back of his throat, he tossed it behind him, shattering the bottle to pieces and causing the witnessing crowd to collectively jump.

"It is I my worshipers," he declared in a muffled voice. He coughed phlegm and cleared his throat before trying again. "It is I, my beautiful servants. Papa Samedi."

At the mention of his name, they all dropped to his feet. One of the drummers got up, lit a cigar and offered it to him. Papa Samedi grinned through Josiah, as he took the cigar. "Merci." He took a long pull from the cigar, and the joy it brought made him close his eyes to savor the sensation. "As I was saying. It is I my beautiful servants, Papa Samedi who has come to you, to bring blessings and good fortunes for all."

A petite older lady ran from the back, dropped to her knees and began to plead with her hands clasped. "Please Papa Samedi have mercy on my husband, Percy. He is fighting for his life right now."

Papa Samedi peered down at the woman, and motioned her to rise as he lifted her chin. "Don't worry my child. You have called me and I have come to answer your prayers." He turned to the crowd and waved his hand. "Let it be known that even though I am father of the fiery spirits, I make certain to take care of my children." Then just as swift, he tossed the woman to the side by mushing her head. "Now where is Malcolm?" He asked as he scanned the crowd. Murmurs of uncertainty went around the room as a path down the middle parted. Malcolm came before the dark spirit and dropped to his knee. "I am here my lord. On behalf of Night Scar Clan what can we do for you?"

Papa Samedi threw his head back and chuckled. "Do not fret Night scar Clan, your merciful master hears your cry and will adhere to your needs. I will bless you all. I will heal you and give you wealth you can't even imagine in your wildest dreams. But I ask only one thing."

Malcolm lifted his head, "What my lord? Anything?"

Everyone in the crowd also leaned in, all curious as to what the Petro Loa could want in exchange for such a blessing.

A delightful smile appeared on his face, as a ceremonial dagger materialized in his hand. "Bring me the heart of a witch!"

Malcolm looked at the blade, and then to him. "Gladly."

13

DANCE WITH ME

*P*atrice was a ball of nerves while she stood at the front of Patty Patty Boom Boom's doorway. As she scanned around the lounge searching for Lorenzo, she became quite impressed by the atmosphere. Patty Patty Boom Boom was a vibrant upscale restaurant that doubled as a lounge, the dining area and dancefloor was separated distinctively by two floors, a classic mahogany dancefloor greeted you upon walking in, a modern crystal sculpture hung in the center, and it looked completely packed from what Patrice could see. Two bars framed the dancefloor from opposite sides, already she could see many young girls hanging on the bar, as older men prowled over them and bought drinks. Upstairs was the dining area, which was decorated in nice black linens, beautiful crystals, modern silverware and soft lighting. Every server, waiter, and host was dressed in tailored all black suits or form fitting dresses. Overall it was a nice find and seemed to be a fitting place for Lorenzo's taste.

She peered down to her phone, which read nine thirty five,

he was already ten minutes late. Patrice was a very punctual person and she already declared to herself he had better have an excuse. She ran her finger through her glorious black tresses and wondered if she had made them too curly or not. A part of her wanted to run to the bathroom again just to make sure she looked perfect. Then suddenly, she felt a slight chill standing by the door. It made goosebumps prickle all along her legs. Patrice tugged at the bottom of her dress, wondering if it was too short. Before she could run more questions through her head, she felt a hand caress her waist.

"Patrice," Lorenzo called over the thump of the reggae music playing. The way he called her name was enough to send shivers down her spine, specifically it was the dark tone he used, that came off his lips as a sensual purr. He leaned into her ear "You look sexy as hell tonight. I'm going to try my best to act like a gentleman." Then his hand lowered as he finished his sentence, "But I won't make no promises."

He can't be serious, Patrice thought as she laughed. She pointed a finger at him, "You're late! And you better behave, or you're really going to feel my roundhouse kick."

Lorenzo held his hand out in surrender, "My bad I was attending to some business. Please don't kick my ass."

The both of them laughed, and the ice was broken, then Patrice exhaled, summoning calm for her nerves.

"Come on let me take you to our table," Lorenzo said as he grabbed her hand.

Patrice caught Lorenzo's line of sight and noticed, his eyes were dancing across her ample bottom again. With her hand in his, Lorenzo whisked her across the sea of dancers on the dancefloor. Just like Patrice imagined, it was barely any room to move, let alone breathe, but Lorenzo carved a path for them to maneuver. From all directions Lorenzo was acknowledged by waiters, the bouncer in the back corner, bartenders at the bar, and the DJ up top at the booth. Once they finally crossed the dancefloor, they went up the stairs to the next floor. He had only to lead her around the corner to their table. It sat on a balcony that overlooked the dancefloor, which was on the right, and had a wide arc sweeping view of Midtown on the left. Lorenzo pulled Patrice's chair back, and she slinked right in.

"Do you come here a lot?" She asked as she pulled herself closer to the table.

"You can say that," Lorenzo responded as he sat across from her. He cleared his throat and said, "I own this joint."

Patrice's brow furrowed. "You own this place?"

He grinned at her, "Yes. I do"

"You're quite a businessman," she said with her brown eyes gleaming.

Lorenzo chuckled modestly, "I try to be."

Just as Patrice peered down at the menu, a waiter casually came up to their table.

"Wah Gwan," he shouted as he stood by their table, pen and pad handy.

Patrice was lost at the greeting. She grinned, "What?"

Lorenzo snickered, "Wah Gwan. It's patois for what's up."

"Okay. Wah Gwan."

Lorenzo smiled, "Yeah Wah Gwan."

Patrice shook her head, "Okay I see. I'm from the 504. A NOLA girl if you didn't know. Where I'm from we say Where y'et."

"Where y'et? Okay I see," Lorenzo repeated as they laughed.

The waiter stood by awkwardly before asking, "Are you ready to order?"

"Let me get the Jerk chicken with some rice & peas."

"No plantains?" The waiter asked

"Come on man. Of course I want some plantains." Lorenzo turned to Patrice who was still studying her menu. "I recommend the jerk chicken, the red snapper, or the oxtail soup. And the rum cake....mmm mmm is the best around."

Patrice folded her menu, "Jerk chicken sounds good to me."

He wrote down the order and then peered up, "Anything to drink?"

"Red wine please," Patrice requested in a soft voice.

The waiter turned to Lorenzo.

"Ginger Beer," He responded.

Patrice looked up and Lorenzo was glaring at her with his alluring gaze. "So what's your story?"

"What's my story?" Lorenzo asked with a raised brow. A tortured expression entered his eyes as he waited a beat before speaking. "Nothing much to tell. Young cat from Brooklyn just trying to get this bread. Don't have much of a family. Did some crazy ish when I was young, and I did some time because of that. And after that I turned my life around."

The waiter came back with their drinks. Patrice wasted no time drinking her red wine. "Nothing much....that sounds like a lot to me."

Lorenzo took a long gulp from his ginger beer. "Well it's pretty simple to me. Life's a jungle. It's all about surviving." Silence strangled the table. A part of Lorenzo felt uneasy telling Patrice about his rocky past. He could sense how uncomfortable she was. "So how about you?"

Patrice took a big gulp of red wine, swallowed, and folded

her arms. "Well my mom was an addict and a dead beat. My father was in and out of my life. I was raised by my grandmother for most of my life. Hurricane Katrina destroyed my home and my family. So I brought my three younger sisters to Atlanta, where I went to Spelman for undergrad, and I've been taking care of them ever since."

Lorenzo raised the tip of his beer bottle, "Sounds like you're a survivor too."

Patrice clinked her wine glass to his bottle. "I am."

He leaned in closer to the table. "Alright enough talking," he said cutting her off. "Let's get up and dance. I want to see you whine for mi baby." Lorenzo said as he got up and took her to the dancefloor.

Lorenzo caught the groove of the music before he hit the dancefloor. Patrice could see it in the masculine way his shoulders moved and she could feel it flow through his hands into hers. It was warm and rousing like a fire. The man moved like an animal on the prowl.

Sleek. Suave. Deadly.

When they walked onto the middle of the dancefloor, he faced her, and pulled her closer to him. Patrice found herself at first stiff when trying to dance along with Lorenzo. But then he found himself behind her swaying back and forth. Eventually Patrice gave into the hypnotic lure of the reggae music, and what started as one dance turned into twenty minutes of hedonic seduction.

Somehow he'd unlocked a feeling of freedom and pleasure that Patrice had long forgotten. Being there on that dancefloor with him, smiling and laughing without a care in the world, made her recall the days of her twenty-one year old self, shutting down the clubs with her line sisters doing the "Uh Oh" dance to Beyoncé. And the longer they danced the more she allowed his hands to explore her body as she did his. Every touch and every caress was gradual and done with care. He would touch and grab then look at her with desire, almost testing the waters, begging for permission, and it was the sensuous smile on her face that told him to proceed.

Lorenzo ran his strong arms along the curve of her waist and behind, and she pulled his face closer to hers, took in his scent, it was Tom Ford. The last man who tried such a bold move with her on the first date got a drink thrown in his face, and almost got his hand broken. He intensified his grasp and she marveled at his strength, the dominance in the grip said this is mine, and I want every man on this dancefloor to know it. Though brutish, Patrice didn't think it was lewd, it was a part of his seduction, just as caressing his face with her delicate hands, and digging her stiletto nails into his back was apart of hers.

With a chuckle that rumbled from his belly, he spun her around, then pulled her waist back to his. She could feel the rising power of his manhood on her back and lengthening to her thighs, practically exposing the thinness of her dress. It was this intimate closeness, along with the call of the music that almost made Patrice lose it. She closed her eyes and surrendered herself to the music and the moment.

"I haven't danced like this in forever," Patrice said between bits of laughter.

Lorenzo spun her around again and placed his hands on her lower back. "If you roll with a boss like me, we will dance like this every night." From the corner of his eyes he spotted waiters arriving to their table with food. "Come on let's go. Dinner is ready."

Patrice grabbed at her chest to calm her laughter. "Good. I'm starving."

Lorenzo took Patrice's hand, lead her back across the sea of never ending dancers and back to the table. Patrice fanned herself as they left the dancefloor and went into the much cooler dining area. She watched his back as he lead the way, shaking her head at how much his shoulders looked like they housed wings. *This man just might steal my heart and my body,* she thought.

14

STORM BREWING

*A*mina had come to the house for one thing, and that was to get her hands on the Legacy. If there was a way to steal her sister's gifts without harming them, it would be in the ancient tome.

She sat on the couch watching some reality show with Makayla as she listened to Makayla's silly high school drama. Even though she had always been closest with her baby sister, she couldn't pay attention to the conversation because all she could think about was getting her hands on the Legacy.

"And that's when she called me a thot!" Makayla shouted with an angry finger. "So that's why I had to fight her. Because if I let one of these girls think they can punk me. All of them will think it's cool."

Amina reached in her purse and blew a puff of yellow powder into her sister's face, yellow mist swirled into the air as strands of Makayla's hair stood out as if she was falling under water, her eyes followed the small specks of dust as they glistened like glitter, and she fell backwards to the couch in a slow motion like a dazed cat. Amina chanted low in her patios. She huffed and blew the dust harder. In one quick snap of a motion, Makayla's eyes slammed shut, and she fell asleep.

"Sorry little bird," Amina murmured as Makayla collapsed onto the couch.

Amina walked through the empty house unable to stop thinking about how she was going to steal her sisters' powers. She rushed through the kitchen and down to the basement. It was far too easy for her to assume Patrice would pack the Legacy away like it was an photo album, or something old and useless. Amina flew down the stairs and found the book sitting there on a grey storage container. She reached for the book and it flew across the room.

"What the?"

Amina stomped across the basement, bent down to pick the book up, and it whirled to the left. "I don't have time for this shit," Amina said in a huff. "No matter if you think I'm evil or not, I am still a Lawson. A descendant of Marie Laveau. I'm apart of this Legacy."

The book slid to her feet. "Thank you."

Amina placed her hands on the thick golden bound book and closed her eyes, hoping to find a spell to help her.

She opened the book, flipping through pages and pages of their family's rich traditions. Inside were stories of powerful family members and their personal spells. She saw instructions on how to work candle magic, lay down root work, how to remove curses, and how to place hexes on an enemy. She saw long lost rich traditions for growth and prosperity, rituals of sacrifice to bless the family wealth, all of which she thought could be useful. It wasn't until she reached the section about potions that Amina found a plausible solution, a ritual on how to drain the gift of a young witch. Amina's lips twitched in delight. She just might be able to pull this off after all.

~

*P*apa Samedi hid in a thicket of trees on campus as he watched Yolanda's dorm. A few students walked by, totally oblivious to the presence of evil so close by them. Frustration was etched all over his face, as he blew smoke, and began to set in motion his new plan. After his taste of Lawson power through Amina, he was persistent now more than ever to possess it. Mama Brigitte sauntered by him as he took a long puff on his cigar.

"He failed. And the sister has not even attained one power."

Papa Samedi pulled the cigar from his mouth, "I know," he grunted. "That's why I always have backup plans."

She smiled at him with a wide tooth grin, "Really?"

Papa Samedi took a slow savoring pull from the cigar and blew out hard. "By tonight I shall have the heart of the third sister. She has the gift of sight. With her gift I can see how to defeat the other sisters. I'll be invincible."

Mama Brigitte cackled and shifted into her snake form. Her bones broke, cracked, and liquefied as she shrunk into a large mass of yellow muscle. She remained coiled on the ground, hissing, ruby eyes glistening, with her head positioned to strike. Papa Samedi wrapped her around his neck while he continued to look out to the campus.

*Y*olanda walked with Malcolm past a dense thicket of trees, and a sudden chill swept through her, sending shivers along the nape of her neck. She had the oddest sensation that she was being watched. She peered over to her left and saw nothing so she continued along, but something was alerting her psychic senses.

Yolanda gazed into Malcolm's darkened eyes. "So bae what did you think about the movie? Did you like it?"

Malcolm looked over and said, "It was powerful. Almost life changing."

She pulled him closely, "I agree. It definitely speaks to the Black Lives Matter movement. I'm so glad you enjoyed it." Yolanda gushed as she buried her head on his shoulder.

Malcolm wrapped her hand in his. "Of course baby. It doesn't matter what I'm doing just as long as I'm spending time with you."

"Aww," she gushed as she clasped harder onto his hand.

Malcolm stopped and looked at her in the eyes. "Yolanda you are the most beautiful girl I have ever met in my life. And you're powerful baby, super powerful. You don't know how strong you are."

She looked at him in shock and awe. There were no words to describe her emotions, so she continued on. Yolanda walked to the steps of her dorm but Malcolm pulled her back. She peered over her shoulder. "What's up?"

A mischievous smile swept across Malcolm's face. "I'm not ready to go back to the dorm." He pulled her into his arms and leaned into her ear. "Baby come take a walk with me. I have something to show you."

Yolanda smoothed her hands over her goddess braids and flashed Malcolm a slight smile. "Okay."

Malcolm pulled her by the hand. "Come on."

Together they strolled to the other side of the campus, under the light of a half crescent moon. Something didn't sit right with Yolanda after walking twenty minutes to the abandoned side of campus. Yet she still walked hand in hand with Malcolm against everything she was feeling inside. She couldn't explain it but there was something different with her boyfriend. He was cold and distant.

"Hey let's go in here." Malcolm said as he pulled himself away from Yolanda and crept onto the stairs of the old chemistry building. It was condemned for two years now and scheduled for demolition in spring, so the school can build a new dorm.

Yolanda just looked at him, then while looking at the dark building, she felt a wave of fear stab her in the chest. Everything in her gut told her to say no. Instead she was silent.

"Come on," Malcolm called again

Yolanda followed him in. The building smelled of old dust, wood debris, and cement. It was pitch black inside and deadly quiet. No sooner that she took two steps inside, a sickening vision slammed into her head. Several images flashed together as a warning that revealed a long hidden truth. Malcolm was praying at some altar. Blood stains covered his face. Then she saw him attacking various girls. A dark entity loomed over him and Malcolm kneeled before it.

"Bring me the heart of a witch," the voice boomed, with its face covered in shadows.

Yolanda gasped as she came out the vision and darkness destroyed her sun-filled heart.

This can't be true? Was the thought echoed in her brain

Malcolm placed his hand on Yolanda's shoulder. "What did you see?"

Yolanda looked back to him, speechless. How could she have not seen this? Why did the spirits reveal this to her now? She felt confused, lost and betrayed. How could she be so blinded by love?

Malcolm leaned in closer. "What did you see?" he asked again as he clutched something shiny held within his jeans.

Yolanda gasped when she peered down. Malcolm had been hiding a knife. She thought back to the images that flashed in her head during the vision. In that moment she realized her boyfriend was a Bokor, demon worshippers who sacrifice to the dark Loa in exchange of power and wealth for their family. Yolanda staggered back.

Malcolm gritted his teeth, "Baby tell me. What did you see?"

Yolanda didn't answer. She ran for her life, convinced that her boyfriend would kill her.

15

BOKOR

*A*fter leaving Patty Patty Boom Boom, Lorenzo and Patrice strolled down midtown, opting to get frozen yogurt for dessert. Her night so far had been something so magical that she couldn't even imagine conjuring anything better. She was spooning her yogurt and exchanging side eye glances with Lorenzo as they meandered the sidewalk.

There had been a moment so perfect, and so endearing that she could feel herself falling for him. It was the moment that Lorenzo went to the bar to buy another round of drinks and his gaze fell heavy on her, all the way across the room. The way he stared made her feel like she was the only person in the whole wide world that mattered. She shuddered at the heat of his hazel eyes, and as she crossed her legs at the table her body moistened. Patrice had been used to the admiring eyes of men. She experienced it whenever she pumped down the street daily. But it had been years since a man looked at her like Lorenzo had.

As they strolled, she turned back to him, to lose herself once again in his alluring gaze.

"You know I can tell from all that craziness in your cup that you're going to be sick." Patrice declared with a mouthful of cake batter yogurt.

"What this?" Lorenzo asked as he used his spoon to point to his cup. "You don't know what you're missing. This is good! German chocolate with fruit loops, gummy worms, pound cake and caramel is the best."

Patrice laughed, "Whatever. You are going to be sick! Do you hear me? Pepto Bismol will be calling your name."

He walked ahead of her and turned to face her, "I'll be even sicker if I don't get the chance to take you out again." His lips curled, and she thought to herself there it goes again. It was the Lorenzo James megawatt smile.

Patrice swallowed a mouthful of yogurt, almost choking. She smiled as cake batter dribbled from the corner of her mouth. "That can be arranged."

"Arranged?" Lorenzo asked. "Let's make sure it happens." He said returning the gesture.

Patrice blushed, she almost felt like a little girl around him. Just ahead Lorenzo spotted a group of bicycles available for rent. "Hey let's ditch the yogurt and go biking," he said as he took off.

Lorenzo was sprinting at a pace Patrice couldn't match in heels. She shuffled behind him with her yogurt cup in hand, "What? I still have a lot."

Lorenzo doubled back and yanked her free hand. "C'mon just toss it. Let's go!"

Patrice took two steps toward him and he held her in place. Lorenzo rested his strong hands on Patrice's lower back as his towering presence swallowed her. The closeness made her shudder. Breaths separated them. Her lips burned with a desire to kiss him. Lorenzo leaned down and Patrice pushed her head forward. Just before their lips could make contact, Patrice's phone goes off and she seethed inside.

Without second thought she broke from Lorenzo's hold, worried it could be bad news.

"Hello," Patrice answered already worried.

"Patrice help me," Yolanda said in a voice barely above a hiss. Her tone was so low, it was almost as if she was hardly speaking into the phone.

"Help you? What's wrong Yolanda?"

"It's Malcolm," She breathed. "He's a Bokor."

~

*A*mina hovered over Makayla with the Legacy in one hand and a crystal in another. She was about to chant when her phone started buzzing. Amina peered over. Patrice was calling. Amina ignored the vibration of the phone and pressed forward with the ritual. She was washing over Makayla's eyelids with oil when the phone vibrated again, dangling on the side of the coffee table. Amina hesitated for a moment and allowed the call to go to voicemail. But as soon as it did, Patrice called again. She cursed out loud before picking up the phone.

"What?" She answered, pissed.

"It's Yolanda," Patrice stated in tone that was urgent. "She's in trouble and I'm all the way across town. You need to get to her."

Amina curled her lips, "Trouble...what you mean trouble?"

"Danger!" Patrice shouted. She is in the Powell building, it's an abandoned chemistry building on Clark Atlanta's campus. She says a Bokor is after her," Patrice whispered.

"Are you serious?"

"I'm all the way across town. The house is fifteen minutes away. I need you get over there. She sounds terrified."

"Wait... wait slow down." Amina said as she pulled the phone closer to her ear.

"Get over to Clark Atlanta University now! I'll meet you there."

Amina paused. She glanced over at Makayla. And then she thought about her deal with the Loa. She sighed. "I'll be there." Amina settled.

She hung up the phone and grabbed her bag from the coffee table. Amina reached inside and blew a puff of brown powder over Makayla's face. Makayla popped up as if a needle injected a shot of adrenaline to the heart.

Makayla dabbed at her eyes. "What happened?" she asked in a yawn.

"You fell asleep in the middle of telling me your story," Amina said with a smile.

"Really?"

"Yes. Go get in bed. I have to leave, Yolanda's in trouble." she said as she patted Makayla on the leg.

~

*P*atrice hung up the phone and walked back over to Lorenzo.

"Is everything okay?" Lorenzo asked with concern written all over his face.

Patrice forced a smile. "It's a family emergency with one of my sisters Yolanda. Rain check on the bike ride?"

Lorenzo nodded, disappointment gleamed in his eyes. "Sure." he agreed.

"Thanks. I had an amazing time," Patrice said all in one breath as she turned to head in the opposite direction.

She had taken three steps off the sidewalk and into the street before he called her name.

"Patrice."

She whirled around to listen to him.

"I want to see you again. Hit me up," he said with his brown eyes tugging the strings of her heart.

"Bet on it," she returned with a smile before dashing off to her car.

16

LOVE BLINDS

*Y*olanda was petrified as she hid inside the cabinet. She lost Malcolm by running upstairs and finding an open lab where she stuffed herself underneath a bench in the back. Not only was she scared but she felt like an idiot. How did she not know Malcolm was a Bokor? All this time! He was the first boyfriend she ever told about her gifts. Now the truth stared her in the face. He was a killer. Bokors gain blessings for their clan through slaughter and sacrifices to the Petro Loa. The stunning revelation brought silent tears to her eyes as her fingers clenched into her thighs that were pulled to her chest.

Her heart stopped when she heard a creak near the front of the room, it was the unmistakable sound of a door opening. Malcolm was there. Inside the room with her. Boots pounded the floor in the old lab and Yolanda's dread magnified tenfold with each step. She placed her hand over her mouth to keep from crying out, and bit into her fingers to hold back the scream for help she wanted to release. Suddenly it seemed as if all the oxygen around her was consumed. Boots pounded to her right. Yolanda held her breath, as a bitter cold wrapped itself around her like a blanket, and she started to tremble.

Boots thudded past the cabinet and then by the door. There was another crack and as she quivered with unease she wondered if he'd left. Stay there her gut told her, don't move. There was another voice that suggested he was gone. But again something told her to remain. Even though common sense told her she should stay, she didn't want to remain in a cabinet hiding forever. Yolanda peeked her head out of the cabinet. Before she could even look over to the door, a hard grip yanked her by the head, and dragged her out of the cabinet.

"Stop!" Yolanda cried as she winced in pain. "Malcolm what are you doing?" she asked as he pulled her out of the cabinet and slammed her against the wall.

"I'm delivering you baby," He declared as he flashed the blade to her face. " I am going to deliver your power and soul over to my lord. You will be the biggest blessing to the Night Scar Clan."

Yolanda struggled within his grasp. He pinned both of her hands against the wall as he maneuvered his knife. "How can you do this Malcolm? I trusted you. It wasn't supposed to be this way." A sob fought to escape her lips as her eyes brimmed with tears. "I loved you. You are supposed to love me. The gods want us to be together. I've seen it."

Malcolm smiled, "I know." Then he stared at her with a blank look in his eyes. For the first time Yolanda saw something she had never seen before. A true monster in the guise of a loving man. "I needed you to trust me. Please don't struggle baby, we can make this so much easier."

"Easier…. You have no idea who you are messing with?"

"What are you going to do?" Malcolm questioned. He chuckled as if her threat was a ludicrous joke. "Yolanda you wouldn't hurt a fly."

Yolanda swallowed her tears and spat, "I wouldn't but my sister is going to kick your ass."

Malcolm smiled, "We'll see. By the time my lord blesses me she won't be able to touch me," He declared to her in disgust. "You know I never thought I could do this until he came. After years of studying rituals and doing the prayers he revealed himself to my clan, about a week ago. With instructions."

*A*mina heard voices as she crept up the stairs of the Powell building. She peered inside the door of one lab and saw Malcolm pinning Yolanda against the wall. Impending doom made Yolanda kick and claw at Malcolm's unyielding clasp. She was helpless as a lamb ready for slaughter. Several thoughts whirled around Amina's head. Deep down she knew that she couldn't harm her sisters, so in her mind it was best if someone else were to carry out the plan.

"Please Malcolm don't do this. You don't have to." Yolanda begged as she broke down to sobs.

Amina turned away as she listened, her heart cringing at the sight of her innocent middle sister, begging for her life. Of all the dirty low down and rotten things Amina had done in her life, she knew she could never forgive herself if she stood by and watched her sister die. Yolanda had always been the pacemaker of the family, the one who would never say or do anything to bring harm on anyone. She was the little light of the Lawson girls, always encouraging everyone else. That was why when it came to problems at school, it was up to Amina to step to any girl who picked on or talked about Yolanda. Patrice was the mother, Yolanda was the peacemaker, Makayla was the baby and Amina was the fighter. With that in mind, Amina knew what she needed to do.

Once she concluded she had to save her sister, Amina stepped into the room. She reached her palm out towards the sky. Her eyes glazed over to a misty white, and dark clouds took shape.

"Thunder and lightning, deliver my sister from evil," Amina chanted.

Like a candle being blown out, the moonlight shining through the room disappeared. Darkness swallowed them all. There was a loud rumble and a sharp crack. Rippling and crashing through the large window panes came a ferocious bolt of lightning, that shattered the glass of the windows, and turned the frame into splinters. Sharp lightning jetted into Amina's hand and she tossed it onto Malcolm's back.

With a loud cry he fell to his knees in an erratic convulsion. Yolanda fell to the floor beside Malcolm, who laid in a steaming slump. She caressed her red and swollen eyes

Amina rushed to her side, "Are you all right?"

Yolanda nodded a yes, with her mouth gaping, her neck still sore, and overall shaken to her core.

"Amina...Yolanda!" Patrice yelled as she rushed around the corner out of nowhere. She ran into the lab and peered down at the steaming slump. Patrice kneeled down to her sisters. "Come on let's get out of here. Let's go!"

Hand in hand the sisters jetted out of the lab and away from the campus in a hurry.

~

*A*s soon as the sisters left, a window in the corner of the lab slid open and Lorenzo crept into the room, dressed head to toe in all black. From the moment Patrice had looked at him during her phone call, he could smell the fear wafting over her. So he followed behind to see what was going on.

He looked down at Malcolm who laid in a heap after being fried by lightning. Plumes of smoke still wafted off his body, as if he had just been pulled out of a deep fryer. Lorenzo knelt down to him and checked his pulse. He was shocked to discover the lucky son of a bitch had still been alive. "Aren't you lucky bruh?"

A glint of silver caught his eye. It was a blade with a veve symbol on it. "So that's why she fried you. You're a Bokor." Lorenzo slapped him against the cheeks, stirring him awake. Once his eyes popped open, Lorenzo proceeded to interrogate him. "Wake up playboy. Whose clan do you belong to?"

"What? Who are you?" Malcolm said as he stared, still in a daze, and then he let out a loud yelp as the pain washed over him

Lorenzo clenched his jaw and pressed him further. "C'mon I'm not stupid. I know all Bokors belong to a clan. Who's yours?"

Malcolm curled his eyes. "I'm not telling you shit!"

Lorenzo shook his head, "Wrong answer playboy. I was trying to let you get through this easy." He cocked his head. "I guess you want me to get gutter on yo' punk ass," he said as his fingernails became talons that stabbed into the back of Malcolm's skull. In response Malcolm released a sharp cry of pain in response. Lorenzo's eyes became golden as he searched Malcolm's thoughts for the info he needed. Then he dropped his nose close to Malcolm and wiped across his clothes, to take in his scent. In one swoop he lifted Malcolm off the floor. "You're coming with me playboy." It was the oldest trick in the book. Date a witch, teach her how to grow her powers, kill her and make delivery to the Loa. Lorenzo had dealt with Bokors before, and he considered them a nuisance that needed to be taken care of immediately. He had plans with the Lawson sisters, plans that didn't need any complications.

It took only twenty minutes for Lorenzo's Ferrari to reach Eternal Sunshine cafe, downtown. The restaurant was dark and the sign outside said closed but he could detect activity going on around back, lots of it. With a shattering kick he knocked open the back door, and all drumming and chanting stopped. Candles and white chalk adorned the back of the restaurant, which was covered in ritualistic symbols, veves. Malcolm catapulted into the room right over a veve, knocking over five large candles. A dozen heads lobbed over to the opened door. Many of the worshippers cleared out earlier, leaving only the higher ranked men.

Lorenzo stepped into the back room, with a grim look on his face. "Does this one belong to you?"

One brother with grey locks that ran down his back stood up. "Yes he does. My name is Josiah. This is my clan, sacred Night Scar, and that's my boy. Speak your peace mister and you better do it fast because me and mine don't like outsiders." Right on cue machetes came out and guns aimed their line of fire towards Lorenzo.

Lorenzo set his jaw hard as his eyes became golden and

primal. "I'm only going to say this once; the Lawson sisters belong to me. If anyone will take their powers it will be me."

Josiah chuckled and laughter swept around the room. "I'm sorry about that mister, but my boy has been setting this up for months now. I was even going to get my nephew to go after the youngest at the high school. Either way, we should reap our harvest soon. And we ain't sharing a damn thing, everything is going to Papa Samedi."

Lorenzo cocked his head. "Your Loa is Papa Samedi?"

"Yes sir and he could use a live sacrifice tonight," Josiah said as he pulled out his own blade.

Lorenzo was silent as he took three steps back, he turned and locked the door to everyone's surprise.

"So, what will it be Mister? We can bleed ya slow or bleed ya quick."

When Lorenzo turned his head, his eyes were red at the center and his claws came out

"I prefer slow!" He growled as he lurched further.

If one was passing through the back alley of Eternal Sunshine they would see and hear many things that would've turned them around. There was the flickering light as gunfire lit up the restaurant. It was followed up by the low guttural growl of a beast as it ripped and tore through flesh. Gunfire continued for a full thirty seconds until the beast howled and the last gunman fell.

Lorenzo rolled out of the restaurant, cool as a cucumber with his face drenched in fresh blood. He popped the trunk of his Ferrari, clicked a button and a secret weapons locker raised up, he grabbed an orbital grenade out of a mass of other weapons. Lorenzo strolled back over to the cafe, pulled open the door, lobbed the grenade inside, closed it and got back into his car.

There had only been a minute between the time he cranked the car and turned the steering wheel before Eternal Sunshine went up into flames that stretched towards the horizon. He would burn the clothes as usual when he got to the penthouse then ask for a cleanup afterwards.

17

SOMETHING AIN'T RIGHT

*B*ack at home the sisters were up late reflecting about the impending doom headed their way. Yolanda was sitting on a stool in the kitchen crying as Patrice padded and consoled her. Makayla sat slumped at the kitchen table with Amina perched across from her. Amina peered up at Patrice who was giving her an icy stare that made her spine run cold.

Amina's face curled in response to Patrice. "What?"

Patrice folded her arms, "How did you get your powers back?"

"Excuse me?" Amina responded, becoming defensive.

Patrice folded her arms and took a defensive stance. "You never told us how you were able to get your powers back after we bound you. That curse should've stripped you of any magic you had."

Amina rolled her eyes. "What does it matter?"

Patrice stood from the table. "We have spent half our life here in Atlanta, monster free and with no magical problems.

Now suddenly zombies show up at Makayla's school, and Yolanda's boyfriend turns out to be a Bokor. Something ain't right. And it all started when you came here. I want to bet that whoever helped you, is after us for something you did."

Amina sucked her teeth. "Not now Peaches. I can't believe you're talking about some bullshit when our sister is in need." She said as she shifted her attention to Yolanda.

Patrice wasn't buying it. She pulled Amina's shoulder to press the issue and to face her. "Look me in the eye and tell me you have nothing to do with this!"

Yolanda could feel a spirit of dissention wafting about the house like an unseen cloud of darkness that made the room tense. This time she dared not step in the middle.

Amina cut Patrice up and down with her eyes and looked at her as if she were about to strike. Makayla called Peaches' name in an attempt to cool her older sister to no avail.

"Human lie detector right here Amina," Patrice declared. "Look me in the eye and tell me you have nothing to do with this. How did you get your gifts back?"

Just like their grandmother, one of Patrice's gift was to read people. She had an innate ability to sense when someone was lying to her. It served her no purpose in her love life because even though she knew some scum bugs she talked to were lying to her... she ignored her intuition. In her career however it made her highly intuitive, and a power house with working clients. Amina knew this about her sister so she chose her words carefully.

"I sought the help of a powerful spirit in New York," Amina declared. "If you must know," She sassed as she eyed Patrice in the eye hard. "But instead of trying to blame me for everything like you always do, let's worry about our sister." She said as she turned to cradle Yolanda.

Patrice still sensed a half truth from her sister. But the look of distraught and pain on Yolanda's puffy red face made her want to drop the issue. She rubbed Yolanda's shoulder. "Stay here tonight. Everything will be fine. I promise you. I will take care of this."

Yolanda nodded as she sniffled. Her heart was destroyed by her boyfriend, and that sad reality made her feel devastated.

Patrice walked to the foot of the stairs. "Let's get some sleep guys and talk about it in the morning." She declared before racing up the stairs to peel off her makeup.

18

A SLICE OF PARADISE

That night Amina rolled around in her bed and moaned as she felt Papa Samedi's ominous presence invading her mind. Papa Samedi's voice boomed deep inside her head. His menacing presence was with her, dominating her senses and flooding her mind with terrible thoughts.

A ruby eyed boa constrictor materialized on her bedroom floor. It flicked its tongue as it worked its way onto the bed burrowing under the covers. Sweat formed at Amina's forehead and coated the dip of her neck into her chest. She gripped the side of the bed ripping the pairs of sheet off the mattress. With two eyes as red as flames, the snake continued to work itself onto the bed. Amina laid on the right side, and on the left the snake coiled itself to a half moon, sizing Amina up like it would any other prey. Slowly it coiled itself around Amina. It's muscles squeezed her tight until she was helpless as a lamb, then the snake reared it's head back, saliva dripped as it's jaws stretched open. In a handclap it snapped into her neck, and

Papa Samedi's voice came crashing into her head like a roaring wave. .

"You dare defy me? We made a deal." Papa Samedi's voice hissed inside her head.

Amina's eyes shot open. "Please! I have a plan. Forgive me. I know how to get them all for you."

Papa Samedi cackled. "You will not cross me again." Then the snake tightened, digging into Amina's neck, pressing against her windpipe.

Panic shot through her as the snake squeezed tighter, crushing her throat, cutting off her air. There was a harsh ringing in her ears, and blood thrummed at her temples. Her eyes bulged as she gasped for air.

"Bring me the powers of your sisters. Do not cross me, mon ami." Papa Samedi hissed.

Amina jerked awake, scared out of her mind and panting, she caressed her neck and glared around. It was still dark, and no one was in the room. This time she realized, she had conned the wrong man.

～

On the other side of Atlanta, Lorenzo laid in bed sleepless with his body oiled in sweat, wondering why Patrice left him standing in the dust. He wanted her. The old lady had revealed her to him in a vision. It took him a long time but finally he fell asleep. Lorenzo dreamed he was getting off an elevator; looking around he was in a swanky bar that had a magnificent view of the city. He didn't know which city or what bar he was in, all he knew was that he was there to see the old lady. Lorenzo looked down, and as always he was dressed in a sharp wool grey suit. Jazz music was playing in the background and the joint was empty as always, except the one bartender, a Latino man that looked to be in his forties with slick black hair.

"Good to see you again Mr. James. Are you having your usual?" The bartender asked as he continued to wipe down the bar.

Lorenzo nodded as he stood by the bar. "As always Eddie."

"I got that coming right up sir," Eddie said with a smile.

How do I know this guy's name? Lorenzo asked himself. Before he could contemplate anymore, Eddie was handing him the drink.

"The Madam is waiting for you at the table."

Lorenzo shrugged. He took the drink and looked over to see her. The old lady. She was sitting across from the bar at the table closest to the view of the city, under a bright spotlight. Lorenzo thought to himself that she was a hot old lady. Dressed in all white. Wrapped in a magnificent fur and dripping in diamonds. She reminded Lorenzo of a Diana Ross or Lena Horne.

"Over here dear," She called.

He picked up his drink off the bar, still confused. Lorenzo walked over to her table and he remembered to give her a kiss on the cheek. "What am I doing here?"

"Just checking in sugar. Have a seat."

Lorenzo sat down. He looked at the lady long and hard. And somehow he knew her even though he couldn't recall her name. He also knew this place. "Where am I again?"

The lady sipped her glass of champagne then looked around. "A little place I like to call my slice of paradise." She swallowed then cleared her throat. "Now. I see you've finally met my Peaches."

A light bulb came on inside Lorenzo's head. "Yes ma'am I did."

The lady smiled, "What do you think?"

Lorenzo grinned, "She's something else."

She took a sip of her champagne and crossed her glossy legs. "She's something else alright."

Lorenzo nodded, "She's strong I'll say that."

The lady cackled. "She gets her strength from me. But don't be fooled, she will still need you. There is a storm coming and you have to protect her."

Lorenzo was stupefied. "A storm? You know, as many times as I've had this dream, you never make any sense. What's coming?"

"An evil that is spreading in the south. And I'm not talking about just any evil. It's powerful. You do know our town sits on a Hell gate? Don't be fooled my dear this battle you are about to face will be only one of many."

Lorenzo furrowed his brow and tossed his drink to the side. "One of many? Lady what do you mean?"

The lady wagged her finger, "No spoilers. I can't tell you too much, just like I can't bring her here neither. But what I can tell you is to get ready."

"Get ready?"

"That's right." She said with a smile. "See you soon sugar."

When Lorenzo woke up everything became a haze again. His heart was slamming into his chest, sweat drenched his clothes, and he hated the fear scent folded into it. The specifics he couldn't remember but what he remembered was the old lady, her message, and his mission to protect Patrice.

19
SHAME

*A*few days later, Makayla came downstairs one morning to find Amina surrounded by oils and herbs at the kitchen table. The Legacy was planted in front of her and she was stirring back and forth in a bubbling pot as if she was making a gumbo. Amina insisted she was trying to figure out a way to protect them all from the evil that seemed to be following them. In actuality she had found a potion that could help rob the sisters of their gifts, but she had to practice making it. Makayla watched her in awe and Amina saw the moment as a great opportunity to help her baby sister perfect her craft. Makayla had just discovered her gift and ever since that night at the high school she hadn't used them.

A spirit of panic and unease had swept North Central High due to Coach Watkins' murder. A murder to which the police just brushed off as gang activity. And that same tense fear was at home, with her sister Yolanda being turned into a shell of herself after falling into depression over Malcolm. Makayla didn't want to feel like the baby, she wanted to feel protected, more importantly she wanted to protect herself. She knew it could only come from mastering her gift. Only problem is that every time she tried walking through a wall she just ended up planting a knot upside her head.

Amina was flipping through the pages. She was reading the part of the Legacy that had biographies of their family members and their abilities. Her lips painted a bright red, curled into a smile as her eyes glanced across the time tinged brown portrait of their great great uncle. "Here he is," Amina said as she slid the massive book around to allow her sister a better look. "This is our great uncle William Lawson. He was the last Levau and the first Lawson. He had the same gift you have. It's called Phasing. He could change his body density, allowing him to become intangible and phase through solid objects. They used to call him Willie the Ghost."

Makayla grinned and grabbed Amina's shoulder. "Phasing...OMG that sounds so cray. But I can work with this." She started tugging on Amina. "Tell me more. How did he control it? And what happened to him."

Amina trailed her hand on the ruffled pages of the Legacy. "It says he mastered his gift through breathing. Somehow through shallow breaths he could make himself hollow and intangible enough to pass through solid objects. It also says that on the opposite end, our great uncle Willie could make his body super dense almost like a brick armor. Around the late 1950's he got attacked by some local racists who shot him up, but were dumbfounded when the bullets bounced off of him. From there he had to leave New Orleans and he changed his name from Levau to Lawson."

Makayla tapped her chin as she stared blankly at her sister. "So does this mean I'm bullet proof too?"

"Could be….who knows?' Amina said with a shrug.

"Well I hope so. That would be A-M-A-Z-I-N-G," Makayla said standing up. "So the Legacy said he mastered his gift through breathing. Theoretically that should help me too right?"

Amina stood up as well. "Sure. You know our gifts are tied to our emotions, our feelings, and our energy. Some abilities are channeled by rage, others by love, but most by calm….an inner peace."

"Just try it," Amina said before glancing up at the echo of footsteps on the stairs.

With wild hair and dark eyes, Yolanda dragged herself downstairs and fell into a chair near the kitchen table with a moan. "Morning," she greeted with a sigh.

" Yolanda….child," Amina said as she patted Yolanda's mess of hair. "It's going to be alright."

Yolanda frowned at her. "What are you doing?"

"Trying to help Makayla with her gift." Amina answered as she turned her attention towards her younger sister. "Come on little bird."

Makayla closed her eyes and exhaled slowly. In and out she kept taking slow shallow breaths. As the air left her lips she felt her stomach fill with butterflies. All along her shoulders was a tingling sensation, one that reminded her of the feeling whenever she hit her funny bone. She could feel the magic inside of her making every fiber and nerve of her being come alive. Then Makayla felt a certain weightlessness almost as if she could float out of the room like a hot air balloon.

"Makayla look," Amina whispered in her ear.

Makayla opened her eyes. She held up her hands. Makayla gasped as she could see right through them. Closely she examined her hands. They were glowing a ghostly radiant color and translucent. She slammed her fist on the table and it ran right through it.

"Oh my god! Oh my god!" She shouted as her breathing returned normal. A sense of gravity came back to her and she was herself again. "Now this is one hell of a gift!"

"What good is a gift if it just fails you and renders you helpless. How could I not know Malcolm was a Bokor?"

Amina curled herself over Yolanda. "Look, get over this shit. Stop beating yourself up. Just like with any woman when you get close to someone you only see what you want to see. Your feelings for Malcolm probably clouded your ability to have any visions about him."

Yolanda looked over to her, "Well how do you explain the vision I had that night just before he was going to kill me?"

Amina shrugged, "Timing. Sometimes the spirits...the energy around us chooses not to reveal things until a certain time." She said as she patted Yolanda's shoulder. "Just like I was trying to explain to Makayla earlier. Our gifts and powers are not our own. Everything comes from the Phoenix. The Bennu. It washes over us and through our craft we channel it. Besides, every girl has to kiss a couple of frogs before they find their prince. Most of these men ain't shit." Amina said with a nudge.

"Well I mean , no shade, but you didn't need to be psychic to see Malcolm was a dirt bag," Makayla chirped in. "I never liked him anyway."

Yolanda forced a fake laugh when really deep down she wanted to cry, thinking about how stupid she was falling for Malcolm and telling him their family secret. Yolanda felt disconnected from herself. How could this happen? She felt fractured and useless and feared that she had somehow let her sisters down.

Patrice was still moisturizing her arms when she asked, "What's going on?"

Amina smiled, "I was helping my little bird with her gift. Teaching her a little bit of the craft."

Patrice sighed. "Well how about you don't. She's currently struggling with her advanced classes and that's all she needs to focus on now."

"What do you mean?" Amina asked, readying herself to go off.

"She is a teenage girl who needs to be focused on school work."

Amina tossed her twists off her shoulder. "But she is a Lawson. She has gifts. Voodoo and magic is her birthright."

"And it's also dangerous and addictive. You don't need to be teaching her hexes and curses. You need to tell her that magic has consequences and karma. It also attracts evil."

Amina fell silent, with the signs of frustration written all over her face. She wanted to slap her so bad, that her fingers twitched. Finally with a sigh, Amina said, "Peaches what do you want to do? There is a big bad fucking with us. Makayla and Yolanda need to learn how to protect themselves."

"I will protect them. I told you before I got this," Patrice said as she stepped closer to Amina.

Amina sucked her teeth, "You know what this is some bullshit. I'm not going to do this with you this morning. Damn....I'm just trying to help." She said before storming out of the kitchen.

Immediately Yolanda swung from her seat at the kitchen

table and shadowed behind Amina's footsteps. "Wait," she called.

Amina whirled around, "Naw, she think she is somebody's momma with all dat'. She needs to calm down. I told you I was gone try and that's what I'm doing."

Patrice stared at them in silence, as Yolanda managed to calm down Hurricane Amina and take her upstairs.

Makayla leaned on the counter. "You know she was trying to help. Why are you tripping?"

"Sure she was. Now go get ready for school," Patrice said with an icy stare.

~

There were many things Makayla was knowledgeable about. She learned how to professionally do her own hair and makeup off of YouTube. She knew how many tattoos Chris Brown had on his body, the date he got them, and what they stood for. She also knew everything there was to know about the Kardashian clan and what was in style for the season. But the one thing that Makayla was knowledgeable about that was actually useful, math. Since middle school she had taken advanced classes. It was the last period of the day and Makayla was sitting perched in her Pre-Calculus class with Mr. Charles. He was a tall well-built black man with a shiny bald skull. Mr. Charles was the most hated teacher in the whole school. His classes were hard. He taught with no mercy. And he really didn't care if students succeeded or not. Some would even argue that any student he didn't like he would do his best to see them fail.

A sense of dread whirled through the classroom as he

handed out graded midterm exams. With a stern look on his face, he walked down the rows of the classroom handing out each exam. "These are some pitiful scores," he said with a shake of his head as he slapped a seventy percent on Brittany's desk. She was sitting two rows behind Makayla and on her left.

"Did anybody study for this? Like for real….. for real?" Mr. Charles said addressing the class with a nasty frown.

Some kid in the back of the class called him a dick, and quickly he twisted towards the voice. Swiftly, the poor boy ducked down in fear. Mr. Charles resumed his trek up the aisle with his right hand full of exams. When he approached Devante's desk he tossed the test right between Devante's arms..

Devante glanced up to Mr. Charles to meet his beady brown eyes. He then stared down to the sixty-eight on his exam. Mr. Charles shook his head.

"Boy you can kiss that basketball team goodbye."

"Come on man chill…." Devante murmurs in a drawl before dropping his head.

Mr. Charles continued slapping one disappointing score after another but when he neared Makayla, she was the only one in the class perky and gleeful. History bored her and Literature was depressing. But above all math was her thing. She was the only sophomore in the class full of juniors. So when Mr. Charles tossed her exam on her desk, he came with a different energy.

"You know Ms. Lawson for a girl who talks so much…You rocked this exam." He announced aloud as Makayla beamed at the sight of the ninety-two written in bold letters.

Makayla held the exam up high as she squealed like a piglet. "Just give me the praise, and hold the shade. Thank ya!"

Behind her Devante took notice of her score and immediately he knew what needed to be done. As soon as class was over and everyone was gathering their stuff out of lockers to head home, he approached Makayla. Makayla glanced over her shoulder. Her breath caught, and she thought she would've passed out at the sight of the caramel dream in front of her.

He leaned on the locker beside her. "Yo what's up Makayla?"

"Hey Devante...um...what's good," she stammered uncomfortably as she grabbed her bag out of the locker.

"I can't help but notice that you are some sort of genius with this Pre-Calculus. Are you trying to help ya boy out?"

Instead of answering, Makayla just stared. Every interaction with Devante was a hi, bye and a what's up, so she was gagging at the thought of being alone with him. Immediately her mind drifted into a fantasy of him on the basketball court shooting a winning shot. Everyone would be cheering his name and he would look over at her. She would be his girl and while there was madness all around them, it would be just them two. He would pull her in his arms, golden biceps that had a cross tattooed on them. A cross that Makayla thought was the sexiest cross she had ever seen in her life. And as he pulled her in his arms with his body all glistening with sweat, he would blow out her flame with a kiss from his large pink lips. She screamed yes god in her mind. Just kiss me.

"Makayla!" Devante shouted.

"What?" Makayla blurted as she jumped up all startled.

"Can you tutor me or nah?"

"Sure. I got you," She confirmed.

Devante tilted his head slightly and licked his lips, "You follow me on Instagram right?"

Makayla shook her head, "Of course."

"I'll hit your DM to let you know when we can meet up. I appreciate it shawty." He said before bobbing away.

Makayla stood there in a daze. "Shawty," she parroted in his southern drawl that she found so cute. Makayla's eyes lingered on Devante's silhouette as she watched him walk away. She found herself in almost a dream state until she was brought back to reality by Erica's hot breath and alarming stare.

"Didn't I tell you to stop talking to my boyfriend?" Erica snapped as her friends Brittany and Amy joined her side.

Makayla shot her a nasty look-*girl bye*. Then she countered Erica's hostility with a look that read unbothered. While admiring her nails, she said "I tried but your boyfriend can't stop talking to me."

Erica squinted at Makayla, stupefied. "Excuse me?"

Makayla smiled brightly. "I didn't stutter Miss Thang. And I also didn't lie. Your boyfriend keeps coming up to talk to me. So the next time you approach me. Check your facts. As a matter fact check your edges and those fake UGGs you have on tap." Makayla spat viciously.

If Erica wasn't embarrassed enough, her other flunky Amy started laughing. She frowned at Amy as if to say shut up, and immediately Amy became silent.

"Since you so hot at the mouth. Let me cool you down!" Erica shouted as she tossed her Venti Frappe chiller right into Makayla's face. She dropped the plastic cup with a sharp thud and it echoed as it bounced on the floor.

Erica exited to the left with her two flunkies Brittany and Amy following behind her, hysterically laughing. Makayla stood in the middle of the hallway with her mouth agape. Her face was covered in sticky wet slush that dripped all over her.

Then it happened. Laughter filled the hallway. She glanced up looking left and right to see numerous faces laughing at her as they walked out of classes. She was mortified. With his bag and jacket in hand, Wallace walked into the hallway to meet Makayla's eyes. He was gagging just as she was. Tears started forming up. His heart dropped as Makayla ran into the bathroom crying.

"Come back Makayla, wait." Wallace called back

He followed her to the bathroom and even though some teacher shouted he couldn't go in there, he disregarded the warning as he went in. Makayla had never been so embarrassed in her whole life. To her right she grabbed some tissue and dabbed at her eyes that were both filled with tears and slush.

"Makayla are you alright?" Wallace asked for the tenth time.

Makayla peered up then pounded the side of the stall with her fist, "I'm going to get that bitch."

20
BOOGALAH

*M*uch later that afternoon, Makayla was upstairs in the bedroom sorting through the pages of the Legacy trying to plot her revenge. She had told Wallace her secret that she was a Voodoo witch and had gifts that defied every law known to man.

Wallace was leaning on her shoulder that was still damped from the frappe chiller splashed into her face. "Where did you get this book from?"

"I told you it's a family heirloom."

"Hmm is there a spell to turn me into a pretty girl?" Wallace pondered.

"Not even Houdini can do that…now boy hush and help me find something we can do to get those skeezers back." She flashed back to the moment Erica tossed the frappe into her face. "Oh my god!" She bellowed. "I swear to God I hate that girl. I am going to get her."

As she huffed and cursed the existence of Erica King, she came across the section for hexes and curses. A sinister smile swept across Makayla's face and her puffy red eyes brightened as she glanced across the pages. The first curse made a light bulb flash in her head. "A hex to induce hair loss," she said reading the text. Then she thought of Brittany Wilson, Erica's best friend who always bragged about her long natural hair. "I will use this one on Brittany to snatch her bald."

Wallace grimaced and clutched his imaginary pearls, "No you can't do that!"

Makayla smiled, "Just watch me." She folded the edge of the page before flipping on through more curses. "Ooh look at this!" she pointed out. "A clumsy klutz curse. This would be perfect for miss acrobatic Amy Lee. I bet she won't be doing all those flips if she keeps falling over her own two feet." Makayla kept scrolling and as she did the book leaped out of her hands and flipped pages on its own. A blinding light flashed in the room and the book jumped again, this time rolling off the bed.

Wallace ran towards the door. "What was that?"

Makayla stepped off of the bed. "I don't know," she whispered as she picked the book back up.

Wallace crept closer to the bed as if the Legacy was a vicious dog waiting to attack. "At first I thought you were playing about all this root work talk, but all of this is giving me the heebie-jeebies. How about we leave this alone, or give it to God?"

"Don't worry I got this," Makayla reassured.

Something glistening on the floor beside Makayla's bed caught Wallace's eye. He bent down to pick it up. "I think this fell out," he said as he picked it up and handed it to Makayla.

Makayla took the small thing out of his hand and examined it. It was a golden bee pendant about the size of a quarter. It was tarnished and old but something about this pendant called out to Makayla. She reached for the Legacy, anxiously flipping the pages until she found a similar looking pendant in the book.

"The Bee-witching charm," she read aloud. "To make boys flock to you like honey and girls serve you like a Queen." Makayla examined the pendant in the light. "Oh this is fabulous. I like this," she stated as Wallace leaned his head on her shoulder. She peered down to the Legacy, "It was used by my great Aunt Estelle. All we need is High John the conquer oil to anoint it and a spell involving Orris root to activate it."

"Let me see," Wallace said as he took back the pendant. He held it to the light as well. "Yes this is cute or whatever. Put this on a nice blazer with some bangles and you can make this work."

"Yass," Makayla agreed as they laughed.

Wallace handed her back the pendant. " It looks like something my mom would wear." Then his face soured. "She is so strict and gets on my nerves. But I love to watch her get dressed and put her makeup on. Ever since I was a kid. That's how I realized I was in love with fashion."

Makayla frowned, "Well at least you knew your mother. Mine passed away when I was two."

Wallace placed his hand on her shoulder. "I forgot about that. I'm sorry"

Makayla sighed as she looked back down to the pendant. "It's okay." She murmured.

One of the most important relationships a girl could have was with her mother. Makayla didn't have that. Neither did she have a father in her life. All she ever had was Patrice and her sisters. Makayla loved her sisters dearly but there was always a part of her that yearned for real parents. Sometimes she felt like an unwanted child. Amina told her the story that just before Hurricane Katrina, their mother, Ruby had shown up on Gran's door with Makayla. Then she disappeared again that same night. Makayla had no clue who her father is. And she envied her sisters for having memories of their mother. Makayla only had one picture of her mother. She wished she could watch her put on makeup. As a child she even dreamed of her mother's scent, but unfortunately, she had nothing, so she turned to reality tv to create an illusion of a glamorous life where she was just as fabulous as her faves on the silver screen.

She blew on the pendant and shined it with her T-shirt. "I'm going to take over North Central with this."

"Wait, let me get this straight. Do you think with this pendant we can run the school? And be like the mean girls?"

Makayla flashed a toothy grin, "Definitely."

Wallace clapped giddily. "What about Erica? What curse are you going to use on her?"

Makayla flipped through the book. She stopped when she saw instructions on how to create a Voodoo doll. In a flash, she ripped the page right out of the Legacy and made Wallace gasp. "This is the one." She said and Wallace agreed with a nod.

Makayla didn't have a clue on what an Orris root was but she figured Amina did, and not only that but she would most likely get it for her. Her instincts told her to make up a good lie, so she reached for her phone. Makayla turned to Wallace, "Be quiet. I'm about to call my big sister to get the hook up on the ingredients."

"Patrice?" Wallace asked. "You know she is not going to let us get into any mischief."

"No. My other sister Amina. Now hush!" She demanded as she fixed her hair and pointed her iPhone.

Makayla FaceTimed Amina. It wasn't no sooner than three rings that she saw magnificent brown legs, sculpted abs, and a luscious chest flash across her screen.

Amina held the phone to her face. Sunlight beamed behind her. Amina's skin shimmers like a faraway star, her licorice-black skin catches the rays of sunlight while she strolls along the sidewalk with people passing her by in the background. "What's up? Can you hear me?"

"Yes I can hear you," Makayla answered. She admired her sister's shape as she walked down the street wearing nothing but a wife beater, shorts, and a shirt wrapped around her waist. Her fresh goddess braids curled over her shoulder. "Come on body!" Makayla complimented.

Amina laughed, "What's up little bird?"

"Nothing much. Just doing some reading. Where are you?"

Amina struggled with her headphones. "Just shopping in little five points."

"Okay. Well since you're out...can you do me a favor?"

Amina whipped her hair, "Shoot."

Makayla leaned in closer to her phone, "Can you bring me some high john the conquer oil and Orris root."

"What for?"

Makayla looked away, trying to quickly come up with something. She saw Wallace and her best friend's face became her inspiration. "It's a potion I'm making to help Wallace's acne."

"Well did you try apple cider vinegar or a cinnamon and honey mask."

"Girl, he has tried everything from Proactiv to Clearasil. Nothing works so that's why I'm trying to hook up this potion for him."

Amina side eyed her sister. "Okay. I got you. Why don't you meet me at Aunt Dot's candle shop? We can do some sisterly bonding.'"

Makayla frowned her nose, "I don't know is there anywhere else we can go? I don't want Aunt Dot telling Patrice."

Amina brushed it off with a wave of her hand. "Aunt Dot ain't gonna say nothing. Especially if we give her a little something extra. Don't worry about it."

Makayla beamed, "I'm down. Is it okay if I bring Wallace?"

Amina paused and then said, "Sure. Why not? Meet me in twenty minutes"

"Bet!"

Makayla ended the FaceTime and turned to her partner in crime. "She wants us to meet her at my Aunt's shop. We will get the ingredients and by tomorrow we will run the school." She exclaimed when she slapped five with Wallace.

~

At around six-thirty that afternoon, Makayla and Wallace joined Amina at Aunt Dot's gifts, oils, and Candle shop. This had been Makayla's first time at the Voodoo shop in many years, yet it was just how she remembered it, somewhat dark, old looking, and creepy. It wasn't long before Amina could sense something was wrong with her sister. With no hesitation, Makayla spilled out the whole traumatic event that ended with Makayla being humiliated in front of the whole school.

Amina was reaching for a candle in the middle of the aisle when she said, "I would've beaten her ass." She snarled.

"I wanted to….believe me," Makayla responded.

"And I would've helped you." Wallace chimed in.

Amina strolled over to the herb section. "Back in my day in high school they gave me a nickname. Boogalah Cunt." She grabbed the Orris root and chuckled at the memory of her high school days. "I hated it so bad, but I was such a hot mess back then."

"Why did they call you that?" Wallace asked.

Amina turned to him with a fiery gaze, "Because anyone who crossed me would end up having a nasty accident."

Wallace clutched his imaginary pearls. "Oh my god."

Amina laughed, "Exactly."

After picking up a few more items they went to the counter, where Aunt Dot had been side-eying them from the moment they walked in. She rang up Amina's items first, but she kept her gaze steely on Makayla. "Does your sister know you're here?"

Amina slammed money on the counter. "No and she doesn't need to."

Aunt Dot tossed up her hands and turned her head. "Well just leave me out of it honey. I don't want no mess around my shop ya hear'."

Amina fastened and put her coin purse back into her Birkin bag. "Just make sure you keep this on the down low."

"You don't have to worry about me beloved. I ain't tellin' nuffin!" She shouted as she began to bag items.

Makayla grinned to herself, "Thanks Aunt Dot. We will see you later," she said as she grabbed the bag and headed towards the door.

Aunt Dot sat back in her chair and picked up her cigarette. "Alright now, bye girls."

At the thought of Amina doing the same thing in high school she was planning to do, Makayla wanted more help. "I just don't know what to do about the situation. I can't get suspended again. Peaches would kill me."

Amina glanced over, "You have to stand up for yourself. I know bitches like that, you have to show them you're no punk. Your Erica King was my Kristine Greenleaf." She rolled her eyes and sighed at the name, as she walked out the store. "Damn, I hated that girl!"

Makayla shuffled behind them, "But how do I do that without fighting?"

"Read her! And read her for filth, my dear!" Amina shouted.

"That's what I'm talking about!" Wallace agreed.

"You insult her in front of everybody. I might not know a lot but I know words can hurt someone much worse than fighting them can....and I'm not talking about a spell. Insult everything about her from her head to her shoes and I promise you she won't try you again."

Makayla smirked, "I think I can do that."

Amina reached in the bag and pulled out a purple satchel full of powder. "And use this too. Blow it in her face and she will have terrible acne," she said before they all erupted into laughter.

"Well if it isn't Amina Lawson!" a sweet southern voice called from across the lot.

Amina looked over and shuttered. "Oh hell naw."

"Who is it?" Wallace asked.

Amina turned, "You remember I told you about a girl named Kristine Greenleaf." She faced forward and pointed with her eyes. "Well that's her."

Makayla frowned, "With all those kids?"

Amina would've barely recognized the cheerleading captain if it wasn't for those high cheekbones, green eyes and perfect hair. Kristine Greenleaf had become very round and jiggly, as she walked with one baby in her arms, three others following behind, and every part of her body rolled like Jell-O.

"Amina Lawson. I would remember that face anywhere," Kristine exclaimed in a very high merry voice. She bounced her baby in her left arms and looked Amina over. "Look at you! You haven't changed a bit."

Amina forced a fake smile. "Thanks." Her eyes scanned Kristine from head to toe, and zoomed in on her gut. "But you sure have changed a whole lot."

Kristine chuckled. It was a chuckle to mask her embarrassment. "I know. I put on a few pounds. Thanks to my little sugar plum, Ray Ray Jr.," she said as she kissed her baby. "So what brings you back to Georgia?"

"Just visiting family, and spending time with my sisters."

Kristine smiled. "Well ain't that nice." She flashed her smile to both Makayla and Wallace. "I see you all in the music videos and I follow your pages. Who would've known you turned out to be such a celebrity. I for one would've thought you would end up in jail."

Wallace turned to Makayla, "No she didn't," he murmured under his breath.

Amina gave her a toothy smile. "Well you turned out just how I imagined." She paused to sharpen the shade that was about to spew out of her mouth. "Fat, with a whole lot of kids."

Kristine's face soured for a minor second, then she smiled again, refusing to give Amina the satisfaction of stealing her joy. "Amina you really haven't changed," She said as she paused for a beat. "You're still a bitch!" Kristine grabbed her kids and walked towards the buffet.

Fiery rage swept across Amina, and fury made her blood run hot. She looked to the heavens and suddenly grey clouds darkened the sun. Thunder rumbled and Amina pointed her finger to the tree covering Kristine Greenleaf's Honda. "Dark clouds do your worst." There was a tremendous roar in the skies, an onslaught of rain fell, then the clouds parted and a lightning bolt came crashing down on one of the tree limbs, and it collapsed on the Honda.

Kristine turned around and gasped. She ran to her car which was all but flattened. She turned to Amina, "Boogalah cunt you evil witch!"

Makayla tugged Amina's arm. "I can't believe you did that."

"What?" Amina asked nonchalantly as rain drenched her face. "You know I'm a bad witch," she snarled.

Wallace wiped his eyes and saw Kristine pull out of her phone. "She might call the cops. Let's get out of here."

Together they climbed in Amina's Porsche to escape the rain and reeled out of the parking lot.

While in the car, Makayla asked, "So in high school. When you did these revenge curses, were you ever afraid of karma?"

Amina raised an eyebrow. "Karma?" She repeated as if the word was a joke.

"Yeah you know... if you do evil unto others, it will return to you. Patrice believes using our gifts just invites evil into our lives. Yolanda believes we were given these gifts to help people. What do you believe?"

Amina turned her attention from the road. "I believe you can't help anybody else until you've helped yourself."

Makayla faced forward in her seat and allowed the thought to sink into her head. "I guess that's true."

~

No sooner than thirty minutes later, Amina dropped off Wallace and they were back home. They walked into an almost empty home, it was dead silent all around, with no sign of Yolanda or Patrice at all.

Makayla was climbing the stairs when she looked back at Amina."Come in my room so we can finish talking," Makayla said as they climbed the stairs, and dried off with towels.

Amina walked into the room behind Makayla and flopped on the bed beside her sister, "Promise me you're not going to do anything crazy with this." She said, yet knowing Orris root is used for most curses.

Makayla chuckled, "I promise you. It's just to help Wallace."

"Good," Amina huffed. "Peaches hates me enough already."

"She doesn't hate you....she just... you know. She's our sister. Our big sister. It's a sisterly thing like big brothers and little brothers." Then Makayla thought about what she said and shrugged. "Look, I don't know."

Amina rolled her eyes. "Yeah, me neither."

"Can I ask you for something else?"

Amina prepared herself for the worst. She took a breath. "Go ahead."

Makayla smiled. "Tell me about her again. Tell me about our mom."

Amina chuckled and her face illuminated with joy.

Makayla curled up to her sister, like a child waiting to hear a fairy tale. "You always seem to have the best memories of her.

Peaches never wants to talk about her. Yolanda has a few. But you always had the best memories."

Amina laid out on the bed, with her eyes to the sky. Just thinking about their mother again, filled her with warmth and good memories. "She was beautiful. Scratch that she was gorgeous. She was the most breathtaking woman I had ever seen."

Makayla sprawled out on the bed alongside her. Fixated on Amina's story. "I know. I just have this one picture. What was she like?"

*A*mina played with the pillow in her hands. "Giggly and girly. She had the most infectious laugh. And just being around her made you want to be wild and carefree like her. She was a charging stallion in the wild, real as they come, and boss of her own. You know they used to call her the black Betty Boop. Because her personality was so Boop Oop a Doop. Her body was real fitness goals. And the craziest thing is she had a touch that drove men crazy. Like literally, that was one of her gifts. Any man she touched would instantly fall head over heels in love with her. Mom could make men do anything she wanted. Buy her clothes, cars, and take her on trips around the world."

Makayla's eyes lit up. "Really?"

"Yes. I saw it myself." Amina said as the memory came to her, just as if it was yesterday. She could envision the beauty that was their mother. The high royal cheekbones. Skin smooth as Magnolia wine. Bountiful black curls that fell down her back. Full lips painted red that could seduce any man.

"I'll never forget she was home one summer around my

birthday, and we were having a crawfish boil. The way she walked into the room," She said shaking her head. "Every man was looking at her. And this one guy....I can't remember his name. I think it was Mr. Jefferson. Mom walked right past him and caressed his hand. And I saw it. He changed. It was like he came alive. A Cheshire cat smile swept across his face as he greeted mom. Then she saw me, so she ignored him and came over to wish me a happy birthday. Later that evening she got into it with Mrs. Jefferson. She didn't like Mom flirting with her husband. Called her a witch and everything. Well that was a big mistake. Mom cursed her into a goat. That's when Gran came. She and mom got into it and mom left."

Makayla studied her sister. "You never told me that story before."

The smile on Amina's face dimmed. "I didn't remember it until just now," Amina said as she stared at the wall, almost watching the memory itself fade away. Quickly she sat up, "I have to go now."

Makayla sat up. "Where are you going?" A grin appeared on her face, " I know you ain't going to see no man."

Amina shrugged, "No. I'm just going to take care of some business." She turned back before she closed the door. "Don't worry. I'll be back before the morning."

Makayla watched Amina climb off the bed and head towards the door. "Alright, be safe."

"Good night little bird," Amina called.

"Goodnight," Makayla responded softly as she reached into her dresser and grabbed the pendant.

21

WHAT ARE YOU?

*a*unt Dot was halfway through her third puzzle book for the day when the doorbell upfront rang, and a tall figure walked through. She took a quick glance up as the man approached the counter and her jaw almost hit the floor as she stared at the chocolate vision looking at her.

On instinct, she slid a Newport into the corner of her mouth as she said, "Well hello handsome. How may I help you?"

Lorenzo blushed as a seductive grin spread across Aunt Dot's face. "I have a few rare items that I'm looking to buy, and I heard around town, you carry the best occult supplies."

Aunt Dot cackled, her voice lowered as her eyes did. His suit did little to cover his bulging muscles, that almost made Aunt Dot's eyes pop out of the socket from staring so hard. "Well you heard right. I got everything you need right here, baby."

Lorenzo chuckled again. It was a nervous chuckle that was

still manly and charming. Her eyes swept over his body again, "Aren't you just a hunk of hammercy?"

He looked over to the far corners of the shop, flickering candles, dust-covered books, and bottles of oil yawned at him, "Do you carry St. John root and holy water?"

Aunt Dot leaned over on the counter "Yeah. It's over there by the candles."

He nodded and went along. A few minutes later he was back to the front to ring up his purchases. Aunt Dot was ringing him up when a dark emotion spoke to her psychic senses. She looked up to him, and all of the seductiveness in her smile faded away. "Beloved, may I ask you something?"

Lorenzo already had his wallet in hand, but he entertained her. "Sure."

"What are you?" she beckoned, her voice almost trembling at the tone.

"Excuse me?"

"What are you?" Aunt Dot asked again, and this time she outed her cigarette. "I hate to be nosey, but I can't help it. I'm an empath, and I sense an eternal darkness inside of you," she uttered as she shook her head. "It's almost like an empty void. And it's strong too, stronger than you think it is, and almost strong enough to consume." she leaned in further. "What happened to you? Did somebody cause this or were you born this way?" Then she peered down at the herbs he bought, as well as the oils, the vials of holy water and pure liquid silver. "And I'm looking at what you're buying. These are items to control bloodlust, hunger, agents to control and bind demons." Then she sat up on her stool. "So what are you?"

Lorenzo's jaw tightened. "Very... rich," he said as he dropped his card.

Aunt Dot was taken aback, "Well let me shut my mouth then." She remained silent as she bagged the items and handed them over to him, moving almost as if she was in the presence of a killer.

Lorenzo took the bag and smiled. "Thank you." He took two steps towards the door, and slowly peered over his shoulder. Aunt Dot held her breath as he turned menacingly. "Why don't you put that smile back on your face."

Aunt Dot forced her lips to curl, as she watched him leave. Soon as he hit the door, she locked it behind him and flipped the open sign to close. She couldn't put her hand on it but what she was sure of, was that he wasn't human.

~

Makayla waited until it was close to midnight to activate the pendant. She peeled back the covers, and her feet softly touched the cool carpeted floor. She walked over to her drawer, pulled the bottom and took everything she needed out. Makayla reached over to the nightstand to use her phone as a flashlight, she turned her beam on low as she held the pendant in her hands. Noise emanated from the hallway and she stopped dead in her tracks, leaned over, and saw nothing. She opened the brown bag and took out the Orris root along with the High John the Conqueror oil. First she sprinkled the Orris Root on the pendant. Then from a small violet bottle she poured the High John the conquer oil, she wrinkled her nose at how fragrant the oil was, notes of lilac and lavender attacked her senses. Makayla wiped her oily hands on her pink sweatpants. She grabbed her phone and shined the light on the spell. "Swarm to me now my hive. One taste of this honey and you'll come alive. Sacred spirits hearken to me. Bless me now. I am Queen Bee."

There was a loud crack and a flash of golden light that filled Makayla's room. It was so loud that Makayla shot up off the floor.

"Is everything alright? Makayla what are you doing in there?" Patrice called from another room.

"Everything is fine," Makayla shouted back. Quickly she jumped back in bed, under the covers and laid her pendent right next to her.

∿

*J*t was after midnight when Amina strolled back into the graveyard. She found something else in the Legacy that could help her succeed in stealing her sisters' powers. It was called the cursed charms of Mombu, a charm bracelet given to enemies to weaken them. Her great grandmother Olia used it to curse a Voodoo priestess who opposed her. The Legacy didn't mention how Olia cursed the bracelet but it did mention that the Voodoo priestess she cursed was extremely powerful, and that was exactly what she needed to deal with Patrice. Amina was sure she could trick Yolanda and Makayla into consuming the potion and she could do the ritual to steal their gifts. She didn't fool herself to believe Patrice would fall for such a trick. And so she needed that bracelet to take Patrice's powers so if push comes to shove she could take her gifts the hard way. This idea lead her to the graveyard to summon Mama Brigitte, a Loa she feared less than Papa Samedi, and would still be willing to help.

Amina came to a clearing in the graveyard, amongst a thicket of four towering oak trees, and began the summoning ritual. First she brought out a chipped wooden bowl and ignited a fire inside. Then she poured in anise, cloves, cinnamon, curry powder, and St. John's wort. On a piece of parchment, she wrote Mama Brigitte's name and tossed it into the flame. On the ground, she wrote the veve for the dark Loa into the ground. Then came the music. Amina brought her iPod. Dancing and rhythm were essential to summoning. One had to break chains and free themselves spiritually to call down the spirits, and the quickest way to lose yourself is in the sound of music. So Amina shed off her leather jacket and began dancing in the graveyard late into the midnight hour, under the veil of moonlight, as creatures of the night stirred and watched in awe. She kicked off her shoes so she could feel the dirt on her feet. The red clay beneath her feet was hard and arid, each bit of loose gravel dug into her soles, but still she kept dancing, as the tempo of the music increased.

Next came the offering. She read Mama Brigitte liked rum like Papa Samedi, so she spared no expense in buying the best bottle she could. She opened the bottle and took one long sip before she chanted.

Spirits open the gates for me.

Spirits open the gates so I may pass through

Spirits open the gates and let me talk to Mama Brigitte.

Mama Brigitte, I summon thee, answer as I call out to you.

With a flick of her wrist, she doused the fire with a dash of the rum. And the fire blew up out of the bowl, in a robust emerald color. There was a loud bang and thunderclap of smoke. Out of the flames came a large hellhound that rolled across the ground and shoved its muzzle into Amina's face.

"Why have you summoned mi gal?" The hound spoke.

Amina's heart skipped, but her gaze didn't waver. "I need your help. I have a plan to get Patrice's power, but I need you to get me something. Here….take my payment," she said as she held out the bottle of rum.

Mama Brigitte shifted into her human appearance. Black fur shrunk as bones elongated, breasts fell and her back straightened. With a scowl on her face, she snatched the bottle out of Amina's hands and drank.

"I need for you to get me the Cursed Charms of Mombu."

Mama Brigitte wiped her mouth, "What do you need it for?"

"My older sister," Amina insisted. "She is way too powerful, and she is not going to fall for anything I come up with."

Mama Brigitte fell silent and pondered. "If you give your sister the bracelet, it will make her weak. And if she is vulnerable then we will attack."

Amina could sense this was taking a turn for the worst. She held out her hand in protest, "No that's not necessary. I can handle it."

Mama Brigitte threw the bottle at Amina's feet; it shattered with a hard clang. "Mama you ain't got it in you!"

"I do," Amina spat back

From out of the darkness Papa Samedi whirled and clutched Amina's neck from the back. It happened so quick that she didn't even catch him out of her periphery. Amina's blood ran ice cold as his rotten breath bellowed on her neck. "It sounds like you finally came up with a plan, witch. I was going to save your big sister for last. But the witch is right," Papa Samedi said looking up to Mama Brigitte. "The oldest sister is too powerful. We have to weaken her. So we'll get you the bracelet. And you'll give it to your sister. Then we will kill her."

"No that's not my plan," Amina whimpered.

"It is now," Papa Samedi roared as he ran his fingers along her neck. "Either one of your sisters dies or I will kill all of them."

"That wasn't a part of our deal!"

Papa Samedi curled a yellow talon in Amina's face, "You said you can get the job done and you haven't delivered yet. Don't force my hand witch! Either we take one or we take all."

"Okay," Amina agreed as he tossed her to the ground.

"Once the oldest sister is dead, it will be easier for you to trick the younger ones." His lips curled into a sneer.

Mama Brigitte walked over to him. "We will get you the bracelet. Meet me back here in this graveyard at sundown."

Papa Samedi pointed his cane. "Don't be late."

Amina cursed herself as she laid on the ground. She just made a bad situation worst. And it finally dawned on her...that there might not be a way to con her way out of this deal after all.

22

QUEEN BEE

*S*treams of warm bright sunshine started a beautiful morning for Makayla. She got up and pinned the pendant on her pajamas, then with a loud clamoring flash of light she was transformed by magic. Her hair fell to her shoulders in a long shimmering ombre unicorn pink, then her skin became tremendously radiant, and she wore a killer outfit that she could've never put together in her dreams. Out of nowhere a music anthem played in her head. She imagined she was a star in one of her favorite teen movies. With this positive energy, she knew it was going to be a good day.

Makayla raced downstairs, whizzing past Amina who was stunned by her pink hair, then she snatched an apple from a depressed Yolanda who was also shaken by her decadent tresses, and she beat Patrice to the door who would've normally fussed about her hair color but she was so blown away, that she simply stared.

Makayla arrived to school with an air of confidence that

made her stride more fierce and powerful. Wallace stopped her before turning the corridor, entering the main hall.

"OMG Makayla you are sitting!"

She smiled at her best friend before saying, "As always." Then she blew a kiss at him, before whipping her hair as he raked his fingers through it.

"It's real!" He uttered, his jaw slack. "I thought it was a wig."

She snickered. "It's everything right?" Then she dropped her bag and took a position on the wall. "Take this picture of me." She commanded before handing over her phone to her best friend and posing on the wall.

Wallace snapped the picture. Makayla took back her phone and posted it on her Instagram. She turned to Wallace, "Okay let's go!"

Makayla cackled before fiercely strutting down the hallway like it was a catwalk, everywhere she turned girls complimented her, then a guy would come up asking her out, and someone else would say how awesome her hair was. The new queen of North Central paid them all no mind, swatting them away as if they were flies as she made her way to her locker. As soon as she reached her locker, her phone began buzzing a hole out of her purse. It was her Instagram. In under one minute she had a thousand likes on her picture and eight hundred new followers to boot. "Now this is what I'm talking about."

It was right around lunch that she began to take out her revenge. Makayla and Wallace shared the same lunch break as Brittany. They were two steps behind her whispering and nudging each other as Makayla was trying to convince Wallace to snatch a strand of her hair.

"I'm doing the spell. You have to grab it," She grumbled.

"But I'm scared," He protested to which Makayla shoved him ahead.

Wallace walked past Brittany reaching out and snatched a lone single strand of hair from her ponytail.

"Ouch, you punk!" Brittany winced as she dabbed her hand over her head.

They watched her from afar at Makayla's locker. Makayla wrapped the hair strand around her finger and repeating foreign words found in the spell of the curse. Soon after lunch, Brittany was pulling her hair back into a ponytail when it fell off in a large heap in her right hand. Brittany ran her left hand underneath the mound that would've been a ponytail and that fell off too leaving a patchy spot. Brittany grimaced, "What the....what's going on?" She cried. She ran out of the bathroom with tears walloped in her eyes.

Wallace started the choir of laughter, it soon swept the hallway as some others joined in laughing or looked away out of shame for her. Wallace pointed and started singing, "She got a bald spot in the front. She got a bald spot in the back. Now break it down...Now break it down like that." Dozens of students in the hallway joined in the laughter and started clapping along with the chant. Humiliated, Brittany ran back to the bathroom, with Erica and Amy running behind. As Amy ran by, Makayla smacked brown dirt on Amy's back and chanted, "Klum Nexus Akee."

Makayla wasn't too sure if that spell was going to work seeing that the Legacy said all was needed was regular dirt rubbed on the one you want to curse's back and reciting the incantation. Just before the day was over she got to see the curse in action. It was around the sixth period, when she noticed Erica and crew on the sideline hating, as senior girls were flocking Makayla asking her about her jeans. Particularly Erica was brushing her head and she placed her brush in her locker before closing it. Makayla paid close attention, knowing that she needed something from Erica to attach to her voodoo doll to make it work. She would have to use her powers to retrieve the bush.

Brittany had covered her head with a polo cap. She stood by Erica who shook her head saying, "Who does she think she is?"

"Someone trying way too hard," Amy said as she approached them with two large Frappe Chillers before stumbling.

Amy splashed both Erica and Brittney before falling to the ground and scraping her knees. In the midst of the crowd, Makayla whirled around and all the students erupted into laughter. She looked over at Wallace whose eyes gleamed in delight like hers. "I told you I was going to get them." She gloated before locking in a fist bump with her best friend.

Mortified the girls retreated to the restroom. As the hallway cleared Wallace leaned into her ear. "I can't believe this is happening. This is the best day of my life."

Makayla smirked, "I know right." She looked around to see who was left lingering in the hallway. Mostly all the students had stopped laughing and made their way to class. She turned to Wallace, "Go ahead to class. I'll catch up."

He nodded and as Wallace trekked to class, Makayla crept over to Erica's locker. She peered all around to make sure no one is watching. Once she looked around and saw the coast was clear, she took one large shallow breath and reached through the locker to grab Erica's hairbrush. Once she retrieved Erica's hair from the brush, a sense of devilish joy swept over her as she beamed in the hallway.

~

akayla walked into the house that afternoon on cloud nine, dancing with the stars, with her energy on ten. She closed the door behind her with soft tap and rested her back on the door before sighing out in joy. Ahead she saw Yolanda on the couch with Amina bringing in a tray of tea.

"Well look who's home early," Amina said as she maneuvered around the living room table and sat the tray containing the teacups down.

"Yeah I got a ride from a few of my new friends on the cheerleading team," She stated with a slightly exhausted breath.

Yolanda perked up and leaned over the couch, "You made the squad? Congrats sissy." she chirped trying to sound her usual cheery self but failing miserably.

Makayla walked closer to the living room, "Thanks."

Amina peered back over her shoulder, "You're just in time for some bomb ass tea," She stated with a pleasant smile. Initially, she had intended to try her power snatching tea on Yolanda but having them both drink at one time would make it easier.

Makayla shook her head as she climbed the stairs. "Oh I don't have time. I have a date with my future husband later, and I have to get ready. I'll be in my room if you need me." The door closed behind with a loud bam.

Amina turned to Yolanda. "Okay, just me and you again."

Yolanda picked up the white teacup, "What kind of tea is this again?"

Amina smiled. "Peppermint, and it will make you feel so much better you won't believe it."

Just as she sat next to Yolanda, there was a knock at the door. Amina got up but before she could reach the door, Aunt Dot came bustling through.

"Hey girls!" She shouted with her hand up. "I heard my beloved is still feeling down, so I came here for some good old fashioned girl talk." Aunt Dot said in her raspy tone as she swerved around Amina and planted herself on the couch next to Yolanda.

She patted Yolanda on the thigh. "How are you doing Ms. Yolanda?"

Yolanda had the teacup to her mouth blowing at it. "Do you really want me to answer the question?"

Aunt Dot raised her brow, "Yes sugar." She looked down at the tray on the table and picked up a teacup. "What is this Y'all drinking?" she asked with an unpleasant tone as she gave Amina a sidelong glance.

Amina cleared her throat, " Peppermint tea…it's good for-"

"Peppermint tea?" Aunt Dot squawked. "This girl don't need no damn peppermint tea," She said with a huff before snatching Yolanda's cup from her hand and placing it on the tray. "She needs some coffee or some hooch. She needs something that is going to put some pep in her step and a sass back in her walk."

Amina walked back towards the couch. "No, Aunt Dot this is special peppermint tea. It's supposed to be relaxing and therapeutic."

Aunt Dot looked at Amina as if she was not convinced. She

picked up the tray of tea. "Here take your peppermint tea in the kitchen and let me have some girl talk with Yolanda."

With a sigh Amina acquiesced to defeat and went into the kitchen. Her second attempt at stealing her sister's powers had been foiled by their nosey Aunt. With her legs crossed in her powder blue jumpsuit, Aunt Dot lit her cigarette. "Okay, so what's going on Miss Yolanda?"

Yolanda shrugged her shoulders. "Nothing much," she said trying to mask the sorrow written on her face. You didn't need to be an empath to tell that she was a wreck.

Aunt Dot leaned back on the couch. "Girl, I don't have time for that today. Go ahead and let it out, beloved."

With that, Yolanda fell into Aunt Dot's lap. "I feel like such an idiot. How could I, the seer, fall for a Bokor? My third eye has been blinded, confounded, bamboozled and it has failed me miserably. What have I done for the spirits to have forsaken me? I was their friend. Their will and a conduit into the land of the living. I really loved him, damn it."

Aunt Dot cradled Yolanda's head in her arms. "Well my dear love is blind."

"But not only that but I have been practicing trying to focus my powers and fine tune my visions."

"Well maybe it's not Malcolm maybe it's you. You pride yourself on being a seer. So what's holding you back."

"I don't know. Could it be my classes?"

"No. What's is holding you back?"

Yolanda rolled her up, "I don't know."

Aunt Dot huffed before asking again, "Let me rephrase this. Who is holding you back?"

"Patrice."

Aunt Dot thumped her forehead. "Ding! Ding! You are your

own woman Ms. Yolanda, and you said yourself you loved Voodoo. You loved helping people. You're a grown ass woman; you can't worry about what Patrice wants you to do. Step into your truth. Step into your destiny. If this family is under attack beloved, did you ever think that it has to be you to save your sisters?"

Yolanda leaned up from Aunt Dot's lap, her tears had stopped. "You're right."

"Instead of pulling down your energy into one lost relationship. Put it into being the best sorceress you can be."

23

HEX COLORED GLASSES

*A*cross town, Patrice shuffled into her office. She did not chit-chat with anyone, nor did she speak to anybody on the way there, she did not pass go but she went straight to her office. She closed the door behind her and had to fight to keep herself from crumbling to the floor. Patrice felt embarrassed after her presentation for the ExFit executives. It was one of the most God awful presentations she has ever given for a client.

Patrice always performed when it came time to present to the clients. She was a shark. Many of them often ready to throw millions at her mid-presentation. But today was different. Lorenzo was there. Patrice was distracted and her thoughts were all over the place. She felt so awkward in front of him after their date, especially since she never called him back. She was busy. Evil was looming. Every time she looked across that boardroom she couldn't help but to wonder how good Lorenzo looked in his grey suit, his shoulders broad, and chest etched in his blue shirt. Patrice tried desperately to explain this strange desire, but there was something about Lorenzo that was so magnetic. Even when Patrice tried to evade thoughts of him, her emotions made him run rampant through her mind.

Nicole strolled into Patrice's office without a word.

"That was terrible," Patrice huffed as she rubbed her temples before dropping into the grey chair at her desk with a huff.

"I'd definitely say that," Nicole attested. She placed her folder on Patrice's rich oak desk. "Patrice what the hell is wrong with you?"

Patrice shuttered, unable to shake off the ominous feeling of nerves whirling through her. "I don't know. I just couldn't stop looking at him. I felt like a deer caught in the headlights." Patrice said using her hands.

"Well maybe you wouldn't feel that way if you called the man. Damn Patrice, send the brother a text or something! It's been a minute since your date. Why haven't you called him? I thought you had a good time?" Nicole asked, leaning in.

Patrice nodded, "We did."

Nicole looked at her sideways, "And..."

Patrice looked at her blankly, "And...what?"

Nicole huffed and shook her head. "Patrice that's a good man. Why are you playing?"

Patrice stood up and paced around the desk, "Hell I don't know. It's just I have so much on my mind with my sister coming back into town."

"Well I thought that was going well."

"It is, but you don't know.... we've had so much bad blood between us. Sometimes it's good then it's war all over again."

"Even more reason you need a piece of hot chocolate in

your life. Patrice listen, you deserve this. You are a good girl that's beautiful, selfless, highly successful, and with a great heart. An Alpha woman deserves an Alpha man. Don't let this one get away."

Nicole was interrupted by a knock on the door. With a click, Lorenzo cracked the door open. "Patrice, can I have a minute?"

Startled by the familiar but unexpected voice, she gasped as Nicole moved aside from the front of her desk. Lorenzo's gaze was intent as he peered in.

Patrice looked at Nicole. "Sure come in," she said as Nicole took the cue to exit left.

Lorenzo strolled over and Patrice grasped at her pearls, as she admired his walk. He had a powerful stride, full of a confidence and casualness that matched his swagger. A boyish grin plastered his face and Patrice was compelled to meet his gesture. She sat at her desk, swallowing hard to subside the heat rising below. "Is there anything you want to discuss further regarding the presentation?"

"No," he said tapping two fingers across his temple. Lorenzo shifted in his seat, and adjusted his gaze as he studied her. His gaze made her wet. It told her that he longed to be with her, to have her in his arms, rubbing his hands across her bottom, and bless her lips with a kiss. She wouldn't allow that. His gaze said he would beg. That made her feel sexy.

"It's been a few days and I haven't heard from you. I wanted to make sure everything was alright with you and your sisters. It seemed pretty serious whatever happened."

Patrice cleared her throat. "Yes, thank you. Everything is fine. One of my sisters, Makayla, ate something and had an allergic reaction. We just had to make sure she was fine."

Concern lined Lorenzo's face. "Is she okay now?"

Patrice took in a breath. "She's fine now." ,

"So what's up," He asked with a long pause. "Why haven't I heard from you? I thought we had a good time."

Patrice smiled, "We did."

Lorenzo arched a brow, "And?"

"I'm sorry I have a lot on my plate lately," she said as she stood and turned to the window.

Lorenzo looked down, "I understand."

Patrice chuckled, "Trust me you have no idea."

Lorenzo stood up and leaned in closer, "You should let me help you lighten that load. How is dinner at my place sound? You can bring your sisters if you want to. I would love to meet them."

Patrice winced at the idea of introducing Lorenzo to her sisters too soon. She turned her head back to the front and demurely pulled her hair over her shoulder. Lorenzo kept staring, transfixed by her lithe but strong legs, "That sounds nice but I would really have to think about it."

"Think about it?" Lorenzo echoed, almost wanting to chuckle. "Patrice why do I think you are trying to curve me? What does a brother have to do? Beg you with some roses in his hand?"

Patrice laughed. "Well, I'm not a rose kind of girl. I prefer orchids," She hissed sarcastically. "And I promise I'm not trying to curve you. Like I said I carry a lot on my plate and I appreciate the offer. I'll think about it and call you. That's the best I can do."

"Ugh woman you are killing me," Lorenzo said with a groan. "But look you make sure you do that," he said an octave lower before turning towards the door. "Don't have me waiting too long," he murmured as he strolled out of the office.

~

*P*atrice arrived home that afternoon to a wafting smell of herbs and spices in the kitchen. *Thank God somebody was cooking*, she thought. Patrice was dog tired. She slung her bags and briefcase on a table by the door before walking into the kitchen. Yolanda had the kitchen counter covered every inch with herbs, spices, oils, and candles.

"It smells good in here. What are you cooking? A Gumbo?" Patrice asked before noticing that there was something different about her sister. There was a certain rosy color to her cheeks and she had actually managed to gel her hair up into a cute bun. It seemed like she was back to being the good ole cheerful Yolanda.

"Not cooking…. working on something." Yolanda corrected as Patrice stood next to her. "Stand back!" she warned before tossing a huge pinch of herbs. Lavender smoke funneled up from the pot and wafted out through the kitchen.

"Bam Bam, thank you mam," Yolanda coughed as she along with Patrice waved the smoke away.

Once the smoke cleared, Patrice could finally see that the Legacy was on the counter. "Yolanda, what is this?"

Yolanda held her hand up in protest. "I know…. I know before you even start. I'm sorry Patrice this is something I have to do. Like it or not Voodoo is a part of all of us. And I know you like to think you can protect us big sissy, but the truth is you can't. I am a beacon of light for the spirits and I have to keep shining to guide them. And in honor of me dating a psycho Bokor, I'd like to do something to prevent any one of us from dating someone like that again." Yolanda reached into the pot, and pulled out Robin egg blue Ray-Ban Wayfarers. She shook all the liquid off of them before handing over them to Patrice. "My dear may I present to you my Hex colored glasses."

"Hex colored glasses? What do they do?"

Yolanda beamed, "They allow you to see magic. That includes magical beings, auras, good, evil and all of that."

Patrice wiped the shades off with a paper towel and put them on. She glanced over at her sister. A lavender aura surrounded Yolanda. Patrice nodded, "Very nice."

Yolanda turned the burner off. "Well thank you very much." She said before dusting her shoulders.

Patrice took off the shades and sat them on the counter. "I understand where you're coming from and you are right. You have a right to protect yourself."

Yolanda was shocked. "Patrice….I'm shook," she gasped.

"Don't be. I'll give you your props," Patrice added. She looked around and took notice that the house was kind of quiet. "Where is everyone?"

"Amina is out shopping and Makayla is upstairs studying with some boy."

"Who Wallace?"

A smile swept Yolanda's face as she cleared the stove. "No sis, some little cutie."

"Really?" Patrice asked as she cocked her head to the side. "Does she have the door closed? I probably should go up there and check on them."

Yolanda held out her hand. "Chill Peaches. She's a big girl. She will be alright."

"Are you sure? You know how Makayla is?"

"Yes. Leave her alone and let her have her little boo."

Patrice gave a sigh of resignation. She stared out of the window for a moment then turned to her sister.

"Speaking of boo. I got asked on another date with Lorenzo."

Yolanda clapped. "Lorenzo huh? So that's who must've had these delivered," Yolanda said as she pointed to the table.

Patrice walked over to the massive white vase full of beautiful blooming Orchids. She picked up the vase and dove her nose right into it.

"I was wondering who the hell sent those. It was delivered to you with no name just a message on the card."

Patrice glanced over, "What's the message?"

"Read it," Yolanda advised.

"Don't make me beg," Patrice said as she read aloud.

Yolanda glanced over her shoulder. "Is it him?"

"Yes," Patrice said as she sat the vase down on the table. "He's asking me out again." Patrice peered down at her phone. "That's the thing, I don't know if I should accept."

"Are you crazy? It's not every day you get asked out by a millionaire on a date. You should go!"

Patrice laughed sarcastically. "So what he is a millionaire.... I'm not some ghetto girl trying to make a come up. I have my own."

Yolanda frowned. "Who cares that you got your own. That's why you're single now. Go out and have some fun."

"Yeah?" Patrice asked with a painful face.

"Hell yes. Go!"

Patrice's mind was finally settled. "Thanks," she said before dashing out the kitchen to call Lorenzo.

Makayla was upstairs, paralyzed with a strange sensation. She was utterly captivated by Devante. She sat there closed jaw, as she ogled his smooth pink lips framed by a thin whisk of a mustache, and he was looking back at her, his gaze intense, as he looked on in desperation. He was frustrated, but she was determined to help him. That's what you do for the one you love, right? *I would cross the ocean for you. I would go and bring you the moon.* Makayla was going to help him pass pre-calculus if it was the last thing she did.

"Do you get it?" Makayla asked.

Devante looked at her. Then down to the question. He closed his eyes, took a deep breath, and shook his head. "No. I don't get it. I don't get it at all."

Makayla sighed, "Okay maybe we should take a break. We have been at this for an hour." She closed the book and reached over to her dresser. "Do you want a bottle of water?"

"Yeah," he responded as he caught the bottle when she threw it to him. Devante cracked open the top and took a baby sip. "Makayla?" he called.

Makayla batted her eyelashes, "Yes?"

"Did I tell you how fine you look today?" he said with a toothy smirk.

Makayla responded with a geisha girl laugh as she said, "Stop it. Boy you so crazy."

Devante licked his lips, "I mean it's not like you was a bird or something. It's just weird lately I have been seeing you differently." He looked down, trying to search his thoughts. "As a matter of fact, I can't help but think of you lately. I thought about you all day today."

"Well I am doing something different with my hair," She said as she fingered her hair.

"It's dope," He responded. Then he leaned in. "My old folks will be out of town for the weekend. I'm throwing a birthday kickback at my spot tomorrow night for my boy Trey. Are you trying to come through?"

Makayla smiled, "I would love to go."

And just the thought of going to a party and being on Devante's arm made her head spin. Immediately she knew she had to call Wallace and put together a fierce outfit. Makayla became so excited that Devante had to bring her back in the moment when he said:

"Can I ask you one more thing?"

Makayla nodded.

"Is it okay if I kiss you?"

Makayla's lips watered. "Yes god."

Her heart pounded and her lips burned with longing. Devante leaned in and teased her lips with his own. She cradled his head as he grabbed her waist. Makayla wanted the kiss to last forever. When he finally drew away, Makayla was left breathless. She looked at him and a boyish grin swept across his face. Then he leaned in and took her breath away once more. And therein her bedroom, as she kissed the boy of her dreams, Makayla died a million times inside.

~

*N*ight fell across the city and Amina was marching her way back across the graveyard. After being away for so many years, Amina thought delivering the powers of her sisters would be easy. She never thought in all that time apart, she had actually missed them. Well everyone except Patrice. A sullen drizzle of rain began to fall, and Amina could feel a storm brewing, as she crumbled inside. She thought of what would happen after retrieving the bracelet. Could she really do it? Could she really play a part in this sinister plan to trap and kill her older sister? Amina had done a number of wicked things. She saw the world for what it truly is. Cold and hard. It was all about survival. Kill or be killed. Scratch and grind to make your way to the top. If not Patrice, then her or maybe Makayla or Yolanda. Amina wasn't ready to risk the lives of her younger sisters. A grim thought flashed in her head. What was going to stop the demon from killing them all? Amina was screwed either way.

Patrice was the easiest pick of all the sisters to sacrifice. There was something about Patrice that had always seemed to get under Amina's skin. They were like oil and vinegar. Black and white. Night and day. The pressure to follow after their Gran, Mother Phoenix, had always been intense since they were little girls. Patrice was the poster girl of the High Priestess and had always been the golden sister, everything she did seem to be blessed by the Gods themselves. And then it dawned on Amina that even though she might not have the heart to steal the powers of her two younger sisters. She had enough hatred for Patrice, to offer her up to Papa Samedi.

Lightning clashed as she stomped through the marsh with her boots. Wind and rain whipped at the flannel she had tied around her waist. Amidst the sound of thunder and rain, she thought back to the moment they bound her powers.

mina could almost recall the smell of Tyrell's Honda, the stench of weed was so strong and pungent, that the little orange air freshener that dangled from the mirror, did little to mask it. Tyrell was the cousin to Marcus, a mortal man whose good looks and charm, enchanted Amina with a spell so powerful, that it shook her to the core. She loved bad boys, and Marcus was the baddest of them all. He stood a six foot five, burly mass of a man, with thick dreads, and an angry mug always plastered on his face, as his gold teeth gleamed. His cousin Tyrell was what the locals would call a weed head, and this was what made him a good getaway driver for the operation. Tyrell looked like a walking joke, he was chubby with chinky eyes, light skin, and wild bushy hair.

Marcus had done time before, doing local robberies, but it was after he discovered Amina's powers, that he set his ambitions higher. He whirled his gaze over to Amina, "You sure you up for this?"

Amina nodded yes, but the way she trembled in the passenger seat of the dented silver, 1993 Honda Accord, said otherwise. "I got the spells and the potion. I can pull this off."

Marcus asked her one more time, "Are you sure? Don't play, this ain't a game. Either you bout' this life or you not."

"Yes," she responded louder, almost offended.

Marcus turned his whole body towards her, and his face lined with seriousness. "If we do this, then there is no turning back baby. Ya heard me? Me and you baby, ride or die."

Amina shook her head, "Ride or die."

Marcus took her face in his and kissed her passionately. "Baby if we pull this off. We ain't ever gotta worry about nothing. We'll be set for life."

Amina's lips quivered. Marcus was the only man who could convince her that she was invincible, that man was her everything, her kryptonite.

Tyrell laughed hysterically in the back. "We about get paid dawg. Let's go set it off in this joint." He clocked his nine mm.

Marcus spun his head around in furry, "Man calm yo ass down."

Amina raised her brows, "Fuck it, I'm ready." She turned to the mirror and pulled out her makeup pad. She ran her index finger along the rim of the powder and chanted, "Bring forth new eyes, so that I may see. Glamour my face and transform me." Once she completed the chant, the reflection in the mirror rippled like a stone being thrown into water. Her dark brown eyes lightened and became the deepest blue, blonde hair stretched from the roots of her hair, and the bones in her face cracked, and rearranged. Seconds later, Amina stared at a reflection that was not her own.

Tyrell leaned up from the back seat. "Oh shit! You really are a witch!"

"I'll be damn," Marcus murmured.

Amina turned and smiled, still under the veil of her disguise. "Remember to give me five minutes, before I release the fog and potion."

Marcus readied his gun, "Go ahead and do ya thing shawty."

Amina got out of the car and walked into the small bank. Just like they had studied there were only two guards on duty and it was relatively slow to be just after lunch. One officer studied her as she strutted along, his gaze lingering and lustful. Amina smiled seductively. She walked to an island of a desk, where a balding Jewish man sat.

"May I help you?" he asked.

Amina dropped her shoulder and placed her pocketbook on the table. "I'm here to make a deposit."

"To the left," he pointed and soon dropped his head.

She walked over to a line of three waiting and stood behind a petite older white woman in a soft pink throw. The woman glanced over her shoulder once she felt Amina's presence, and smiled. Amina was waiting to be served when she spotted Marcus creeping outside on the corner. It was time to put the plans into action. "Excuse me I have to go to the bathroom," She said to the lady in front of her as she exited the line.

Amina's eyes glazed as she chanted. "Murky fog I command you to swarm and blind my enemies to my will." Smoke formed into a ball in her hands then wafted off her body. The smoke became thicker and dense, almost a heavy smog. Within seconds it filled the bathroom and crept out of the door, like massive crashing waves the fog built and whirled into the main bank room. The security guard whirled around looking around. "What the hell is that."

Amina slowly peeled open the door. Both Marcus and Tyrell put on their masks. She pulled the stunning potion out of her bag and rolled it into the main bank room like it was a grenade. "Now!" she screamed. Right on cue both Marcus and Tyrell slammed their eyes shut, just as the potion vial erupted, and there was a bright stunning flash. Everyone in the room stopped dead in their tracks.

Tyrell was the first to open his eyes. "It worked," he said with a childlike smile plastered on his face as he snapped in front of the security guard.

Marcus opened the bag, "Stop playing around fool and let's get this money."

Then the two hopped behind the counter and started filling up their bags.

Amina sashayed her way into the front. "Hurry up you two. You only have about one minute before the stun wears off."

She was looking down at her watch when suddenly, something unbelievable happened. Gran used her eternal power to push through the veil of death, and her voice came slamming into Amina's head. "Don't do this child. You're going to ruin your life, for a fool."

Tears fell down Amina's face, as a kinetic force pulled her to the knees, the same force Gran had used to keep her from stealing that Mercedes, years ago. "Gran," she murmured in disbelief. "Is that you?" she questioned. She sat for a moment waiting for a response but got none. She was able to rise to her feet, sensing the hold on her had been lifted. Amina sighed out in relief as she glanced in the glass window, before standing on both feet. Quickly she rushed back to the window, she had seen something. Oh no. Short black hair and dark brown eyes reflected back to her. The spell had worn off.

"Fuck!" she screamed.

"What?" Marcus screamed as he rose.

She turned to him, fear tingling down her spine. "We have to get out of here now."

"Why?"

"I think my spell is fading."

The security guard rose to his senses. Once he saw the two going at it, he pulled out a gun.

"Freeze! Put your hands up."

Three shots ran at the guard's head. "Come on let's move!" Marcus shouted. He ran towards the door and reached for Amina. She took his hand and together they dashed towards the door.

Amina whirled her head, looking for Tyrell. She found him struggling to follow behind. "Come on!" she called.

He ran towards them and then BAM! A loud shot echoed in the building. Tyrell's face froze as he dropped to his knees and fell to the ground face forward.

Amina cried out as Marcus pulled her out of the bank. Amina was so shook the whole ride to Marcus' place. That night she just needed to get the rest of her clothes so she and Marcus could disappear into the night. Amina was sneaking into the house late that night to get her clothes so she could flee Atlanta. She walked into a dark apartment. Little did she know Patrice and Aunt Dot were waiting for her.

"Amina I can't believe you helped him rob a bank," Patrice shouted

Amina shook her head, "What are you talking about?"

Patrice clicked the remote, "It's on the news. I can recognize Marcus anytime I see him and they found Tyrell dead."

Amina turned her head to the screen, too shocked for a rebuttal.

Patrice stared with her jaws clenched, steam practically come from her ears. "Not to mention Yolanda saw everything in a vision."

Aunt Dot walked over and grabbed Amina by the hands. "Beloved, your grandmother has told you too many times. You're going to end up in trouble with this path you have taken." Aunt Dot cried.

Amina snatched her hands back. "Ya'll need to pipe down. Marcus is a good man, he's just in a bad situation, and he wants to do better for himself and his family. And I could help so why not?" She looked around at faces that stared in disbelief. "He did this for me because he loves me and wants to be happy with me."

Patrice jumped in front of Amina. "You must've lost your mind." Patrice paced the room as she raked her hair. "This time you have gone too far. I'm not going to let you hurt anyone else or bring any more shame to this family with your reckless decisions."

"Well bitch, you don't have to worry about me anymore. I'm leaving with Marcus tonight and this time it's for good," Amina spat with venom as she grabbed at her bag that was tossed on the couch.

Amina headed towards the door, but Patrice blocked her path. With stern eyes she said, "Do you think I will just let you leave like this? Amina you are scaring me. You are becoming just like mom. Using your powers for evil.... following behind some crazy man..... It won't be long before you end up addicted to black magic too."

Amina removed the hair from her face and pointed a threatening *finger towards Patrice. "Well that's my decision and it's my life and my gifts. There is nothing you can do about it."*

"Wrong," Aunt Dot declared. "I'm sorry beloved. But you leave us no choice. We have to do this as a tribe."

Aunt Dot looked to Patrice who looked at Yolanda as she crept down the stairs. " I'm sorry Amina," she muttered as she held Makayla's hands. Makayla began to moan as they all enclosed Amina.

Patrice reached around her back and held up a wooden Voodoo doll with Amina's picture on it, and a strand of her hair. "You can leave but I won't dare let you leave with your gifts. You will cause no more havoc with your power. We bind you by the spirit, declaring you unfit to wield your gifts. It is not I who makes this decision, but it is the spirit that will cause this shift. We summon all ancestors who have played a role in this tribe. Revoke this witch's magic, clean her heart, and straighten her tongue so she may no longer tell lies." She then chanted patios across the doll and set it ablaze with her eyes. "I bind you by the spirit, and revoke your access to the wonders of our tribe."

"Wait a minute," Amina cried and she turned back to Aunt Dot.

Aunt Dot was also holding a voodoo doll. "I'm sorry beloved. I bind you by the spirit Amina, and revoke your access to the wonders of our tribe."

By the bedroom door, Yolanda joined in with the chanting. Amina slumped as she looked at her sister. "Yolanda you too?"

Yolanda was crying. "I'm sorry....I'm so sorry."

There was a pain in Amina's chest, that seemingly crushed her heart, strangled her lungs, and robbed her of breath. It was the dagger of betrayal. How could her own family turn against her? Suddenly there was a loud crack and whooshing grey winds whirled and engulfed Amina. Once the smoke cleared from around her, Amina was stripped of her gifts. Her hands trembled as she looked down at them. "I hate you!" She screamed, her voice so filled with emotions, that it seemed to make the room crumble. "None of you ever loved me. And none of you ever gave a fuck about me." Her jaws were shaking now but she refused to let them see her cry. "But you know what? You don't ever have to worry about me again." She grabbed the door and never looked back after slamming it.

∾

Tears welled in Amina's eyes. She let them fall across her cheek along with the rain. She never felt so betrayed in her life. Amina knew she had always caused her beloved Gran hell. But she also knew that had Gran been alive, she wouldn't have allowed that to happen. Six years later and Amina still felt the constant burden of her sister's anger and her grandmother's disappointment. Revenge was a dish served cold, Amina thought as she waited. It takes two or more out of a tribe to bind a witch's powers, so Amina didn't have anyone to do the same to Patrice, but the bracelet would come close to it. Rain smacked her against the head as it fell all around her. Out of the corner of her eye, she detected movement. Amina wheeled around, instantly engulfed with fear at the single gritting sound...a footstep.

Mama Brigitte crept from out of the cover of a large oak tree with hanging moss.

"Do you have it?" Amina asked.

"Yes," Mama Brigitte said before placing a silver bracelet with golden pyramid charms on it. "This bracelet is cursed. It will leave whoever wears it powerless."

"Perfect." Amina murmured as she took the bracelet, and

stuffed it into her pocket. She turned to walk away and the demoness called her by the name.

"You know there is no turning back after this?"

Amina took in an aching breath, as her face became stone cold. "I'm ready."

~

*W*hen Amina arrived home, Patrice was on the other side of the door dolled up and ready to go out. "Somebody is looking gorgeous," Amina smiled.

"Thank you. I'm going to Lorenzo's penthouse for dinner."

Amina stepped in, "Sounds fun."

"I hope so," Patrice said as she stood in the doorway.

"Peaches!" Amina called, pulling her back. "I bought you something," she said as she fastened the bracelet around Patrice's wrist. "It's for protection."

"Wow thanks," Patrice said slightly surprised. "Man my sisters have my back. I love you guys. Goodnight!" Patrice shouted.

Amina closed the door. "Goodnight," she waved with a malicious smile.

24

VIEWS FROM THE...

*P*atrice maintained a nerve-wracking silence as she whooshed up the elevator to the seventy-seventh floor. Her hands were shaky and her mind was all over the place. She wondered if this anxiety was from the anticipation of going on a more intimate date with Lorenzo or fear that she had chosen the wrong outfit. At work she had become accustomed to wearing powerful suits and designer blouses, but when it came to dating she had been drawn to a sickeningly short black dress. She thought wearing a daring number would send the wrong signal. He might be fine, but she would not be sleeping with him anytime soon. So instead she chose a simple yet stylish cream colored top, blue jeans, finished with red pumps, all wrapped in a stunning Burberry coat.

Patrice had felt as though she'd walked into a dream as she stepped into the lobby of the Clark Tower. The lobby itself was breathtaking with wall to wall marble, eye-catching modern decor, a grandiose chandelier that hung in the center. Everything from the seating in the lounge area to the main desk was adorned in a luxurious ivory color that combined with the strong lighting made Patrice feel as though she had walked past the pearly gates of heaven. As the elevator continued to ascend to Lorenzo's penthouse, she recalled the article that broke the news that someone had purchased the twenty eight-million-dollar penthouse in the newly erected Clark Tower. It was a 5,425 square foot pad that faced south of the Tower, offering a magnificent view of Atlanta's skyline, three bedrooms, five and a half baths, a chef's inspired kitchen, dining room, den, living room with a fireplace, and infinity pool. Reading the paper, she imagined the owner to be some rich old European business tycoon. Little did she know it was a hot brown skin brother from Brooklyn that would walk right into her life.

Moments later, the elevator doors parted and Patrice's heart skipped a beat. Lorenzo was there waiting in a black V-neck, with a smile on his face.

"Patrice. Come on in," Lorenzo welcomed with a steely gaze.

Patrice stepped into an all-black foyer, and a wonderful aroma hit her as soon as she walked off the elevator.

"Sorry I'm late. I had to make sure my sisters were all right."

"That's all right," he said as he looked her down. Her curves inspiring life in his pants. "You look magnificent as always," he said with a boyish grin. "Come on through," Lorenzo grabbed her hand and peeled back double doors.

Patrice's mouth fell to the floor as she scanned all around. Lorenzo's house was breath taking. On the walls were dark moody paintings softly illuminated by rose gold lighting, modern black furniture made up the interior, and the kitchen which was far left, featured rich wood and stainless-steel surfaces that complemented the statement-making stove. His penthouse reminded her of a million-dollar bat cave with its stark and calculating architecture.

Lorenzo led her straight across the veined marble flooring to sixteen-inch floor to ceiling glass windows. Lorenzo's living room had a mind-blowing, 360-degree view of downtown Atlanta. Patrice pressed her face close to the glass like a little girl at an aquarium. The coolness of the glass felt pleasant against her warm skin, and she felt butterflies in her stomach as she took in the view.

"Oh My God Lorenzo... this is amazing. I love your place," Patrice gasped.

Lorenzo grinned as he crept behind her. "Isn't it beautiful? As soon as I saw this view, I knew I had to have the place."

"I could imagine," Patrice purred as she continued to gaze out into the lights of the city. "You're a lucky man."

Lorenzo pressed himself closer and leaned into her ear. "More than you think. You know I have a great eye for beautiful things. And right now I'm looking at the most gorgeous thing in the world."

Patrice poked her head around the window, "Where? What are you looking at?"

"Come on girl. You." He said as they shared a laugh.

Patrice shook her head, reeling inside. An unbearable heat made her strip off her coat. His living room featured a central custom gas fireplace finished in mirror-polished stainless steel. Inside, the fire was roaring and made Lorenzo's apartment feel like the swamp during a Louisiana summer.

"My bad. Let me take your coat," Lorenzo asked as he grabbed her coat. He walked over to a closet concealed in the wall by the projector style curved tv screen. A few steps to her

left, the seating area hosted a pair of sculptural sofas and a
live-edge wood coffee table. Patrice walked over and tossed
her purse on the sofa. Around the corner she spotted a door
that lead to the master bedroom.

She watched him walk into the kitchen and pick up two
large glasses of red wine amidst wafting pots. "I hope you're
hungry. Food is almost ready. And trust me... you will be
licking the plate. Ya boy can throw down." He declared as he
handed her a glass of wine.

She laughed, "Okay Chef Ramsey. What do you have
cooking?"

"Italian sausage with some penne pasta in a red wine vodka
sauce. A side salad of arugula, figs, blue cheese, prosciutto, and
garlic crostini." He boasted.

Patrice nodded with a wide grin in between sips of red
wine. Tucked away in the corner she spotted a pool table, and
she went over. "Nice pool table. Do you want to get a game
going?" She sat her glass down on a wooden table and grabbed
a pool stick.

"What do you know about playing pool?" Lorenzo asked,
with his voice coated in cockiness.

"Enough to take all of your money." She sassed as she
racked the balls. Patrice took the stick and bent over to
take aim.

"Wait... before you embarrass yourself let me show you
how to aim." Lorenzo declared as he pinned himself over her.
His hips against hers, and his arms on top of her.

Patrice shuttered at the closeness. She could feel the craft of
his abs on her back. The smell of his cologne danced into her
nostrils. Damn she loved a man that smelled good. "What are
you doing?" she protested, still bent over the table.

Lorenzo grinned. "I'm trying to show you something."

Patrice turned around and leaned on the edge of the pool table. "Well I don't need your help."

"Okay I'm lying," Lorenzo admitted as he licked his lips. He rubbed his hands together. "I really wanted to do this," Lorenzo declared before setting her lips on fire with a kiss.

Patrice fell into the embrace of Lorenzo's arms. His lips were soothing like cocoa butter yet burning with a passion like a never ending flame. She allowed him to run his hands along her feminine curves as she clasped at his chest and neck.

Lorenzo pulled away leaving her yearning for more. Then he trailed his mouth up and down the nape of her neck. "Damn girl."

Patrice caressed his strong masculine jawline and marveled in his brown eyes. Somewhere in his eyes she saw the broken promises and expectations from every man she ever dated. It was as if he was sent to her by the Gods to make up for every tear she had to cry and all the pain she had to endure. She felt a strange ownership over him as well as an instant kinship. It was as if Lorenzo belonged to her. Maybe he was a lover from another lifetime. Some strange intuition made her believe he was made for her and her to him. Lorenzo gave her a cocky smile, and inside his arms she wanted to crumble.

～

*L*ights from the television screen flickered as Yolanda laid on the couch, knocked out in a deep slumber. She was stirring, wincing and kicking as the spirits whispered into her ear. Rapid images flooded her head as she harkened to the indistinguishable murmurs of the spirits.

189

Yolanda was walking through a graveyard with the ominous feeling that evil was near. Moss rose high on the trees and night insects sung all around her as she trekked further. She detected movements between the darkness and shadow of the moonlight. Her pupils dilate and her muscles tightened. It was a demon. A voice whispered the name Papa Samedi. She had no idea of his name and no recollection of ever seeing him before, but the spirits assured that he was the one after them. Yolanda studied him closely. She peered into the deathly gaze of his eyes, the yellow snake around his neck fell from his shoulder and slithered towards her in the grass. At the whim of his hand, dead men and women clawed and crawled from out of their crypts.

Rising from the dirt and ashes they stood as mannequins in the graveyards. Solid and stiff with glowing eyes. They all stood idle awaiting a command. Yolanda stood watching in terror. Suddenly one voice in her ear became clear. All the creatures in the graveyard were people who sold their souls to the demon. And now in death they belonged to him. Yolanda tiptoed around rotten flesh and unearthed crypts. One creature looked familiar. She walked closer to him. Once in front of his half rotten face, Yolanda recognized him as the same zombie that attacked Makayla at the high school.

In a flash she was out of the graveyard and then she could see her ex-lover Malcolm killing for Papa Samedi. As these frightening images and creatures filled her head, she continued to stir back and forth on the couch.

Yolanda was back in the graveyard. Hundreds of zombies everywhere. Holes and crypts all around were empty. This time she wasn't in the graveyard alone. She was with her sisters and they were fighting for their lives. Powerful winds swarmed around Amina as she soared into the sky. A large beast with golden eyes and jet black fur dashed across the graveyard to sink its claws into a group of *zombies. She looked over to her younger sister Makayla whose body was encased in a crystal like armor. When she saw herself, Yolanda was on her back crawling backwards from a hell hound whose jaws drooled in anticipation. Finally there was a bright light. She shielded her eyes. The light was burning and alive. A scream as sharp as a needle stabbed Yolanda's ears. Peeking from around her hands, she could see eyes in this consuming flame. It was a Phoenix.*

Yolanda jerked, then she sat up on the couch. A bolt of pain went through her neck and she grabbed at the cramp there. It took Yolanda a minute to process what happened. It was one hell of a vision, and the dread she felt upon waking was deep and rich, it made her quiver in a cold sweat. The book she thought, throwing off the blanket and swinging her legs off the couch. She had to go to the Legacy. She had to find that demon and warn her sisters. Yolanda called out for Makayla and Amina before dashing upstairs to gather her sisters.

25

GOLDEN EYES

*I*t seemed to Patrice that she had found a decent guy in Lorenzo. He was incredibly funny, dangerously charming, and the mere sight of his brown eyes made her stir. There was a certain ease she felt with him around, an ease she hadn't felt with anybody in a long time, let alone a man. Dinner had gone well. She was highly impressed that he could cook his ass off. Yet, in her head a nagging voice insisted that something had to be wrong with him. What thirty something millionaire that had a nice body and decent personality, would be single?

"So what kind of movie do you want to watch?" Lorenzo called from the kitchen, his back turned as he piled dishes into the sink.

"I'm a big romantic comedy type of girl," She called back as she thought about the enchanted shades Yolanda had given her earlier.

Her inner voice insisted that she put on the shades. Lorenzo was good looking, charming, and interested in her so something told her he had to be evil. Patrice decided to give into the demands of her conscience. She knew her bag was on the side of the couch. Inside were the shades Yolanda enchanted to see magic. Patrice scooted to the edge of the couch and dug around in her bag for the shades. She did this all the while keeping a suspicious eye on Lorenzo.

Lorenzo was pulling pints of ice cream from his freezer. "I got that new Kevin Hart movie is that fine?" he asked.

Patrice spotted the shades buried underneath old receipts and make up. "Perfect," she shouted back as she put on the shades.

"Good," he settled as he closed the freezer door. "Now are you ready for dessert?" He asked as walked from out of the kitchen carrying pints of ice cream and spoons.

Lorenzo turned to her and through the lens she saw his pupils flash primal, and she grimaced as a black aura swallowed Lorenzo's shape. The aura shifted, changed, and took the shape of a beast. It wrapped it self like an armor around Lorenzo. Patrice examined closely. Golden eyes stalked her as golden claws wrapped around Lorenzo's chest. Patrice could feel the hairs on the back of her neck stand up. As Lorenzo walked towards her, the black aura that surrounded him became more aggressive. Patrice climbed backwards on the couch like a mouse being cornered by a cat. As she began to etch out the claws and the eyes of this beast to give it form. Suddenly it let out a guttural roar that made her jump, and Patrice snatched off the enchanted shades. She had seen enough. How could she have been so foolish?

"I should've known." She said as she sprung from the couch. In one long flash it all came back to her. Was he the one after them this whole time? The thought made Patrice cringe, and she grabbed her purse and started towards the door.

"Patrice what's wrong?" Lorenzo asked, dumbfounded. He was looking at her like some crazy lady.

"Stay away from me!" Patrice shouted as she dashed to the double doors.

"What did I do? What's going on?" Lorenzo asked as he followed behind. "Come back here!"

He tugged her arm, and she whirled around and shoved a finger in his face. "If it's been you that's been behind all of this, I will kill you myself. I will make you regret the day you ever tried to come for the Lawson sisters."

Lorenzo held his hands up in protest. "What the hell are you talking about?"

"I know what you are! Just stay away from me!" She shouted as she slammed the double doors behind her and hopped into the elevator.

"Wait Patrice! Where are you going?" Lorenzo called as he watched her descend in the elevator.

Lorenzo was utterly confused. He tossed one pint of ice cream on a wooden table in the middle of the foyer as he peeled open another one. "These damn women are crazy."

~

Makayla was kissing Devante when she heard a loud banging on the door. She opened the door to reveal Yolanda on the other side. She went out into the hallway and closed the door behind her. "Um excuse you Miss Thang? Why are you banging on my door?" She asked with an attitude.

"Get rid of your little boyfriend. We have demonic problems. I just had a major vision." Yolanda murmured in an agitated yet low voice, trying not to let Devante hear on the other side. She looked down the hall. "Amina!" she called for her older sister.

Makayla curled her lips, "Demonic problems? Girl, what are you talking about?"

Yolanda grabbed at her hands, "Just listen and get rid of your little boyfriend. Then meet me downstairs in the basement."

Makayla sighed, kicked, and cursed under her breath as she went back in her bedroom.

Devante laid across the bed, his long legs dangling off, and an aloof look spread across his face. "What's good? Everything cool?" He asked in his heavy drawl.

Makayla screamed on the inside, but she smiled thinly. "My sister is a little cray cray, and she's having some issues right now. So we need to pray for her and have a little sister time." She said in an uneasy tone as she gathered Devante's books and calculator.

Devante stood up. "Okay, so do you want me to leave?"

Makayla nodded, "Yeah, she's acting up right now... so it's best if you leave."

Makayla opened the door and Devante slung his backpack across the shoulder. "Alright well thanks for the help... shawty." he said as he walked in the doorway.

She blew kisses his way. "No problem boo."

Devante nodded as he walked past Yolanda.

"And don't forget the party tomorrow night. I want to see you there," he said as he started down the stairs.

"Oh trust me I will be there." Makayla said with her voice sweet as honey.

Yolanda side eyed Makayla, "Party?"

Amina entered the hallway, "What's going on? You called me?"

Yolanda turned to her sister with a grim face. "Yes. I just had a major vision. Let's go down stairs. We will need the Legacy. We are in for the fight of our lives."

～

*P*atrice was furious as she stomped into the Clark Tower parking garage, her heels clicked loudly against stone and rung out in the half empty lot, as her quick pace whipped hair in her face. It was cold, and the air was dry and brittle. Goosebumps prickled on her arm and she ran her hands across them, she left so quick that she didn't have time to grab her jacket from the closet. She was zipping open her purse to look for her keys when the presence of something sinister brought her to a pause. Patrice was not alone. All around the garage was an eerie quietness yet still, an inkling of doom brought a shiver down her spine. Evil was looming around, and she could feel a shift in her spirit that caused her to look out across the lot, alert and ready.

Scanning across the garage she saw few cars. No people. Creeping around the corners came a rolling fog. Again Patrice wished she had put on her jacket because the temperature plunged to the point she could see her breath blow cold and hard. Thick and misty, the fog continued to fill the garage until it enveloped her. She whirled around to see a familiar thick red surrounding her, even peering down it came up her thighs. It was as if Patrice was knee deep in a Louisiana swamp.

Patrice took three cautious steps forward, still trying to remember where she had parked her car before the fog came rolling in. Slowly her heels clicked against cement until she stopped dead in her tracks. Standing a few feet in front of her was a dark figure. And she knew this figure was the source of the ominous dread she felt. Unable to make out anything from this menacing silhouette it suddenly disappeared into the fog. And her dread magnified tenfold.

"Good evening mon cher," A gritty baritone greeted.

Patrice whirled to the right and gasped as she looked into the face of evil. "A demon." She grumbled. "I should've known. What do you want?"

"You, my cherie." Papa Samedi cackled as he walked out of the shadows to give Patrice a glimpse of himself in all his evil splendor. "More specifically," he said with a pause. "Your powers along with your sisters'." His gritty baritone was sinister and haunting, like the voice of doom itself

Patrice stared the demon in his eyes to let him know she didn't fear him. He might be able to scare any of her younger sisters, but she was not the one to play with. "So it was you sending zombies after my sisters." She spoke before folding her arms. "Now I know whose head I need to collect. Nobody comes for my family. Ever! Do you hear me?"

Papa Samedi chuckled. "Such fight in you. I see why you are the most powerful of your sisters." He unbuttoned his blazer and spat out his cigar. "And I'm going to enjoy taking that power."

"Who are you?" Patrice asked as her eyes narrowed. She demanded an answer.

"I am the master of necromancy. The demon of the cross-roads. Lord of the Dark Loa. And I am your end." With a pound of his cane an orb of light appeared in the mist. Patrice watched as the orb bounced all around the garage and vanished into the fog.

Violently, the ground shuddered underneath her and Patrice covered herself as she buckled down to the floor. Loose gravel fell over her head, and car alarms went off. After a momentary quake everything became still again. Once the shaking subsided, Patrice stood back to her feet. Again her eyes darted out into the thick fog that filled the garage. Her heart beat fastened. Adrenaline rushed. Patrice gasped as she looked at silhouettes of the dead, standing in the fog like glowing statues. She let out a half scream before covering her mouth with her hands and forcing herself to remain calm. She was surrounded by half rotten faces and pale grey skin that stretched across gaunt bodies that were half clothed. They did not move or flinch. They stood stiff and their faces were emotionless. Patrice knew they were waiting for command and mentally her guard rose.

It was time for battle. Patrice knew the only way out was to fight. "Raging fire, I command you to devour my enemies." She swirled her hands around each other, trying to summon embers of fire into a ball of flame. But she was disappointed when nothing happened. Okay, no fire power she concluded. Her second thought was to knock this demon on his ass with a wave of her telekinetic fury. She waved her hand to strike Papa Samedi. Again she was further embarrassed when nothing happened. She tried again yet still nothing happened. Something was not right, Patrice concluded.

Patrice peered down at her hands, "What's wrong with my gifts?"

Papa Samedi laughed. He tapped his cane against the ground. "Bring me her heart!" he commanded

Papa Samedi's will came surging into their bodies with the force of possession, as their eyes glowed with an emerald fire and their bodies sparked into motion. The demon compelled them to kill, so they rose to life and inched out of the fog. It was more of them than Patrice had originally counted. They were coming all around armed with knives and blades, closing in on her. Patrice rummaged through her purse and clicked the alarm. Out to her far right she heard the familiar sound of her Mercedes jeep shrieking. Like a bat out of hell, she dashed to the source of her alarm. She traced out the black body of her car, hopped in and locked the doors. By the time she went to put the key in the ignition there was a loud slap against the driver window. Patrice jumped in fear, and her keys fell. A round woman with red hair knocked and clawed at her window. Patrice cursed as she bent and felt around. While she patted around for her keys, she heard another slap on the passenger side and along the body of the car. Like bees, the zombies were swarming around her car. She had to get the hell out of there.

Overhead she heard a loud thump as one of them pulled itself on top of her car. More and more slaps to her car made her hand tremble as she tried desperately to put her keys into the ignition. Patrice fumbled with the keys until she got them in. She started the car and threw it back so fast, she heard bones break as they rolled under her tires. Like bugs on the window, she still had two zombies slapping at her window and others walked stiffly towards the car in the garage. Patrice jerked the car forward and barreled down the garage with her car pummeling through whatever stood in her way. Her engine roared as she punched on the gas pedal. Zombies covered her windshield with their arms flailing and legs kicking. Patrice could no longer see but she continued to mash the gas. She could hear her tires screech as she barreled through the garage. Then she jerked at a loud bam as her car flew somewhere she couldn't see and became blocked by a wall.

When Patrice came to, her car was crashed into the building outside of the Clark Tower Parking garage. She was being pinned by the airbag. Patrice rolled her hands to remove her seatbelt. Once free, she rubbed her fingers at the sharp pain throbbing at the top of her head. With one eye she confirmed that there was no more movement in front of the car. Just torn body parts. She looked into the eyes of one zombie's head which was separated from the body and it still snapped at her from there outside of the window.

Patrice tried to start her car again. She turned the key, and the car gave two pitiful rumbles before crapping out. Just what she needed. She pulled herself out the car wincing, first unbuckling her seatbelt, then pulling her legs out the door once she had it open. It was dark outside. A lot darker than she suspected, and it was still raining. There was a pain in her thighs that matched the throbbing in her head. It was quiet around except for the hum from the car as it smoked. Rain drops pounded at the top of her head. A neon light pointed to the Clark Tower Parking Garage. There was a dead end on her right. She looked to her left and faced a long driveway up to the next building and the main street. Patrice knew she had to move. Any moment that demon would return. So many thoughts ran through her head. Adrenaline surged through her veins and made her anxiety level soar. She had to get out of there, and if she couldn't escape she had to warn her sisters.

Patrice started the slow trek down the driveway when a sharp pain slammed into her side. She darted around and came face to face with a dead bride, her face still made pretty but her jaw missing. The bride held a knife that was lodged into Patrice's side. She had been stabbed. Now she felt pain all over. Patrice was pulled in closer as the zombie placed its hands on her. With everything she had, Patrice summoned strength to push the zombie back. Once she had space between them, she kicked the zombie bride in the head and sent it to tumbling back into the car.

Patrice's guard went up. The zombie bride stood back to its feet unbothered and unfazed. From the corner of Patrice's eye she spotted a dozen of the zombies trailing out of the garage in a slow stiff walk. When one of them locked eyes on her, the others quickened their pace. There was no way she could take them all. Patrice started backing up towards the dead end. With every cautionary step she took, more of the zombies appeared out of the fog. Dozens upon dozens came until she could no longer see her car but zombies as they filled the alley.

Patrice cringed as she held the wound at her side which had already drenched her shirt and leg. She turned around and spotted the trash bin and the railway that lead to a fire escape along the adjacent building. If she could get some height, she could escape the situation. Patrice ran for her life, with waves of pain all over her body. She was throbbing everywhere.

Bullets of rain pelted her face as she dashed down the alleyway. She jumped and climbed upon the bin. Zombies came running after her, pulling their limbs as they staggered along. These zombies did not roam the streets like the flesh hungry undead, she had seen in the movies, slaughtering and attacking at will. Because they were resurrected, their movements were coordinated. They exist to obey his will and operated in a hive mind like bees. Soon they surrounded the bin. She reached for the railway but as soon as she jumped, the pain in her stab wound made her crumble backwards. Patrice encouraged herself. *Come on you have to get out of this. You have to warn your sisters. Protect the family,* she declared to herself. She reached again and this time she grabbed a bar. Patrice pulled herself. The bar was cold and slippery. As she did, a cold grip yanked her foot. She looked down in horror. Few of the zombies had climbed onto the bin. Another hand reached for her leg. With a strong pull Patrice fell.

Jaws chomped at her nose. She swept two of the zombies off their legs with a swift kick, and they fell tumbling back on the ground. Patrice scanned around. She was trapped! Hands of rotten flesh clawed up the bin at her. Panic overwhelmed Patrice as her breaths became shallow and static. Vision blurry and her heart pounded. Out to her far left she saw the demon with a snarl on his face. He was enjoying this. This was bad... real bad. Dread burned at the pit of her stomach. All was lost. But still something inside told her to keep fighting.

Patrice refused to die.

Out of the corner of her eye she saw movement. Shouldering its way down the side of the Clark Tower came a massive black panther. Patrice was speechless. It was the biggest panther she had ever seen in her life or even on tv. Black fur with golden symbols etched on top, it moved with feline precision as it crept down. She gasped as the panther's golden eyes locked in on Papa Samedi, Patrice blinked and in a motion quicker than the eye, the panther leaped from off the building and pounced right on top of the demon. With the force of its paws, the panther pummeled the demon right through the adjacent wall.

Could tonight get any worse? The thought occurred to Patrice as she held onto her wound which was bleeding faster by the minute. She focused so much on the giant panther that she hadn't notice one zombie had pushed itself on top of the dumpster and was pulling itself up by grabbing her leg.

"Get off of me!" Patrice bellowed as she kicked and scrambled on top of the dumpster. She dragged herself against the wall as scarred and decayed hands were all around grabbing and cutting towards her.

As she scrambled against the wall, wounded and helpless, the Panther stood on its hind feet. Stretching over seven foot tall, the panther filled the air with a roar that made Patrice's blood run ice cold. With its claws reaching towards the sky and its jaw crushing fangs exposed, the panther set its golden eyes upon Patrice. She looked at the beast petrified. It charged towards her.

A whirlwind whooshed across Patrice knocking her off her feet on top of the dumpster. She fell with a loud and resounding thud. She peered up and half of the swarm of zombies had been sliced to shreds. There was no sign of the beast. Coming from her right came another whirlwind. Again she peered up but found all the zombies lying all around her in a bloody heap.

While on her knees Patrice glanced over the dumpster. All the zombies had been slayed but there was no sign of the creature. An uneasy spirit overwhelmed Patrice and brought shivers down her back. Patrice knew the panther was not gone but she could not find him. At a snail's pace she looked further below the trash can. She had almost reached underneath when she fell back as the bin shook underneath her.

Golden eyes of the panther locked with hers. Patrice felt its breath blow onto her face as drool fell on her thigh. It slapped a right paw that ripped into the dumpster and then a left. Patrice had nowhere to go.

She was trapped by the panther.

26

INTO THE MOONLESS NIGHT

*H*er heart was pounding out of her chest as she stared into the golden irises of the panther, while lodged between its massive paws that shredded the sides of the bin, like a hot knife running through butter. She panted as the panther's warm breath swept across her face. Then the strangest of things happened. As the markings of the panther continued to glow, the look in the monster's eyes softened, and Patrice saw something that was a resemblance of humanity. The panther looked at her as if it had known her. She let out the breath held stifled in her chest.

"Grab on to me," she heard a smooth baritone voice say, not aloud but in her head.

Patrice was dumbfounded. She took her bloody hand off her wound and caressed the Panther's cheek. A shudder danced down her spine as she felt a strange intimacy between the two.

"He will summon more zombies," his voice came trailing

into her head telepathically in a soothing baritone. "Grab on to me and I'll get you out of here."

Patrice looked out across the panther's shoulder and saw Papa Samedi starting to work his dark magic. The panther laid its shoulder on top of the dumpster. With a groan she fell over the panther and wrapped her legs around its back.

"Hold on to me," the voice bellowed in her head.

Patrice buried her face into the soft fur of the creature's neck as rain pelted her back. With a rumbling purr, the panther fell on all fours and leaped into the sky. Rain and wind whipped at Patrice's face, as it soared through the air, agile and quick. The panther's claws landed in a crash on the side of the building, then it dug its paws deeper and leapt again. In two hops the panther had reached the rooftop, from there the panther became one with the night as it leapt from building to building to put distance between the two of them and Papa Samedi.

Patrice was losing a lot of blood. It drained on the back of the panther as wind and rain continued to belt at her face. She was falling in and out of consciousness as she stared up into the grey moonless night. Lightning struck down from above. She buried her face into black fur that felt so soft on her face. Cool air kissed her cheek and a sense of euphoria overcame her, she felt safe with the panther, the tenderness in its eyes reassured her. They had been running for about thirty minutes, when the panther stopped, and laid her on the ground. Patrice rolled on gravel in pain. She looked up and saw golden eyes and black fur transform into the brown flesh. With roars and grunts he shifted from beast to man.

Rain fell harder from the sky. Her vision blurred as her

body grew weak, she was losing consciousness. Strong arms pulled her close.

Patrice wiped the water out of her eyes and was floored. "Lorenzo, that was you?"

"Patrice….. Patrice listen to me," He called as he shook in fear. "You are losing a lot of blood. But I won't let you die!" Lorenzo said as he caressed her face. There was a groan, and she was being cradled to a chest. "Drink my blood and you'll heal faster."

"No," Patrice protested. Her voice frail and weak.

"You are going to die!" Lorenzo shouted as he shook her. Patrice dropped her head and Lorenzo began to panic. With a flick of his wrist, his fingernails grew into thick talons. He took his index finger and ran it along his chest. When crimson red came out, he shook Patrice and put her lips to his chest.

"Patrice just drink it. I heal faster and with my blood you will heal you too." Lorenzo looked back down into his arms and he shook her. "Patrice? Patrice?" he called as he shook her.

She rested in his chest, lapping at his wound. As Patrice's head rested in his chest, her arm fell and the cursed charms of Mombu rolled over into the gravel. Lorenzo examined the bracelet. He had seen it before. Lorenzo scooped the bracelet into his pocket and then he picked Patrice up. He carried her back to his penthouse where he knew he could keep her safe.

~

*B*ack at the house, the sisters were finally gathered in the basement. Yolanda had the Legacy in her hand, trying desperately to find answers to the horrible vision she saw in her dreams.

"That's him!" Yolanda shouted as she pointed to a figure in the Legacy. "That's the Loa I saw in my dreams. He is the one after us."

Amina glanced over, "Papa Samedi is a dark spirit that is a part of the Petro Loa. He is known as a crossroad demon who can make a deal for one's soul. He is a master necromancer and can be called on to aid in resurrection. It says he even taught some of our ancestors how to bring people back from the dead as slaves."

"Papa who?" Makayla asked, dragging her fingers through her flowing hair.

"I don't like that name. Can we call him Papa Tutti?"

Amina paused, "Hmm Papa Tutti... I like it."

Makayla sneered, "Yeah me too."

Yolanda smacked her hand in the middle of the book. "Hello? This is not the time to be playing around. This is for a real, for real. The spirits have called me and alarmed me of the danger threatening us. A demon and not just any demon, a Loa is set on killing us."

Amina sighed, "How do you know that? C'mon Yolanda you've read through this book a dozen times. You probably saw this scary picture of this demon and it showed up in your nightmare."

Yolanda turned to Amina, "That was no nightmare. I know the difference between a vision and a dream."

"Alright chill," Makayla resolved. She stepped in front of her two sisters "Let's just say Papa Tutti really is after us. What do you think he wants?"

Yolanda shook her head, "I don't know. This is a demon that collect souls so maybe he wants ours. Maybe if he gets our souls, he gets our gifts."

The childlike grin vanished off of Makayla's face quicker than ice melting. "Well if that's the case. How in the hell are we going to beat him?"

Yolanda turned back to the book and closed it. She placed both hands on top and closed her eyes. Inside she hoped and prayed for an answer. It wasn't until she opened her eyes again that she noticed she had already turned the pages of the Legacy. And the spell she came to was called Conjure the Spirit.

"We have to conjure the spirit," Yolanda murmured.

Amina shrugged, "What the hell does that mean?"

Yolanda turned, "We have to summon the Bennu, the phoenix, the creator spirit. It makes sense. The Loa of Voodoo are like the saints. They themselves are not deities but they are not just spirits neither. We never summoned Papa Tutti... I mean Samedi so we don't have the power to banish him only the Phoenix can do that. If there was a reigning Mother Phoenix, then she would do that. But since there is not, we are on our own."

"How do we conjure the spirit?" Makayla asked.

Yolanda looked down at the book. "Well besides having a Mother Phoenix, there is a ritual that involves channeling all five elements."

Makayla laughed sarcastically, "Well then you're right we're screwed. Only Amina and Patrice have elemental powers with fire and air." She looked over at Yolanda, "Me and you need to step our game up."

"Not necessarily," Yolanda inserted. "The spirit is a fifth element in Voodoo. My visions are a connection to the spirits. Also I think your powers may further into an elemental gift."

Yolanda stated, thinking back to the armor of ice she saw in her vision.

Makayla pointed to herself. "My power? Let's hope so, because there is but so many walls I can walk through. I want to kick some ass."

At first Amina was worried about her sister's discovering the identity of Papa Samedi. But now she had a way to destroy the bastard. She was pleased. "What do we need for this ritual? I can run to the store tonight and get it."

Yolanda looked down, "Just a few things. I can write them down."

Makayla placed her hand on her hips, "Well I guess this sounds like a plan. Conjure the spirit to take out Papa Tutti so hopefully he won't send no more zombies and crazy boyfriends after us. I'll go call Peaches and let her know." Makayla said before starting up the stairs.

"No, No!" Yolanda yelled. "I don't want to ruin her date. We will tell her in the morning."

Makayla threw up her hands, "Okay girl, whatever." She turned and trekked up the stairs.

"Here you go Amina," Yolanda said as she finished scribbling the needed ingredients on a piece of paper. As she handed over the list to her sister she was startled as a vision jolted in her head.

She saw Amina laying on the floor surrounded by a pool of her own blood. Papa Samedi entered the scene through shadows. He dragged Amina helplessly when the vision ended. Yolanda opened her eyes.

"You good?" Amina asked with concern written on her face.

At first she was speechless but the look on Amina's face let her know she was worried. "I'm okay just tired and worried. Go! Go get the supplies and let's get rid of this demon."

Amina nodded, "I'm out. I'll be back in twenty minutes."

"Okay," Yolanda said as she watched her sister climb the stairs. She was stunned. Unsure if the vision she had seen was that of the past or if it was a preview of the future. Either way danger was headed their way.

27

SAFE IN THESE ARMS

*P*atrice woke up warm and comfortable. She kicked her legs. They were covered in thick blankets. She laid on top of a bed that felt like a large cloud. She opened her eyes, and the room was dark. Lorenzo entered the room holding a glass of water. He eased onto the bed with his chest bare, and his heat powerful.

Patrice sat up, "What happened? Where am I?" she asked.

Lorenzo sat next to her, "Take it easy. You're in my penthouse. And you're safe," he declared in a smooth tone. He laid his hands on her and she jumped back, almost frightened. "It's alright. That demon that attacked you won't get in here. I made sure this place is warded. It's protected from evil." He handed her the glass of water. "Now drink up."

Patrice took the glass of water and sipped. Her throat was dry and the cold water seemed so cooling and refreshing as it went down. She eyed Lorenzo suspiciously.

Lorenzo adjusted himself on the bed. "You got stabbed pretty badly. But I took care of your wound."

Patrice lifted the covers. She touched the bandage at the side and flinched.

"Hey!" Lorenzo said as he removed her hand. "Give it some time and you will heal. I gave you some of my blood. You will feel like new in no time."

"You what?" Patrice said as she shot him a nasty look. She turned to the nightstand and saw her blouse laying on the side. She rolled out of the bed in one swoop grabbed her blouse then descended the stairs. "Stay away from me!" she yelled as she folded her blouse under her arms. Lorenzo had removed her shirt to dress the wound.

"Hold up, where you are going? "Lorenzo shouted as he pounded down the stairs after her. "Give yourself some time to heal."

Patrice turned to him. "That beast out there... that was you. Wasn't it?" she asked as she edged closer to his face. "What the hell are you?"

Lorenzo sighed, "I'm a Were-panther."

Patrice shook her head. "A what?"

"A were-panther," Lorenzo repeated.

"How did this happen to you?"

Lorenzo grinned. "I was born from a family of weres. I turn at will. Sometimes I roar and go on a rampage." Lorenzo pulled her into his arms. "Other times I'm sleek and purr like a kitten."

Patrice was speechless. She felt allured in his steely hazel gaze.

"I can take many forms," he continued. "Sometimes I can morph into a regular panther. Then I can change into a half human and half panther shape. Most times when I'm threatened I take on my savage form which you saw last night."

Patrice ran her hand across the bandage covering her wound, the pain had eased tremendously. Patrice ripped off the bandage. No cut. No scar or bruise. It was as if it never happened. "You gave me, your blood?"

"Yes. Were-Panthers heal fast. So I gave you some of my blood to absorb my ability." He said nonchalantly as if the whole thing didn't sound absurd. "Don't be surprised if you temporarily become more strong and agile."

"Thanks for saving me, but I wish you hadn't force fed me blood. Have you ever heard of blood borne pathogens?" Patrice said as she pulled herself back from his arms. Over the over-look she spotted her heels, she went over and scooped them into her hands. This made holding up her blouse and covering herself more difficult. "This is way too crazy for me. I'm leaving now."

"I'm sure it can't be any crazier than being a Voodoo priestess."

Patrice's shoes fell out of her hands as she gagged. "How do you know?"

Lorenzo held his hands up. "This will sound crazy but I have been having these dreams."

Patrice raised a brow, "Dreams?"

"Of you," Lorenzo continued. "I came to Atlanta with a purpose. To help and protect you. Patrice there is a storm coming. Something evil has set its sights on you and your sisters."

"I know. It's the demon we encountered tonight. Once I go home and find his name then his ass is grass." Patrice spat. "But go back to these dreams. What did you see?"

"You." Lorenzo declared. "Well this old lady showed me you

and she told me you were in danger. And I don't think the threat she was talking about was that demon. It's something more powerful. More malicious than you can imagine."

"Old lady. Malicious evil." Patrice said vaguely. "You are not making any sense."

"I know it made little sense to me either." He took her hands and pulled her back into his arms. "It's hard to explain but when I saw you Patrice, I knew I had to protect you and now that I know you…. I want to love you."

Lorenzo rested his hand on the back of Patrice's waist. It was a smooth and casual gesture. It was a knock on the door to see if she would let him in. She gazed over at him. Her thigh pressed against his and Lorenzo's heart began racing. Her glare was so intense that Lorenzo felt as though he needed to restrain the panther inside of him.

"Look, I know you're strong. I get that." He said as he ran his firm hands over her shoulder. "But let me take care of you," he said as his voice dropped to a low sensual groan. "As long as you're with me. You will be safe."

"I've never been safe," she interrupted. There was no hostility in her tone, just simple truth. "I've been fighting all my life. For me and my sisters. That's all I know how to do, and what I will continue to do, to make sure they are safe, and live long lives full of happiness. I had to watch greed, evil, and black magic tear my family apart. Me and my sisters are the only ones left, and we are the only ones who can continue our family's legacy."

Lorenzo pulled her closer. "I'll tell you what. Since you protect them. I'll protect you."

*P*atrice felt herself melt in Lorenzo's strong embrace. He smiled and with no shame she let her blouse fall to the floor. Lorenzo caressed her lower back, and the way he held Patrice made shivers run down her spine. To the left, the fire crackled as the heat in the room went up another notch. She caressed his cheek and the mere touch sent a surge to his pants that made him gasp at the intense stimulation. His bulging chest burned with desire to be adorned with the delicacy of her kisses. Golden eyes stalked Patrice, and she bowed to their mercy, her lips trembled as she prayed he would kiss her, with his brown eyes sparkling gold and his magnificent beard glistened in the darkness.

Finally, the moment came when they exhaled and gave into their yearnings, Lorenzo kissed Patrice and every cell in her body purred. She yanked at his pants and they fell exposing more of his body. Built like an African war God, his beautiful brown skin stretched tight over solid muscle. With ease he lifted her up and she wrapped her legs around his waist. Lorenzo pinned Patrice against the floor to ceiling window. He buried himself in her neck and she moaned in ecstasy as he presented their love to the world for all to see. Patrice pulled Lorenzo from her neck. He gave her his tongue as he dropped her to the floor so she could step out her jeans. Once bottomless, Patrice yanked down Lorenzo's pants. He wore black Calvin Klein boxer briefs that curved perfectly under his muscular butt.

She grabbed at his manhood. He was throbbing and the fact she had it firmly in her hand made her body wet in anticipation.

"Condoms?" She asked.

He hurried over to a draw near the kitchen. "Got em!" he shouted back.

"Good, because I've had enough fluid swapping after drinking your blood." She ran over and jumped in his arms.

Lorenzo caught her and pressed his lips against hers, then he caught her gaze, her eyes were golden and primal like his. Once he noticed this, a naughty laugh escaped his throat as he carried her back over to the overlook, shoved her against the window, and squeezed her throat before dragging his tongue along her neck. Patrice's nipples ached in mind blowing ecstasy as his beard tickled her collarbone and his tongue wrote a sweet love song on her neck.

Patrice was still in his arms as she dropped her head back and released a moan that she didn't know could come out of her body. "Kiss me," she commanded. His tongue and lips moved lower, adorning every inch of her chest with kisses. With her right hand she pushed up her breast, directing him to where her agony of desire hurt the most.

Lorenzo eyed her, "If I kiss it, then it's mine."

Patrice raised a brow, "Take it."

Lorenzo took her breast in his mouth, greedily like a savage, better yet a barbarian. She moaned again, but this time loudly, as she clenched her fingers around his head. Then Patrice noticed that there was something growing inside her, it was a type of passion far from human, and more primal. His panther strength, sight, and power was coursing through her veins, and heightening her lusty desires. "Devour me," she screamed, and the words came out her lips so fast, they surprised her.

"Tonight you belong to me," he growled as he pulled her hair.

"Yes," she moaned.

In one fluid motion, he lifted her by the bottom, placed her legs on his shoulders, and dove his face between her legs. Patrice died a million deaths in the moment. His fat wet tongue ran, far, and deep inside of her, making her legs quake. A growl rumbled deep in his belly, the low sensual sound drove her to insanity, as she ran her hands across his shoulder, and felt the growl vibrate all over his body.

It wasn't too long before waterfalls came crashing down hard and like being dipped in the river of Jordan, Lorenzo was baptized in her glory.

Once Patrice quieted from the pleasure of coming so hard, he set her legs down and turned her over. Lorenzo brought their bodies together, as he ran his hands over hers on the overlook, and Patrice cocked her neck to the side so that he could kiss her. They stood there for a moment, just enjoying the unbearable heat their bodies made together. Then his tongue ran down her back as he put the condom on, the latex made a loud slap around the base of his shaft. He stood behind her to behold her beauty, and was breathless at the Queen that stood before him. A Queen worthy to carry his heir and give him enough power to become Alpha amongst his pack.

Patrice looked back at him and tried to search his thoughts. She ran her hands along his throbbing shaft, it was the size of an arm. With a firm grasp she pointed it to the gates of heaven. Lorenzo entered her and just the tip was enough to make her moan.

Lorenzo kissed her. "Take a deep breath," he commanded.

Patrice inhaled and when he entered fully, she rejoiced as she felt a worthy King had marched through the gates of her kingdom. She had found a dragon who could burn down the frozen wall that guarded her heart. The prince that was promised to her by the gods, had finally made his way into her life.

Lorenzo and Patrice made passionate love that went from the window, to the walls and finally onto the living room floor by the fire. With Lorenzo's hands on her, Patrice was floating on the highest wave of ecstasy. Before she knew it, his lips were blessing hers again, and she welcomed him back into the gates of heaven.

After the first thirty minutes of love making, she became a maniac. She straddled him, wrapping her hands around his neck, proclaiming her dominance. He did the same by guiding her hips up and down on him in a steady rhythm. Lorenzo started moaning real loud when she tightened the muscles in her sweet sex around his dick.

Patrice rocked him and he set free a rumbling grunt, then he flipped her over. Patrice was on her hands and knees, she whipped her mane and looked back at him. He shuddered at her gaze. She was challenging him. He entered her again as she wailed. Then he fucked her good. Hard.

And Patrice had wanted that. She connected with that feline spirit. For so long her soul cried for her love, but her body yearned for the release of orgasm. Patrice felt him growing inside of her, becoming engorged, lengthening and stretching her sex which opened for him.

When it was over and they both came crashing down, Patrice laid on his chest as they cuddled on the floor.

"Patrice you don't have to worry. With every breath I have.

I will protect you." Lorenzo said to her as he kissed her forehead.

As she laid on his chest, his voice became a soothing rumble. Patrice looked him in his eyes and she knew by his tone that he meant it.

28

WE HAVE TO FIGHT

*P*atrice was greeted by the warmth of the sun when she woke up. She woke up that morning with a certain renewal. Smiling ear to ear, Patrice stretched out to the morning sun and glanced over to a mink blanket covered Lorenzo. She rolled under the blanket and kissed him on the cheek, slowly he opened his eyes and smiled. Patrice returned the gesture.

Lorenzo wiped the crust out of his eyes. "Good morning."

Patrice's smile, widened. "Good morning."

Just as bliss entered, her mind returned back to the imminent danger near, the evil spirit had made his move last night, and she had to warn her sisters. She had her fun, but now that was over, this demon had to be dealt with. With that in mind, she got up clutching the blanket to her chest.

"Where you going?" Lorenzo asked with his hand blocking out the morning sun.

"A demon, remember? I have to warn my sisters."

Lorenzo sighed out heavily as he got up. After two years of

celibacy, Patrice was surprised she hadn't blacked out from feeling so good. Lorenzo rose from the floor and then marched to the kitchen while Patrice was scooping up her clothes. She whirled over her shoulder to glance at him. His ass was a perfect mountain of brown muscle that she wanted to clasp against her in the early mornings, then again at dusk, and once more in the middle of the night. He walked over with green goodness juice in hand.

Patrice pulled him to her. She wrapped her arms around his waist and buried her head against his chest. "Thank you for saving me. I don't need saving often. But it's nice to know someone has my back."

Lorenzo lowered his head and kissed her. He lifted her off the ground and Patrice kicked her legs like a little girl. "You're forgetting something."

"What?" She asked.

"You wrecked your car last night."

"Damn it."

"Don't worry I'll call my homie Brian to tow your car to the shop."

"I don't want to put you through that much trouble."

"Don't worry ma I got you," he said as he walked over to the kitchen. He was still naked as the day he was born. And as he wagged, Patrice delighted in her view. For a brief second she wanted to stay. The need to protect her sisters made her feel guilty for such a selfish thought. Lorenzo went to the counter, grabbed keys and tossed it to Patrice.

"You can use one of my cars until your car is fixed. It's the black Range Rover parked in the garage downstairs.

Patrice shook her head. "I cannot accept this. You can't just give me a car."

"Borrow," Lorenzo corrected. Then he shrugged. "What? You think I'm just going to give you a car?" he asked sarcastically.

Patrice smirked then she grabbed at her clothes. "Okay well thanks. I have to go. I got to get back home."

~

*W*hen Patrice got home, the first thing she did was look for her sisters. "I'm home!" she called out loud to the house.

Makayla pooched around the corner from the kitchen. Her hair was tied up in a bun and her face covered in Saturday morning laziness. "Well look who decided to show up. You must've had one hell of a date last night."

Patrice smiled before nodding, "Trust me you won't believe me."

Footsteps pounded from above on the stairs. Yolanda peered over the staircase, "Peaches whose Range Rover is that parked outside?"

"It's a long story. I'll have to explain."

When Amina came from around the corner, she was stunned silent. Surprised that her sister somehow managed to survive the trap laid out for her. Another one of her plans thwarted. "Peaches....you are home," she said wide-eyed and solemn.

Yolanda flopped down on the couch, "How did the date go sissy?"

Patrice looked to her sisters grimly, "Last night after my date with Lorenzo I was attacked."

"Oh hell no," Makayla gasped.

"Yes." Patrice said through tight teeth.

"What happened?" Yolanda asked.

"Demon surprised me in the Clark Tower Parking Garage. He looked like a New Orleans mack daddy with his outfit and cane. But he was hideous in the face and powerful. Summoned a swarm of zombies to kill me."

"Zombies as in more than one this time?" Makayla asked.

"Yes," Patrice returned with her voice sharp. " There were dozens of them. I've never seen anything like that in my life. I don't know who this demon is. But he's powerful."

The seriousness of the danger the sisters were in left them all quiet. This was no longer a question of maybe or what if. But danger was indeed knocking on their door. And if the demon was not dealt with, then they will all be killed.

"So how did you escape?" Amina asked, breaking the silence.

"Lorenzo. He is a were-panther."

"A what?" the girls sang in unison.

"A were-panther," Patrice repeated. "It's his Range Rover parked outside. He let me borrow it after I crashed my Mercedes trying to escape."

Makayla grinned, "Lorenzo must really got some money. What did you do Peaches for him to give you a car? You always said nothing in life is free. You pay on the front end or the back. Either way you are going to pay," she suggested, trying to be messy.

"Listen we don't got time for that. There is a demon after us." Patrice took a deep breath and searched for the words in her heart to say, "I thought I could handle this, and tried to. I wanted to protect you guys, but I realize I can't. So there is only one option. We have to fight. First we start off by finding this demon's name."

Yolanda leaned forward. "It's Papa Samedi."

"Aka Papa Tutti," Makayla corrected.

Yolanda turned towards Patrice. "I had a vision of him. He's been after us this whole time. We found a spell that might help us take him out. If we can conjure the spirit of the Phoenix. We might be able to banish this demon for good."

Patrice grimaced and looked down. Gran had been warning her and pointing her in the right direction, in all pride, Patrice didn't listen. She sat there; trying to piece together everything that was going on, to make sense of it all.

Makayla stepped over Amina and sat near Patrice. "Peaches what gives sis? We have a plan, so why are you stressed?"

Patrice turned her head slowly, as worry lined her face. "You're too young to remember, but that's what mom did. She conjured the spirit of the Phoenix and couldn't control it. It killed her along with Gran and the others."

For once in her life, Makayla was speechless.

"I think this is the only way," Yolanda interjected.

Amina stood. "Maybe with the four of us we can control it."

Yolanda shrugged, "It's worth a try."

"Perhaps," Patrice reasoned. "But either way this ends tonight. We can no longer wait for him to come after us. We are going to go after him with everything we have." Patrice turned to her sisters, eyes burning with fury. "If he wants a fight. You better believe we will give it to him. Get dressed ladies and wear…"

"Black?" Amina interjected.

"No," Patrice corrected. "White. We wear all white. It's our tradition. We have to tap into the spirits of our ancestors."

And under the cadence of Patrice's voice the Lawson sisters began to plot out their plan of action to stop the diabolical evil that threatened them.

"First things first. We need to protect this house," Patrice said as she strolled through the kitchen. Her sisters trailing behind like soldiers. "He has been attacking us all over but we need to make sure our home is covered. And we also need to carry something around with us for protection. Incense and salt won't work. We need something stronger!" Patrice declared.

Yolanda held her finger like a student with a brilliant answer. "From the Legacy I learned that brick dust protects you from your enemies."

Patrice shrugged, "That could work."

Buried in an old box of family hoodoo items Makayla found the brick dust. Together each sister spread out handfuls along the doorways of every room in the house.

Yolanda held up her finger again. "What about gris gris bags? I can make some with herbs and oils so we can carry around with us for good luck and protection." Yolanda added.

When she made the bags, the foul odor was so grotesque that Makayla just tapped the small black palm sized bag to her nose, while her face curled in disgust. "Oh no ma'am. There is no way I am carrying this thing in my bag."

"It's for good luck and protection." Yolanda protested in a cheerful voice.

Makayla flicked the bag, "Yeah it's gone protect you from ever getting a man in your life. This thing smells horrible."

"Now that we have protection. We need to learn how to fight," Patrice announced. "I'm not going to lie I have been shielding you guys from a lot. I thought I could protect you, but I was wrong, and I'm sorry. Gran and our uncles used to be ruthless with my training. They taught me how to fight and I'm going to teach you guys too."

"We will teach you," Amina corrected.

Patrice agreed. "We."

Amina folded her arms. "Knuckle up bitches."

They were in the basement surrounded by oils, herbs, and powders that spread all over the place. Majestic and powerful the Legacy was opened and planted in the center. "This is going to be our biggest defense. Especially for you without assault powers." Patrice said as she held a six inch vial that looked like a salt shaker filled with powder. "Its golfer dust mixed with hot foot powder. To any other mortal this would be used for hexing. But for us!" she shouted as she tossed the vial to the basement floor to erupt in small explosion.

All of the sisters flinched as the smoke wafted into the room. "For us it's like a grenade." Patrice said as her sisters examined the hole in the floor.

"We have to make full use of our precious gifts. Yolanda you and Makayla don't have defensive gifts, but that doesn't mean you're defenseless. Yolanda if you focus your visions will allow you to anticipate your opponent's every move. If you open yourself you can see where danger will come from in every direction."

"I never thought of it like that. But I don't know. My visions have been very shaky. One minute I can't get a vision to save my life….literally and the next I can get a major prophesy like the other night."

"That's because you're trying too hard. Don't think, just feel and allow your gifts to flow through you. Your clairvoyance gives you supernatural instinct. Trust it sister."

"And you baby girl." Patrice said as she turned to a bag full of knives. She paused suspiciously, and in a flash the knives rose up and darted towards Makayla.

Screaming, Makayla became hollow as the knives whizzed right through her and landed in the wall.

"Peaches have you lost you everlasting mind?" Makayla screamed at the top of her lungs.

Patrice nodded in approval. "Seems like your power works through fear. Use that." She stepped closer to her baby sister. "Let me tell you this story written in the Legacy. One of our great aunts could literally reach into a chest of a demon and snatch out his heart. And with your power. You might be our back up to defeating this demon."

Makayla gagged, "So you want me to reach into Papa Tutti's chest and grab his heart. Eww that's disgusting. I can't do that."

"But what if you have to? To save our lives?" Patrice asked, trying to be snarky. "Look I've been trying to protect you guys but now you have to fight for yourselves."

"Any tips for me?" Amina asked with her hand on her hips.

"Just do what you do best. Bring the hurricane. If that demon can resurrect a whole graveyard we will definitely need some crowd control." Patrice paced around in the circle. "This is the plan. Yolanda go upstairs and look for some chalk or hell a sharpie so we can draw veves."

"What are veves?" Makayla asked.

"Veves are drawings used in rituals like a pentagram in witchcraft. They can be used to summon spirits, for protection, for sacrifices and for trapping. We want to trap this demon. My plan is we have Yolanda find this demon. We attack whatever forces he has luring him out, we trap him in a veve, then banish him by all of us hitting him with hot foot bombs.

"Me?" Yolanda cried as she pointed to herself. "You want me to find Papa tutti?'

Patrice ran her hands on Yolanda's shoulders to inspire courage. "Yes you. You're the one who found out his name. I'm sure you can find him."

"Yeah," Yolanda agreed. "But who knows what if spiritually looking for this demon, I don't just draw him straight to us."

"Even better we will still go on with the plan." Patrice answered.

Amina raised her eyebrow. "Even better? Okay Patrice you're tripping now."

"I'm not," Patrice snapped. "It's very simple. Either we can go after Papa Samedi or he will kill us. Either one by one or all. It's so simple. We must fight or die." She paused to let her words settle in their mind. "I am serious guys. We have no other options. This demons wants us dead."

Amina knew Patrice had a point. She thought to herself and realized her best option at this point was to align with her sisters to banish Papa Samedi. Amina sauntered around her sisters like a cat, "I hear you and I think this is a good plan and all. I just think our best bet is to conjure the spirit. Why else would Yolanda be lead to that spell? The spirits are trying to help us and we should let them."

Patrice's face tightened and she said, "Conjuring the spirit is a powerful ritual. Its black magic and it is dangerous when it's not done by a Mother Phoenix. Very few of our ancestors have successfully done it. What the Legacy didn't mention is that the spirit, once summoned can consume. It can literally burn you inside out as well as cause a natural disaster. It's nature. It's raw untamable power. That's what happened to our mother. Do we really want to do the same?"

Makayla stood by Amina. "I think Amina is right. Yolanda wouldn't be lead to that ritual if we weren't meant to do it."

Yolanda looked up to Patrice, "And you did say that we have fight. This is our best shot sissy."

Patrice was out numbered. And even though she agreed with them, her inclination to protect still made her hesitant. "But what if something goes wrong?" Patrice proposed.

"Well let's practice it." Yolanda suggested. She turned to Amina, "Did you get everything last night?"

Amina groaned, "I did."

Yolanda looked to Patrice. I think we should practice this.

Patrice looked to each of her sisters. "Okay let's do it."

29

A CIRCLE OF SISTERS

*T*ogether as one, all of the Lawson sisters sat with their hands clasped inside a circle. As smoke from the incense swirled into the air, a spirit of unease wove in and out of the sisters' circle.

Patrice looked over to Yolanda, "Hand me the rattlesnake blood."

Yolanda grabbed the bottle and handed it across Makayla, who was frowning. Patrice took a deep breath as she looked to her sisters. "Ready?"

"Come on with it." Amina cheered as Yolanda nodded.

Patrice gazed down at the Legacy and began chanting. "By broken chains free me. From solid ground mold me. From the depths of the ocean seek me. With wind lift me. By fire consume me. Creator spirit we conjure thee. Grace us with your presence. Take this humble vessel and breathe on thee. Spirit we conjure thee. Spirit we conjure thee. Spirit we conjure thee."

Swirling through the living room came a large gust of

J. MOON

wind. Each of the sisters squeezed hands as the wind blew around them. There was a stirring sensation in the air and in the pits of their bellies, they could all feel a presence near. Some being that was fully alive. Some entity breathing its breath over them. As the Lawson Sisters began to give into the presence of the spirit. The doorbell rang.

Amina cocked an eye open, "So is that the spirit or nah?"

Everyone turned towards the door, from the living room. Makayla was the first to hop up.

"Don't worry I got this." She said as she ran to the door.

Patrice looked at Amina, "You felt anything?"

Amina shrugged. "Goosebumps. But it could be that I'm cold."

Patrice turned to Yolanda. "How about you?" she asked her sister who still sat with her eyes closed. Yolanda fell silent. "Yolanda?" she asked again.

"Peaches come to the door. Your man is here!" Makayla yelled down the hallway.

Both Patrice and Amina peeked around the corner in sync. Patrice was the first to get up, and Amina followed behind. Butterflies filled Patrice's stomach as she saw him. She couldn't believe he was here at her door. Lorenzo fine as ever.

Makayla circled Lorenzo, "So you must be the man my sister has been talking about."

"Good things right?" Lorenzo responded cockily.

Makayla sucked her teeth then looked him up and down. "Real good things. I can see why she didn't come home last night."

Lorenzo laughed at the girl who stood a foot under him, but circled him like she was intimidating. "You have to be Makayla."

Makayla raised a brow, "How did you know that?"

"Your sister tells me you have a smart mouth." Lorenzo said before laughing as Patrice strolled over.

"Hey. What are you doing here?" Patrice asked as Yolanda and Amina shuffled behind her.

Lorenzo's face went serious. "I had to check on you. Last night was very crazy. I can't believe we made it out alive."

Patrice cracked a wry smile as she eased her hands into her pockets. "I can't thank you enough."

"Well I told you I would protect you." Lorenzo said with a toothy grin.

Amina cleared her throat. "Well aren't you going to introduce us?" She turned to Patrice but before Patrice could say a word, Amina stepped forward with her hand out. "What's good? My name is Amina. I'm Peaches' younger sister."

"Peaches?" Lorenzo gasped.

"Family nickname," Patrice blurted under her breath. She turned to her other two sisters. "This is Yolanda and Makayla."

"Nice to meet you ladies," Lorenzo said with a slight head nod. He paused then he became tense as he said, "Patrice there was another reason why I came here. I have something important to tell you."

Patrice nodded for him to continue but Lorenzo fell silent as he also noticed the listening ears of her other three sisters.

"Do you think we can speak in private?"

"Sure," Patrice said as she led him into the kitchen.

While watching Lorenzo walk away, Amina leaned over to Yolanda. "I would let that panther climb on top of me any day." She said as she admired the swagger in his stride and the way his shirt clung to his body.

"Can you believe Peaches has finally gotten a man?" Makayla sneered as she leaned in.

"This explains why the world is ending," Yolanda quipped.

In the kitchen Patrice turned to Lorenzo, "What's up?"

Lorenzo reached into his pocket and pulled out the bracelet. "I found this on you last night. After the demon attacked."

Patrice was silent as she picked up the bracelet out of his hands.

"It looked familiar so I looked it up," Lorenzo continued. "It's called the cursed charms of Mombu. It drains magical power."

*D*ull anger came to Patrice as she studied the bracelet. She then dropped it as if it was burning hot.

"I remember you said you couldn't use your powers," Lorenzo continued. "Well this is why," he pressed.

Patrice was stunned, as a flurry of emotions hit her all at once like a whirlwind. Amina had given her that bracelet. Everything made so much sense. In her gut she knew her sister had been up to no good, but she wanted desperately to give her a chance, this time she hoped things would've been different. But they hadn't, and quite frankly she wasn't surprised. Patrice's blood began to boil. All around her she saw nothing but red. How could she? After giving her another chance, Amina did what she always does. Bring trouble. But this time she went too far. Patrice marched out of the kitchen and back into the foyer. Lorenzo followed behind, getting the clue that something was up.

Patrice glared over at Amina. "You did this didn't you? You set me up. You knew it was a trap."

Amina was silent as inwardly everything came crashing and burning down. Caught in the web of lies she had spun. She wanted so desperately to say something as all eyes in the room stared at her. There was nothing she could say. The truth was out. The damage had been done.

Patrice edged closer to her sister, "Is Papa Samedi coming after us because of you?" she asked with a furious brow. "Is he?" Patrice continued. She waited for her sister to speak up and the longer silence filled the air, the more pissed off she became. "You gave me this bracelet to strip me of my powers. You knew Papa Samedi would come after me."

For once in her life she felt guilty. The girl who normally gave zero fucks had finally found one to give. Amina looked away for a beat, a hundred emotions competing for dominance in her mind as she was confronted with the truth of her treachery. She had planned to betray her sisters for power. Now Amina realized coming back and being with them was a big mistake. She thought she could do it, steal her sisters' powers and give to the demon, then move on. Of all the plots Amina conspired, she didn't think she would fail because she actually cared.

Amina took a long breath before she said, "Let me explain."

Makayla stepped forward and cut her off "Is she telling the truth?"

The rest of the sisters sat wide-eyed and mute, their stunned gazes going between Patrice and Amina and back again. All eyes were on Amina and she began crumbling under the pressure. As Amina crumbled in the hot seat, the spirits lifted the haze off of Yolanda's eyes and she had a vision of the past.

Amina laid on the floor with desperation written all over her face. "Save me and restore my powers. Then I can help you get the greatest power there is." Amina drew a deep aching breath, as she thought of home, and everything she had been running from. "I can get you the power of all the Lawson sisters, power of the Bennu... the Phoenix."

"It's true." Yolanda proclaimed as she strolled into the room. "You know last night I had a vision. I couldn't see everything until now." She turned to Patrice. "She was stealing from Magnum and he shot her. She almost died, so she made a deal with the crossroad demon to save her life and return her powers. In exchange she promised him all of our powers."

"No ....hell no," Makayla stomped as she shook her head. "I don't believe it," Makayla said almost gasping.

Amina's heart pounded. "I didn't mean it." She groaned. "I didn't mean to hurt you. I was only going to give him your powers."

Patrice felt weightless, standing there face to face with her sister. True they have had their battles in the past, but nothing like this. Nothing that would have resulted in either one of them dying.

"Do you hate me that much that you will plan to get me killed?" she asked with her throat thick and filled with emotion.

Silence strangled the room and Patrice's eyes met Amina's in a hard glare and then she glanced at her phone as if she was waiting to leave.

*P*atrice stood there saddened, and surprisingly not angry. She should have felt more anger. More righteous fury. Betrayal. Her sister planned to have her killed. After everything Patrice had done for her. How could she? Patrice wanted to slap her.

"And how did you think he was going to do it?" Patrice shouted. Veins popping in her neck. Her voice in a loud shrill. "How did you think he was going to get our powers? You know I really wanted to be wrong about you. But you're still the same selfish, reckless, hot mess"

"Fuck you!" Amina spat back.

Patrice lifted her hands to use her power to knock Amina on the floor. But Amina raised her hands as well and deflected the force. Tension rose in the room as the sisters engaged in a power struggle.

"I told you I'm not as weak as I was before!" Amina proclaimed. "I am the mistress of the winds. The commander of thunder and rain. I'm the fucking hurricane bitch!"

"I don't care who you are. You are not welcomed here anymore!" She roared as she pointed a finger in Amina's face. "If you're not with us then you stand against us. I might not be a Mother Phoenix, but you bet your ass that I will find a way to bind your powers again." Patrice bellowed as she lowered her hands.

Winds barraged through the front door. Everyone shielded themselves from the powerful gusts that swirled with force. Amina stood idle as her braids blew all around her, whipping back and forth. Rage filled her soul and the winds lashed at everyone as she stood in the middle of the foyer. "It won't work," she said as she turned to the door, giving her sisters her back. Her eyes glazed over to a misty white as tears began trickling down her cheek. She looked over to her baby sister Makayla whose tearful eyes ripped through her gut like a jagged knife. "I'm sorry," she moaned. Then she turned to Patrice and her lips turned up into the ugliest curl. "You better watch out. There is a storm coming." she said as she lifted up in to the winds and soared out of the house.

A final gust of wind nearly buckled them all to their feet. Patrice dropped her hands to see nothing but dust in the path of her sister.

"What the hell just happened?" Lorenzo shouted.

Patrice turned to him. "My sister, like always. She causes a big mess, runs away, and leaves me to clean up the broken pieces."

Makayla's eyes filled with tears as she dashed up the stairs. Tears stung her eyes and then fell without shame as she ran up to her room. Patrice called behind her but she was so filled with emotion she dashed up the stairs and locked the door behind her.

Lorenzo waited a beat before he spoke to Patrice, gathering his words with care.

"Well I'm just going to let you have your moment. Hit me up if you need me." Lorenzo said as strolled out of the door.

"Well that's two for two," Yolanda murmured as she strolled next to Patrice by the staircase.

Patrice raised a brow "What?"

Yolanda leaned on the staircase. "I'm two for two. My powers were blinded by someone I loved. Amina was lying to us this whole time. You picked up on that early. But I didn't. I wanted to-"

"Believe that she has changed," Patrice finished. She took a deep breath as she choked back emotion. "I wanted to believe that too."

Yolanda tried to purse her lips into a somber smile.

Patrice rubbed her shoulder, "Don't beat yourself up."

"I'm not," Yolanda returned. "Everything is going to hell around us. Somehow we have to figure out how to stop the madness."

Patrice grabbed her hand and leaned on her shoulder. She glanced over to Yolanda and said, "We will somehow."

~

*N*ight fell and Makayla was still sitting up in her room. She had run in an hour ago, slammed the door, leapt to her bed and wrapped her arms around her head then wailed. Her emotions ran high as she laid in disbelief, tricked by her older sister Amina. Everything around her became solemn and grey to the sound of her own grief. Another hour went by when the silence was interrupted by a text.

Wallace: Are we still going to that party tonight?

Makayla: No. Don't feel like it.

Wallace: Quit playing.

Wallace: Your bae Devante will be there.

Wallace: Come on! We have been talking about this for a long time.

Wallace: Don't leave me hanging sis.

Makayla studied Wallace's words on her phone screen for a long time. To her right she could hear the slams of both sisters' doors as they went into their respective rooms. If she wanted to go it had to be now.

Makayla: Meet me in 20

Once she clicked send on the message Makayla got dressed then walked through all of the doors of the house like a haunting spirit. She left with no sound or notification that she was gone to the party.

30

CONSEQUENCES

*M*akayla's heart raced with excited nervousness as she and Wallace snaked through the crowd that gathered around Devante's door. All chatter ceased around the porch as eyes followed her path. It was her first "in crowd" party and she dressed to be the showstopper. The bee-witching charm had inspired her picture perfect outfit, her simple yet luxurious ponytail, and the golden beat on her skin that made her look like the most decadent cinnamon bun.

"Well it's already looking like it's a movie in there," Wallace says as he pulls Makayla along.

Makayla pulled her ponytail over shoulder. "And every movie needs a star. The dolls is ready tonight."

"Let's go in!" Wallace says as he opens the door.

A shiver of anticipation made her heart lurch as she stepped through the door. The living room overflowed with sweaty bodies. A strong stench of weed assaulted their senses. Suddenly all eyes rolled over to Makayla, and the living room rumbled with whispers, clatters of pictures snaps, and echoes of jealous gossip.

Girls who recreated her earlier outfit, rush from the other side of the rooms like bees, pulling her into selfies.

Before she knows it, the crowd overwhelms her and a dozen or so bodies separate the two of them. Makayla reaches out her hand, "Wallace, help!"

Wallace pushes through the sweaty bodies, grabs Makayla, and heads toward the kitchen.

"Like damn just get your life. Fall back," Makayla sassed as Wallace pulled her through the front door and to the kitchen. Makayla thought being a socialite would be so much easier, little did she know just how annoying fanboys and fan girls could be. Before she could even walk into the house she had been pulled into selfies with people she didn't know, she had been given explicit compliments she didn't like, and more annoying than anything, she had seen over a dozen girls copying her exact outfit and hair color from earlier. This made Makayla respect her idols Rihanna, Beyoncé, Kim Kardashian, and Tamar so much more. It was difficult being a trending topic.

Wallace turned to her, "Not having fun Queen?" He asked sarcastically.

Makayla sighed and rested her hand on her forehead. "Well I mean it's cute or whatever but this is becoming annoying. I lowkey miss being a regular schmuglar girl."

Wallace shook his head and stroked Makayla's shoulder. "But this is everything we always wanted." He reached on the table and grabbed two red cups. "Here sis have a drink." He said as he offered the cup to Makayla.

Makayla grimaced as she swallowed the spiked punch

down. She glanced across the kitchen to see a girl with a red brimmed fitted looking at her. Makayla turned to talk to Wallace again, but she could feel the girl staring a hole in the side of her head, she looked back over. Makayla gasped as a name came to her. "Brittany?"

"Hey Makayla," she murmured as she stepped out of the shadow of the door corner.

"That's a nice hat," Wallace commented, his tone dripping in shade.

Nervously she adjusted her cap, "Thanks." she said before peering down.

Makayla sat her cup on the table. "Are you alright?" she asked.

"Yeah," Brittany said with a shrug as her voice cracked with emotion. "Actually no. It's my hair." She said as she pulled the cap off revealing a smooth yellow skull. "It keeps falling out and I don't know why." Brittany said before erupting into sobs.

Both Makayla and Wallace at once covered their mouths as they grimaced at the sight of Brittany's bald head.

"We went to several doctors and they can't figure it out either. They think I have some sort of disease," She said as she placed the cap back on her head. Sobbing, she turned to look back up to Makayla, "I look just like my mom when she had cancer."

"Oh no sis, put that back on." Wallace said.

Makayla stared into Brittany's bleak eyes, and guilt cut through her like a sharp twisting knife. She closed her eyes. But still she could only shudder at the mental image of Brittany's snatched scalp. "I'm so sorry," she cried as she cupped her hands around her mouth.

"Come on," Wallace said as he dragged Makayla away.

As they walked backed through the living room, it seemed more people came as the house was now packed to capacity with little room to breathe let alone move. Wallace pushed and pulled until they were far away from the kitchen and at the base of the stairs, "Did you see her scalp?" he asked.

Makayla nodded her head yes. Her actions made her want to leave.

"Makayla you have to fix this. You know.... before I never used to believe in all this hoodoo and whatnot like you do. My grandma did. And one thing she always taught me is that whatever you do comes back around times three."

"Meaning?" Makayla asked.

Wallace grabbed both her hands. "If you don't reverse the curses you put on those girls, something bad is going to happen to you."

Makayla sucked her teeth. "Don't get me wrong I feel bad for miss thing or whatever but I got this. Don't worry about it." She argued.

From the corner of her eyes she spotted Devante as he descended down the stairs. He entered the room and his gaze blistered her skin. Makayla looked over, and she gasped as he licked his lips. A flush of nerves climbed from her stomach to her chest, fluttering like butterflies.

She raked her hair and batted her lashes as he came to her. "What's up?" he called as he pulled her into a hug, and she inhaled him deeply. Devante carried the scent of cedar, cardamom and musk. It was masculine and intoxicating. Makayla closed her eyes and smiled.

"Hey Devante," She said in a demure tone. Makayla took a step back and looked him over, "You look fly tonight."

Devante chuckled then licked his lip, "Shawty you do too." Devante tugged at her hand as he grinned. "I've been waiting for you. I'm glad you made it."

"You know I had to come through, for you." Makayla returned with a bat of her eyelashes.

Devante nodded at Wallace before pulling Makayla's hand. "Come over here. Come dance with me."

Makayla looked over to Wallace and signaled for him to get lost.

Wallace sucked his teeth. "I guess I'll just go make some new friends then."

Devante pulled Makayla to the middle of the floor. He looked over to the corner of the room where a pudgy sweat-drenched boy dee-jayed. "Hey Dj Chubby, slow it down."

The Dee-jay nodded, scratched the turn table and changed the rattling hip-hop song to a slower 90's R&B jam. A collective sigh released over the room as boys got behind girls and pulled them closer. Devante's lips curled into a boyish grin as he pulled Makayla's hips to his.

Makayla sighed. "This is my song." She gazed into his eyes realizing they were a golden brown like honey. Her heart hitched as they swayed to the beat.

"What you know about Usher?" Devante asked with a frown.

Makayla sucked her teeth. "A lot more than you do. Him and Brandy are my faves. I watch nothing but Moesha re-runs on Saturday morning."

Devante arched his brow. "Oh yeah?"

"Yes." Then a joyful memory filled her with glee. "You know this reminds me of? The Pajama Jam episode."

"What happened?"

"Well you know," She began. "It was the highlight of their relationship. Moesha and Jeremy went upstairs and went from friends to boo'd up."

"Hmph," Devante smirked as he stopped dancing. "Let's recreate that then. Why don't you follow me?"

"What do you mean?"

Devante tugged her hand. "Come up stairs I got something to show you."

Makayla exhaled slowly. "Okay."

Devante's hands were warm and sweaty. With every step she was shaking, and trembling with nerves. She walked in the room looking around as he closed the door behind with a soft tap.

"Have a seat," he commanded as he flopped down on the bed.

Makayla sat down with butterflies in her stomach. She dreamed of this moment with him and it finally came to pass. The two of them alone. "You have a nice house," Makayla said as she looked away from Devante's hazel brown eyes.

"Thanks... my folks are pretty loaded." He said as he scooted over to her.

She looked around at the large room featuring every spec a teenager could want, a PS4, large flat screen, and decked out Macbook. "I see," she responded.

Then suddenly he grabbed her by the shoulders and said. "Look I don't know how to say this but I'm obsessed with you. Like I swear to God I don't know what it is, but I think about you all the time. I get nervous when you're around. And I don't even trip off no female ya heard me. It's just…..you are so damn fine," he concluded as he caressed her cheek.

"But what about Erica?" She asked.

"What about her?" Devante said with a shrug. "I ditched her to get with the hottest girl in the school."

Makayla nearly died. Her cheeks flushed with redness. To hear Devante declare love for her in his southern drawl, made her feel like butter melting on a hot biscuit. Makayla cackled, "Aww me? Little ole me. Stop it."

"No, real talk. You're the baddest chick at the school right now. And I don't know why I'm just now seeing you."

"Well you know sometimes a good thing can be right under your nose."

"Exactly," Devante whispered before pulling her into a passionate kiss.

Makayla felt as if the whole room started spinning. She kissed him back. Then he nibbled on her neck as he climbed on top of her. Devante began kissing her again this time more forceful and aggressive. As he did, Makayla struggled to breathe.

"Wait slow down," Makayla murmured between kisses.

He climbed further on top of her and nudged her legs further apart as his hands went all over her body. Makayla felt hot and not in a good way. "Slow down," she called again.

"Chill," he spat back before pulling off his shirt.

Again he dove to her neck, planting kisses. He started tugging at her skirt. His hands became more aggressive. Makayla felt less turned on and more vulnerable. She pushed at him. "Okay I'm not feeling this. You need to get off of me."

Devante continued his onslaught of kisses as his hands pulled and tugged at her body. Makayla pushed at him again until she slapped him in the face. "Yo shawty what's your problem?" he snarled in one of the ugliest faces Makayla has ever seen him make. Then he buried his lips between her neck and shoulder, so once again she pushed him off. "Look I know you want this as bad as I do. I see how you look at me." he shouted.

In that moment as Makayla looked into Devante's eyes, she saw a guy she had never seen before. They were pitch black and void of any human emotion, he was possessed. Makayla's heart sank when she thought of the spell. It had to have been doing something to him. She knew that if she didn't get up now, Devante was going to rape her.

"I've had enough. I'm not playing with you anymore. Get off of me!"

He looked at her sideways. "Don't fight this. I want you baby. I need you," Devante gritted in his teeth as he forced all of his strength on her.

Makayla screamed and he covered her mouth with his hand, as he reached up her skirt with the other. Every second seemed like an eternity of horror as she stared up at him frightened. Then as his hand reached to grab her underwear, Makayla closed her eyes and exhaled, a cooling sensation swept over her skin, her tummy filled with butterflies and her whole body felt light as a feather. Once her power was activated, she fell through the bed and hard on the floor.

"What the hell?" Devante screamed as he jumped up.

Makayla crawled from under the bed and struggled to her knees. If there was any a time for her phasing power to come through it was that one. She looked on the table and grabbed her bag.

"How did you just do that?" Devante asked, his mouth agape.

Makayla started to the door before turning to him, "I don't ever want to see you again. I can't believe you just did that." she cried through staccato breaths.

"No wait, don't leave!" Devante cried as he grabbed her shoulder.

Makayla yanked his hand off. As she did a freezing strength ran down her arms. She felt Devante's bones buckle underneath her grip. He yelped in pain. Makayla pulled her own hand back startled. She flew down the stairs.

Erica was waiting at the bottom of the stairs. Erica stared Makayla down with her arms folded. "What were you doing up there with my man?"

"Girl, you can have your man. I don't want him," Makayla said as she nudged past Erica.

"I knew you were nothing but a thirsty thot!" Erica spat as she walked away rolling her eyes.

The insult stung Makayla in the chest like a dart. She froze in anger. Her eyes fashioned on Erica's back like an eagle studying its prey. Makayla saw nothing but red. She reached in her bag and pulled out the voodoo doll. She grabbed a five inch pin and stabbed it into the doll's chest. Instantly, Erica fell to the floor.

"From now on you're gonna watch what you say about me trick. And you gone keep my name out your mouth!" Makayla growled.

Erica gasped out loud as she clenched her chest, a searing pain ripped through her, and she didn't know how to respond. Blood formed at the corners of her mouth. Makayla stood there enjoying the sight. Lost in a place of darkness as she continued to ram the pin into the doll. Wallace walked over as others began to take notice of Erica's condition. A crowd of individuals formed around Erica, completely oblivious as to why she was in pain.

Makayla stood her ground at the base of the stairs as she inflected her revenge on Erica. Wallace loomed over Makayla's shoulder. "Stop!" He cried as Erica screamed loudly in pain.

Makayla dug the pin deeper into the doll. Enjoying the pain she was inflicting on her enemy. Frightened, Wallace shook her and pulled at her hands. "Makayla!" he bellowed, snapping her out of the trance.

"What?" she answered, stupefied.

Wallace pointed to Erica laid out on the floor. "Look at what you are doing."

"She looked down at the doll and pin in her hand." She was stabbing the pin into the doll so hard that she began to cut up her own hand. As blood flowed out of Makayla's hands, a whirlwind of emotions came crashing through her. She took deep breaths and the anger faded to grey. "Let's get out of here." She declared as she dropped the doll back into her bag.

They made their way from the crowd that gathered around Erica to the door. As they walked out, they heard people talking about Amy.

"Amy you're so clumsy now. Like Steve Urkel," a tall blonde boy chuckled with his group of friends on the porch.

"I don't know what it is. It just seems like I have bad luck." She said as she backed off the steps to the porch. "Anyway, I'm about to go home. See you guys Monday," She called as she backed into the street.

Wallace was taking the first step when he saw the bright flashing lights. "Amy watch out!" Wallace cried.

Without warning, a jeep came flying past and sent Amy tumbling through the air. With a loud screech, the jeep came to a halt, a few feet from her body. Wallace along with a few others ran to the middle of the road.

"Somebody call for help!"

Wallace looked back to Makayla in fear. She stared back as he mouthed what have you done. Overcome with fear and sorrow Makayla dashed down the stairs. She ran from the house. Makayla had no clue how she was getting home, but she wanted to get far away from here. She was almost half a mile down the road when she picked up her phone to call her sister. After a long pulse tone, Patrice picked up the phone.

"Peaches I need your help. I messed up," Makayla yelped

"Makayla? Where are you?" Patrice asked, confused.

"I'm near Buckhead. Down the street from Devante's house. Look, I did some spells I wasn't supposed to be doing and I messed up big time. People got hurt. I need to fix this. I need you to help me fix this...please."

"Don't worry just let me come get you?" Patrice proclaimed.

"Okay...okay," Makayla breathed. "Please just come. I'm sorry. I'm ready to go."

"Just give me fifteen minutes," Patrice said with a rumble as she grabbed her pocket book.

Makayla breathed a sigh of relief. She turned to walk back towards the house, then froze as she saw something move in the shadows, out in the open field to the left side of the road. She looked forward, and a form appeared in between the trees, barely a silhouette, and the barest etch of a shadow.

"Wait a minute, hold on" Makayla said as she dropped the phone from her face.

She looked out and her breath caught as she saw slow moving figures heading her way. There was a quick rumble in the weeds that made her look back. Something wasn't right, she could feel it. Her stomach knots as a surge of panic struck like lightning.

Everything in her body was telling her to run but she couldn't understand why. Then Makayla narrowed to see the green eyes of the demon. Papa Samedi stood a few feet away from her grinning.

Once Makayla recognized the demon she dropped her phone. Patrice was still calling her name on the other side. Then Makayla noticed the figures weren't just people they were zombies. And it seemed the field and the street held a dozen of them heading her way. Thunder cracked across the sky and unleashed an onslaught of rain. Slowly the zombies inched forward in the darkness with their eyes glowing. The sound of the thunder along with the groans of the undead magnified Makayla's dread by tenfold. She had to go back. She had to escape.

NO WHERE TO RUN, NO WHERE
TO HIDE

Makayla's feet pounded the pavement as she ran for her life. She looked over her shoulder as rain assaulted her head from the sky. Zombies poured into the dimly lit street, their eyes glowing with a thirst to kill, as they marched towards her, each holding a weapon in hand. Her immediate thoughts were to get back to Devante's house and hold out until her sisters could get there.

A glimmer of hope entered her heart when she spotted the lights of Devante's house. The rain made it almost impossible to find her way back, everything was a total blur as she ran, wind and rain whipping at her eyes. She wiped her eyes with her sleeve, peered up and saw lights from the house. There were still a few people outside. She whirled over her shoulder and saw death inching its way towards them all. "Get back in the house!" Makayla shouted, her voice a half desperate cry.

Out of the figures still standing in the street, she spotted Wallace. "Wallace go back inside!" She shouted, out of breath.

"Why?" Wallace yelled before cursing as he spotted the horde that followed Makayla.

Panic swept the few left standing outside as they screamed looking upon the impending doom heading their way. A few members of the basketball team carried Amy's unconscious body back into the house. Once inside, they killed the music and locked the doors.

Papa Samedi stepped out of the shadows in front of the house, as Amina grew stronger so did he, and the taste of Lawson power was invigorating. He needed all of their powers. Mama Brigitte stepped out by his side. He looked over to her, "Go bring me the girl?"

She turned towards him, "Her heart?"

"No. Alive." He corrected.

Mama Brigitte raised a brow, "Why alive? Just kill them if you want to steal the power."

"I need the witches alive. In order to get the phoenix, I need their blood to conjure it. From there I will drain them. Now go!"

Mama Brigitte took off in the shadows as the horde of zombies descended upon the house. By sheer number they covered the front of the house and slapped on the sides and banging on the windows. They swarmed the craftsman home like an army of ants devouring a crumb of cake. Each zombie was someone who was loved, who had lived, and had a family. But now none of that mattered as they all rose with their eyes gleaming green, their will belonged to Papa Samedi.

*P*apa Samedi lurched his hand, and pushed. "Kill them all. Get in there and drag her out." His will came flooding into the zombies, so they swung, chopped, and tore into the house with an increased frenzy.

Inside Devante's house was sheer chaos, as a spirit or terror dominated the teens that packed the living room. Steady incessant knocks surrounded the house, and disoriented them all. Some were too drunk and high to move. Others, mostly girls just screamed frantically and buried their hands in faces, trying to convince themselves such a nightmare couldn't be true. Then there were the cocky and brave souls, largely football players, who tried to go outside to fight, against the more reasonable ones' wishes.

"Barricade the doors! We have to stop them from getting in!" Makayla shouted, her voice lost in the sea of dread.

A dozen faces stared at her with blank expressions.

"We have to keep them from getting in!" Makayla ordered. Some continued to stare frozen before her like deer in headlights while others took to their phones and social media to call for help and record. "Screw it," Makayla snapped before buckling down to push the couch to the door. Beads of sweat dot her neck. Once seeing what she was trying to do, several large boys helped her. After she got the couch to the door, next she ordered an entertainment set to block the windows. And once everyone had orders, and structure they continued to slow the entry of the zombies.

Devante walked over, "What do you want me to do?"

"Die slowly," She spat as she darted the ugliest of looks at him. A large crash erupted somewhere along the right. She pointed, "Go make sure they are not getting in through the side."

Glass shattered in the back of the house, and Makayla's heart sunk, but yet her adrenaline surged. With no hesitation she ran to the back, only to find an axe wielding zombie corner a girl. Makayla reached right through his hand and grabbed the axe, she pulled it into her grasp, reared back, swung and in one fell swoop chucked off its head. More glass shattered on her left. Two zombies were entering the back kitchen door, both nothing more than bones and slimy flesh. She reached, and pulled them through the wall but stopped before pulling them all the way through, trapping them.

Makayla looked back to the girl, a pale redhead who became a screaming mess. "Get your ass out of here. Go into the living room with everyone else."

"Oh my God! Thank you." The girl said before jumping to her knees.

Then it dawned on Makayla what she just did. She exposed herself to the girl. What if she told everyone in that living room about Makayla's gifts? Before Makayla could think of the trouble that put her in, she spotted the body on the floor. A girl with a cap covering her bald scalp with a gnash at her neck. It was Brittany. "Oh god," Makayla shuddered, as her knees buckled. She stared into her lifeless eyes. There was a part of her, that couldn't help but feel responsible. It was her fault. Her pettiness had caused this girl grief in her final days. And if she hadn't come to this party, Papa Samedi wouldn't have lead this horde to attack the party. Before she could succumb to the guilt, Wallace crossed her mind. He was still back in the living room with everyone else. She had to protect Wallace and everyone else she could until her sisters could come. Makayla dashed back into the living room.

She spotted Wallace at the foot of the stairs, facing the door which the football team fought desperately to hold against the zombies. Makayla grabbed Wallace's hands, "Come on let's get upstairs."

As they climbed the stairs, the lights went out, and darkness swept through the house. Everyone in the house let out a collective scream.

"We are going to die." Wallace whimpered.

Makayla reeled around, "Look at me. We are not going to die." At this moment she wanted to slap him, but instead she shook some courage into him. "We will stay upstairs and wait until my sisters get here. Then everything will be fine, you know my big sister doesn't play games. And neither do I, so calm down."

"No, I think we should make a run for it!"

Makayla's eyes grew large. "Boy, we just came from outside. It's too many of them." Then she ran upstairs and Wallace followed.

He shouted behind her. "It's way too many of them but I've seen enough horror movies to know when the monster comes you don't hide upstairs Makayla."

"We will be safer up here," she declared.

As the words left her lips, there was a loud clatter and thump in the room right behind them. And their blood ran cold as they slowly turned heads to the closed door. Wallace was the first to tread down the hall and Makayla followed behind him.

"What was that?" he mouthed shockingly.

Makayla shook her head, "I don't know."

Wallace stood by the door, listening. There was nothing but silence on the other side, an unnerving silence that intensified his fear. Makayla grabbed his hand and phased through a bedroom then into a closet.

"Stay here. Don't move until I come back," she whispered.

"Where are you going?" he probed.

She pointed towards him. "I will take care of it."

"Are you crazy?" he asked as she phased back out of the closet.

"Makayla!" he called back in a half whisper, to the door.

*M*akayla phased out of the closet and treaded back down the hall to the room where the noise came from. She took three silent steps towards the door, and her heart pounded all the way up her throat the closer she got. She was scared, but also ready to face anything that was about to attack her. She was tired of being the baby of the family. This was a battle she would take on her own.

Makayla grabbed the door knob, and the door squawked loudly as it opened.

She stepped in. It was the master bedroom. Most likely where Devante's parents slept. Further she stepped into the room and looked around.

Nothing. Silence.

Makayla took one step back then she heard something that made her shudder…. breathing. *Where was it coming from?* She wondered. Then she peered up and screamed as a dark figure fell on top of her.

Makayla was quick to knock her attacker off of her. With no hesitation, she scrambled to her feet, and spotted a Royal

Oak bookcase to her left. She phased her hands to the side and returned it to form to pull the bookcase on her attacker. As it fell, Makayla's breath caught when she caught a glimpse of her attacker.

Mama Brigitte bounced the bookcase to the other side with an elbow. "Come yuh pretty girl," Mama Brigitte called as she lurched towards Makayla.

Makayla's blood turned into frozen daggers as she looked at the woman who looked more reptilian than human. At that moment she wished she had listened to Wallace. The mere stare of Mama Brigitte's elliptical shaped pupils and hissing tongue, told Makayla she was in grave danger. *We definitely should've ran out the house*, she thought. Makayla looked around the room as Mama Brigitte inched closer. She was being backed into a corner with nowhere to go, then she clocked a window to her right.

Butterflies fill her stomach as her blood cools

She took a deep breath and then barraged straight through the window and came cascading down to a long fall. Seconds stretched to minutes as she kicked and swung on her way down. When she got close to the ground, she phased, and dirt surrounded her, then in one huge breath she surfaced on top of grass. Makayla's power made her landing soft as she phased through the ground. This took her by surprise.

For a split second, she laid on the ground stupefied, but she knew she had to move as the demoness was soon to be on her. A haunting breeze pushes it way through as the moans of the undead filled the air.

Mama Brigitte crashed through the window with blunt force. Glass shattered all around her. As she descended mid-air, she shape shifted into a terrifying Rottweiler hound.

Makayla shouted a loud shrieking scream as she darted towards the woods with Mama Brigitte barking behind her.

*W*hen Patrice arrived at Devante's house, she stopped the car with a screeching halt, zombies swarmed the house in dozens and she feared the worst. Patrice hopped out of the car and readied herself to battle. She slammed the door behind her and a smaller zombie, a girl with a doll in her hand, turned from the house. Patrice didn't care how many zombies stood in her way, nothing was keeping her from getting to her sister. With her hands she called fire.

"Makayla I'm coming!" Patrice shouted as gradually the zombies turned from the house and came towards her, moaning.

"Fire, I call upon you to lay waste to the wicked," Patrice shouted. Out of thin air, bright embers ignited around Patrice and she formed them into her hands. Then in an eloquent motion, she drew back like a snake preparing to strike, and honed the flames. When she attacked, the flames came shooting out of her hands and blasted across the swarm of undead that covered the house. With their bodies covered in fire, the zombies dispersed and walked aimlessly, until they fell on the lawn, writhing as they turned into ash.

Patrice walked closer to the house as the ashes of zombies swirled into the air, creating a grey haze. Dog barks clamored in the distance, and she turned the corner to witness Makayla being chased by a Rottweiler.

"Makayla!" Patrice shouted.

"Peaches help me!" Makayla shouted back as Mama Brigitte came so close she nipped at her heel.

∼

*A*cross town, Yolanda dashed into Aunt Dot's candle shop, wild and out of breath. She stormed through with such a haste that she made Aunt Dot jump up and knock over her puzzle book.

Aunt Dot reached under the counter and picked up her bat. "You picked the wrong shop to rob today!" She shouted

Yolanda held her hands up in protest. "Hold up Auntie....just calm down."

Aunt Dot frowned as she slowly lowered the bat. "Great God girl, don't be rolling up on me like that."

"I'm sorry...I just...I just..."

Aunt Dot put her hands on Yolanda's shoulders. "What's wrong? Just calm down beloved and tell me what's going on."

Yolanda closed her eyes, chest heaving. "I think something bad is about to happen. This monster... demon... or whatever. I think Patrice has been underestimating it. I have to do something but I don't know what."

Aunt Dot wagged her finger. "You know what I've been sensing some darkness for a while." She pulled Yolanda. "Come with me to the back."

They went past the curtains to the back room. On the floor was a large veve painted in white. Yolanda walked through with her eyes wide. "Woah I never been back here."

"I know because I don't let people back here. It's sacred." Aunt Dot pointed to the floor. "Sit child."

Yolanda did as told and sat across from Aunt Dot, who

reached in a satchel and scattered dust around the circle. "What are we doing?"

Aunt Dot lit candles. "We must reach out to our ancestors and the divine spirits for answers. They shall reveal truth to us." Then Aunt Dot sat in front of her. "Take my hand beloved."

Yolanda took her hand.

"Mothers, daughters, uncles and fathers. Guiding spirits, we call out to you. Come to us in the night. Come to us in this hour. We seek truth. We require your divine power." Aunt Dot said, with the words crackling like electricity as it fell off her lips. Aunt Dot shook Yolanda's hand. "Say it with me."

"Mothers, daughters, uncles and fathers. Guiding spirits, we call out to you. Come to us in the night. Come to us in this hour. We seek truth. We require your divine power." They chanted together until a stirring presence rippled the air around them. Stars exploded between the two of them with so much force their hands tremble.

All of the walls in the room folded. Then suddenly both of their spirits soar out of their bodies, and ascend amongst swirling, twinkling stars. Yolanda felt as though she was caught in a whirlwind until they arrive at a field, where they saw him.

Papa Samedi.

"It's him," Yolanda murmured. "Papa Samedi."

Papa Samedi watched from a distance as the dog chased Makayla. Then her turned his head. Slowly and menacingly.

Both Yolanda and Aunt Dot gasped.

Suddenly they were thrusted back to the candle shop. Both of them looked around the back room, scared and out of breath. A red fog swirled around them, and Yolanda quivered in fear. A red glow covered Aunt Dot and she spoke. "Silly witches. You will only see what I want you to see.

Know what I want you to know." He spoke through Aunt Dot.

Yolanda stood up, scared. She backed up. "Get out of her!" she shouted.

Aunt Dot laughed. She stood and smiled menacingly. "Pretty soon I will have you too Yolanda. You were always the weakest weren't you?"

"No," Yolanda murmured.

"A power in you that you can't even master. I will rip it from you."

"No!"

Somewhere deep inside Yolanda rose a strength, one she didn't knew existed. She thrusted her hands, "Get out of her!" she shouted.

Blinding light exploded between them and sent the both of them spiraling. A sharp pain ran through Yolanda when she opened her eyes. There was silence in the room until she heard a crazy girl screaming.

It took a long while to realize that crazy girl was her. She was looking at her aunt in horror. Aunt Dot laid crumbled on the floor with head was split wide open. Yolanda could not believe this. Blood splattered everywhere. Then she ran a hand across her face. It was on her. She had Aunt Dot's blood on her. There was no need to check a pulse.

Aunt Dot was dead.

Dead as a doorknob.

Yolanda stood there paralyzed with fear and blinded by disbelief. Her throat tightened. She couldn't breathe. It was if all of the oxygen got sucked out of the room. Her bright eyes refused to register what they were seeing. Seconds later her screams began again. Aunt Dot was gone and nothing will ever by the same. Silky red shadows slipped into the room like fingers reaching out. Then she heard Papa Samedi's dark laugh rumbling around the room.

"Pretty soon I will be coming for you too, cherie."

She ran out of the shop, not calling the police, and not looking back.

Yolanda ran for her life.

~

*F*aster Makayla ran but Mama Brigitte's muzzle remained close on her feet. Makayla grew slower as she continued, she struggled to breathe, and began panting. Makayla was looking back to see how far Mama Brigitte was from her, when she felt a crushing blow pummel her off her feet. Savage breath blew on the back of her neck like the sigh of a great furnace, and Makayla turned. Out of the Shadows Papa Samedi appeared. Mama Brigitte bit into Makayla's leg and snatched her like a doll.

"Makayla!" Patrice called as she rounded the path.

When Patrice arrived, the demon had Makayla in his arms. And then with a menacing smile he and Makayla disappeared in the shadows. The Rottweiler came snarling behind her and Patrice tossed fire at the hound. It ran off into the woods, whimpering. Patrice drew in a shuddering breath as she watched the dog run away.

Before her eyes they vanished, and it took Patrice a long time to believe what she just witnessed. She sunk to her knees, as the world collapsed, and a massive weight of emotion crushed her soul. She felt as if an elephant had stomped on her chest, it was a pain that was unbearable. She had failed. Patrice had failed to protect her sister. Now she was officially scared, so scared she didn't want to admit it to herself. It was the kind of fear that could drive you insane, and make you choose death rather than to suffer the dread haunting you. While thunder clashed and rain fell, she remained there on her knees. Sunken in her defeat.

32

THE STORM COMETH

*A*mina cursed to herself as she stood on the edge of the W hotel rooftop. She looked out to the lights of the city like a lioness standing at the top of Pride Rock. As she looked out over the Atlanta horizon, the shiny pinpoint top of the Westin to her left, the Ferris wheel at Centennial Park on her right, and bright lights of the Coca Cola building center, she manifested her inner turmoil. When she reached out her hands, lightning came down over the distance.

In her mind she pictured Patrice's face. Fury filled her and the surrounding wind stirred, dark clouds blocked the moonlight and swelled with rain. When Amina cried the clouds unleashed rain onto the city. Amina was full of emotions. She was sad. Angry. Pissed. And most of all she felt stupid. Her web of lies had finally unraveled. Of all the selfish and dumb things she had ever done in the past, this had to have been the worst. She had fooled herself into thinking she could con her way out of her deal with the demon. Her motto was if they give you an inch.... snatch a

266

yard. But this was one deal she couldn't break or worm her way out of.

The rain came down hard. Cold wallops of water, pelted her head, and Amina grabbed at her braids. They felt spongy as they absorbed the rain. She was getting soaked. She wiped her eyes, as lightning fell sharp, and icy winds viciously whipping her leather jacket around, her hair grimly floating out from her body in a shocking electric charge. With her head thrown back she screamed, and allowed the storm within her, to release more rain on the city.

The demon had fulfilled his end of the bargain. Amina's powers had returned by tenfold. She let out another roaring shout before breaking down into tears. She exhaled and spoke peace to the storm. As commanded, the wind and rain subsided. And there was not a dark cloud in sight.

Once satisfied with her release of emotions, Amina turned to go back to her hotel room. She knew inside that the best thing she could do was what she had always done. Run away. Now more than ever, all she wanted to do was get as far away from Atlanta as she possibly could. Then she remembered all of her clothes still at the house. For a second she thought of going back, or maybe getting Makayla to meet her with her stuff. But what was the use? None of them probably wanted to talk to her, anyway. When she reached for the door to go back down to the hotel, a pain throbbed in her back slamming her on the ground. Amina looked up to dark eyes looming over her.

"Where you headed, mon ami?" he said as his lips curled into a smile with the rest of his face cloaked in the shadow. Papa Samedi walked towards her. "You wouldn't be thinking about running, now will you?"

Amina backed away, "How the hell did you find me?"

Papa Samedi grinned, "You can't escape from me. I own your soul, cher."

Amina pursed her lips, "Who said I was running?" She reached her hand back to call lightning.

But before she could attack the demon, he motioned his hand and enacted his dark hold over her. She clenched her belly on the ground. Papa Samedi pulled her within his clutches and disappeared into the shadows.

~

*A*t the sound of the door slamming shut, Yolanda popped up off the couch. "Patrice where is Makayla?"

Patrice walked past her, shoulder slumped and chest heavy. "She's gone. The demon took her."

"He took her?" Yolanda gasped. "What do you mean he took her?"

Patrice turned to her sister. Her eyes were broken and sullen. "Papa Samedi was at the house when I got there. Another demon was with him. And they took her." She said with her lips trembling. Patrice was so numb she didn't even notice the blood on Yolanda's face.

Yolanda grabbed her. "Patrice, Aunt Dot is dead. He ki….he killed her."

Patrice closed her eyes. Tears fell down but she didn't move.

Yolanda bit her fingers. "So what do we do? I know this is bad but what can we do?"

Patrice was silent. Her eyes still closed.

"I know you have a plan. We can go get Amina. Rescue

Makayla and the four of us can bring Aunt Dot back right? It might be hard but we can do anything together right?" Yolanda shook Patrice again. "Right?"

A tortured expression entered her eyes and a defeated spirit shrunk her shoulders. With no other words, Patrice walked past her sister and trotted up the stairs.

Yolanda held her hand at her mouth as if to keep herself from crying. She watched her sister march up the stairs and into her room. Her door closed with a loud bam. *This is terrible*, Yolanda thought. She'd never seen her sister so defeated, even after working two jobs while going to grad school, Patrice always had a tenacious spirit. And the woman who marched up the stairs in defeat, was not the sister she knew.

Yolanda took one step forward to follow her, and a vision slammed into her head. She was in a graveyard brimming with people dressed in white. Blood of a goat was being poured on an altar. Candles of all sizes lit. Gold and fruit was placed in bowls to be offered to the Loa gods. Then she saw her sisters. Both Amina & Makayla were trapped inside veve circles, she was there with them, in the graveyard. Yolanda walked closer. Both of their eyes rolled back as drums banged and the marked ones in white danced. She kneeled near Amina, then felt darkness loom over her. Yolanda stiffened as fear rose in her chest. She looked up, and Papa Samedi strangled her throat.

"I can sense your presence witch!" He growled in a sinister voice.

Yolanda screamed as she stared right into the eyes of terror. And then she came out of the vision. Her head spun, as she struggled to make sense of it all. The demon had grown more powerful than they had figured. This had been the second time he detected her presence. How were they going to defeat an enemy who is always a step ahead?

"Sheesh, this just got real!"

It was down to Yolanda. Patrice was not herself. She had to come up with a way to save her sisters, but she had no clue on how she would bring Patrice back around or tell her about the rest of the vision. Yolanda had to figure something out. Fast. Because they would be next if she didn't.

~

*U*pstairs, Patrice clung to her pillow. Brokenness was all that could describe her spirit. Normally she was always the fearless sister, always in control, always leading the way. She was the one who raised them. But this pain… this despair struck her like a sword in the gut. And she couldn't pull it out. She hadn't felt this helpless since Hurricane Katrina. When her mother conjured the spirit and caused the devastation of the hurricane.

Patrice could remember it like it was yesterday.

She and her grandmother had just gotten back from grocery shopping when they walked in to Yolanda and Amina sitting on the couch tense, with two men dressed in black overlooking them.

"Girls, I hope you're ready. I'm going to make my world famous jambalaya-" Gran said before pausing at the scene in the living room. She looked at Yolanda who sat on the couch scared stiff, then peered to the grim men who loomed over them.

Her voice remained sweet southern honey. "Well I don't recall inviting over company. Who might you two gentlemen be?"

One of the grim men, the darker of the two said, "We are friends of your daughter."

Gran chuckled, "Friends you say?" She echoed with a raised brow. "I know my daughter has a taste for bad men. What I didn't know was that she liked hanging with demons."

Patrice gulped as she whirled from around the corner of the kitchen, dropping off the grocery bags on the corner, and taking her grandmother's side.

From the moment she saw the darkness in their eyes, Gran could sense the evil dripping off of the two men. She could also smell them a mile away. A pungent scent of burning sulfur, it was one of the gifts of being Mother Phoenix, the ear to the spirits. After Gran exposed them, the two men armed themselves, dark energy coiled into their hands, ready to attack.

Patrice stepped past Gran, "Gran what are they doing here?"

Gran held her granddaughter back, "Now, now Peaches...settle down. We don't want to be rude to our guests. Everything is alright, sugar." She said with a smile before looking down to her younger granddaughters. A teenage Amina, and nine-year-old Yolanda. "You girls alright? Did they harm you?" She asked as she whipped her shawl across her shoulder

Amina shook her head as Yolanda began to whimper.

"It's okay sugar. Everything's gonna be sweet. Gran will make sure of that." To the demons overlooking them she said, "Now listen here and hear me good. I don't allow any demons or bad spirits in my home. I don't know why my daughter summoned you but you best be on your way."

"She summoned us because her time is now you old witch!" The lighter shouted before both aimed and tossed the dark energy towards Gram.

With a mere wave of her hand, Gran deflected the attack. And with a swift slicing motion through the air, the heads of the both demons came rolling off. Both demons burned to ash and nothingness, screaming as they disappeared into thin air.

Immediately Gran rushed to her granddaughters' sides. She pulled the crying Yolanda in her arms first. "You girls alright?"

"I was so scared." Yolanda said between sobs.

Patrice was pissed. Years of her mother's antics made her ask, "Grandma why is our mom back in town?"

Gran looked over, concern written on her face. "I don't know sugar, but it seems like she's up to no good."

"She's downstairs with a bunch of those bad guys," Amina spoke up. "They are doing some kind of ritual."

"Oh lord," Gran groaned. She turned to Amina, "Take your sister, go upstairs and lock yourself in the room with the baby." She looked backward, "Peaches you too."

Patrice shook her head. "No. If my mother is here, I want to talk to her."

Gran knew there was no reason to argue with her. Peaches was twenty-two and had already accepted the nasty truth concerning their mother. "Very well let's see what this mess is about."

They trekked downstairs to hear chanting over the sound of drums. An altar had been erected in blood and bones, adorned with various animal carcasses and oil still dripping wet. There were at least a dozen men dressed in black with Patrice's mother, Ruby, in the center. She was dressed in black as well. Her hair sleek and skin radiant. She had almost looked as good as Peaches remembered when she was a child.

Gran screamed as she saw the body laying at the foot of the stairs, "Pete get up," She whimpered as she held the man with coffee brown skin and peppered hair in her arms.

"Uncle Pete!" Patrice cried.

While Gran held Pete in her arms, Patrice took notice of the other bodies in the room. Most of their family, around a dozen or so of the matriarchs laid dead in the basement. They had been slaughtered, brutally.

Ruby walked over to the foot of the stairs where Gran was on her knees as she cradled her dead son. "Hello mom, it's nice to see you. And Patrice my lovely daughter, it's nice to see you too."

Gran cut her eyes towards her daughter. "Ruby what the hell are you up to now? What is this wickedness? Why would you kill your own brothers and family?" She asked with her voice full of rage and pain.

Ruby stood defiantly and said, "This is not wickedness mother... I have simply decided to step into power."

Gran cast a sidelong glance at her, " Tuh. It's bad enough... two years ago you dropped a baby on my doorstep. Now this?" she asked her voice dripping with disgust. "What kind of power cher? What do you want that would make you kill your family? " Gran asked with despair.

"Power of the Phoenix..... My birthright. What belongs to me," Ruby said with her voice rising to a rebellious scream.

"Belongs to you? The title of Mother Phoenix is not just given, it's a duty and that you have to earn."

A handsome man appeared by Ruby's side "Royal blood runs through her veins," He was about six feet tall, dark chocolate skin, bald head and a long beard.

Gran shook her head, "My wicked.... wicked daughter. You done fell in love with a demon. Tell me something?" She waited a beat as she took a step closer. "What have I ever done to you for you to behave this way? Where did I go wrong? For you to open your legs to married men, sleep all around like a harlot and get addicted to dark magic."

Tears and rage welled into Ruby's eyes as her face twisted. "You hated me! You always hated me you old bitch. You treated me like I was something to deal with, you were everyone's mother but mine. Everything came second to the tribe, including me. Your daughter!" Ruby gave them her back as she turned to the shaman. "And now I take what's mine," She shouted before chanting.

The house shook. Gran turned to Peaches. "Go upstairs and get your sisters now! And bring me my purse!"

"But Gran." Patrice protested.

"Don't back talk me! Go now!"

Patrice dashed upstairs even though she could hear crashes and sounds of struggle in the basement.

"Come on then, with the lot of you!" Gran yelled as Patrice ran up the stairs.

Up the stairs, and on the first door of the right, she opened it up with the wave of her hand. Inside Amina was holding baby Makayla as Yolanda stood by the door still in tears.

"Let's go! We have to get out of here?"

"But Gran told us to stay in here," Amina sassed back as she rocked baby Makayla. A loud explosion erupted from downstairs. Thunder clashed and the emergency alarm siren sounded off in the city.

"What.... what's going on?" Yolanda cried.

"Grab the baby bag and let's go!" Patrice ordered. Behind her, Amina came with Makayla and grabbed Yolanda's arms.

Strong winds picked up, and the house trembled as all the sisters stampede down the stairs. Patrice spotted her grandmother's purse on the counter. Swiftly she ran over and grabbed it. She turned back towards her sisters, "Meet me outside. Get out of here!"

"But what about mom and Gran?" Amina asked.

"I will get them. Just go!" Patrice shouted.

Patrice rushed back down to the basement, her foot creaking the old boards with each step. When she came downstairs, she saw no signs of the demons. There was only her mother and grandmother.

Flames crowned Ruby's head as she stumbled about the room. "I can't control it..... I can't control it!"

"Don't worry I'm here. I'll get it out of you." Gran said as she held her hand.

With tears streaming down her face, Ruby fell to the floor crying in agonizing pain, and Gran fell by her side.

"Gran what's wrong with her?" Patrice asked.

"The spirit is too much for her. Its' cooking her from the inside out." She grabbed Patrice's hand, "Listen to me Peaches. I need you to be strong for your sisters. You are a very special girl. I knew it ever since I laid eyes on you. You will lead our people to greatness. And I know it, sugar. No matter what happens, just know you'll never be alone. I'll be with you forever, showing you the way, loving you all, and giving you my strength when you need it."

Patrice looked at her as if she was crazy. "Grandma .... what do you mean?"

*G*ran pulled out a powder from her bag, blew into Patrice's face, chanted and clapped.

Next thing Patrice knew she and her sisters were out on the street, and in the middle of hell. Wind and rain surged all around as the streets flooded. "Wait!" Patrice called as she went to step back to the house but instantly the whole house erupted into flames. Darkness took over the clouds as the winds grew stronger. An energy released that powered the storm, and everything around her became a blur, as cars flew, water crashed into the streets, and parts

*of houses ripped away. Patrice fell to her knees as the strong wind,
practically dragged her down the street.*

That despair, that helplessness was the emotion she felt as
she currently laid on the bed sleep.

"I can't do this alone...." Patrice declared to herself. And she
cried. She cried like she never had before. She cried for all the
family she lost. For all the hardship she endured. For her lost
innocence and twenty-two year old peaches, who had to grew
up quickly.

Out of nowhere, she heard a small still voice say. "You're
not alone."

Patrice stood up and peered over her shoulder. And as she
matched the face to the voice, she became speechless.

33

NOT ALONE

Standing a few inches from Patrice was her Gran. She was there not as a ghost or apparition, but as brown flesh bathed in white lights. Patrice thought the vision in front of her was a dream but it was all too real, her hair popped to perfection, the royal cheekbones, and the scent of White Diamonds danced into her nostrils.

"Gran is that you?" Patrice asked on a shallow breath.

Gran strolled to her bedside, "What do you think, sugar?" she asked as the swarming lights dimmed.

Immediately Patrice stood up and wrapped her arms around her. She was shocked to discover a warm, firm body. It was her grandmother, and she was there for real. Patrice glanced at her, "I don't know what to say. I have so many things I need to say."

Gran grinned, "Well you know cher, that death is only the beginning. And of course I am Mother Phoenix. Well at least I was." She said as she took Patrice's hands. "It is your time now Peaches. It's okay to be down but eventually you've got to get up. Ya hear me? I've been watching over you Peaches, and you've done a real fine job of taking care of your sisters. A real fine job. Now it's time for you to step into your destiny, sugar. Gather your sisters. Conjure the spirit and send that demon packing. When the time comes you must declare yourself Queen. Declare yourself as the lead priestess and the Phoenix will come to you."

Patrice sobbed, "I can't."

Gran's upper lip stiffened. "Why not?"

Patrice shook her head. Disdain filled her at the thought of her treacherous sister. "Amina has done some unspeakable things. She has gone too far this time. I don't know if I can forgive her. Aunt Dot is dead. Papa Samedi has Makayla and....I just can't."

Gran sat down on the edge of the bed and motioned for Patrice to scoot beside her. "You see this?" She said as she balled her fist. "You curl this fist and you can knock out anything. You girls have to stick together. I don't care what she did. That is your sister. You have to love her and help her do better." Gran said with a smile as she turned to look away. "My only regret in my life was that I pushed your mother away, instead of giving her the love and help she needed." She turned back to Patrice and looked her dead smack in the eyes. "Don't make that same mistake. You need to pull her in closer instead of pushing her away."

Gran continued, "As far as black magic goes. Cher ain't nothing wrong with a little gris gris. Sometimes you have to lose yourself in the darkness to find yourself in light. That's what being Mother Phoenix is about. High priestess. You have to be willing to sacrifice. That's what true love is, it's sacrifice.

You also have to possess the discipline to utilize both light and dark magic. As well as have the tenacity to lead."

Patrice could feel the emotion in her throat before the tears swelled in her eyes. "But how am I going to do all this?"

Gran being both regal and resilient, stood up. "You have to be strong." She said the words simply as if it was something as easy as ABC. She walked to the furthest corner of the room before looking over her shoulder. "Us black women…. especially the Lawson women. We have been given the strength to move the heavens and the earth. Remember that."

Before Patrice's lips could utter another word, her grandmother vanished. She was gone just as if she was never there and she left Patrice with her strength, with that strength, Patrice knew she could carry on.

*T*here was a loud bam on the door and Yolanda hopped up from the couch again, she opened it up to see Lorenzo peeking from the other side.

"Everything alright? I've been calling Patrice ever since I left."

"No it's not alright," Yolanda said shaking her head. "Everything is very… very bad. Come in."

Lorenzo stepped inside, his face stern and serious. "What's going on?" he asked as Yolanda closed the door behind him.

"He killed our aunt." Yolanda said as she looked away.

Lorenzo frowned. "Who?"

Yolanda could feel tears brewing behind her eyes again. "Aunt Dot," She hiccuped. Finally she looked at him. "I was there."

Lorenzo took a step forward and placed a hand on her shoulder. "Are you alright?"

Yolanda noded. "I'm fine. But that's not it."

Lorenzo rubbed his temple. "What else?"

"It's Makayla," Yolanda said as she took a deep breath. Her chest was heavy from the weight of the emotions she was feeling, just thinking about her baby sister in the hands of the demon. "She's gone. Papa Samedi took her."

"Gone?" Lorenzo shouted. "How did he take her?" he asked as he brushed past the doorway.

"She snuck out of the house to go to a party. He attacked her and a bunch of other kids." Yolanda started pacing the floor with the sleeved arms of her oversized sweatshirt stretched across her head. "I don't know what the hell to do. Makayla's gone. Amina's gone. And Patrice is not even talking to me right now, so she might as well be gone too."

Just when Yolanda was close to losing it, she heard footsteps trail down the stairway. She glanced over her shoulder to see her sister.

"We are going to fight." Patrice boldly stated as she stomped down the last step.

"I'm down for that…. but all I want to know is how?" Yolanda asked in a half whimper half defeated tone. "It's only two of us. And we have no way to find them."

"Three," Lorenzo said as he spoke. "I'm down for the cause. That's if you will have me?" he asked as he looked over to Patrice.

"Three," Patrice repeated as she nodded and turned back to Yolanda.

Yolanda turned back to her sister, "So how are we going to find them?"

"You," Patrice proclaimed.

"Me?" Yolanda questioned as she pointed to herself.

"Yes. I don't see no other powerful seer here."

Yolanda froze in terror. " Oh my god you can't be serious. Don't do this to me Peaches…. I can't. He's already sensed me twice."

Patrice grabbed her by the hand, "Don't say that. Yes, you can. We don't have anybody else. You were born to this, the spirits choose you. All this time you've doubted yourself. Holding back. Letting me hold you back. Now there is no one holding you back. Believe in yourself, because I believe in you."

Yolanda stared at her sister. She was full. Full of fear. Full of worry. But now full of confidence. As she tried to sort through all of those feelings, there was a certain confidence that washed over her. When she faced forward her eyes rolled back and a white haze glazed over them. She could see Makayla and Amina. Yolanda knew where to find her sisters.

34

BONES & ASHES

*M*akayla woke to the pungent smell of sulfur in her nose, and a sharp throbbing pain near the front of her skull. She was lying on her stomach, her cheek pressed against the ground. Slowly she raised her head. Her mind drifted fuzzily, trying to figure out where she was, blinking twice, she saw feet kicking up dust. Insects called all around her. She was outside and laying on the ground as far as she could tell. Suddenly there was a loud beating. It was the sound of drums. She got up, but it seemed the more she rose, the more everything hurt.

It took her awhile but Makayla could identify her surroundings, she was in a graveyard, filled with people dressed in white. "Help!" she moaned.

She started her lips to mouth for help again, but then she watched them go back-and-forth lighting candles and adorning an altar. She looked down to her foot and noticed she was standing on top of a veve she had never seen before, and entrapped in a circle. Makayla lifted her foot to step across, and was knocked back on her behind, like a fly zapped by a fly trap. Again she stood up, but this time gingerly. As she regained balance, she felt a cold, ominous presence loom over her. Makayla knew it was him, the demon, and so she kept looking down.

Papa Samedi grinned, "Foolish gal. This here veve is to keep you in there forever.... well at least until the end of the ritual."

"Ritual?" Makayla echoed. She turned around and stared into the eyes of death itself. Her lips trembled, "What are you going to do?"

Papa Samedi's face curled into a diabolical sneer, "Why my cherie, I plan on draining you. I'll use your essence to invoke the spirit of the Phoenix and I will possess its power."

Makayla nodded, "And then_"

"And then what?"

"You can't tell me you want a massive amount of power if you don't want to take over the world or something."

Papa Samedi waved his hand to show how many souls he had under his will. "Look around child. I plan on raising an army of the dead. And with each person they kill... I gain another soul and another willing body to be a part of my army."

"That sounds like as good as any evil plan goes," Amina said as she folded her arms.

Papa Samedi turned towards Amina. "And I sure couldn't have done any of this without you." He threw his head back, and cackled menacingly as he toyed with her. "Lawd have mercy I sho' have met my share of bad witches, but never have I met a witch willing to sell her own sisters down the bayou for her own hide." Again he laughed and looked over at Makayla.

Once he saw his seed of discord had taken root he walked away towards Mama Brigitte.

Makayla sunk back down to her knees and glanced over to her sister. "So it's all true?" she asked through tight teeth.

Amina softened, took an embarrassing breath, and shook her head. "I'm sorry," she said her voice humble and true, stripped of its normal bravado. "I was desperate. For the first time in my life, I was truly scared and didn't know what the fuck to do." She looked over to Makayla, seeking sympathy. "I fucked up."

"No, I was stupid," Makayla said as she shook her head. "You know I always take up for you, Amina. When everyone else talks bad about you, or make you seem like the worst of us, I defended you, because I loved you, because you were my sister. Damn Amina! I don't know our mother. You, Peaches, and Yolanda are all I have. How could you do this to us?" she growled as tears wet her cheek.

Amina sat up and straightened herself. "Don't worry, I can fix this. We will get out of this. Do you hear me?" Amina boasted through pounding fists.

Mama Brigitte rounded the corner with her hands wrapped around a flapping chicken. "You shouldn't lie like that mama," she sassed as she slashed the chicken's neck and whipped Amina's face with blood. It was warm as it splashed on Amina's face, she raked her eyes, and spat a salty metallic on the ground. Mama Brigitte did the same to Makayla, and commanded all the disciples who gathered for the ritual to dance.

"It's time," Papa Samedi said. From his waist he pulled out a small curved knife. He went to Makayla and yanked her hand. She screamed and tried to pull herself away but the demon had a cold unyielding grip. With the small knife he slashed the inside of her palm.

"Get the hell away from my sister!" Amina shouted as she punched at the barrier.

Papa Samedi was silent as he held on to Makayla's hand. One disciple, an older lady with many wrinkles and grey eyes, came with a small bowl. Papa Samedi squeezed Makayla's hand over the bowl and allowed the blood to drip down. Once the blood spilled into the bowl, he tossed Makayla to the side like a used towel.

Then he went over to Amina, who by this time began to punch and kick at the barrier that trapped her inside the veve. "Don't even think about it. You better get back!" she shouted, half cocky yet half afraid.

With a raised hand Papa Samedi rendered her limbs stiff, as she levitated in front of him. Amina felt powerless. She tried to move, but her body just wouldn't do anything her mind was telling it to do. Then her right hand raised against her will, turning over to her right palm. Swiftly he sliced her hand and her blood was added to the mix.

Mama Brigitte took the bowl from the disciple holding it and anointed Papa Samedi's forehead, "Blood is power. Blood is of the spirit. The spirit is the Phoenix." She said as Papa Samedi grinned, to which she returned the favor. "What about the other sisters?" Mama Brigitte posed. "Do you think they will come?"

The smile disappeared from his face. Though he had grown more powerful, the Lawson sisters still threatened him, especially Patrice. "I know they will, that's why we will do much more than just invoking the spirit. We need to conjure something nasty. As Amina lives and grows more powerful, I do as well through our pact. I can resurrect this whole graveyard if I want to, but that will not be enough for these sisters." He said as he turned around and walked to the mausoleum. Near the mausoleum was an altar adorned with candles, herbs, and offerings.

The gate cracked with a loud squeak as he peeled it back before going inside. When he came back out, In the palm of his hand he carried a large horned skull. Some disciples gasped and fell to their knees as he held the skull with horns extending out to his shoulders.

Mama Brigitte flashed a wicked smile. "A Behemoth. That's defiantly nasty."

Fear paralyzed Makayla as she stared at the skull and watched the reaction between the two demons. She had no clue what a Behemoth was, but she knew she was about to find out. Makayla curled herself into a ball as the maddening thump of the drums intensified so did her fear.

~

*P*atrice stood over Yolanda's shoulder. "Do you see her?" she asked before biting her nails, her nerves were shot, She had to rescue her baby sister and she would not rest until Makayla was home. Her mind raced to all the bad things that could happen as they stood at home, clueless. Papa Samedi could torture her. She could be scared. He could use black magic to turn her into another one of his zombies. Then the worst scenario of all, came to the forefront of her mind. Makayla could be dead. And that thought brought a shudder down Patrice's spine that made her eyes close. "Find her.... you can do this." Patrice cheered.

Yolanda was unresponsive. Her hands were out almost as if she was seeing though Makayla and reaching out in the environment.

"Do you see her?" Patrice asked again, louder.

"It's dark and kind of blurry. But I think I can see around her. Patrice it's a lot of people here. Candles are everywhere." Yolanda said in a half sure whisper.

Patrice's eyes grew large. "Can they help her? Are they trying to hurt her?"

Yolanda shook her head, "No, it looks like they are doing a ritual."

Lorenzo turned to Patrice, "Ritual?"

Yolanda gasped as her pupils returned to their normal color. "He has Amina too. Both of them are trapped in some sort of barrier. And that's not it... I think.... from what I sense... they are invoking the spirit."

Yolanda's words hit Patrice with a thud as her eyes widened and her mouth fell agape. Patrice went to the kitchen table and grabbed vials of hot foot powder. "Come on we have to go get them."

Lorenzo grabbed her hand, "Wait, where are you going?"

Patrice jerked back, "I don't know. But I'm going to find my sisters."

"Listen to me," Lorenzo rationed in a calm voice. "I know how bad you want to find your sisters. Trust me, I do. But we can't just go there without a game plan."

"We have one," Patrice said as she looked at him right in the eyes. "We are going to rescue my sisters or die trying. That's it. It's simple," she declared almost begging him to tell her something else.

Lorenzo fell silent as Patrice's gaze hardened on him.

Yolanda stood between the two with the Legacy clasped between her hands. "We have to conjure the spirit Patrice…. It's the only way," she muttered.

Patrice waited a beat. "How do we buy the time to do the ritual, while he attacks us?"

Lorenzo's eyes gleamed at the thought of action. "I can hold them off," He suggested.

Patrice turned to him, "In that first vision Yolanda had, she said she saw hundreds of zombies. A whole horde. I wouldn't dare put you in that danger."

Lorenzo flexed. "It's all good. I'm a Were baby. We don't get tired." he spoke in a rough bravado.

Yolanda was struck with sudden inspiration. She slammed the book on the table with a loud thud, and flipped pages. "I think I know how to buy us time. Something I saw in the vision. It was a light I couldn't identify. But I think it's this…. a shield. It could protect us."

Patrice looked down at the book, and raised a brow. "Do you think you can conjure it?"

"Well… um… yeah. I think so, I'm sure I can." Yolanda said in a reluctant tone.

Patrice turned to the door with no hesitation, "C'mon then, let's roll out." She ordered. Yolanda and Lorenzo marched right behind her to face the inevitable to save their sisters.

35

FORMATION

atrice drove in silence. Lorenzo sat beside her in
the front, every now and then he looked over at
her to gauge her mood. Lorenzo had to admire Patrice's
resolve in the face of such overwhelming despair; most women
would have succumbed to either hopelessness or folly, but
Patrice wasn't like most women. She was driven further by
despair.

Patrice was gripping the steering wheel tensely as she navi-
gated the long dusty back road leading to the unknown.
Yolanda, had led them to a narrow snaking road in the woods,
far away from the city, in an area of town long forgotten. A
rolling fog covering the road made her visibility limited. They
were all trying desperately to find her sisters, and she was a
mixed bag of emotions. Patrice felt like she dropped the ball.
She should've went after Papa Samedi herself and nip this all in
the bud. There was nothing she could do to change the past, so
she had to soldier on in the name of love. Though she was
unyielding in her resolve to find her sisters, she was also still

afraid of this demon. Fear infected every fiber of her being. It made her hands tremble, so tighter and tighter she gripped the steering wheel. Even though she was afraid, there was still a spirit of tenacity that made her press on. It was her grand-mother's strength. Patrice could feel her spirit and that made her confident. Just up ahead of the long curling road she could see an opening.

"Zombie hunting will be hard to top on our next date." Lorenzo said, breaking the silence.

Patrice grinned, "I think so. But I'm a simple girl. A Kevin Hart movie is good enough for me."

Lorenzo's face tightened. "Are you scared?"

"Yes," she responded with a solemn look on her face.

"Over there!" Yolanda pointed from the back seat. Patrice rolled the car to a stop when she could see a graveyard just beyond a thicket of trees.

Lorenzo narrowed his eyes and his pupils became golden, "I can detect multiple signatures of body heat over there with in his feral vision. Something is definitely going on." Lorenzo's feral eyesight cut a golden swath in the darkness beyond the grove of oak trees, as he scanned the area.

Patrice became dazed as she studied his golden cat like eyes. "We are in the right place then," she concluded. Patrice pulled up sharply in the graveyard at the end of the road, turning her headlights off, as she parked under a towering oak tree.

She looked back to Yolanda, "Are you ready for this?" she asked.

"No turning back now," Yolanda declared. "We have to save our sisters. Let's bring them back."

Patrice turned to Lorenzo, "How about you? Again... you don't have to do this?"

Lorenzo gave a head nod of approval. "Didn't I tell you I will always protect you? I got your back."

Patrice turned the car off, with her hands shaking as she took out the keys. Be strong she could hear her grandmother say. And she took deep breaths to subside the rising panic in her heart. All together they got out the car and closed their doors with soft taps. Outside a full moon hung overhead, and the night air was stone cold. It was the kind of cold that stung your face and made you blow breath in your hands. Yolanda zipped her light track jacket while Patrice rubbed her hands. Night creatures stirred as they skirted along the edge of the cemetery gate. Flares from a fire grew brighter and more visible in the dense cover of the fog. The closer they crept, they took notice to an ungodly smell permeating the graveyard. It was the stench of sulfur and incense; black magic was being worked.

Lorenzo led the pack as Patrice followed behind, armed with a flashlight. As Yolanda followed her sister, her dread intensified with every step. Together they were a powerful team, Patrice could throw fire, Lorenzo could turn into a ferocious Were-panther and she herself was one with the spirits. Still as they stepped into thickets of overgrown grass and as insects of the night hummed all around them, she couldn't help but to be afraid. She reached in her purse and took hold of multiple vials of the hot foot powder. It was comforting to know she had means of protecting herself.

Lorenzo switched to his feral eyesight again and his vision became clear in the dark. "I can see them," he murmured as he motioned for Patrice and Yolanda to come to his location.

"There is at least a dozen people. I spot the demon, your sisters, and some funky looking witchdoctor. It looks like they are just starting." Lorenzo said with his face raised to the cold, feral eyes gleaming.

Patrice listened, and she could hear the chanting from across the field. She turned to Yolanda, "They are invoking the spirit," she declared, her voice barely audible.

"We have to stop them," Yolanda exclaimed.

Forward they marched into overgrown grass and broken tree branches. The grass, thigh high and still wet from the night's rain, soaked their pants. Grasshoppers and other insects leapt out of the way as the group trekked deeper, the brighter the fire grew as they stepped closer, and the rhythmic beating of drums intensified. When they made it to the center of the graveyard, they paused as they watched the ritual take place.

Makayla and Amina were trapped on top of Veve circles on opposite sides of the altar. One figure, an older woman, with as much wrinkles on her brown skin as rings inside of a towering tree trunk, chanting. She chanted with her arms raised and her head turned up towards the sky, another one of the smaller women held a headless chicken over a brass bowl, laughing as life poured out.

As the chanting grew louder, the drums became more robust and infectious. Once the ritual went into full swing, a spirit swept over them and the people danced around the fire in a frenzy.

Yolanda covered her mouth as she looked into the eyes of one of the older men, toothless and yelling as his eyes rolled to the back of his head. She fell to her knees as drums pounded and the tribe continued chanting. There was a heaviness in her chest and strange fog on her senses. The level of black magic in the graveyard was dominating her psyche. She could feel the presence of the Loa.... the ancient voodoo spirits had been awakened, and they were not happy.

Patrice reached for her sister, "Yolanda what is it?"

Yolanda stared past Patrice with her eyes wide, and breath caught in her chest. "You can't see them?"

"See what?"

"The Loa," she said as she struggled back to her feet, casting her gaze around. "They are all around us."

Whirling streams of white mist leapt out of the fire, spirits swirled about, and made blood curdling screams as they whizzed by. Worshippers danced faster around the flames, as they continued to pound their feet, the Loa continued to wake up and possess them.

Patrice turned from the fire and focused on Makayla and Amina, they were trapped side by side in two veve circles. Just like the disciples, their eyes rolled back to a devastating white glow and their bodies twitched as they laid on the ground.

"By broken chains free me. From solid ground mold me. From the depths of the ocean seek me. With wind lift me. By fire consume me. Creator spirit we conjure thee," Papa Samedi chanted with his head cocked back to the sky. His voice rolled across the graveyard like thunder, it was a sound that conjured fear and could shatter the heavens.

Patrice reached into her bag. It was now or never. She tossed the vial with everything she had, the vial hit Papa Samedi square in the chest, thrashing him into the far wall of the mausoleum. Mama Brigitte turned to see where the attack came from.

"Get the hell away from my sisters!" Patrice shouted, her voice as threatening and fierce as the roar of a lioness.

Mama Brigitte raised her staff, "Kill them!" she snarled.

On command, the possessed disciples stopped dancing and turned to them with machetes raised. Wasting no time, Patrice unleashed her telekinetic fury with a wave of her hand, and in the air they scattered like rag dolls, dropping in all different directions.

Papa Samedi popped up to his feet, "I knew you would come. You have to know this will only end in one way."

"Yes. With us sending you back to the spirit realm," Patrice declared.

Papa Samedi's face curled into a snarky grin. "With your heart clenched in my fist!" he shouted as he soared into the air. Thanks to the conjuring of Mama Brigitte's root work, he felt Makayla's and Amina's power surging into him. To the middle of the graveyard he glided, there he stretched out his hands and emerald streams sparked life into the graveyard.

*T*wisting and crawling out of their graves, the dead rose to their feet. The sisters buckled as the ground shook and all around them they heard pounds and moans as the resurrected struggled to free themselves from their graves.

"Peaches what are we going to do?" Yolanda cried.

"Never mind them let's get our sisters," Patrice ordered.

Mama Brigitte disrobed and took a battle stance before them. "You will have to go through me," She declared before shifting into one of her more sinister forms. Mama Brigitte fell on all fours and her bones cracked and changed the structure of her body to a larger shape, around five feet at the shoulders.

Golden fur stretched over her skin, her eyes enlarged and turned primal. Sharp fangs replaced her teeth and from her hands, grew brown claws that raked the ground. Stretching out of her back curled a large and deadly stinger. She had become a fully fleshed feline creature armed with a scorpion stinger, and she hissed as she stalked, daring them to cross the line.

"Go ahead, I got this!" Lorenzo shouted as he ripped open his shirt and shifted into a were-panther. His muscular body twisted, contorted and grew as black fur stretched over his chiseled brown flesh, then he fell on all fours, and let out a guttural roar from his belly. The golden etches on his midnight fur, made his coat look extra sleek and shiny. With his jaws stretched he exposed his deadly teeth, as he shouldered his way in front of the sisters.

Both of the beasts locked eyes and circled each other. Mama Brigitte was the first to swipe at Lorenzo, but the agility of the panther didn't allow her paws to connect. Her jaws curled into a sinister grin as her fangs wet with the appetite for Lorenzo's blood. Lorenzo walked in a tight circle, never taking his eyes off her, he was waiting for the perfect opportunity to strike. But before he could, Mama Brigitte struck as fast as lightning, this time she uses her acid dripping stinger. Lorenzo rolls out of the way with feline agility.

Once he was out of line of fire from the stinger, Lorenzo dove in, burying his powerful jaws into her side. She yelped in pain. Panthers have been known to have the most powerful bite in all the animal kingdom. Enough strength to crush bone easily, and a stronger hold that was more unyielding than a pitbull. Lorenzo ripped into Mama Brigitte's flesh, and with her stinger she stung him. The first sting made him wince, but the second made him lose his grip on her side. Lorenzo shook her in his jaws, and Mama Brigitte cried out as her wound deepened. She stung him again, her stinger moved like lightning, and was hard for Lorenzo to avoid as he held his grip. Lorenzo felt weaker with every sting, with his strength fading, he wailed a primal scream.

As the two beasts continued to battle, Yolanda and Patrice rushed to the aid of their sisters. Yolanda paused as she stood by the barrier of the veve Amina was trapped in. "How do we break this?" she asked turning back to Patrice who stood in front of Makayla.

Patrice reached in her bag, "Salt…. we must purify this circle." she said as she grabbed a box carton of salt. She poured a handful and tossed it into the circle. Once the barrier collapsed, she tossed the carton over to Yolanda who caught it and did the same for Amina. Patrice fell to the ground and scooped Makayla in her arms. Her body was still twitching and her eyes glossed over. She shook her sister, feeling her heart in her throat, "Makayla wake up. Come on! Wake up baby girl!"

Makayla gasped for air as if she had been drowning. Her eyes returned to a normal color, and she came back to her senses. "Oh my god Peaches…. I have never been so scared in my life. I want to get out of here." she cried as she buried her head into her sister's arms.

Patrice cradled Makayla's head as she caressed her shoulder. "I know baby girl. But it's almost over," she reassured. She pulled Makayla to her feet, "Come on get up. Stand up."

"I feel so weak." Makayla responded with a long sigh.

When Amina came to, she turned over and struggled to her feet. "Yolanda…. Patrice," she said looking over at her sisters. "It's about damn time. It's nice to see y'all."

Patrice glanced over, "You too. Can you fight?" she asked.

Amina wiped the dust off her jeans. "No. He was draining us to summon the Phoenix."

"Well you better get ready because they are coming!" Yolanda said, as she focused her eyes through the fog to see the haunting silhouettes of the zombies heading their way.

As they took breaths, readying themselves to fight, the doors to the mausoleum behind them broke open. Out came two zombies wearing civil war outfits. One grabbed Makayla from behind and she screamed before phasing, the zombie clasped his arms and fell through her. Patrice shoved an elbow to its rotting face, when it fell to her feet, she put her heel right through its skull.

The other went toward Yolanda and Amina. He was carrying a rifle with a knife tip. Amina wrestled the gun out of the zombie's slimy decayed hands. Once she had the gun in her possession, she kicked it in the sternum before running the sharp tip through its skull.

"They are coming!" Yolanda warned before throwing the first bottle of hot foot powder. It detonated and burned a first group flanking their left.

Amina got down on her knees and took aim with the rifle. Side by side, the Lawson sisters took their stance. As Amina shot, Patrice and Yolanda hurdled rounds of hot foot bombs at the surrounding zombies, creating a haze of ash as decayed bodies keeled over. A strong odor of death hung in the air. At first it seemed as if their attack was effective, but soon they realized the more zombies they obliterated, the more came back. Closer and closer they were gaining on them. Papa Samedi continued soaring above, cackling at the helplessness of it all. Soon Amina ran out of bullets, and there were no more bottles of hot foot left to throw.

"What are we going to do?" Amina asked as she tossed the rifle to the side. "We can't hold these things off forever. We need to attack the demon."

"Can you conjure a storm?" Patrice asked.

Amina shook her head, "I am still too weak."

Patrice sighed in despair. She looked back up and it was another group of six zombies charging towards them.

"Raging fire, I command you to swallow my enemies!"

With her lips to her hands she blew a wall of fire that engulfed them. Before she could delight in her short lived victory, Lorenzo still in panther form was being tossed over their heads. All sisters ducked, as three hundred pounds of black fur whirled over them, then the panther tumbled until it was back on all fours.

With his head held low, his shoulders blades arched to attack, Lorenzo leapt into the air, shifting into half man half panther form. He fell on Mama Brigitte hard, wrestling her. With his paw like hands, he ripped off her stinger.

Yolanda grabbed Patrice's shoulder, "I think we should head back to the car."

"No. We have to finish the demon here or else he will keep haunting us." Patrice declared as she tossed fire to and fro, protecting her sisters.

Patrice looked around, there were ashes and smoke everywhere. A sea of decapitated and mutilated zombies stretched out before them on the ground, littering the graveyard where they'd fell. But yet the restless zombies kept rising out of graves. Against her own will Patrice had to admit there were too many of them to handle. To continue fighting would be like sticking her hand into a fire ant pile, or wrestling a honeycomb from a swarm of bees. They had to escape if only to fight another day. She had rescued her sisters. That's all that mattered. Now she needed to protect their lives. She turned to the right, "To the car. Go!" she cried as she pulled Makayla along with her.

A charging horde of zombies faced them as they ran to the car. Patrice punched her way through, with the use of her telekinesis, sending brittle bones slamming against the trees every which way. Blood trickled down her nose as she clenched her chest. Patrice could feel her own energy drain after such heavy use of her gifts. Makayla followed stumbling to her side while Yolanda and Amina ran to her right.

Moans called from beyond a thicket of trees on their left. Lorenzo curled further behind the sisters, taking the rear and checking his back to keep the swarming horde away. On his right shoulder three came running from the side, each wielding a weapon. They closed in on the escaping group. Lorenzo spun and swiped his claws across their necks. With one whirling slice, he removed three heads from neck and shoulders. All three of the zombies collapsed as their heads swiveled into the air, and their emaciated bodies crumbled.

For a brief second Patrice looked back and saw that death loomed all around them. Her panic became undeniable. They had to get out of there. Back to the car they ran, stepping through the overgrown grass as they pushed back tree branches and moss.

"Let's speed it up!" Lorenzo yelled. He could hear footsteps gaining behind them.

Floating above, the demon watched them as they tried to escape. In his hands he held the behemoth skull. With his long talons he opened his hand and out came a liquid dark as the foggy moon night. On the skull he marked a veve and chanted.

*Y*olanda stiffened as her psychic senses made her aware that danger was near.

Just before Patrice could hop the ditch to the other side. Yolanda pulled her back, "Wait."

"What is it?" Patrice asked gasping for air.

And just as she asked, Papa Samedi tossed the skull on the ground near the car. The skull shattered into pieces, and those pieces dissolved into the Earth. Where the pieces remained, the earth cracked and then fire consumed the car. Ominous rumbling made the sisters fall back, and within seconds something massive climbed out of the fissure. A low, warning snarl echoed up as the beast climbed further out of the hole, exploding the remains of the car, setting ablaze to the trees nearby, and quaking the woods surrounding.

Amina gasped, "Oh hell to the nah!"

Intense emerald flames rose, and then a beast made of rock and fire, that stood around eight feet tall, stepped out of the curtain of flames. Its eyes were green like two emeralds and its horns both gold and sharp curled out. It had massive shoulders and arms thick as the trunk of small trees. It took two small steps and the weight of its hooves was enough to make its footsteps sound like the stomp of an elephant.

From behind them Lorenzo crept until he stood on his hind feet. "Go!" Lorenzo roared as he pushed the sisters back. With his eyes full of primal rage, Lorenzo charged to combat the Behemoth. Swift and agile, the panther leapt into the air. When he came down to pounce on the monster, brute force met him in the face. The Behemoth backhanded Lorenzo squarely across the face with enough force to send the were-panther airborne, cartwheeling, and splitting a large oak some yards away.

Patrice gagged at the strength of the foe dead set on destroying them. "C'mon let's get out of here," she shouted as she and her sisters took to the woods, knowing there was nowhere to run, and nowhere to escape. But somehow if only by the Phoenix itself, they may survive the night.

36

INTO THE WOODS

*F*urther into the woods they ran to escape the wrath of the Behemoth monster. From behind them, they could hear hooves stomp as it incessantly marched behind. Patrice and Lorenzo lead the pack and fended off the stragglers of the zombie horde while Yolanda, Makayla, and Amina brought up the rear.

"Come on. Keep up!" Patrice pleaded as she wrestled with a zombie who was no longer flesh but mostly bone. With both hands she wrestled the bony creature to toss him into Lorenzo's sharp claws to be dismantled.

Makayla was next to Yolanda and could barely see Patrice and Lorenzo turn the corner a few yards ahead, "Girl, I'm about to die. Where are we going?" Makayla huffed as she gasped for air.

Yolanda came sprinting from behind Makayla, "If you don't run… you will die," she emphasized as she pulled her sister by the shoulder. "C'mon move it missy."

Heavy footsteps cracked twigs and broken tree limbs

behind them. Yolanda turned around and became a deer in headlights. Her brown eyes met the dark solemn circles of the Behemoth's eyes, with his silhouette masked by the cover of trees. As the demon drew nearer, the woods grew colder under the icy moon.

Yolanda was so drawn to the terror of the Behemoth, that she didn't feel slimy hands pull her down to the ground. She hit the back of her head with a sharp thud and let out a scream. She gasped desperately for her breath as the zombie chomped and gnarled at her. It was missing one leg and with the aid of a jagged knife it pulled itself on top of her. Yolanda elbowed her way back, but the zombie was unyielding in fulfilling its command to kill. She looked back and saw no one around. She screamed again and this time so loud that it brought a raw pain to the back of her throat and she could taste sour metallic.

With blood lusty eyes, the zombie forced itself on top of Yolanda. Its elbow pinned her throat as it rose a knife high. Even though she could no longer scream, everything inside Yolanda was calling out for help. Tears swelled her eyes as she tried to fight the weight of the zombie on top of her. The zombie's blade came down swift but before it could connect, Makayla blocked the blow and redirected the knife into the skull of the zombie.

"Yolanda, get up. Let's go!" Makayla screamed as she gave her sister a hand up.

"Are you guys okay?" Patrice asked as she came circling back with Lorenzo and Amina.

Yolanda was the one this time struggling for breath. "That was close. But I'm okay," she said with a hand across her chest as she panted.

Makayla turned and gasped. "And that's the least of our

worries," she said as she pointed towards the Behemoth demon, who peeled back branches as it made its way towards them. Its lips curled into a malicious sneer, revealing sharp and pointy shark like teeth.

Amina walked towards the Behemoth.

"Come on Amina!" Patrice shouted. "We don't know how to kill it."

Amina turned back and said, "I am tired of running. We have to try something! And if we don't kill it, then I know how to slow him down," she boasted as she felt the returning of her strength. With her hands raised towards the gods, she floated into the foggy midnight sky. When her eyes opened they were a washed grey. Dark clouds formed in the sky and the dim light of the frosty moon faded away. "Now this is going to fuck him up. Lightning reign down and destroy my enemy." She cried as she channeled a powerful bolt of lightning, that came cascading down, and surging to her target. It was a bolt so powerful that wind blew around them and the sound of thunder that followed echoed throughout the woods. Electric charges made Amina's braids rise from her shoulders as her fingers sparked, and her arms glowed.

When the smoke cleared from the bolt, the Behemoth demon laid crumbled in a crater dented into the ground with steam all around him.

Amina turned to her sisters as she floated to the ground, "See we did all of this running for noth—," she said before being cut off by the sharp pain that came across her right shoulder. Amina swiveled her head and saw a bearded zombie in overalls, who had stabbed a pitchfork near her shoulder. In shock, Amina looked at her sisters as her mouth filled with warm metallic and her shoulder agonized in pain.

CONJURE

"Amina!" Yolanda shouted.

Patrice burned the zombie with flames from her lips as Amina fell to her knees.

Two zombies fully decayed and rotting, stalked Makayla. She saw a decaying, man buried in a crisp navy suit now covered in mud, the other a round female in a flowery white gown. She tugged at Patrice's shoulder. "Look, here they come again."

Lorenzo tackled and shredded them both at once. He turned to Patrice, "Don't worry about your sister. I'll take care of her. We need to keep moving."

Patrice nodded as she marched forward. Lorenzo shifted back to his normal appearance and scooped Amina in his arms before following the group. Deeper into the woods they ran.

"Where are we going?" Makayla shouted from behind.

"I don't know but we need to find shelter or a space where we can have time to complete the ritual." Yolanda shouted as she pushed past moss and broken branches.

"We will," Patrice said, but her usual cool, in control tone absent. Her voice was shaking. She snapped her head around to gaze at Yolanda. "A vision would be so clutch now. Can you find some place for us to hide?"

Yolanda closed her eyes. In a flash she saw an old white rickety house hidden in the woods, nestled in a clearing nearby, surrounded by overgrown grass and covered in vines. The paint was chipping and the screen on the porch ripped and ragged. She opened her eyes and ran up to her sisters, "There is a house somewhere in these woods."

"Where?" Patrice asked.

"I don't know," Yolanda responded frantically.

Patrice glanced over her shoulder and could see more of

the zombie horde heading their way. Guttural moans echoed from her left and right. At any moment the undead minions of Papa Samedi were about to swarm on top of them. She wondered to herself what to do and begged herself to think quickly. When she looked to the hills, she saw a light. It was a strange white light, that made her raise her arms to shield her face. Patrice lowered her arms and looked closer. It was her Gran, and she was pointing to the left across a small stream.

"This way!" She called behind as she led them to the direction she had seen Gran pointing to. Further into the woods and across the pond they went.

Their feet splashed as they marched through the pond with Amina swearing through clenched teeth as she lay helpless in Lorenzo's arms. The fog was thick now, almost solid. Everything in the woods became a tangled blur of trees, fog, moss, and dirt. Finally they reached the edge of the woods and came to a clearing. In a grove of ancient Holly trees stood the house just the same as Yolanda saw in her vision. With not a second to waste, they ran to the porch, huffing as danger hung in the air, sounded in the night, and chased after them. Just as they reached the doorstep Papa Samedi appeared out of the shadows and he didn't come alone. The Behemoth Demon came marching behind, accompanied by Mama Brigitte and hundreds of zombies.

"Hurry up. Let's get inside!" Yolanda shouted. The moans of the zombies intensified as they came in every direction out of the woods and towards the house.

37

PEACE IN THE STORM

$\mathcal{M}$akayla walked through the door and opened it from the other side. They all went rushing in. Lorenzo was following behind with Amina in his arms. With the aid of his panther senses he heard a blade whoosh through the air. He sensed the danger but he could not react until the blade landed in its target. An axe landed dead center between his neck and left shoulder. He fell to his knees and groaned in pain.

Patrice reached for him. She turned to Makayla, "Close the door!" She pulled in both Lorenzo and Amina as they both fell to the floor.

"Come on... come on." she pleaded as she pulled Lorenzo who struggled in pain.

Patrice slammed the door behind and with her hands, she used her powers to move an old dusty couch to the door.

"Don't worry about me. I'll heal. Grab her... she's losing a lot of blood." Lorenzo said through grinding teeth. He was in unbearable pain, it was the type of agonizing pain that made it hard to breathe.

Makayla and Yolanda grabbed Amina by her hands and feet then placed her on the floor.

With his hands clasped over his shoulder, Lorenzo said "Patrice you need to pull it out."

Patrice tried to remain focused and calm. She grasped the axe with both hands and yanked it out of Lorenzo. In agony, his scream resounded, a mix of both human and animal. Patrice took off her jacket and placed it at Lorenzo's wounds. Her heart pounded as his blood flowed. "Look, stay with me…" she said as he wheezed.

Lorenzo put his hands over hers as he held her gaze. "I told you I'll be fine," he stammered. "Don't worry about me. Save your sisters."

From outside they could hear dozens of footsteps on the porch. Then there was a banging at the door and all across the front of the house as the zombies tried to fight their way in.

"Peaches that's not gonna be enough to hold all of them back!" Makayla whimpered.

"It will have to be enough until Yolanda can get the mojo going," she shouted and as the words left her lips, there was a crashing at the windows. Patrice looked to her left and saw decayed hands clawing into the house. Then the door in front of them rattled. "Yolanda that shield would be handy right about now."

Yolanda sat Indian style on the floor. She pulled out a small bowl from her bag and filled it with the contents of a pouch that contained several herbs and powders. "In this space we call our home. Where goodness dwells and no evil shall roam, mothers, sisters, fathers, brothers, all family spirits rise from the ashes and come to me. Protect these walls, protect us against evil, join your hands and protect thee."

A whirlwind stirred and rattled within the room of the rickety house. All of the sisters became speechless and trans-fixed as spirits entered the room, covering in shimmering white lights.

It was their family.

The roots of their legacy came to the aid of the branches.

Gran led them all as uncles, aunts, cousins, and other family members, some of which were unknown, rose and swirled around the room. They brought peace to the chaos and formed a blue light.

*W*hen Yolanda finished the chant, an arc of blue light went outward in every direction. It filled the room and shot outwards, outside it repelled all the zombies off the porch, they were zapped back like flies. Then an energy rose to form a dome of protection.

Outside the house, Mama Brigitte shifted back human. "The sisters are up to something," she told Papa Samedi as he fell to the ground.

Papa Samedi snarled as he turned to her, "Bring that wall down." He commanded, his voice furious.

With her staff raised, Mama Brigitte chanted as the Behe-moth demon pounded fists to the barrier.

Makayla was looking outside when she turned to her sisters and asked, "Umm Yolanda how long is this barrier of protection supposed to last."

Yolanda wiped her knees as she stood from the floor, "I don't know….a few hours… maybe all night."

Makayla looked back outside, then she turned back to her sister. "Girl, you might want to think again. Rocky and Mama Odie are already working on bringing it down."

Yolanda smacked her head. "Then we're screwed!"

Amina laid helplessly on the floor. It was Deja vu all over again. After everything she did, she was about to die the same way. Laying in a pool of her own blood on the floor, in an abandoned house.

Patrice appeared over her. For the first time she didn't see her sister, she saw her grandmother. It happened so quickly that Amina had to look again.

Patrice grabbed her sister's hand. "Amina don't you die on me. Stay with us. We need you. We love you."

Amina smiled, "I love you too." she said, and the words surprised her when they came out of her mouth. Her strength faded. For a brief second she closed her eyes.

Patrice shook her awake. "Oh no you don't. You're not going to ditch us now."

Amina sneered as her eyes rolled open and Patrice helped her sit up. Patrice looked over to Yolanda, "We need to do it now. We have to conjure the spirit. It's our only chance."

"Can she even say the spell with us?" Yolanda asked.

Makayla knelt to the floor, "Get up Amina, we need ya girl." She said as she aided Patrice.

"Just get in a circle and let's do this!" Patrice barked.

Together in a circle, the sisters clasped hands, hoping this creator spirit will hear their desperate plea and rescue them. Patrice started, "By broken chains free me. From solid ground mold me. To the depths of the ocean seek me."

Patrice was cut off by a thunderous clash that surrounded them. Lorenzo darted towards the window. Footsteps marched onto the porch again. Lorenzo looked outside and his heart sank, "They got through the shield!" Lorenzo called back.

"Aw hell naw!" Makayla cried before a fist pounded through the front door.

It was the hard rocky fist of the Behemoth monster. Lorenzo then raced to the door, which lurched as the monster fought its way in. Then there was a crash from a side window and when they looked to it they heard something rustling around back.

"Continue the spell!" Lorenzo said as he perilously held the demon back. The Behemoth continued to work on the wooden door, it crumbled like a cookie as he peeled it back.

They grasped hands and chanted together, "With wind lift me. By fire consume me. Creator spirit we conjure thee. Grace us with your presence and breathe on thee. Spirit we conjure thee. Spirit we conjure thee. Spirit we conjure thee."

From the heavens the spirit of phoenix reigned upon them. There was a shift in the atmosphere. All the noise and clatter turned to silence. Yolanda's hair stood up on the back of her neck. Something was entering the room. All four sisters could feel it coming, it was a presence that was both massive and powerful, that came around the corners in a sweeping light that forced itself through their eyes and mouths. Coursing through their veins was the essence of life. The magnificence of the spirit peeled off their clothes and adorned them with golden and ivory armor both feminine and strong. Their skin was radiant like the purest gold and their beauty magnified to perfection.

Once the spirit filled them, the sisters went to the door to battle with their strength renewed and their gifts multiplied. Lorenzo looked at the sisters in awe as he stepped aside.

Gently Patrice touched him and he was healed. Standing in front, Patrice held her hand out towards the door and it shattered, tossing the Behemoth monster and all that surrounded, back.

The Lawson sisters took one step outside and Papa Samedi knew he was too late. The Lawson sisters were one with the Phoenix.

RISE OF THE PHOENIX

The Lawson sisters stepped off the porch to feel the haze of glowing eyes from the reanimated corpses that surrounded the old house. Death was in the fog. Low guttural moans filled the dead air and surrounded the old rickety house. Their only way out would be to fight and destroy the evil that stood against them. Silence hung in the air as the sisters strode forth.

Patrice crossed hands across her shoulders. "You should've returned to the spirit realm when you had the chance demon."

Her gaze was stern and her will unyielding. With the power of the Phoenix surging in her veins, she felt assured. Papa Samedi could see the difference in the sisters, he could sense incredible power dripping off of them, and this made him afraid. As they stepped off the porch, the fog crept back, as if driven away by the magnificent light that radiates around them, the divine splendor from their ivory armor was blinding, and made the night creatures want to crawl back into darkness.

*P*apa Samedi's eyes narrowed. "That power belongs to me, mon cher…. and I want what's mine." He pointed a long pointy finger at them. "Amina, you will pay what you owe. And you will pay it with blood."

Amina shook her head, "Fuck that."

Yolanda nodded, in a hell yea manner. "We are one with the creator spirit… the Phoenix flows through us. Don't be foolish demon."

Makayla stepped out with a hand on her hip. "Yeah stop trippin. We about to send that ass packing."

Patrice side eyed her sister, and eased her back. The look on her face said, I got this. "If you know what's good for you, then you will leave now."

Papa Samedi considered the threat for a moment, then he turned to Mama Brigitte and his army of undead, who gathered around him. Their numbers now were no longer in the dozens but the hundreds. "Bring me their hearts!" he demanded. At the orders of Papa Samedi, the zombies came at them from everywhere grunting with their weapons raised.

"My pleasure!" Mama Brigitte declared with a sardonic grin as she shifted into her feline form.

Patrice turned back to her group. "Amina and Yolanda I need you to control this horde. Round them up and don't leave one left standing." She turned to her left, "Makayla and Lorenzo handle Mama Odie and Rocky," she said channeling her sister's words.

Amina wasted no time in floating to the skies, with feminine hands that conjured the surrounding air, she commanded the winds to swirl. "Goddess wind unleash your breath of destruction. Come to me, your mistress, and destroy my enemies."

When Amina called for the winds, they came blowing from all directions, swirling larger, blowing past treetops, rising from the ground, and funneling into a cone of destruction. A tornado. Amina unleashed destruction below to the group of zombies that encircled them, the gusts of wind came tumbling through the woods and whooshing below, sucking in anything in its path. Zombies blew left and right and flew all around as Amina controlled the motion of the tornado, around them, with her hands outstretched.

On the ground, Patrice blew fire that swept and consumed. As Amina cleared the zombies that tried to encircle them, she burned her way through the horde with brilliant orange and crimson flames, that engulfed everything in sight. Papa Samedi locked eyes with Patrice and peeled back his robe as he levitated and charged towards her.

"You want a piece?" Patrice murmured as she elbowed a zombie that tried to sneak up on her and tossed another that crossed her path.

Papa Samedi came at her with dark energy clenched in his fist. Patrice leapt to the air and knocked him back with a fiery spinning kick, the demon tumbled across the grass and got back to his feet. He attacked explosive streams of dark energy, and the two began exchanging blows.

A zombie, a girl in t-shirt and jeans, smiled a black gooey sneer at Makayla. Makayla rushed forward, meeting the charging zombie and snatching her blade before redirecting it into her skull. Another zombie crawled towards Makayla, she spun and caught him in the skull with the same blade.

Mama Brigitte had her predatory eyes set on Yolanda.

Somehow Yolanda got separated from the group and was struggling with a female zombie who held a butcher knife in her hands. With a push Yolanda fell back. Even with her powers intensified by the Phoenix she still doubted her abilities. A trio of dead turned to Yolanda who was now backing towards a tree.

"Can I get some help over here?" Yolanda called.

Patrice saw her sister out of the corner of her eyes, as she continued to exchange blows with Papa Samedi. She turned to Yolanda, only for a brief second, "You have to fight back. Fight!" she beckoned.

Yolanda nodded before she stood up, still terrified, and not sure of what she had to do. Her fear only paralyzed her for a moment, but soon Patrice's fighting spirit came over her. She swallowed hard before ensuring herself, "I can do this. I am one with the spirits..." she continued as zombies ran towards her.

Yolanda stomped and her feet rippled the ground beneath, causing the group to stumble, as the ground shuddered. "I am mother earth!" she said in surprise. Again she stomped, and the zombies toppled before her.

Mama Brigitte in her feline form leapt across the crowd of zombies. Yolanda's second sense kicked in and she reacted lightning fast, picking up a nearby shovel to deflect Mama Brigitte's jaws. Yolanda fell on her back with the beast on top of her. Summoning every bit of strength she had she pushed Mama Brigitte off her and pummeled the demoness with the blunt end of the shovel.

"I don't believe in harming animals but you're evil!" she shouted as she continued to wail on Mama Brigitte. After a few strokes to the back and chest, Mama Brigitte transformed back. Yolanda stood confidently over the demon. "See I knew I could do this."

*L*orenzo let out a loud roar before transforming, he vaulted over and came crashing down to the Behemoth demon with a pounding fist. The Behemoth blocked and countered with a jab from the left, to which Lorenzo swiftly backed away from. The two began exchanging blow for blow with Lorenzo out maneuvering the brute strength of the monster with his swift agility. Irate and angered at Lorenzo, the Behemoth huffed and pulled Lorenzo into his massive arms. Trapped within the demon's arms, Lorenzo whirled and slammed the Behemoth to the ground.

Before Lorenzo could blink, the Behemoth snarled and was back on its feet. Using his hind legs Lorenzo kicked with his powerful panther feet. As the demon stumbled back, Lorenzo slashed and ripped into its hide. The Behemoth then caught both of Lorenzo's hands and head-butted him. A sharp pain dominated Lorenzo's head from the force of the demon's hit, allowing the demon to take advantage of this moment and uppercut Lorenzo, knocking him senseless. Lorenzo struggled to get up. Charging with curled fists, the Behemoth reached back to deliver a finishing blow, when suddenly his fist was held back.

*C*overed in a hard icy armor that resembled the hide of the demon, Makayla matched the Behemoth's strength as she forcefully snatched his fist back. Surprise etched the monster's face as it looked down to the girl who looked almost like a pixie next to him.

"Not today Satan!" Makayla shouted as she delivered a mouth breaking punch to the Behemoth's jaw, which sent the demon soaring overhead.

With his advanced healing kicking in, Lorenzo rose to his feet and delivered the final blow in a roundhouse kick to the Behemoth's temple. "Now stay down!" He said cockily.

Papa Samedi was knocked to the ground by Patrice when he noticed the Lawson sisters were defeating his forces. Bellowing his rage, Papa Samedi shot Amina down from the sky with a ball of dark energy.

Reeling from the blow, Amina cursed as she tumbled to the ground. Still, her combat instincts kicked in when she spiraled down from the sky to the battlefield, and she tossed a bolt of lightning at Papa Samedi.

In a blur of motion, Papa Samedi dodged the bolt and blasted both sisters with dark energy. With a sickening crack, Amina toppled into a tree as Patrice reeled alongside her.

The demon waited for the sisters to get up but once he saw that they were still, a smile swept over his face.

39

WRATH OF THE QUEEN

hrough the chaos Makayla spotted both of her sisters lying unconscious. "Patrice!" she called. Fighting her way through the maelstrom, Makayla rushed to her sisters' sides, but the horde of undead became a never-ending sea. The more the Lawson sisters killed, the more they kept rising with their muddy brown suits and gowns, even those who didn't even have proper burials but the remains laid on the ground, they all rose with missing limbs, decayed flesh, and broken bodies, inching to destroy the sisters.

Patrice's rage was white-hot, as she rose to her feet. There was a hard pain in her back. But as she got up, far past Papa Samedi, she saw a light. Gran came to her again. Not as she remembered her but as a younger woman. She was adorned in white and gold, her cheeks brown and her head held high looking regal.

"The time is now. You have to do it." She heard her grand-mother's voice in her head, even though her lips didn't move.

Patrice watched everything through a daze, the battle scene

stood before her, and it was all slowed down. Right then and there Patrice knew what had to be done to win this battle. To her left and right, she saw her sisters and Lorenzo continue to battle relentlessly. It wasn't enough. Everything had led her to this moment, her grandmother's love and strength, the antics of her mother, her uncle's training, her heartache at the devastation of Hurricane Katrina, her struggle to protect and raise her sisters. All of these things both good and bad molded her into the queen she was meant to be.

"Spirit come to me...the Queen. I am the MOTHER Phoenix." She declared, her voice loud and boisterous seemed to echo off the trees and into the heavens.

With those words the spirit of the Phoenix left the rest of her sisters. Inside Patrice all the power surged. At first she felt overwhelmed. Her senses heightened and her body vibrated with life. Before her very eyes she saw the stars, the earth, moon, people, nature, life and death. It all came flooding to her brain rapidly with the wisdom of the ancient spirits. It wasn't until she took several deep breaths, that she concluded she could withstand the power.

Soaring through the air, a bird of white light and fire manifested. Long and stalky the bird called out as it soared above them. Fire danced in the sky as it trailed behind the phoenix's wings. To the skies Patrice and the Phoenix connected with her hands stretched, the wings of the Phoenix opened and in a strike, it banished Papa Samedi and his undead army. Engulfed in flames Papa Samedi went back to the spirit realms, as all the risen undead burned down to ashes.

Witnessing the destruction, Mama Brigitte crept to the

woods and disappeared into the night, as the fire destroyed all that was evil.

The forest was washed in silence. Papa Samedi was gone as well as the Behemoth and the zombie horde. As if sensing that it was no longer needed the bird disappeared, Patrice felt the power of the Phoenix no longer. She fell to the ground weakened but strengthened by victory.

"Well that's it..." Makayla said as she walked over to Patrice.

"That's it!" Patrice murmured. "He's gone."

"Amen to that," Makayla said as she rested her head on her big sister's shoulder.

Yolanda joined her sisters to their left. "Don't know about y'all but I'm ready to go home."

Makayla looked up and nodded, "Me too."

Patrice looked to Amina. "So are you going to join us or nah?"

Amina smiled and embraced her sisters in a group hug. They all let out a collective sigh. Evil had thrown its worst against them and they survived. Only because they stayed together. As the Lawson sisters beamed at one another, Lorenzo walked towards the group.

"Damn girl!" Lorenzo shouted. "I knew you were bad but not that bad."

Patrice smiled as she brushed her hair off her shoulder. "Well you know, what can I say?"

"So does this mean we are finally going out on a third date?"

Patrice pulled Lorenzo in and kissed his brown lips.

"Okay can we get the fuck up out of here?" Amina said slightly grossed and jealous, as she looked at her sister.

"Yes please."

"Well how are we going to go? We don't have a car."

Lorenzo pulled out his phone. "Just walk to the road. I'll call my driver."

"Driver? Oh Patrice I like him. You came up girl," Makayla quipped.

The Lawson sisters laughed as they walked out back towards the main road in victory.

40

MISSING YOU

They buried Aunt Dot on a sullen grey day at the end of October. It was about one-week shy of Aunt Dot's birthday. All together they gathered graveside at Rest Haven cemetery along with Aunt Dot's bingo buddies, and dropped beautiful white roses in her grave. Together they held hands, crying and weeping. Although sad, Patrice wished such pain wasn't the catalyst to bring them together. But it did and they were stronger because of it.

Patrice took some time from the office to plan the funeral arrangement. She picked out the flowers, the ivory casket, and the silky gown Aunt Dot wore. Makayla had a hand in picking the right wig from Aunt Dot's collection. She picked the curly brown one because it matched the gown and it was Aunt Dot's favorite, her "party wig".

Amina shook her head. "This is some bullshit."

"I can't believe she's really gone," Makayla said as she leaned on Amina's shoulder.

Patrice sighed. "Like it or not, all we have is each other."

Then she looked over to her sisters. "We have to look after one another."

Yolanda sniffled. "And try our best to be nice to each other." Of all the sisters, Yolanda took Aunt Dot's death the hardest. Patrice did the best she could to comfort her. She held her close like a baby as her heart broke into a million pieces.

Lorenzo rubbed Patrice's back. "Are you going to be alright?"

"I will," She answered. "We will."

He'd been there at her side the whole time and arranged to pay for everything, since Aunt Dot had no insurance and her candle shop was barely breaking even. Lorenzo held Patrice's hand and comforted her throughout the whole ordeal. At the back of the shop they did find a note saying that if anything were to happen to her, everything will go to her girls evenly.

The whole funeral Yolanda prayed for this nightmare to go away. She looked at the casket but all she could think about was the blood. The blood that was everywhere, on the floor, splattered on the walls, and swept across her face. Yolanda trembled as a wave of nausea came to her. She erupted in tears again, and pulled Patrice's shoulder as she crumbled to her knees.

Amina sighed. "We need to put her back in the car."

"I got her," Lorenzo said as he pulled Yolanda to the side. Lorenzo practically carried Yolanda out of the graveyard as she screamed for Aunt Dot to wake up. Cold air brushed her face as he pulled her away with steaming hot tears rolling down her cheek.

The whole ceremony was too much for Yolanda, so while the others stayed for the end, she waited in the car by herself, watching from the window. There she sat in her sadness, shaken to her core, when something stirred in her belly. She looked up in the hills and she swore she saw a lady in white waving.

That made Yolanda smile.

She knew then that everything would be alright.

41

SISTERS

*A*mina woke up early Sunday morning, with her mind dead set on taking out her braids. She was looking in the mirror long and hard, before she reached for the comb, and began to unravel her braids. With a wide tooth comb she began working on her strands, nipping at them and untangling until her hair was free. Amina starred at her reflection and she was completely baffled. Somehow, she woke up that morning with a spirit of peace, a peace that she had not felt in a very long time. Peace she couldn't remember after Hurricane Katrina, where her mother tried to overthrow her grandmother, the spirit came, and the surge of power brought the levees down. Ever since that day she spent her life running and fighting. It was then that the hell inside of her was born, her rebellious and fiery nature.

It was no wonder that her powers manifested itself in storm & rage to match the pain she felt inside. When she was old enough, she left Georgia to be with Marcus in Chicago. Then after double crossing Marcus she fled to Detroit. Then once she got tired of Detroit, she went to New York to make a name for herself.

Amina was tired of running. Tired of searching for a tribe or a place to call home. She has been chasing peace for a very long time and finally she found it here, with her sisters. She looked at the mirror satisfied with her work. There were a few braids in the back she couldn't get loose, so she went downstairs to go find Yolanda to help her.

She came downstairs to be met with the sounds of joy and laughter. Yolanda was walking back and forth from the kitchen as she cooked. Patrice was drinking coffee and checking the blogs on her iPad. Makayla was watching tv trying to get all of their attention about some silly reality show. It was right then and there, when she saw the love and joy on her sisters' faces that Amina was sure that she would stay awhile.

"Come on y'all I got the food ready, and it's time to eat down," Yolanda called from around the kitchen.

The sisters all got up from their respective corners.

Makayla turned the tv off. "Please don't tell me it's none of that vegan crap. Girl, I'm hungry."

Yolanda came around the corner, holding a pitcher of mimosa. "Oh hush. It's all natural and all good for you. Plus I made Aunt Dot's shrimp and grits." She grabbed Amina's shoulder once she got a look at her. "You took your braids out?" she asked as she examined and admired.

"Most of them, but I need some help getting some in the back out." Amina said as she pulled the stray remaining braids in the back.

Yolanda waved a hand, "No problem sissy. I got you after brunch." she said with a smile.

Then Makayla passed her, "I don't know about you but I'm

hungry down girl. I'm about to hulk smash this brunch. Yolanda made Aunt Dot's famous shrimp and grits and I know you remember how good they used to be."

Amina laughed and nodded, "Yes girl. I sure do."

Makayla headed to the kitchen. Patrice passed and said, "Come on. Are you not ready to eat?"

"Peaches can I talk to you for a minute?"

"Sure," Patrice said as she went and sat on the arm of the chair across from the couch.

Amina felt hot and uneasy. She knew if she didn't keep it all the way one hundred, the words and feelings she felt in her heart wouldn't come out. So without thought she began spilling her heart out. "I just want to say I'm sorry." She began.

Those two words almost knocked Patrice out. After all the fights, all the shade, and the lies it was a big moment for Amina to finally own up to her mess. More than vindication she felt proud.

"I know sorry doesn't even cover all of the things that I've done but that's how I feel. Truly," Amina continued as she rung her finger.

With a deep breath, Patrice folded her arms. "No. Sorry is a lot coming from you."

"You welcomed me back in and I betrayed your trust. I'm mad at myself for being so selfish and stupid, but it felt like I had no choice. Starting right now I swear I'm going to change. I'm going to do better."

"Well nobody changes over night, but the fact you can see what you did was wrong speaks volumes."

Amina's lips curled into an uneasy smile. "I know we've had this rivalry for too long. How I felt about mother and how you felt about Gran. I was always jealous because it seemed I would never be as good as you. In school or life. Regardless of that, you did a lot for us Peaches, and you really did a good job caring for Yolanda and Makayla. I don't know how you feel about this…" Amina started before a single tear trickled from her eye. "I really did miss you guys and I'm tired of running. If it's okay can I stay here until I get on my feet and get a place of my own?"

Patrice grabbed her hands. Inside her head she heard her grandmother's voice. *"Pull her closer…Pull her closer."* With those words echoing in her head she pulled her sister in a warm embrace and said, "As long as I have a place you will always have a home."

"Oh ain't that sweet," Aunt Dot said.

Amina and Patrice looked over and gasped. "Aunt Dot?" Patrice asked as she stared at her. " What the hell are you doing here? Didn't we just burry you?"

Aunt Dot pulled out a cigarette. "Chile I know."

"Can y'all hurry up I'm hungry!" Makayla shouted. She came from the kitchen, took one look at Aunt Dot and passed out.

"What is going on?" Yolanda said. She walked around and dropped the pitcher of mimosa on the living room floor. Glass shattered everywhere. "Aunt Dot what are you doing here?"

*A*unt Dot stood before them hollow and translucent. "Beloved, I want to know the same damn thing." She took a puff on the cigarette. "But the spirits told they weren't ready for me yet. They told me I was needed here to be with you. For some reason I can't leave."

Amina stood up. "So you're a ghost?"

Aunt Dot shrugged. "I guess something like that."

Patrice laughed. Her laughter was so odd that it became infectious and spread to the rest of them.

"Now that that's over, somebody pick Makayla up and let's get this brunch rocking." Aunt Dot said. "I don't even know if I can eat but god darn it I'm gone try." She said as she walked with Yolanda around the corner. "Did you put enough pepper in the etouffee?"

"I did just like you used to." Yolanda said.

"Well let me see for myself."

Patrice and Amina both turned towards her and laughed as they remained embracing each other. A few more tears trickled down each of their cheeks and the doorbell rung.

"I'll get it. Go eat," Patrice told Amina before heading to the door.

Patrice opened the door to find Nicole on the other side.

When Patrice cracked the door and Nicole saw her tears, she immediately thought the worst. "Is everything alright?" she asked.

"Better than alright. Everything is perfect. Life is wonderful." Patrice gushed.

"Uh huh okay," Nicole murmured with her eyes wide.

"I just had a moment with my sister. She is going to stay for a while and finally I think we are good. I mean we were good before but now I think we're good good."

"How about your aunt? I'm sorry I couldn't make it but I heard the bad news."

Patrice glanced over to the kitchen.

"Ain't enough pepper in this damn stew!" Aunt Dot shouted.

"I'm okay now. It's almost like she never left." Patrice said.

Nicole raised an eyebrow. "And Mr. James?"

"Let's just say I can definitely see a third, fourth, and fifth date in our future. If you know what I'm saying."

"Good...that's all very good." Nicole said. Then she looked down at the files in her hands and remembered her reason for visiting. "Speaking of Mr. James. Your signature is needed ASAP for this deal so I brought them over."

Patrice grabbed the file, "Thanks Nicole. Do you want to come inside and join us for brunch?"

"No thanks girl. Watching my figure. But I'll talk to you later."

Patrice smiled, "Thanks love. See you tomorrow." she said before closing the door and heading back inside.

*I*f it wasn't for Patrice's genuine happiness she would've noticed a few things about Nicole. Nicole wasn't really happy for Patrice and it was evident in the frown on her face. If she really thought about that she would re-think their friendship. That would lead her to question why in only a year did the two become so close. It was as if Nicole was forcing herself on Patrice who at that time didn't have many good girl friends. And above everything, had Patrice stood in the doorway a while to watch Nicole leave she would've seen the scars on her back. It was a little warm that Sunday morning and Nicole was wearing a halter top. One that barely concealed the large bite marks that healed on her back. And if that didn't make Patrice curious, watching Nicole get into the back of a black Suburban that was strangely parked across the street would have.

Nicole got into the back of the black Suburban. As soon as

she sat on the warm leather seat, she shifted, her skin peeled and morphed from brown flesh to pale yellow skin. Mama Brigitte didn't need her cover anymore. Of course she was always loyal to Papa Samedi who was now destroyed, but she had been planted to watch Patrice by someone else.

The lady who sat across from her had glowing golden brown skin. She was wearing all black, with her legs crossed. The lady's mere presence brought fear to Mama Brigitte. She was wearing a large black widow's hat that covered her eyes. She lifted her hat ever so slightly. "And so?"

Mama Brigitte cleared her throat. "She's done it. She declared herself Mother Phoenix, and the power resides in her now."

The lady in black smiled, her red lips twisted up. "Who knew my daughters would be so strong...so powerful?"

"They are very powerful," Mama Brigitte continued. "Papa resurrected a whole graveyard full of zombies. He even had a part of the Phoenix to himself thanks to the Amina, and yet they still destroyed him."

The lady in black cocked her hat, "Impressive... very impressive. Well I hope they're ready." She said as she lifted her hat and exposed her black eyes. "Momma is back. And she's coming for her sweet girls along with the power of the Phoenix! I didn't sell my soul and overthrow that ole crone for nothing. Hell could not hold me, nor will the heavens stand in my way. That power is mine and there's only room for one Mother, and that's me." She smiled as she raised a glass. Ruby cracked the window and observed her daughters eating. "Get ready girls. Because I'm going to shake Atlanta like a nine point five earthquake on the Richter scale."

The sisters had no idea what was coming, but now that

they had joined together they must keep their bond to defeat everything in their path or lose it all if they fall apart.

Patrice beamed as she looked out to her sisters and aunt who all sat across the table. She raised her mimosa, "Here's to the Lawson girls."

The End

If you enjoyed this book and you can't wait to read the next one, I'd like to hear from you and hope that you could take some time to post a review on Amazon or Goodreads. Your feedback and support will help this author to greatly improve his writing craft for future projects and make this book even better. You can find this book on Goodreads and Amazon by searching "Conjure + Voodoo Vixens"

 *lso join the Moonsquad by visiting Facebook.com/jmoonwrites*

ALSO BY J. MOON

Book of the Anointed

Coming Soon

Smite

Book of the Weeping Prophet

PREVIEW OF SMITE

Old man Willie, the head of security, sat in his chair by the main door, puzzle book and flask by his side. After a grueling nine hour shift, the number of customers dwindled down and the Black Friday sale at J&K mega clothing store was over. The vast showrooms were tiddy again, most of the floors were dark and silent, and a few lights shined on the main floor.

Jerrell and Shanice were the only employees left to close the store. Shanice walked to the back room to find Jerrell checking his phone.

Jerrell looked up, "Son, I'm so ready to roll up out of here."

Shanice huffed, "For real. Me too," she said as she dropped her bags.

Jerrell reached into his pockets. "You trying to hit this?" he asked as he pulled out a small bag of weed.

Shanice snickered, "Right now?"

Jerrell nodded, "Hell yeah. Let's go out back."

Jerrell lead the way and Shanice followed. Soon they were

rolling up and letting all of their troubles blow into the wind. Jerrell passed the blunt to Shanice and grinned as he admired her features under the dim light of the back alley. Shanice stood under him around 5'5. Her skin a magnificent almond brown, her hair was midnight black and always curly, just as if she had just came out of the shower. And whenever she smiled, you could see her dime size dimples sticking out of the corners of her mouth.

Jerrell leaned over, "You know I'm feeling you right?"

Shanice grinned, "No. What do you mean?" she asked sarcastically, blowing smoke in his face. As he waved the clouds away, Shanice passed the blunt back to him.

"I'm trying to be your boyfriend. Your whole swag. I can see myself being with you."

Shanice looked up and said, "I guess. You're cute or whatever but right now I'm just trying to take care of Pop."

Jerrell sucked his teeth, "Are you trying to curve me or nah?"

"It's not like that…. it's just that I don't have time for a boyfriend."

As the mood became tense between the two, they heard a shuffling coming out of nowhere. Both Shanice and Jerrell looked back, "Did you hear that?"

"Probably someone trying to get back in. Don't trip…. I got it." Jerrell said as he passed the blunt back to Shanice.

Shanice stopped him."Isn't Willie still at the front?"

Jerrell frowned at her, "His old ass has probably passed out by now."

Shanice giggled as Jerrell moved passed her.

When he left, she sighed out in relief. She took a long pull from the blunt then exhaled. Suddenly there was movement in the alleyway and her bones stiffened. Shanice leaned over and saw nothing, so she paid it no mind. The weed was making her paranoid, she assumed. Then came the sound of boot steps. Heavy boots pounded around the corner and she looked out in the faint light of the back alley, still she saw nothing. "Jerrell is that you?" She called to an echoing dark alley. "Boy stop playing."

Without warning, white lights crackled and whirling out of thin air came an armored soldier with his gun raised. "Target identified. Twenty-one-year old Shanice Ebony." It said in a cold stoic voice

Shanice dropped the blunt. "It's not mine. I was just holding it for my homeboy I swear." she declared under the impression she was being held by a police officer. She held her hands up to shield her eyes from the bright light flashing on her face. She peeked over the corners of her hands to examine the soldier closer. He was covered head to toe in a gunmetal grey porcelain armor, four stripes of glowing beams placed where the eyes should be on his helmet, and an assault rifle that looked alien .

"Target identified. Shanice Ebony is now in custody of the League and is to be handed over to Legion." The voice was very harsh and metallic.

Shanice was dumbfounded. "Look son, chill it's just some weed." She pleaded. Then came two others appearing out of thin air. They uncloaked themselves and aimed red beams to her head. Shanice had an outer body experience as she tried to wrap her mind around what was going on. It's strange how you can see something on t.v or read it in a book, but when it's staring you dead in the face, you still can't recognize it. Then

Shanice realized these weren't police officers at all. Nor were they men. They were cyborgs.

"You will follow the League or face annihilation."

Shanice backed up. "Wait please. I don't want no problems." She begged.

"Follow the League or face annihilation," it repeated.

"Please...please c'mon just chill,"

As the heat of the weapons fell on her, a man appeared from out of nowhere. "I don't think so," He declared in a raspy baritone before burying a blazing sword into the cyborg.

Sparks flew out of the chest of the cyborg as it fell to the ground in a heap. It thrashed on the ground, spewing black liquid until it exploded. The remains disintegrated into the air. Immediately the two others behind shot at his head. The man clutched his left wrist to his chest and a blue shield of light covered him and deflected the bullets being fired his way. He charged the soldier on his right with the shield, knocking the weapon out of its hand. With his right hand he used the sword and claimed the other soldier's head. Then he elbowed the one closest to him, ran his sword through its chest, and swirled with his sword aimed at its neck. Both of their helmets rolled off leaving two sparking corpses behind.

Shanice screamed as everything happened so fast around her. "What the hell?" she exclaimed as she stared up to the dark eyes of the towering man.

Radiant sparks of light casted an alluring glow against the man's toffee brown skin. He had wooly hair trimmed into a magnificent fro hawk and eyes of blazing fire. Shanice became transfixed by his beauty.

"My name is Gabe. What's your name?"

She was almost too stunned to speak, but somehow she managed to say "Shanice."

Gabe took a step forward. "Shanice come with me love if you want to live."

White light crackled in the alley, and more of the cyborgs appeared. "Target identified. The League will apprehend."

Gabe put his sword back in the cover of his long camel coat. He held out his hand. "Come on!" he commanded.

Shanice grabbed his hand and together they dashed down the alley. Bullets of light shot over their heads and Shanice winced as the mysterious man lead her away from the menace of the League. She looked up into the man's eyes and again saw fire in them, and it was obvious he was not afraid of danger. And the more she followed him, the more she became intrigued. It was obvious that he was older. Somewhere around mid-thirties. Around six foot four with a perfectly chiseled face, and an intricately styled goatee.

Shanice peered over her shoulder. The League was gaining on them. "Who are they?"

"Grunts from the League," Gabe responded. "Hurry… my ride isn't too far from here."

They came to a halt as an eight foot gate stood between them and the exit of the alleyway.

Shanice looked to Gabe in fear, "It's too tall to climb."

"We can jump it." Gabe said calmly.

Shanice looked at him like he was stupid, "Jump?"

Shots flew over their heads and they buckled to the ground. "Now. Jump!" Gabe barked.

Together hand in hand, they jumped and leapt over the gate with a single hop. Shanice gawked, "How did you do that?"

"Firing Missile," a metallic voice called from behind them.

A shrill whistle stung Shanice's ears as the missile whooshed by them and blew up the large green garbage bin in front of them. The heat of the flames kissed her face and hit them like a bus. Her legs felt riddled with shards as she struggled to get back on her feet.

Gabe spun and pulled out his eagle eye handgun from his coat. It was a sleek pistol adorned in black and gold, that shot photons of light. He focused on the Grunts that fired the missile and sank two shots in their helmets before they could fire again. He pulled Shanice closer. "We have to get out of here."

They continued running, and Gabe glance over his shoulder to see that the League was hot on their heels. With the gate blown to pieces the Grunts marched behind with their guns raised. "You will not escape The League. Hand over the target or face annihilation".

Gabe and Shanice scaled the end of the alleyway, and he led her around the corner. Shanice saw a long vintage black Cadillac, "I hope this ain't your ride. Because we ain't getting nowhere fast in this old thing."

Gabe ran his hand along the glistening side of the car, with the tenderness of a man caressing his lover. "This baby still has a lot of purr in her. And surprises too. Get in!"

Bootsteps pounded from around the corner as the Cadillac roared like a panther awakening from its sleep. Shanice whipped her head and saw that death was upon them.

"The target will not escape The League. Fire missile!"

"Oh snap!" Shanice shouted as she pulled open the door and hopped in. "They are about to fire again. We have to get out of here!"

Gabe was gripping the steering wheel when he looked over

and said, "Hold on tight." He punched the gas, and the Cadillac lurched ahead. Shanice rolled down the window. The League soldiers fired another missile, and it was heading their way. Gabe shifted the car and mashed the gas harder, and with the agility of a Ferrari the car side stepped the missile and crawled alongside the adjacent wall. The missile whooshed passed the car inches away and detonated a parking garage to their left.

One grunt looked to the other. "Fire a tracer."

The League grunt took a knee as it peered into the scope and shot through the plumes at the Cadillac speeding away. "Tracer has landed, "it said as it stood and turned to the others.

"We will reconvene and then continue pursuit once again." The other Grunt stated before they pounded their chests and teleported away in a crack of white lights.

The explosion filled the alleyway with an acrid cloud of noxious smoke coming from the garage. Shanice choked on the fumes as she pulled her hoodie up over her burning nostrils and pulled herself out of the window. With her heart thumping from her chest to her throat, she looked at the ruggedly handsome stranger who had just saved her. "Who the hell are you?" she asked again, her mind in total shock.

The man sneered, "My name is Gabriel. And I'm an Archangel."

ACKNOWLEDGMENTS

I thought I told you that we won't stop. First of all, I want to thank my lord and savior Jesus for helping me make this dream continue, and continuing to feed my inspiration. I hope my inspiration never runs out. Next I want to thank all of my Moonies! Moonsquad where you at? If you haven't joined the reading fandom yet. What are you waiting for?

I want to send a huge thank you to my parents who believe in me and love me. Thank you Grandma Olia Mae, I miss you so much but you have given me enough love for a lifetime. Thanks for always saving me my own Sweet Potato Pie. I can make my own now thanks to you.

The biggest thanks to my best friend April, I love you so much and your support means everything to me. Thank you Anique, for doing a wonderful job editing. I can't wait to work with you again. Shout out to my HU homies Trigga Trey, Dr. Nene, Moneybags Marcus, Grandma Samone, Kayla bear and her precious bundle Amari, Always on time Adiana, Ashley, and Lovest. Shout out to my road dogs Zorian (Zozo), Omar

"Sweetdaddy ellis", Amanda the panda, Nique, and Jaspy. Get to know the name Jasper Bracely ladies and gentlemen because my friend is a star, and I can't wait for us to storm Hollywood. He's the Michael B. Jordan to my Ryan Coogler.

For those that don't know, all of my fantasy stories are written in the 7th dimension. A world that is parallel to ours but just a "little" different. I wrote Conjure, previously titled Black Magic, two years ago. It was after AHS Coven aired and I missed the daily dose of LIFE auntie Angela Bassett gave every week. After writing a male centric story, which I hope will still see the light of day, I wanted to write a story that celebrated the bulk of my readers. Powerful Black women.

All my life I've been surrounded by strong black women. I grew up in a house with my mom, grandma, and aunt. Most days it was beautiful and others it was a hot mess....lmao. But that's life. Also with this story I wanted to marry the spirits of my favorite heroines like Buffy, Xena, Jean Grey, and Storm to the women that surround me daily. Hopefully you can relate to each sister in this story or they remind you of the women in your own family.

I know some of my Moonies were mad that Book of The Anointed came out before Conjure. I came up with the concept of BOTA in high school but I actually COMPLETED Conjure first. So for those of you who've been waiting, I hope you are satisfied. Also check out Book of the Anointed if haven't yet. And get excited for SMITE which is coming sooner than you think. SMITE also has a pretty dope heroine by the name of Shanice Ebony. And that Josephine Baker "charcter" is something else too.

You know I'm a Marvel fanboy so instead of just focusing on one series I'm giving you the first book of each series

Voodoo Vixens, Saga of the Sons, and Legend of the Archangel. We will call this phase one lol. It will end after the release of Book of the Weeping Prophet.

With that being said, thanks for all the love and support. Please don't stop tweeting, texting, emailing, and writing fan fic. I love it all. And stay tuned! I'm so excited for the journey I am about to take these characters. Are you? What happens after Patrice becomes Mother phoenix? Where does her relationship with Lorenzo go? Speaking of relationships will Yolanda ever find love again? Has Amina truly changed for good or will she be a bad witch forever? What does Ruby have planned for her daughters? And will Makayla ever stop being a hot mess? For all these answers and more please continue reading. There is A LOT coming to this series including dragons, African Gods, more weres, and a return to New Orleans.

Happy Reading!

The Lord of darkness

The king of Litasy (Lit fantasy)

J.Moon

CPSIA information can be obtained
at www.ICGtesting.com
Printed in the USA
LVHW011619071218
599658LV00001B/70

9 781732 081338